Jean Echenoz won France's prestigious Prix Goncourt for *I'm Gone* (The New Press). He is the author of seven other novels available in English and the winner of numerous literary prizes, among them the Prix Médicis and the European Literature Jeopardy Prize. He lives in Paris.

Mark Polizzotti has translated over forty books from the French, including works by Gustave Flaubert, Marguerite Duras, André Breton, Raymond Roussel, Patrick Modiano, and Jean Echenoz, and has written six of his own. He directs the publications program at the Metropolitan Museum of Art in New York, where he lives.

Linda Coverdale's most recent translations for The New Press were Jean Echenoz's *1914* and Julia Deck's *Viviane.* She was the recipient of the French-American Foundation's 2008 Translation Prize for her translation of Echenoz's *Ravel* (The New Press). She lives in Brooklyn.

Liesl Schillinger is a New York–based critic, translator, and moderator. Her work has appeared in the *New Yorker*, the *New York Times*, the *Washington Post*, and many other publications. She is the author of the illustrated lexicon *Wordbirds*, and her recent translations include the novels *Every Day, Every Hour* by Natasa Dragnic and *The Lady of the Camellias* by Alexandre Dumas fils.

ALSO BY JEAN ECHENOZ

1914

Lightning

Ravel

I'm Gone

S.: A Novel (in collaboration with Florence Delay, Patrick Deville, Sonja Greenlee, Harry Mathews, Mark Polizzotti, and Olivier Roth)

Plan of Occupancy

Chopin's Move

Double Jeopardy

Cherokee

Three by Echenoz

Big Blondes, *Piano*, and *Running*

Jean Echenoz

With an introduction by Liesl Schillinger

NEW YORK
LONDON

The New Press gratefully acknowledges the Florence Gould Foundation for supporting publication of this book.

Published in the United States by The New Press, New York, 2014
Distributed by Two Rivers Distribution

LIBRARY OF CONGRESS CATALOGING-IN-PUBLICATION DATA

Echenoz, Jean.
[Novels. Selections. English.]
Three by Echenoz : Big Blondes, Piano, and Running / Jean Echenoz.
pages cm
"Distributed by Perseus Distribution"—T.p. verso.
ISBN 978-1-59558-983-5 (paperback : alk. paper)—
ISBN 978-1-62097-002-7 (e-book) (print)

I. Echenoz, Jean. Big Blondes. II. Echenoz, Jean. Piano.
III. Echenoz, Jean. Running. IV. Title.
PQ2665.C5A2 2014

843'.914-dc23 2013043221

The New Press publishes books that promote and enrich public discussion and understanding of the issues vital to our democracy and to a more equitable world. These books are made possible by the enthusiasm of our readers; the support of a committed group of donors, large and small; the collaboration of our many partners in the independent media and the not-for-profit sector; booksellers, who often hand-sell New Press books; librarians; and above all by our authors.

www.thenewpress.com

Composition by dix!
This book was set in Minion

Printed in the United States of America

CONTENTS

INTRODUCTION

BEYOND THEIR CONTROL

Liesl Schillinger

What do a murderous hard-boiled blonde, a hard-drinking, neurotic concert pianist, and a record-breaking Czech runner have in common? Seen through the potent, essentializing lens of the French novelist Jean Echenoz, the answer is: most everything. People often talk of writers having a "voice"—the chopped, deadpan earnestness of the sci-fi noir auteur Philip K. Dick; the wryly mellifluous fugue precision of Nabokov; the garrulous, judgmental sentimentality of Dickens. But the distinctive seam that runs through the fictions of Echenoz is not so much a voice as a preoccupation or even an obsession: the idea that the individual has next to no control over his or her own motivations, duties or choices, and that identity is a tragicomic construction projected largely by others.

The complaint of one of Echenoz's protagonists, the alcoholic Parisian pianist Max Delmarc (the antihero of his 2003 novel *Piano)* could be the refrain of all his characters: "No one understands my project. Not even me." Max, though he lacks any clear notion of what he's trying to achieve, stubbornly lurches ahead, taking unconsidered actions whose consequences will shape his life, death, and afterlife, "with no discernible method" or objective. In this, Echenoz seems to suggest, he resembles most of us. As Max pushes through a revolving door on one of his many unthought-through moves—an escape attempt from a sterile limbo called "the Center"—he asks himself, rhetorically, what the point is of his breakout: "To go where?" he wonders, and answers his own question "No idea." No matter; he continues his undirected journey all the same, until his minders (with Echenoz, there is always a minder) catch up with him. Soon, Max will be brought back to the Center, and be given a new face (via plastic surgery) and a new name (via the Peruvian underworld): Paul Salvador. As Paul Salvador, Max will return to Paris, but not to the "real" Paris: instead he will inhabit a kind of replica or "twin" Paris, "smothered under a black, synthetic rain expelled by clouds of pollution, brownish and swollen like udders"—where he will come across everyone he knew in his former incarnation. Most of them will not recognize him. But when one of them does, Max's chief minder from the Center, a man called Béliard, will show up on the spot, in a rage. "You let yourself be recognized," he shrieks. Even-temperedly, Max/Paul responds, "You can't blame me for that." In the world of Echenoz, this is the sole rational response to the absurdity of the human predicament.

The three books in this Echenoz gatherum—two short novels, *Big Blondes* (1995) and *Piano* (2003), and the fictionalized biography *Running* (2008), about Emil Zátopek, the Cold War–era track superstar from Czechoslovakia—all partake of Echenoz's dark, fantastical sensibility and indulge his penchant for geographical dislocation. In *Big Blondes,* a different Paul Salvador—that is, a Paul Salvador who was never Max Delmarc—sets off the book's noirish chain of events. This Paul Salvador is a Parisian television producer who wants to create a series of documentaries about the lives of women he classifies as "big blondes," to explore his vague conviction that "tall blondes possess an acute awareness of their singularity . . . of being special, of constituting the product of a mutation, a genetic phenomenon, even a natural catastrophe," though he brings no rigorous methodology to his approach. "What is it we call blondness?" he muses. In his bland offices, Paul mulls the categories he wishes to collect in his survey—"warm tall blondes" versus "cool tall blondes," Hitchcock blondes, Soviet blondes, "the emblematic Monroe-Dietrich-Bardot triangle," not to mention the "solar," "incandescent" and "artificial" blondes. "Every blonde, one day or another . . . faces the suspicion that she's a fake," he explains to his bored, curvaceous brunette assistant, Donatienne. "Every one of them is exposed to this doubt; each one runs the risk they'll be suspected of being artificial." Donatienne yawns, "Whatever you say," and keeps filing. What is it all for? Salvador cannot explain: "When you get down to it maybe they don't even need to be blonde. I don't really know yet," he admits. What he does know is that he definitely wants to track down one big blonde in particular, a flash-in-the-pan French singer known as Gloria Stella, who vanished (intentionally) after serving several years in prison for the suspicious death of her "lover-cum-agent," who had tumbled down an elevator shaft. Salvador hires a band of detectives to find the ex-con blonde, but Gloria Stella resists discovery. So profoundly does she desire to remain anonymous that she has moved to the sticks, dyed her hair mouse brown, and adopted a disguise: she affects a hunch, wears shapeless tracksuits, and paints her face with "violent makeup" that makes her look like a demented clown. The first gumshoe, a man named Kastner, accosts her by accident while seeking directions, and wary Gloria (for it is she) soon pushes him off a cliff—an action approved by her minder, a parrot-sized homunculus named Béliard (who has the same name as Max Delmarc's minder in the later novel, *Piano)*, who shows up when he feels like it to abet or thwart the murderous muse. "At best, Béliard is an illusion," Echenoz writes, "an hallucination forged by the young woman's deranged mind. At worst, he is a kind of guardian angel." Fleeing the prying eyes of Salvador's hapless goons, Gloria (called Gloire now), will fly to Australia, India, and other distant lands, accompanied by Béliard, until the plot draws her back to Paris, where she will submit, for no good reason, to the spotlight Paul Salvador yearns to turn on her. "He wanted her consent, she has granted it," Salvador reflects, as Gloire at last walks into his office, "a tanned tall blonde" whom he barely recognizes. But who she is (or was) scarcely matters: "Feminine, masculine, neuter; if the sun's gender varies from one language to another, its character also changes depending on the skies." The two of them, hunter and hunted, will end up high in the sky, on a ski lift in the Pyrenees. Will they fall in love? Or will Paul Salvador, like so many of Gloire's previous pursuers, fall into the void? There may not be much difference—as the other Paul Salvador will later observe in *Piano:* love "is not only evanescent, but soluble. Soluble in time, money, alcohol, daily life, and a host of other things besides."

It is one thing to bring philosophical abstraction and post-structuralist happenstance to characters who never drew breath; but in his novel *Running,* Echenoz carries his fictional principles and focus into the real world. Widening his aperture, he takes in the improbable rise and equally improbable fall of the gangly Moravian factory worker Emil Zátopek—a sport of nature who won three gold medals in long-distance running at the Helsinki Olympics of 1952 (the 5,000 meters; the 10,000 meters; and the marathon) and broke scores of speed records in his prime. Born in 1922 in Czechoslovakia, Zátopek came of age as the troops of Hitler's Wehrmacht overran his country (which they called the Sudetenland and wanted to seize for the Third Reich). When Nazi youth organizations compelled "raggedy Czechs" to compete in running races against highly trained German athletes, Zátopek, who loathed all sports (in Echenoz's account), had no choice but to run and surprised himself and everyone else by winning handily. His form was "impossible," Echenoz writes: "Emil advances laboriously, in a jerky, tortured manner, all in fits and starts. He doesn't hide the violence of his efforts, which shows in his wincing, grimacing, tetanized face, constantly contorted by a rictus quite painful to see." His arms windmill and twitch, his tongue sticks out, he moves "as if he had a scorpion in each shoe, catapulting him on." Yet he wins at meet after meet, breaking Czech records at Brno, at Zlín, at Prague. After the Germans lose the war, he keeps on winning, in Oslo, then in Berlin; only now, his country has become a satellite of the Soviet Union. The once-reluctant runner becomes a world-famous Olympic sensation, applauded in the public square, adored—and imprisoned in this role. The Czech Republic's new Soviet minders want Zátopek to serve as a poster boy for the triumph of socialism and swiftly curtail his traveling privileges for fear he might defect (though he has a wife at home, a well-connected javelin thrower). Deftly, indelibly, Echenoz shows the humble hero's helpless progress to prisoner of the state—gawky Zátopek might as well be one of the author's pure inventions, like a big blonde hunted by a mad television producer or a weak-willed pianist tethered to a purgatory whose rules he can neither obey nor violate. He becomes, in essence, an individual with next to no control over his own motivations, duties, or choices, whose identity has been stolen by his minders. He becomes, like so many of Echenoz's characters, a tragicomic construction created largely by others.

In this omnibus of three definitive novels by Jean Echenoz, each of them deceptively light and quick to read yet cumulatively resonant when read side by side, readers will feel the patterns of the author's thought replay and interplay, reinforcing the vitality and power of each portrait. With *Big Blondes, Piano,* and *Running,* Echenoz deftly captures the transformation of personality, as it flutters between the two forces that struggle to constrain it—imagination and history, in all their obdurate caprice.

Big Blondes

Jean Echenoz

Translated by Mark Polizzotti

1

You are Paul Salvador and you're looking for someone. Winter is coming to an end. But you don't want to do the looking by yourself, you don't have much time, and so you contact Jouve.

You could, as usual, arrange to see him on a bench, in a bar, or in the office—yours or his. For a change of pace, you suggest he meet you at the municipal swimming pool at Porte des Lilas. Jouve is glad to oblige.

On the day in question, you are there at the appointed hour, at the appointed place. But the Paul Salvador you are does not usually show up early for his meetings.

Arriving particularly early that day, Salvador first walked around the large black and white building containing five thousand hectoliters of water. Then, following the slight incline of Boulevard Mortier, he passed in front of the gray constructions that bordered the southern face of the pool building and contained five hundred employees of the French counterintelligence services. Salvador took a stroll around that, too, until, not far in the distance, the bells of Notre-Dame des Otages rang the hour.

He and Jouve met in the pool cafeteria, above the grandstands that hung over the lanes, beneath the wide, transparent sun roof.

The only people in that area wearing business suits (light gray for Salvador, navy blue for Jouve), they watched the bathers flail about at their feet, observing the women more closely than the men, each establishing a private mental typology of their swimwear: the one- or two-piece kind, bikinis or thongs, models with pleats, smocks, ribbons, even flounces. They hadn't yet begun speaking. They waited for their Perrier and lemons.

At the time, Salvador was working for a company that produced TV shows, in charge of entertainment programs and news magazines—entertainment programs and news magazines that Jouve watched every evening with his wife. Salvador, a tall, thin individual of about forty, didn't have a wife. His long pale fingers played with each other constantly, whereas Jouve's hands, more carpenter- or butcher-like, ignored each other, carefully avoided contact, each one ensconced most of the time in one of Jouve's pockets.

Heavy-set, ten years older than Salvador and four inches shorter, Jouve prudently sipped the contents of his glass: the carbonated water and lemon blended with the chlorinated air of the natatorium to gently cleanse his nostrils. "So," he finally said, "who is it this time?" He shook his head when Salvador uttered a woman's name. "Mm, no, I don't think so," he said. "I don't believe I've heard of her."

"Take a look anyway," said Salvador, handing him a ream of press clippings and photos depicting the same young woman, always on the point of departure, with captions mentioning the name Gloria Stella.

Two kinds of photos. On the four-color ones, cut from the glossy pages of weekly magazines, one could see her leaving the stage, or bursting from a Jaguar or a jacuzzi. On the other, slightly more recent ones, in poorly screened black-and-white garnered from the Society pages of the daily press, you could see her exiting a police station, leaving a lawyer's office, or walking down the steps of a courthouse. If the first batch of photos, perfectly lit, abounded in dazzling smiles and triumphant looks, the second was filled with averted eyes behind dark glasses and closed lips, flattened out by the flashbulbs and hastily centered. "Hang on," said Jouve, "wait a moment."

While waiting, Salvador excused himself. On the door to the toilet stalls, amid various propositions, an exasperated felt pen had inscribed THOSE WHO CAN'T DO, TEACH SWIMMING. "I've got it," said Jouve when Salvador retook his seat in the cafeteria. "Now I recognize her. I remember that story. Whatever happened to that girl?"

"No idea," said Salvador. "Vanished four years ago. I'd like you to handle this for me. It shouldn't be too complicated, should it?"

"Shouldn't be," said Jouve. "We'll have to see."

Soon afterward they headed out on foot toward the city's outer boulevards. "Right," Jouve said. "I'll start a file. It would be good if you could write down everything you know about her."

"Of course," said Salvador, pulling another paper from his pocket. "I drew this up for you. I've put down everything I could find on this sheet."

"Nice-looking girl, in any case," Jouve pronounced as he leafed through the photos. "Can I keep them?"

"By all means," said Salvador.

With Jouve, Salvador walked once more past the counterintelligence headquarters, of which only the upper floors were visible behind a protective wall bristling with barbed wire and fixed cameras aimed at the sidewalk. At wide intervals, enameled signs bolted to the wall discouraged people from photographing or filming the area, which enjoyed military classification and bore witness to successive styles of administrative architecture from 1860 to 1960. A tall, skinny metal tower supported a number of antennae directed toward the four corners of the earth, and the only means of ingress was a heavy gateway mounted on rails, through which French vehicles containing vague individuals entered and exited nervously. Two uniformed sentries guarded this gateway, with similarly deterrent expressions and somber appearances, their eyes masked by mirrored shades.

"To tell the truth," Salvador said, "this might not be too easy. We looked around a bit ourselves, but came up with nothing. It's as if she hasn't been in touch with anyone in, as I said, almost four years."

"We'll see," said Jouve. "I'll get somebody on it for you right away. But who?" He wondered. "There's Boccara, who wouldn't be bad; I'll see if he's free. Or else Kastner, maybe. Yeah, better Kastner. Nice guy, and he could handle it just fine. First off, is that the right identity?"

"Excuse me?" said Salvador. "What identity?"

"That, her name," said Jouve, putting his finger on Gloria Stella. "Sounds kind of like a fishing boat, don't you think?"

"Oh, right," said Salvador. "Oh, no, no of course not. But you'll see, I put all that down on the sheet."

2

Late in the afternoon, Jean-Claude Kastner reached the small industrial zone that gave some preliminary idea of Saint-Brieuc. He parked his car in the lot of a pet food factory, then searched in the glove compartment for an opaque plastic pouch, fastened with Velcro, which he set on his knees without opening right away. First he pressed his eyes, with just the tips of his fingers, but hard, to rid them of the 250 miles of highway.

The pouch contained the documents Salvador had given Jouve the day before yesterday, along with Michelin map number 58, detailing Brittany between Lamballe and Brest. In a fold of the peninsula was slipped a handwritten list of port towns swarming up and down the coast, as well as others farther inland, from here to Saint-Pol-de-Léon. According to the first cross-checks that Jouve had done, it was there that the woman might be living—a tall, beautiful, intimidating blonde woman photographed in various angles and various climates. Tracing his route for the next few days, Jean-Claude Kastner joined together in red pencil, directly on the road map, the townlets that he would have to visit. Once the latter had been connected by a broken line, as in certain magazine games, the route formed no discernible shape, and Kastner found this vaguely disappointing.

Having folded these materials back into their sheath, he started up and returned to the highway, continuing on to Saint-Brieuc. With his car parked in the center of town near the covered market, Kastner dined on a deluxe couscous at one of the Maghrebi restaurants that compete with each other near the old station; then he found a room in an unrated hotel opposite the new one. Gloomily lit by a single overhead bulb, the room was a windowless cube with no television or refrigerator, and no toiletries in the bathroom, since there was no bathroom: in a corner they had simply grafted an elementary shower under a tarnished, foldable plastic device, fragile and leaking. Kastner fell asleep fairly quickly.

He woke up just as quickly two hours later, tossed several times in his bed without managing to fall back asleep, turned on the overhead light, then tried to get back into a sci-fi novel whose whys eluded him even more than its wherefores. The room was too hot, then too cold, and Kastner alternately shivered and perspired, unable to keep his mind on what he was reading. Taking up his road map again, he reworked the itinerary established in the parking lot: it didn't change very much, but this time the resulting drawing vaguely suggested a sea horse lying on its side. In desperation, he ended up swallowing a sleeping pill, dozing off after twenty minutes.

Incoherent dreams passed through him, concluded by a familiar nightmare. The classic vertigo dream: Kastner clings with all his might to the top of a vertical mass of disjointed girders and rusty crossbars hanging over an abyss. It's a precarious scaffolding with peeling paint, which a strong wind is threatening to knock down. Kastner doesn't dare look at the void below him; he feels his energy flagging and his strength deserting him, knowing full well that he is about to let go. The situation is already very distressing, and normally the dream ends there; it's there that his terror generally wakes him. But not this time. This time Kastner loses his grip and falls, falls into the endless void. He wakes up, drenched, just before hitting the ground.

Ordered for seven o'clock, his breakfast consisted of watery, mass-produced coffee, orangeade, and pastry. Kastner didn't have the stomach to finish it. The sleeping pill had left his mouth dry, cut his strength just like in his dream, along with most of his appetite. He was achy, feverish; his fingers trembled a bit. He proceeded to do a few half-hearted deep kneebends, after which his sweat gave off a chemical odor that persisted after a careful shower, persevering even through the eau de toilette. Then he put on the same clothes as the day before: brown polyester suit over a wine-colored polyester polo shirt. In this way, Kastner was dressed like some salesmen or door-to-door canvassers—professions that he had more or less held in the past, as well as several others that enjoyed a similar level of prestige in the social scale of employment.

All day long, at the wheel of his car, the Michelin road map folded out on the right front seat, Kastner followed the prescribed route. Stopping in each little town, he showed his photos to bartenders, service station managers, tripe butchers, or bakers not yet done in by the large supermarkets. He convinced himself he was being discreet. Kastner said that the woman in the photos was his sister, or sometimes his sister-in-law. Once he got up the nerve to pretend she was his wife, but it bothered him, upset him, and he didn't risk it again. In any case, the small shopkeepers shook their heads and pouted negatively, and so Kastner also canvassed the large supermarkets. But in vain all that day, and all the next.

On the third day it rained, and Kastner got lost. In fact, it rained without really raining; minuscule droplets dotted the windshield—not heavy enough to make it worth using the wipers, not light enough to do without them. The blade smeared the glass instead of washing it. No doubt because of that, while trying to get to a village named Launay-Mal-Nommé, he missed a junction on Route D789, somewhere between Kerpalud and Kervodin, only to find himself smack in the middle of a cluster of anonymous gray houses. He parked on a platform in front of a massive church, with a monument to the dead to the left and a small seaside graveyard to the right, which was scarcely more lively: nothing to inspire any joy in the man sitting in his car. He tried to decipher his road map, which by now was more like a rebus. Then he vaguely sought out his name on the monument to the dead, but as usual it was a total loss: only patronyms of local vintage were listed there, which did not include the Kastners.

His glance drifted toward the church, behind which an elderly man no sooner emerged than disappeared; then two minutes later a woman skirted the church door. Kastner, despite all the wrong-way streets in his life, had never liked asking directions of anyone, but this time the ambient dampness, loneliness, and silence led him to lower his window and, as the woman was passing nearby, apologize for bothering her:

"Excuse me," he said, "but I think I've lost my way. I'm looking for an intersection. You wouldn't know anything about an intersection around here, would you?"

The woman was young, slightly stooped: little flat shoes, dull mid-length hair that for lack of a better word one would call chestnut brown, large eyeglasses on a small aquiline nose—the whole thing covered in violent makeup and wrapped in a sweatsuit whose halves didn't match. Closed, perhaps fearful expression, nothing attractive, didn't seem mean. She stopped without immediately coming closer, her body leaning to one side under the weight of a bag of groceries. "An intersection," Kastner repeated, "a crossroads."

She appeared at first glance to have no particular ideas on the subject, then not to have very many ideas at all. Doesn't seem all that bright, judged Kastner, slowly repeating himself in a more articulated voice, pressing his finger onto the map that he presented upside down through the lowered window. "Launay-Mal-Nommé," he specified. "That's where I'm going."

"Launay," the woman finally said without looking at the map, "I know it. It's on my way. Wait a minute and I'll tell you."

A pause, then, in a monotonous tone, a succession of first rights and first rights, of lefts before a light, of thirds after the traffic circle, you couldn't miss it; Kastner had quickly stopped following.

"Listen," he said to her, "if you're heading that way, I can give you a lift if you like. You can tell me where to go. Get in—if you like." Another pause, then she gave only a small nod; as she walked around the back of the car, she said something about a bus which Kastner didn't understand. She got in, setting the bag down by her feet. It was in her way for the entire ride, but Kastner didn't dare suggest putting it on the backseat.

The ride offered a uniform vista of scattered gray houses, few of which seemed inhabited, a fair number of which were for sale—but who would want them, Kastner wondered, who would want the ones whose narrow windows didn't look out to the sea? Not me. Not really a place for me. I prefer the sun, and anyway, when you get down to it, I don't have any money. On the bloodless facades one could sometimes see traces of water from a flowerpot or hanging laundry, a sign of life that dripped from the wash and irrigated the flowers. Other facades were barely still breathing, bearing the old skins of advertisements painted fifty years before, the ghosts of hernia trusses and phosphatides.

Immobile on her seat, lips almost still, his passenger indicated the route step by step for Kastner—who, ostensibly watching the road, used his peripheral vision to take in the harsh makeup: apple-green eyelids, two violet lines under the eyebrows, two circles of terra-cotta blush on the cheeks, and extraterrestrial garnet-red lipstick. All of it against a rather pale background. His peripheral vision even made out the time on the kind of little wristwatch you can win at a local fair—something-or-other to seven—and spotted a few red traces that flaked on the half moons of chewed fingernails. Upstream from one of them, Kastner thought he identified a wedding band—but no, the object, having turned, was decorated with a cheap little green stone flanked by three brilliants.

They headed on toward Launay-Mal-Nommé; the young woman was now completely silent. To fill that silence a little, Kastner decided to divulge the reasons for his presence. Employed by a small private company, they had dispatched him into the sector with the mission of finding someone. For reasons that weren't clear to him, he specified—probably some miserable matter of debt repayment, as was too often the case. Careful not to touch his passenger, he stretched out his arm toward the glove compartment and pulled out by feel two or three photos of the someone in question. You wouldn't have seen her, by any chance? She was barely listening or didn't understand it all, said no the way she might have said yes; she didn't seem too happy or too stable. Kastner felt a certain sympathy rising in him, not far removed from a vague solidarity.

Around a bend, the young woman pointed her finger (there, I'm getting off there) at a small, isolated house near the road: Kastner braked while downshifting. The house was gray and squat, like so many others in the area, with a small garden on the side. Won over to the wild state, timorous flowers encircled a yellowed palm that, half-dead from cold despite the microclimate, looked like a large janitor's broom that had been planted in the ground and started growing. "It's not too much farther," the young woman said. "Straight ahead about another half mile."

"Thank you," said Kastner. "Thank you very much."

"Thank *you*," said the young woman. "Can I offer you something to drink?"

"I don't want to impose," said Kastner.

"Oh, come on," she said with a new little smile. Then, as she bent down to get her bag, her left hand seemingly accidentally brushed Kastner's right thigh. Who shuddered imperceptibly. Who then said sure, OK, and parked his car on the verge. "Don't leave your car out here," said the young woman. "I'll open up for you."

"Sure, OK," repeated Kastner, whose auto then crossed through the gate and rounded the house toward a small courtyard that mirrored the garden. Kastner switched off the engine, got out of the car, and slammed the door without taking his keys from the ignition.

The sea was not very far away. Through a side window, in the absence of a clear horizon line, one could almost see it blending with the sky in the waning daylight. Kastner was now sitting in a not overly comfortable wicker armchair, a glass in his hand, piles of brochures at his feet. The furnishings in the living room were rudimentary, mismatched as in the kinds of houses one rents on vacation; a socket hung bulbless from a wire in the middle of the ceiling. After a first glass, Kastner had accepted another, then a third, before the young woman had suggested, given the hour and since he was there, that he stay for dinner. It would be a change from the usual steak and fries swallowed alone and at top speed; he hadn't put up much resistance. They didn't speak much more after that. Kastner heard the woman moving glass and metal objects in the kitchen. The idea—incongruous, immediately dismissed—crossed his mind that he could spend his whole life this way.

While waiting, he took stock of the brochures: always the same magazines in last month's issues, a television guide, the almanac of tides for the current year. Leafing through the latter, he looked for today's date, scarcely familiar with these phenomena. Nonetheless, he seemed to understand that corresponding to today's date, at eleven twenty-four p.m., there would be a record level of high tide. The young woman passed through the living room from time to time, restoring the levels in the glasses until dinner was pronounced ready.

She had prepared only white foods: peeled shrimp, noodles, and plain yogurt, seasoned with sauces in tubes whose colors were no less vivid than her makeup. White wine. As Kastner asked a few questions about her life, she claimed to have worked the previous year in a canning factory, to have lost her job, to be currently unemployed, like a fair number of people in the area (unfortunately that seems to be the case all over, Kastner commiserated gravely), but that she helped out twice a week at a fish market in Ploubazlanec (I worked in fish too, Kastner informed her, without specifying further).

After dinner—rather drunk, to tell the truth—Kastner reeled out a few tortuous phrases from which one could deduce that he found the young woman quite pleasing and that he was, indeed, rather attracted to her. As she smiled while refilling his glass, he judged that the situation was advancing nicely. As she did not pull her hand away from his, he figured it was in the bag. Kissing her voraciously a bit later as he leaned against the door, he was forced to admit that he was having a hard time standing up. Then, with a snicker, his fingers blindly sought an opening in the uncooperative textile; he was starting to get excited when he broke out in a cold sweat. The woman laughed and shook her head; she gently caressed Kastner's cheek before her hand slid down to his neck, against his chest, and when she passed over his belt the man trembled from head to foot and turned pale. Then, although she was still pressed tightly against him, Kastner continued to shake. "What's wrong?" she asked in a low voice. Kastner found it hard to explain. "Come," she said, "let's get some air. It will clear your head."

"OK," said Kastner, "sure."

He hadn't paid much attention to the time passing during dinner. He was surprised that night had already fallen, so black, opaque, and dull, solid as concrete, devoid of stars as if its consistency were blocking out the celestial vault. Far off in the corner a moon just barely hung, reduced to its thinnest shaving. Scarcely out the door, Kastner put his arm around the young woman again and took the liberty, encouraged by the fresh air and the darkness, to explore matters a bit further. She did not seem to mind this development, and so Kastner was pleased. "Wait a minute," she said. "Come—we'll be more comfortable over there."

To get over there, away from the road, they took a dirt path between two artichoke patches. The young woman went ahead while Kastner followed by guesswork, stumbling to the rhythm of the potholes, disoriented by darkness, horniness, and white wine. Unable to see even his feet, the man discovered at the last second that the sea was right there, thirty yards below. You couldn't see it from the top of the cliff he had just reached, but Kastner divined its proximity by its habitual low growl, punctuated with convulsions. Crashing here and there on the rocks, a larger wave exploded like a bass drum, dissipating afterward in shudders of studded cymbal. The woman seemed to be disappearing toward the silhouette of a small blockhouse, the size of a sentry box for two—perfect, stammered Kastner's consciousness.

But an instant later she had vanished behind the pillbox. Kastner reached it, walked around it without finding her. He tried calling out to her, realizing only then that he didn't know her name, and timidly emitted a few exclamations of the *hey, hello* variety—followed by a prolonged *euhh* for his own benefit, bending toward the sea but leaning with one hand against the sentry box wall.

Then, as he tumbled into the void under the impact of a violent shove, his groan was transformed into a strangled cry, a horrified whimper that stretched out while, in fast motion, the sensations of his last dream rushed toward him. During his fall he barely had time to hope he would wake up again before hitting the ground, but not this time. This time his body would shatter for real against the rocks. Of the man named Kastner only his clothes would remain intact, transformed into a sack of broken bones. Two hours later the tide would rise to take care of them; then its record level would carry them far away from the coast, and six weeks afterward the sea would bring them back, beyond recognition.

That Jean-Claude Kastner should manage, first, to lose his way in a civilized and well-marked region already suggests that he was not the world's sharpest investigator. That he should have to ask directions of a passerby says a lot about his ingenuousness. But that he should not recognize her as the very person he was seeking disqualifies him once and for all. Even if that person had changed a lot.

The fact was, she had completely transformed herself. Judging by the documents they had given him, Kastner had pictured some tall, elegant blonde with interminable legs and high heels, the delicately pitched gait of a tightrope walker, and a clear gaze sloping gently down toward him. That was how he had visualized her. That was no longer the case. She no longer fit a single point of the description. On the other hand, it's true that, since the day she had disappeared, things had had plenty of time to evolve.

3

And the next day, you are someone looking for Paul Salvador. Your vehicle carries you toward the eastern part of Paris, near Porte Dorée, not far from the Bois de Vincennes. You park in front of the modern building that houses Stochastic Films: six floors of offices and studios, sixty million francs in yearly revenues, rising from the corner of Avenue du Général-Dodds and Boulevard Poniatowski. You walk in without attracting attention. Airtight as a bunker, the lobby is decorated with green plants and lit by indirect spots; in its center rises a tall, polychromatic abstract sculpture, a totem planted slantwise in a gravel doormat. To the right, a row of exceptional receptionists, all nails, lashes, and breasts; to the left, nothing special. Just ahead, the elevators. Forget the receptionists, head straight for the elevators.

You cross the lobby; no one asks you anything. Secure in their three-day beards, the young men in boots and leather jackets barely even jostle you. Your eyes would also like to linger on all the unstructured girls who come and go here, but you ignore them as well and proceed straight ahead. You enter the elevator, press number 3.

The elevator door opens onto a hallway that you follow to the first open office: that's it. Enter. Stand quietly in a corner. Wait.

Whatever happens, no one will notice you. In any case, Salvador's office is empty for the moment. It's a large room whose double-thick panes calmly overlook the avenue traffic. Armchairs and conference table, as well as large oval mirror and sofa. On one wall, two paintings by who knows who; against another, volume lowered, six stacked televisions broadcast the day's programs. The walls are dark green, the carpet warm sand. Not a folder lying around, not a sheet of paper; all the data is digitized. Only on the table do a few files rest, ongoing projects that Stochastic will deliver, made-to-order and ready-to-wear, to public and private TV stations.

And here comes Salvador, seeming not very busy. He walks around his office, stares at but doesn't really see the specters wriggling onscreen, nor the avenue through the window, nor his reflection in the oval mirror. Distractedly he leafs through the files while awaiting his assistant. Here she is now. Let's go.

37-24-36: no matter what the season, Donatienne stands out by wearing clothes that are supernaturally short and miraculously low-cut, sometimes so short and so low-cut at the same time that between these adjectives almost no actual fabric remains. Endowed with the energy of a breeder reactor, Donatienne throws an envelope quilted with plastic bubbles onto the table before dropping into a chair and expressing herself in a rapid voice, sharp but fragile like a fishbone made of chalk. It sometimes happens that talking, for Donatienne, consists in reeling off a single, unending sentence without catching her breath, without period of comma or pause—a performance that, as far as Salvador can tell, only Roland Kirk has matched on the saxophone, and perhaps also Johnny Griffin to a lesser extent—all the while beating, in triple time, the arm of the chair with her right palm. It also happens that once in a while she speaks more soberly.

Salvador rips open the envelope that she dropped on the table. It contains two 45s recorded five or six years earlier, when vinyl was still the coin of the realm. Both carry the name Gloria Stella in boldface, followed by the title of the A-side ("Too Too Too" for one, "We're Not Taking Off" for the other) superimposed over a color photo of the singer. Donatienne, meanwhile, describes all the trouble she's had procuring these two records, now out of print. She seems to be stressing—Salvador is barely listening—the gap between the breadth of her research and the value of its object. To underscore her point, she makes a disdainful gesture with her left hand while shrugging one shoulder, causing a strap of her brief garment to slip down the other shoulder. As she frequently shrugs her shoulders, a strap of her dress slips one time out of two, and the next time it's the other strap; Salvador averts his eyes two times out of two. But just then the telephone rings, allowing him to busy himself elsewhere. "I'm listening," he utters.

At the other end of the line, Jouve sounds concerned. The evening before, his employee Kastner neglected to call in with a progress report, as he was instructed to do daily, no matter what, and fruitful or not. "I'm a little worried," he says. "That's the first time. It isn't like him. Anyway, I'll see if he calls tonight."

"All right," says Salvador. "Keep me posted." Then, after hanging up, "To work," he says. Donatienne opens the Gloria Stella file.

Usually, Salvador's programs appeal to collective memory. Where are they now? That's the formula: a good, reliable formula that has proven itself time and time again. You go in search of a name whose posterity has faded, whose echo has died out. Retired talk-show host, single-role actor, overachieving crook, radio game-show champion, vanished top-of-the-bill amnestied by memory. You exhume a one-time instant celebrity who had soon dissolved into neglect, someone people remember so little that they don't even remember having forgotten him, but who is there nonetheless: stored like the others at the back of a closet, in memory's oldest boxes. Those boxes are still there, way in back, even though a few have been damaged by a leak in memory's ceiling. The labels pasted on them are now a bit hard to read. Salvador's programs consist in repainting the ceiling, refreshing the memory, opening those boxes.

But this might take a more intimate and personal turn. So it was, for example, with *From the Bottom of My Heart*, a ratings hit with the pre-retirement crowd in the provinces, or with *The Prettiest Girl on the Beach* ("You once saw the prettiest girl on the beach and you remember her. You remember her all too well, though you didn't dare talk to her. Do you remember her name? Write to us. We'll find you that prettiest girl on your beach."). It was another matter entirely with Gloria Stella, whose case fell into a broader category. Indeed, first as a popular singer, then as the heroine of human interest stories, she had gotten herself pretty well noticed five or six years ago, for a few months.

Career brief: Born Gloire Abgrall, precocious teenage fashion model. Entered the world of variety shows under the pseudonym dreamed up by Gilbert Flon, her lover-cum-agent.

Bottom line: those two 45s, a shot at the Olympia, a few tours as special guest star, number three on the hit parade for "Excessive"; photographs, autographs, fan club, movies on the horizon. It all looked very promising until Gilbert Flon took a suspicious dive down a fourth-floor elevator shaft.

Since then: suspicion, investigation, prosecution witnesses, indictment, trial, verdict (five years; extenuating circumstances), prison, release for good conduct, disappearance.

So that, having covered the ground in the teenage weeklies, then in the women's monthlies, having cleared herself a little place in the Arts and Entertainment sections of the dailies, it was more and more in black-and-white that they then transferred her from the Celebrity news to the Legal columns, before she sank into the deep column of Forgotten.

Where, indeed, was she now? Not a peep in four years. She must be thirty by now. The perceptible path of Gloire Abgrall stopped dead the day of her release from prison, the date on which any relatives and allies she had left stopped receiving the slightest sign of life from her. She disappeared into the woodwork like a good thousand other persons a year who are never seen again. Still, Salvador and Donatienne are hopeful. While waiting for Jouve's men to find her, they put the finishing touches on their project: specifying the order of documents from the video library, archives, news of the day, interviews with those closest, specialists' viewpoints—courts, mental health, and show business.

Naturally, Salvador is not the first to look for Gloire Abgrall. Numerous paparazzi have tried, with no other result than, for one who was a little more brazen than the rest, the outline of his body deeply embossed in the roof of a Peugot parked in front of Rouen cathedral (Seine-Maritime region), at the bottom of a two-hundred-foot drop.

After their work has ended and Donatienne has left, Salvador makes the rounds of his office one last time. Noticing, next to its envelope, the recorded opus of Gloria Stella, he slips a 45 from its pouch and drops "Too Too Too" onto the turntable. Standing near the window he watches, on the boulevard, a leather-clad woman extricating herself from a diesel automobile. The song plays and he listens to the words, popping the envelope's little plastic bubbles between his fingers, one by one, the way he had treated, on family vacations thirty years before, the little bubbles of algae growing on the submerged rocks off the Giens peninsula (Var region).

4

On the morning of that same day, the woman who had sealed Jean-Claude Kastner's fate awoke a little before nine o'clock. She had opened her eyes on the grayish ceiling, then, recognizing it, got up and slipped on a shapeless green fleece-lined bathrobe. But immediately afterward, in the bathroom mirror, she had trouble recognizing her face.

Hurling a man into the void being the sort of thing that can make you forget to remove your makeup, it was a contracted mask that appeared to her in the glass, petrified by sweat and suffocating under the greasepaint. She restored her image with scant consideration, using cold water and household soap, as delicately as one sandblasts a facade. Her hair was not a pretty sight, but she, who hardly cared, brushed it back violently. She gave the mirror an evil grimace that bared her teeth, which she then brushed no less brutally—until her gums bled, the handle of the toothbrush snapped in two, and the young woman swore out loud while spitting a pinkish froth onto the sink's yellowed enamel. She rinsed her mouth endlessly before putting on new makeup that was only slightly more discreet than the day before, tying her hair with a brown rubber band. Back in her room, she haphazardly chose a sky-blue blouse with feather prints and a bright red skirt, throwing a large navy-blue smock over the whole thing.

Standing in the kitchen, Gloire Abgrall then emptied a large bowl of coffee in one gulp. On the sides of the bowl, pochoir silhouettes of fruits and vegetables chased after each other beneath the cracks. She glanced out the window to check the weather: silent light-gray front. The windows hadn't been cleaned in some time, and it was hard to make out what was happening outside, but even in the kitchen it wasn't that easy to see either, as if the air itself hadn't been cleaned. Setting the bowl on the table, she then gathered some food scraps onto a page of newspaper—crusts, tops, peelings—before going out.

Behind the house, the back of the small courtyard ended in a shed in which a one-eyed, formerly white Renault R5 stood parked, and a few rimless tires, two caneless chairs, and an enucleated lamp grew mold. A first-generation washing machine and an antique boiler framed a hutch in which a rabbit, fleshy and trembling, pondered the short term with an opaque eye. The young woman crossed the courtyard with her food, a grating little wind brushing at her temples. Then, as she was about to lean toward the animal: "Personally," said Béliard, "I don't disapprove."

Gloire Abgrall turned her head and Béliard was there, sitting on her shoulder. Well, what do you know, he was back. Casually posed on her shoulder, legs dangling and eyes looking elsewhere, Béliard leaned with one hand on her collarbone, and with the other rubbed his chin.

"Ah," she breathed, "there you are." Béliard nodded contentedly. "And anyway, so what?" she said. "Disapprove of what?"

Béliard crossed his tiny legs and doubled over with a sharp laugh: "The guy last night," he said. "Others might disapprove. Not me. You were within your rights, Gloire, you've had enough to deal with. They've given you enough to deal with. I'm just calling it as I see it."

"I don't give a shit how you see it," Gloire declared.

"It's my duty to tell you," Béliard observed in a pinched voice.

"It's part of my job. Afterward, you can do as you like." Then he fell silent, sulkily folding his arms and staring straight ahead.

"All right, fine," said the young woman, "don't pout."

"I am *not* pouting," Béliard said coldly. "If you only knew how little I cared."

"Come on now," she said. "Come on now, Béliard."

Béliard is a skinny little brunette, about a foot tall and with a slightly receding hairline, part on the side, drooping eyelids and upper lip, muddy complexion. He is wearing a brown cotton suit, dark purple tie, and shiny little brown shoes, spit-polished. Rather disgraceful spineless face, though with a determined expression. Arms folded, his fingers stick out of sleeves that are a bit too long for him, and drum on his elbows.

At best, Béliard is an illusion. At best he is an hallucination forged by the young woman's deranged mind. At worst, he is a kind of guardian angel, or at least can claim some kinship with that congregation. Let us envision the worst.

If he really is one, created too ugly and too small to be officially recognized by a fraternity overly preoccupied with its movie-star physique, they must immediately have dumped him on Social Services. That is, unless they simply abandoned him on the side of a highway during a move, a parade, or an angels' convention abroad, cuffed with his standard-issue halo to a roadsign. Whatever the case, from a very young age he had to get along by himself, taking advantage (despite everything) of whatever gifts and qualities his birth conferred. Ignored by his own kind, renounced by his hierarchy, perhaps even slapped with a prohibition, he is compelled to ply his trade as a freelancer, outside normal channels and as discreetly as possible.

Moreover, he isn't always there, or at least not always physically present: the frequency and duration of his visits with the young woman vary. Sometimes he stays away for two months, sometimes he shows up every evening like a regular at the local bar, sometimes for two hours in the middle of the night as if with some girl. Always he seems rather self-centered, not too observant of principles, often in a surly mood. Occasionally he keeps office hours, a cruising little nine-to-five, but he might also spend three weeks grounded on his little corner of shoulder, immobile, nervous, taciturn, looking hunted, as if hidden away or wanted by the authorities. In short, he's pretty irregular. The only general rule is that he shows up when Gloire is alone, which has not been an uncommon occurrence in the past four years. Lately he hasn't been too constant, coming by only two or three times a week. Not that he does anything in particular when he's there, but at least he's there.

At the moment, he was clearing his throat, patting his lips with a balled-up handkerchief. He seemed to be lost in thought. "Did it feel the same?" he said in a distracted voice, without looking at the young woman.

"What do you mean?" she said in the same tone. "Did what feel the same?"

"The guy last night," specified Béliard. "When you pushed him. What did it feel like? Compared to the other times, I mean."

"Fucking little asshole!" hissed Gloire. "Goddam little asshole piece of shit! We agreed we'd never bring that up."

"Just doing my job," Béliard reminded her.

As Gloire leaned toward the hutch, Béliard, to keep his balance, slid toward the back of her shoulder, almost to the shoulder blade. When she stood up again without warning, he nearly went tumbling head over heels, but regained his equilibrium just in time: "Ah," he grated, "*that* was smart." Then, having settled in again, "So, what's the plan for today?"

"You'll see," said Gloire.

"I'd like to be a little more involved in the decision-making," Béliard declared energetically. "I'd like to have my say in all this. I mean, after all, that's what I'm here for, isn't it?" She, having turned around, now walked resolutely toward the house. "Hey, what are you up to?" he worried. "Where are you going like that?"

"I have to take a piss," Gloire said abruptly, "and maybe a shit, too. I don't know yet."

"All right," said Béliard, averting his gaze, pinching and knotting his nostrils and brow. "Fine. I'll just step out for a moment."

"Now there's an idea," said Gloire.

As soon as he had evaporated, she automatically brushed off his spot with the tips of her fingers, as if to dust herself off when there wasn't anything to dust, the immaterial Béliard neither leaving any remains—spit-out fingernail, sweat, textile debris—nor having any weight on her shoulder.

He returned to his position around noon, as Gloire was getting rid of the last traces of Jean-Claude Kastner. He had watched her work, at first grumbling in a low voice, then shutting himself up in a meditative silence, without offering the slightest opinion or advice: miniservice. The day passed, waned. Late in the afternoon, Gloire settled into a folding chair under the palm tree, intending to leaf through some magazines. The dried palm leaves surrounding the tree's lower hemisphere clacked like wooden rattles, or the way a band of feverish birds might shiver with the tips of their beaks. Not so easy to read with that idiot sitting on your shoulder and naturally reading along with you—and to make matters worse, not necessarily at the same speed: "Hang on a minute," he said once as Gloire was about to turn the page, "just two seconds, all right? OK, you can turn now." Then, when night had fallen: "Well," he said, suddenly shivering, "I should start thinking about leaving soon."

"You're right," said Gloire, glancing at her watch, "you'll have to start getting ready."

Béliard shook himself, stretched, then gave a long yawn. Sighing contentedly after his yawn, not seeming especially eager to move, he stared at the setting sun, blinking his eyes as if he'd just awoken, going over events in his head, doublechecking the rest of the plan. These days he always left at about the same time—and as for where he went, the subject was never broached. If he hadn't been incorporeal, he probably would have asked for a cup of coffee, or one for the road. But in his state of substance, he had never yet shown the least sign of hunger or thirst. "Well," he finally murmured, "I'm off."

After his evaporation, Gloire spends a typical evening alone. Serves herself some wine, some bread and butter—the first is hard because it's a day old, the second because it has just come out of the fridge. Chili heated in the can, yogurt with exotic fruit flavors that she eats without transition, mechanically, while standing up, taking no more of a pause than the soundtrack of spots, jingles, and flashes spewed out by the radio. Sometimes in a low voice, an octave down, she picks up the refrain of a song. Cursory dishwashing before turning off the radio and switching on the television, which she can't bring herself to watch.

Impossible to watch it, as if Gloire had forgotten how. A TV movie starts, which she forces herself to follow to the bitter end—but it was just the opening sequence, the movie is really only starting now; that's discouraging. She tries to concentrate on the plot, but in vain: as nothing in her retains them, the images pass through her like X-rays, like an undifferentiated electronic wind, monochromatic and smooth, tepid and muted. Gloire summons the strength to switch off the TV before total hypnosis sets in.

Silence. A glance at the alarm clock creeping grudgingly toward ten p.m. Outside, not a single animal around to give a sign of life, not a single car passes on the road. Only a deafening silence in which all kinds of parasitic thoughts, a word, a name, an incoherent refrain of words and names, develop and become amplified: an insane melodic loop whose echo comes and goes, distorts and twists around, as if in a machine drum, in Gloire's mind as she sits in front of nothing. To break out of it she turns the radio on full-blast, then immediately snaps it off again, horrified. She gets up, walks a few feet only to sit down somewhere else; every evening it's the same thing. Ten thirty and no desire to go to sleep despite the spread of multicolored soporifics splayed out next to her bed, asking only to be of service. Suddenly Gloire stands and grabs the collar of her coat.

She heads to the Manchester, only ten minutes away with the Renault. It's the kind of rural nightclub that you sometimes find on the fringes of small towns, sometimes even in the middle of the countryside; the kind that make you wonder what they're doing there. Inside the straw hut made of concrete is just a bar that closes a bit late, containing a small floor on which the only dancer, two mornings a week, is a cleaning woman with a broom. This evening there's no one at the Manchester except three young guys busy making noise near the bar. The young guys resemble each other like brothers, sporting bomber jackets and wide French-made jeans, tow-colored hair, and checkered shirts. They are the crossbred product of farmers, workers, and fishermen, and two of the three are unemployed; Gloire doesn't know them. She orders a drink, standing not too far from these guys who have already had a few drinks themselves. As one of them, the tallest one, begins talking to her rather familiarly, the two others split their sides in the background. We gather she doesn't much care for such behavior.

Indeed, she is not in the mood and things could turn ugly, at least for the tall guy who has moved nearer and is now trying to put his arm around her. Lucky for him, not far away, nonchalant as you please, Béliard, who is invisibly keeping an eye on all this, is not about to stand idly by and let Gloire unleash her violence again so readily. Extra hours and overtime rates, but no matter—the homunculus decides to step in.

5

Donatienne reappeared the following afternoon, dying of thirst. The weather had changed (light drizzle), and Donatienne had changed too. This wasn't immediately noticeable but, after she had shed her raincoat, what she was wearing revealed itself to be still scantier than the day before—so short and so low-cut that this time these adjectives tended to blend together, with a view toward shacking up in the same entry of the first dictionary they could find.

In a corner of his office, Salvador had a small refrigerator containing all the necessary accoutrements, but as for glasses he possessed only cups of the disposable picnic variety. And the sound of ice cubes in the plastic was dull, cheap, without resonance, without the elation of real glass glasses, in which the ice may clink and glint proudly: the gin and tonic's rhythm section.

"Too bad," Donatienne resigned herself. "Did Jouve call?" Salvador shook his head. "Call him," Donatienne suggested.

Salvador called, but the line was busy. "I'll try again later," he said.

Before him, in scattered folders and envelopes, lay his main project: tall blonde women in the movies, in the arts in general, and more broadly, in life. Their histories, their characters, their roles. Their specialties and their variations. Their whole significance in five-times-fifty-two minutes. While the project mainly involved splicing together existing works, the fifth episode was to be devoted to a specific case. They had sought out a living example of a bizarre tall blonde, eventually settling on Gloire Abgrall.

Indeed, after they had reviewed all the classical formats, Gloire embodied, by her evolution, her life, and her work, a special case within the framework. She could represent the anomaly, the oddity, the indirect example, one way among many to illustrate Salvador's thesis—to wit, that tall blondes constituted a group apart, neither better nor worse than anyone else but special, governed by specific laws, following a separate plan: an irreducible category of humanity. In short, tall blondes versus the rest of the world. A firm conviction, an obvious postulate in Salvador's mind, but somewhat difficult to demonstrate. Every day new arguments presented themselves to his brain, and every day he struggled to shape them, to establish the overall order in all of this. For Donatienne, once more, he tried to clarify his thinking.

"OK," said Donatienne, "I can see this hasn't progressed very far. Don't you want to try Jouve again?" He tried: still busy. "Let's just go there," proposed Donatienne. "The best thing would be to just go there. I'll drive."

They took Porte d'Ivry to reach the left bank of the Seine and followed it in a westerly direction. In a car with Donatienne, life itself became convertible. As on the previous day, she couldn't stop talking, her uninterrupted discourse standing in for the car radio. Moreover, once past the Pont Neuf they had to take several tunnels—that series of short, cold, underground passageways that border the river—and at the entrance to each tunnel her voice progressively faded out, her words stopping until they had come out the other side: a phenomenon car radios know all too well. Then her outflow resumed as soon as they were back in daylight, but without picking up where it had left off, having continued underground in suspension, probably as an interior monologue. Salvador then had to splice the two halves together, to reconstruct the buried missing portion.

Ten bridges later, near Bir-Hakeim, they turned left into the fifteenth arrondissement: a boulevard, an avenue, then a maze of small, quiet streets up to Jouve's building behind the Kinopanorama. One of those small, quiet, distinguished streets that knows how to behave, whose dapper, freshly remodeled buildings never raise their voices inconsiderately. Parking lot, entrance code, intercom, elevator, doorbell, spyhole (dark for two seconds), bolt.

Then Jouve, looking rather tired. "Ah," he said, "it's you." Voice sluggish and motor functions circumspect, with perhaps a hint of anisette. His eyes kept watch as best they could above their ringed sockets, ready to sink into them and go back to sleep. "Still no news from my field agent," he immediately informed them. "But come in, come in." They moved into the living room: geometric wallpaper and skin-pink vase containing a potted flower; a few paintings on the walls (wedding scene in Charente, full-length portrait of a puffin); distinct undertone of Airwick eucalyptus. At Salvador and Donatienne's entrance, a weeping Mrs. Jouve rose from her end of the sofa to turn off the VCR and briefly greeted them before leaving the room. Salvador had already met her; Donatienne, who came in after him, saw only a thin, translucent silhouette, hypersensitive and hypertense.

"She's been watching TV all day," Jouve apologized. "She gets very emotional about the soaps. You'll have something to drink?"

Motioning toward two armchairs, he dropped onto the other end of the couch, facing the television that he designated with a brief movement of his chin. "Not always the same taste," he sighed. In fact, on either side of the sofa lay two remotes: while Jouve measured out the pastis, Donatienne imagined the remote control wars every evening in front of the TV.

"I have to say, I'm a bit surprised," Jouve reiterated. "This isn't like Kastner. We'll wait another day or two."

"It's just that we can't let it drag on too long," Salvador worried. "Don't you have anyone who's a little more competent?"

Jouve stared at his glass as he thought. His glance always drifted very slowly toward things, then adhered to them, stuck there, seemed to have trouble becoming unglued.

"How about Personnettaz?" suggested Salvador. "Couldn't we try with him? He was really good."

Jouve continued to examine his glass before dragging his eyes away, with the sound of tape being ripped off cardboard, and training them on Salvador.

"I'd rather not bother him for so little," he finally said. "I'd prefer to put someone else on it first. Maybe Boccara; I'll call him later on. If that doesn't work, then we could try Personnettaz."

Night was falling when they left Jouve's. After they'd had a little something at the restaurant at Invalides station, Donatienne returned home, but Salvador didn't. A taxi carried him to Porte Dorée. No one left at that hour at Stochastic: in place of the receptionists, under an anemic spotlight, there was only a young watchman rubbing his eyes over a Xerox of international law. "That's not enough light, Lestiboudois," Salvador said in a paternal voice. "Go get a lamp. You'll ruin your eyes that way."

Having returned to his office with the idea of working a bit, Salvador gave up the idea fairly easily. Hardly had he poured himself a few fingers than he began drinking and undressing, a sip, a piece of clothing, a sip, another piece of clothing, such that the glass and he became, at the same moment, respectively empty and nude. That done, he opened a closet and pulled out a blanket, which he spread over the couch before slipping under it in the company of a book entitled *How to Disappear Completely and Never Be Found* by Doug Richmond (New York: Citadel Press, 1994). But scarcely had he opened the work than he shut it again, pressed the switch, and six seconds later he was asleep.

6

One can envision sleep in various forms. Gray scarf, smokescreen, sonata. Gliding flight of a great pale bird, open green portal. Plains. But also slipknot, asphyxiating gas, bass clarinet. Insect retracted onto its brief life, final warning before repossession. Rampart. It's a matter of style; it depends on the way each one sleeps or doesn't sleep, on the dreams that scare or spare one.

At the moment, everyone is sleeping. Salvador, on his couch, poorly. Donatienne, tossing in her huge square bed. Jouve next to Mrs. Jouve, soundly. Jean-Claude Kastner, definitively. As for the woman who hurled Kastner into the big night, judging from the tubes of benzodiazepines and buspirone hydrochloride scattered over her nightstand, she is sleeping chemically. She snores a bit from time to time. She has left a lamp lit nearby, or maybe she simply neglected to turn it off. At the foot of her bed a few books lie open, one on top of the other: detective novels, works by Freud in mass-market paperbacks, and a series of small volumes in English devoted to the identification of common birds, European trees, and wildflowers. In the shadows, not far away, sit an empty flask of cheap rum, a half-empty liter of cane syrup, and a full ashtray. It's the same every night; nothing seems to change very much. Since

Kastner's visit, only two small things are different: one on Gloire's body and the other on the table.

On one of the young woman's ankles, a large Band-Aid protects a cut dating from the day before yesterday, as she was getting rid of Kastner's car after emptying it of its contents: rags, bungee cords, tools, and minor spare items, old rubbish from the glove compartment, Jean-Claude Kastner's personal effects and vehicular registration, which she had gathered in a box—except for two tools, the pliers and hammer. Except, too, for the pouch in which Kastner had kept his itinerary, photographs, and road maps. The pouch isn't bad. Emptied, its contents burned in the sink, washed and disinfected, it now rests on the table.

Behind the wheel of the thus-cleaned car, Gloire had then taken the road to Tréguier and deposited the box in the town incinerator, after which she headed north, the pliers and hammer resting on the seat next to her. Past Larmor, another bit of cliff overhung a very deep ditch, filled with water no matter what the tide. The promontory was relatively steep, rarely visited—ideal. Gloire had parked the car facing the void, using the pliers to remove the plates and the hammer to erase the engine and chassis numbers. Then she had lowered the windows, released the handbrake, and pushed with all her might. In vain, at first: the vehicle resisted. Then, after having moved an inch, slowly another inch, it had suddenly accelerated as of its own volition, to get it over with, and everything had gone smoothly—although at the last moment the young woman's leg had gotten caught on the bumper, an end of which had scraped her ankle. Gloire had cried out and cursed rudely as the car foundered. Bent forward, holding her ankle in one hand, she had leaned grimacing over the cliff. Then as she watched the vehicle sink her face had grown calmer: as if she were under anaesthesia; as if the fall of bodies brought her some peace, like Anthony Perkins pondering the same spectacle in 1960—except that Kastner's vehicle was a compact beige Renault registered in the Paris suburbs that immersed itself obediently and without a fuss, while

Janet Leigh's had been a big white recalcitrant Ford, license number NFB 418.

Then she returned home on foot, limping, following the coastal paths dotted with red and white lines painted on boulders and markers. She buried the plates between two stone blocks, under a mattress of gravel. Back at the house, she had bandaged her ankle and then, while she was at it, converted the pouch into a new medicine kit.

She is still asleep. She does not move in her slumber, even though in her dream, for hours, she has been straddling a powerful motorcycle. Day breaks imperceptibly. Day breaks slowly, delicately, the way an illuminated Boeing softly leaves the runway, the way a string orchestra begins the last movement.

But soon this movement ends and the sun shines, motionless. Gloire climbs down from her motorcycle. She heads toward a phone booth, and it's then that she awakens. Eyes wide open, she remains still for a moment before confronting yet another day: she gets up and puts on her hideous green bathrobe. The kitchen, the electric coffee pot. As the coffee drips, the young woman's gaze falls on a sheet of yellow paper, the back of a flyer lying on a corner of the table with a drawing on it that she must have sketched the evening before—she doesn't remember very clearly. It's the embryo of a portrait, somewhat shaky, perhaps even (worst of all) a self-portrait. Whatever it is, Gloire immediately rips it up with her eyes shut, rips it again into minuscule squares which she dumps into the toilet bowl, flushing them down without looking.

In the bathroom, two tiles are missing on the floor of the shower, a third is cracked, and the rest are coated with tan and brown grit. Gloire has hung her bathrobe on the hook screwed in behind the door. She is naked in front of the square mirror above the sink, a mirror too small to let her see her body, which she has no desire to see in any case. No desire to see her long, flawless legs, her high, round, firm breasts and high, round, firm buttocks that, decked out in their tracksuit, Jean-Claude Kastner would never have imagined.

Had he envisioned such a body, Kastner would never have dared to desire it.

She washes quickly, practically a cold shower, before slowly putting on her makeup. A first layer of moisturizer followed by an almost white base coat, applied evenly the way one prepares a canvas. Having penciled her eyes in almond, she repaints her lids turquoise. Then with the help of a chrome device like snail tongs, Gloire accentuates the curve of her eyelashes before making them very dark and very thick with very greasy mascara. Soon her eyes are the only living things in this face; only they show movement in this immobile mask. Gray-green, they shift from green to gray depending on weather, place, light, and mood. After that, outlining her lips with a red crayon, she overruns the edges, then saturates the inside with a brush. Two orange circles on her cheeks, two swipes of a black pencil on the arches of her eyebrows, and that's that. Beneath this makeup, Gloire Abgrall could pass for a circus performer committed after a nervous breakdown—but not too depressed to perform her little skit as part of the festival organized, family members in attendance, for open house day at the clinic.

We can understand how Gloire, a woman on the run, would wish to disguise herself, how such a mask would help make her unrecognizable; but we might wonder nonetheless whether making herself ugly doesn't also afford her a certain pleasure. Thus bedizened, inspecting her face in the mirror until she feels like vomiting, she is in fact quite content—exulting, guffawing, grimacing—and her contentment increases tenfold when she hears herself utter a few obscenities in an unusually shrill register.

Moreover, that excess of makeup must rub off when someone kisses her—but hardly anyone kisses her, she makes sure of that. Of course, she occasionally finds herself obliged: to get rid of Kastner, for example, no way to avoid it. And indeed, then it rubs off but good. Kastner never saw himself after the kiss, falling into the dark void joyously smeared with garnet, apple green, and brown.

Now Gloire has calmed down a little. She has just noticed a

groundswell of light gold threatening the roots of her drab hair. Remember to color it this weekend. Change the Band-Aid. Find something to put on. Strap that watch to her wrist: a quarter to ten. Hey, and what about Béliard? Still naked as a jaybird, Gloire lights a cigarette along with the television, for television in the morning is just as stiff as gin on an empty stomach. But she dresses before the set as if it were someone. She slips on another of her impossible getups: a jacquard decorated with hoarfrost crystals and green, yellow, and mauve bear cubs on a chiné background, over a pair of navy-blue sweatpants crimped at the ankles.

On the television, a female newscaster reports that old people who drink wine have 27 percent better reasoning capacity than old people who don't. Good news for the wine industry, the newscaster comments, and Gloire wonders if that gloss is unintentional humor or not. She ties back her hair, puts on her glasses. A harsh glint in her eyes flashes over the lenses; she is frightening to look at.

Another flash of pale sunlight crosses the dusty windowpane toward the unmade bed, making the rumpled sheets look even dirtier than they are. It is now almost cold in the room; Gloire summarily straightens her bed to warm up the atmosphere. Then she goes out to check the contents of the mailbox: not much, various flyers and papers that she discards without looking at them, keeping only an envelope with the letterhead of the Bardo law firm on Rue de Tilsitt, Paris, which contains a check signed with the name Lagrange. Ten thirty, eleven fifteen, Béliard really is late today. In his stead, someone knocks at the kitchen window: Alain.

Alain, a retired sailor in the fifty-five range, looking less knowledgeable than his age would warrant. Compact, not very tall, face made of scarlet box calf, Gitanes-blue eyes and short reddish hair. V-neck pullover, pants of the same faded blue. Limps a bit because of an accident, but remains stable on his short lower limbs.

Alain stops in on Gloire from time to time, gladly lets himself be served two little glasses of rum, chats with her about benign subjects, the weather, the tide, the locals, the shopkeepers; sometimes he brings her a fish. A big one or a little one, depending. When he smiles, the wrinkles bunch up around his eyes. Though willingly talkative, he speaks in a hesitant, almost interrogative tone and, because of another accident, the movements of his lips are not entirely synchronized with his words. Such as: "How's it going, Christine?"

"Going OK," said Gloire, "going OK. Want some coffee?"

This time, Alain puts on the table a midsize mullet—not the best fish in the world, mullet, but what can you do? Then he talks about the weather, which he deems normal for the season, then about the tide, which was exceptional the other day, as we know, over 380, nearly 400.

This phenomenon comes, he informs her, from the alignment of the earth with the moon and the sun. It's what they call a syzygy.

"A what?" says Gloire.

"A syzygy," repeats Alain, who throws his head back the more briskly to down his coffee. Then come several familiar memories of his travels and more precisely of Australia. Australia where, Alain assures her, not so long ago they still ate their steaks with jelly. From there he forks off onto other fleshly preparations, generalizes about edible meats, then about the controversial personality of the local butcher.

"And is he a good butcher?" Gloire pretends to care, she who lives mainly on dairy, canned goods, vegetables, an egg in a crepe, or nothing.

"He knows what he's doing," says Alain. "He's good."

He reflects a bit before developing his thought, an opportunity Gloire seizes to pour him a little more coffee.

"He's good," Alain continues, "but how can I put it? The animals are always a bit, with respect to what one would like, always a bit too old, that's it. You ask for lamb, you get mutton."

Gloire smiles, then snickers nervously.

"You go for veal," Alain pursues, "he just about gives you its mother. He prepares a good cut of meat, got nothing to say against that, but he likes to take them a little aged."

Gloire has begun to laugh in silence, in small, irrepressible waves that soon begin to swell dangerously; that rise, curl, and finally crash before the sailor's uncomprehending eyes. Now Gloire hiccups, unable to stop. Alain tries to intervene, but with her hand she desperately signals him to be quiet. "Stop," she goes between two spasms, "stop, please stop. Shut up. Get out." Unnerved by this familiarity, the other stops talking, stares at her curiously, then makes up his mind to leave. He leaves, brooding. He knew she wasn't entirely normal, but to *that* extent . . .

He goes on his way, toward his little home which is not far from Gloire's. In his concern Alain fails to notice the metallic blue-gray Volvo 360 parked in front of her house. Body pearly with dew, windows smothered with mist, it seems that there is no one inside. But, equipped with a case of Vittel, a carton of Pall Malls, and a radiophone, someone *is* inside.

7

That radiophone crackled a bit, but it worked: "Boccara here," went a voice. "Can you hear me?"

"Roger," said Jouve. "That was fast. Are you sure it's her? All right, I'll tell the client. Don't move, just wait for my instructions. What's that? Yes, I know it's cold out. Bundle up."

The day began at around nine o'clock. Continental climate. After having made an appointment with Personnettaz—noon at the office—Jouve had put on his coat to cross the city in a southwest-northeast diagonal, by Metro. At the Botzaris stop he got out to take a wide, calm street of provincial character, bordered by plane trees and surrounded by private villas, with few passersby and few shops: walking toward a small police station, Jouve passed by a modest hairdresser's salon, an empty pharmacy, a grade school, and the headquarters of some charity organizations and general contractors.

A rather humble police station served the Amérique quarter. A graceless building in need of renovation, windows with rusty grates, flea-ridden facade in the middle of which the three colors of a dirty national flag, twisted around the pole like an old curtain, overlapped each other. An insignificant outpost far removed from worldly affairs—only rookie officers must have been assigned here, or officers on the verge of retirement, or those found guilty and demoted. The main door had all the allure of a service entrance. Jouve pushed it open.

They seemed to have made some small effort since his last visit, bought a few sticks of secondhand furniture and painted the reception area green; in any case, Jouve didn't visit often. Behind a sort of counter, a young functionary recorded complaints on a fat typewriter which seemed to date from before the advent of electricity. Jouve awaited his turn on a bench while gazing over the bulletins tacked onto corkboards, skimming the map of the arrondissement, pondering two wanted posters, and lending an ear to the various plaintiffs.

Among the latter, a civvie with a short, nervous beard was complaining that a taxi driver had added, after the fact, a large 5 before the number 100 on a check for a hundred francs.

"Didn't you write out the amount?" queried the functionary.

"No," went the other, confused. "Just the number."

"Shouldn't do that," scolded the policeman. "Shouldn't ever do that. Anyway, it's against fiscal regulations."

Then a beautiful young woman with a perm, sunglasses, and tanned shoulders, the kind who drives an Austin Mini, reported to the intimidated policeman the disappearance of her Austin Mini. Jouve, waiting, studied her from top to bottom. Then, when it was his turn: "I'm here to see Inspector Clauze," he said.

"Second floor, room twelve," said the policeman.

"I know," said Jouve. They hadn't repainted the stairway.

Nor the offices. At least not number twelve, in which the guilty and demoted Inspector Clauze presented the terrier-like face of a French character actor. Sinuous voice and filament of mustache, eye squinting over slantwise smile that displayed as frankly as you please the personality of a complete phony. The perfect picture of the kind of backstabbing little crud you might see hanging around casting departments: sarcastic, obsequious, sometimes dangerous, believing himself to be clever, moreover often being so, more than you'd suspect, but ultimately not quite clever enough, since his schemes always manage to backfire. The kind they'd hire to play the shady stockbroker, blackmailing former colleague, or brother-in-law cop. And in fact, he *was* the brother-in-law cop. "So how's Genevieve?"

"She's just fine," said Jouve, "just fine. But you know how emotional she gets."

"Sure do," Clauze said with satisfaction. "And to what do I owe the honor?"

Jouve told him about Gloire Abgrall's disappearance, mentioned her two identities. Clauze was at first hard-pressed to remember, then:

"Oh, right, the singer—I remember the trial. Whatever became of her?"

"That's the point," said Jouve. "I'm asking *you*."

As usual, Clauze started waving his arms around and rolling his eyes heavenward. "Always the same," he summarized, "you know damn well I can't do anything for you. She paid her debt, all right? You can look for a missing person when it's a minor, but for adults there's nothing we can do. Adults have every right to disappear."

"Robert," uttered Jouve.

"Even when it's the family who's looking, you know it never works out. If somebody doesn't want to be found, there's nothing we can do. Nothing I can do."

"Forget about that," said Jouve, "find me everything you can about her, Robert. Find it now."

"Careful how you talk to me," Clauze suddenly stiffened. "Watch it. You can't make me do anything."

"I think I can," said Jouve.

"Don't be an asshole," said Clauze. "*I* paid my debt, too. I strayed, they found out, and they put me back to zero. I paid through the nose."

"You know damn well," Jouve pointed out, "that they never knew the half of it. You know I've kept the receipt."

So as to fill the heavy silence that followed, an automobile considerately drove up Avenue du Général Brunet.

"One day we'll settle this," Clauze said venomously.

"For sure," said Jouve. "One day we'll have to."

After another car had gone down the avenue in the opposite direction, Clauze finally stood up—I'll be back, I have to make a phone call—leaving behind his detective odor: essence of cafeteria and office, perfume of jail and slum, effluvium of hovel, oil of dump, everything a policeman passes through, everything a policeman must pass through. While awaiting his return, through the window Jouve watched the branch of a plane tree limply beat the air. Ten twenty-five.

Clauze reappeared with an appeased face, without apparent grievance, as if settling a perfectly normal matter, paper in hand and pride all swallowed. "Not easy to find," he said in a detached voice. "The guy I called at first thought she was dead, but I guess not. Anyway, we came up with this. You can give this a shot." Jouve glanced at the piece of paper: the address of a law firm near the Champs-Elysées.

"Thank you, Robert," he said. "I won't forget it."

"Fine," Clauze said calmly. "Now go to Hell."

At around eleven o'clock, Jouve returned to his office, a former building manager's domain with very little light and a gray-painted window facing the street. He had kept the original furniture: tubes and latex, bottom of the line and not particularly comfortable. Not much better, in small business terms, than the police station of the Amérique quarter. Jouve read the paper and organized some files; Personnettaz appeared at noon sharp.

Personnettaz hadn't put on any weight. Unhealthy-looking as ever. Still that not-very-reassuring air of a soldier-monk. Jouve explained the situation: Kastner's disappearance, his replacement by Boccara, Gloire's personality. "She won't be easy," he said. "The kid can't handle it. What do you say to taking over?"

"I have some free time at the moment," Personnettaz uttered after a long silence. "In any case, I'll need an assistant."

"Take Boccara," Jouve offered. "He's young, but he'll make you a good little sidekick."

An hour later, in the lobby of Stochastic, Jouve's appearance clashed with the employees of that enterprise, and his teeth gnashed in their direction. He entered Salvador's office as the latter was going over the next episode of *The Prettiest Girl on the Beach* with Donatienne. "I've got this for you," said Jouve, holding out his brother-in-law's paper. "Excuse me, old friend," said Salvador, "but I'm a bit—you see." "I'm not your old friend," observed Jouve. "Beg your pardon?" said Salvador. "Oh, forgive me, Jouve, it's stress, I'm awfully sorry." ("OK," said Donatienne, "so there's a Mr. Yvon Querson who gave the name of a Miss Anabelle Fleury, who we found.") "No harm done," said Jouve. "Here." ("Who recognized herself," Donatienne continued, "who is now Mrs. Annabelle Schnitzler and who's agreed to come on the show.") "What *is* this thing?" Salvador grunted, glancing over the paper. "Hey, hold on, Jouve. Hey, wait a second. Hey, come back!" ("We'll have to notify the families," Donatienne projected, "and we've found some of her friends. We even found the lifeguard who was on duty that day at the beach.") "Shit," muttered Salvador, sitting back down in his chair after Jouve had gone, dignity ruffled, door left open behind him.

Salvador reread the paper that he'd stuffed in his pocket, tried to make heads or tails of it, then: "OK, that's fine—you can take care of that on your own. Let's get down to the important thing."

The tall blondes. Let's recapitulate. We'll proceed by auteurs. We have the Hitchcocks. Then we have the Bergmans. Then we have the ones from Soviet films, satellite nations included. After that we're not sure. Let's start over. Perhaps we'll proceed geographically instead. Mainly American, European, let's say from across the Atlantic to the Urals: tall blondes mostly populate the northern hemisphere. Yes. That's not a very good angle, either. We could begin with a classic reference, everyone included. Let's say the emblematic Monroe-Dietrich-Bardot triangle.

"Isn't that a little overdone?" wondered Donatienne. "Haven't we seen that a hundred times already?"

"Have it your way," said Salvador. "Fine. So we'll organize it by personalities. Let's forget the three classic tall blondes and turn to the oddities. Let's look at the special cases, like Anita Ekberg, you see, or Julie London in another genre. Hand me that file. Let's see. We have the solitary types, the marginals, the failures. We've also got a few insignificant ones. Plus we should mention a couple of comediennes. And take into account the very small number of ugly ones. How do we establish an order? How do we classify the whole thing?"

"Actually, she wasn't as tall as all that, Monroe," Donatienne observed, leaning over the file.

"Nothing to do with it," answered Salvador without raising his eyes, "you don't get my methodology. They don't absolutely need to be tall to fit into the category of 'tall blondes,' not necessarily." (He reflected.) "When you get down to it, maybe they don't even need to be blonde. I don't really know yet."

"Ah," went Donatienne, "forgive me. Forget I said anything. I guess I don't get it."

"My fault," said Salvador. "I'm just getting worked up. But maybe I'm getting off the track. Maybe I should make my criteria a little stricter. Honestly, what do you think? What do you *really* think?"

8

Another late afternoon, almost evening. Gloire is sitting at the kitchen table, elbows on the waxed cloth, two fingers holding a cigarette whose end she taps more often than necessary against the rim of a Martell promotional ashtray. Today she isn't made up, except for her lips, saturated with a violent red that makes her face look even paler than usual. And re-dyed brown as planned, held back with a pink terrycloth loop, her hair is no better styled than last time.

She is not beautiful to behold, but fortunately there is no one there to behold her. Even so, why doesn't she fix herself up a little? She has her reasons, of course, but she could at least buy herself some new clothes once in a while, something a little more flattering, no?

No. She's wearing her sweater with its frosted bear cub pattern, and her feet are in dirty white and blue sneakers bearing the inscription *Winning Team.* Since it is not very warm in the kitchen—the only heat comes from a gas device with a reddening grill over which a brief tongue of magenta flame occasionally runs, producing a dull, vaguely frightening *whump* of air—Gloire has kept on her royal-blue ski parka, polyester and cotton with a polyamide lining, size 4.

It's now seven p.m. and she is alone again. Vexed, Béliard has left after yet another argument. The transistor radio still plays quietly on the table. Sometimes the young woman underscores three notes of a song in a low voice, sometimes she emits a kind of cluck that might make you think she's a little drunk. But no: into the mustard glass with Bugs Bunny's effigy sitting before her, Gloire has dipped her lips only once.

We can see little in that kitchen with its two anemic wall lamps and tube of neon over the sink. We can make out two folded, faded lawn chairs shoved into a corner, the cube-like refrigerator and greasy stove, the massive buffet table, the plastic flowered tablecloth, and two frames on the wall containing a photo of the Maréchal de Lattre and three sunflowers on canvas. The walls haven't been any particular color since the dawn of time and Gloire is sitting in the shadows, how bored she is tonight, oh my God tonight how bored can she be.

When they handed her the keys to the house, Gloire didn't change a thing, preferring not to impose any of her own tastes, which she abandoned. On the contrary, it was herself, her own person that she tried to make conform to the house, letting herself be impregnated, remodeled by this small, poorly lit, badly heated lodging, in a village of ninety-five souls squeezed between an arm of the sea and acres of cereal. Instead of replacing that tablecloth and turning the Maréchal de Lattre against the wall, it was the tablecloth and the photo that she let turn and replace what they wished in her. Rather than repaint the kitchen, Gloire asked the kitchen to choose the color of her blush and eyeliner, dictate her choice of clothes, words, and inflections, define the angle of her stoop.

Gloire Abgrall's life might not seem very happy, but that's the way she wants it. In the four years since she decided to disappear, erase herself from the face of the world and go underground, she has performed all her actions with this in mind, trusting her instincts. She cut all past ties, changed her name for the second time, to Christine Fabrègue, and transformed her appearance as we have seen. She has kept relations with her neighbors to a minimum, the only one allowed to converse with her being Alain. And in fact, there's a knock on the door and here he is. "Well, well," she thinks, "shit-head's right on time."

So Alain enters, still wearing the same pullover—only, the temperature having dropped, a triangle of brown wool now emerges from the dip of the V. Stocky, condensed like a battery, electric-red hair; just add a socket and you could plug a lamp into him. Hesitant, he remains standing in the doorway, an uncertain smile floating over his lips. At the end of his arm dangles a live crab fat as a handbag. Berthaux has just given it to him, he explains, he himself doesn't know what to do with it, would Christine like it?

At first Gloire doesn't answer, distrustfully eyeing the tannish creature whose right front claw, bulkier than the left, convulsively pinches and releases the void, emitting signs. "Something to drink, Alain?" she says with some delay, after the crab is installed in the sink and has begun producing tiny bubbles of drool. About as mobile as a vaguely free-willed pebble, as a man fallen in his armor and trying to stand, the crab labors in vain to climb out of the sink. Moving in clumsy lateral jerks, it skids against the smooth sides and falls back onto its flank, secreting its fluid with the noise of a soggy mineral.

After sitting down, the ex-sailor resumes the tale of his maritime memories: expeditions, voyages, and injuries that might add up to a full life. He has always been a sailor: navy, merchant marine, fishing. He returns to his impressions of Australia, the country that seems to have left the deepest impression on him. Still, he's lacking his usual verve: he pauses, sends expectant looks Gloire's way, no doubt waiting for the young woman to address him familiarly like the other day.

When Gloire gets up after a while to fetch some more ice cubes, Alain's fuzzy gaze follows her toward the refrigerator. He stands in turn and walks up behind her as she's foraging in the freezer. "You know I really like you, Christine," Alain declares in a strangled voice. Gloire does not answer immediately.

"It's important for neighbors to like each other," the man frantically continues, "it's good to really like each other. How can I put it—it's better."

The young woman turns around slowly, a wide mask-like smile on her lips, in her hand two ice cubes that burn her palm. "What are you saying?" she asks.

"Nothing bad about doing something good," the man stammers, happy to see this smile, "that's what I meant."

"What are you going on about?" Gloire repeats softly while walking toward Alain, who is ready to beat a retreat and suddenly grows worried. But too late. Grabbing the collar of his V-neck with her free hand, Gloire pulls him close and kisses him roughly, for two or three long seconds, before violently pushing him away. "Get lost," she says. "Get out of here now." As Alain tries to pull her back by one arm, Gloire wrenches free before bringing her ice-filled hand down on his face. A sharp corner of one of the cubes scrapes the forehead of the ex-sailor, who lurches back, lifting a hand to his face and staring at the short smear of blood on his fingers. Then scarcely has he raised his eyes back to Gloire than she rushes forward, shoving him with punches and kicks toward the door, and this man who has stood up to life's hardships, the fury of nature, physical confrontations, and adversity recoils before this unexpected force that pursues him even beyond the door, which is then slammed shut behind him. He flees down the road, toward his home, still without paying attention to the Volvo 360 parked in the same place as the day before, while Gloire, beside herself, goes to find a hatchet in the storeroom.

Back from the storeroom, tearing through the kitchen in a sweat, she spots the crab at the bottom of the sink. Spinning around, she hacks it in two with a single blow of the hatchet. And as she rushes toward the door, the animal's two halves continue to wave feebly each on its own side, in the mad hope of pulling closer and resoldering themselves, leaking shreds of transparent flesh.

Gloire reopens the door, bursts onto the threshold, tries to make out in the darkness the silhouette of Alain, who hasn't waited around for her. In both directions, the street is deserted. The only unfamiliar object is the Volvo 360 parked not far from the house, apparently empty, on which Gloire's gaze rests for a moment, and from which that gaze would immediately have come away if it hadn't been for the intermittent glow of a Pall Mall behind the fogged windows. *There they are again, back to get on my fucking tits.* The young woman's eyes narrow an instant before she begins walking with determined steps toward the car.

From inside that car, Boccara sees her approaching. Hatchet in hand, face of a Medusa, in the shadows she appears to surge from a barbarous pantheon, a Symbolist painting, or a horror film. She moves much faster than the mental processes of Boccara, who at first doesn't have the slightest reaction. By the time he finally moves his hand toward the ignition key, the hatchet crashes down onto the windshield which explodes just as the engine turns over. In a deformed voice, Boccara emits an inarticulate cry of terror, hastily shifts into first as he stomps on the gas pedal. Gloire jumps away in time. After two clumsy swerves, the Volvo finds the direction of the road and disappears with its lights off. Not until five hundred yards later does Boccara remember to switch them on. The cold air rushes in through the absent windshield, cauterizing the little cuts on his face caused by shards of safety glass. Still, lucky for him he didn't take his chances by the cliffs: no doubt he would have fared much worse. But Gloire knows no means of cleansing the world other than the void.

9

Over the following miles, while shielding his eyes from the cutting night air and posing the pad of a cautious middle finger on his fresh wounds, Boccara hurled numerous loud imprecations against Gloire. Worried, dissatisfied, contracting his jaws, aching from his wounds whose gravity he hadn't assessed, Boccara demonstrated a fair amount of invention in his volley of curses.

Forced to drive at a reduced speed, he also took a fair amount of time to reach Saint-Brieuc. At the city's entrance a service station was open, its functions diversified enough for them to handle his windshield problem. While they attached a temporary plastic film in its place, Boccara headed for the toilets to assess the damage—four or five very superficial cuts, nothing serious. He examined himself in the mirror: still the same young fellow, a bit chubby but with the eyes of a pretty girl, an alert air, not short enough to be short, not fat enough to be fat, not yet thin enough on top to be truly bald, but all that would happen soon enough. All that would surely happen, and so it bothered him. No matter what he did, in twenty years his future was settled: lotions and wedge heels, diet pills, jogging—nothing would help.

Still, he tried to smile almost all the time. Even in that moment of defeat before the mirror, alone in the gas station bathroom, batting his eyelashes, looking like he could let the world go for a song, he forced out his lighthearted smile, dusted with insouciance and topped with nonchalance. He brushed off the lapels of his beautiful prussian-blue jacket with its violet sheen. Always well dressed, Boccara chose his garments with care, from inside which he observed with troubled eye the mediocrity of the world, and of others' clothes in particular.

He headed back to the service station, settled the bill and asked for a receipt, then drove off. On the road back, the landscape as filtered through the plastic film was hazy, as if in a heavy fog, its motions jerky as in an old television. Prevented from driving at his usual speed, Boccara bore his cross patiently. Stretching out his lumbars, draping his forearms over the wheel, he enjoined himself to stay calm even though irritated by that slowness, by the hypocrisy of that slowness, majordomo of death, that feigned to ignore the brevity of existence.

Twenty miles back, Gloire also forced herself to calm down. After smashing the windshield and watching the Volvo flee, she took refuge inside her house, door double-bolted and shutters latched. Then she secluded herself with a glass of wine in the windowless bathroom, closing the door behind her, switching on the fluorescent light above the sink. The light, like the rest of us, had a hard time waking up; coughing and spitting up a little glimmer, it sputtered for a few seconds before glowing its entire length. Having lowered the toilet lid, Gloire sat down on top, chest forward, head dangling between her elbows which rested on her thighs, her hands joined in front of her around her glass. What's the situation?

Apparently they've found her. Located her, recognized her, followed her. Not only does Gloire have not the slightest idea as to the identities or intentions of the men who have tracked her down, but not the slightest curiosity either; for her, the only question is how to get rid of them. In the long term, any overt resistance seems vain: making Jean-Claude Kastner disappear has proven useless, and scaring off tonight's intruder will surely serve no purpose either. They seem to be well organized. They are obstinate. There might be many of them. They will be back. Despite all the care she has taken, the young woman's retreat now appears compromised. No more anonymity, no more peace, no more prolonged social coma. These men on her tail represent a rejected past, but one that has just surged up from the depths of time, propelled by a fat rubber band. Others in a similar situation might try to come to an understanding, negotiate with these men, get information about their plans, and then act accordingly. Others, perhaps, but not Gloire. The idea does not even occur to her.

She thought she had been there for only a moment, sitting under her neon, when an early bird began to moan and stretch, yawn while opening a first eye in the palm tree. Back in her room, four filaments of dark gray daylight already delineate the frame of the shutters. Then another moment later, lying fully dressed under a blanket, her eyes remain staring into the darkness. The sun as it rises finds her in a canvas chair in the middle of the garden, under the same blanket. Béliard appears at around nine thirty.

Béliard looks beat. Hasn't shaved or changed since the day before. Although preoccupied with other worries, Gloire has to restrain herself from asking where he spent the night; besides, he never tells. He seems not very talkative in any case, ill disposed to conversation. One might suspect him of having come just to get some rest, to doze peacefully nestled on the young woman's warm and supple shoulder. As the latter tries after a moment to bring him up to date on the night's events, the homunculus at first answers only in pouty, sometimes sarcastic, generally dismissive monosyllables. It seems that today isn't the day.

Today isn't the first time Béliard looks out of sorts, ignorant of what's been going on and its import. But it's always like this: sometimes he knows everything that has happened in his absence, even mentioning details that Gloire doesn't know, and sometimes he turns up aware of nothing, looking dazed, like this morning, and she has to explain everything to him—of course, it's also possible that Béliard might be faking it. Gloire shakes her shoulder to rouse him a bit.

"Listen to me, at least," she says. "It can't go on like this."

"What can't," grouses Béliard. "A lot of things can't go on like this."

"They were back again," says Gloire. "Another one, last night."

"Yeah, yeah," goes Béliard, barely sitting up, with a more or less informed smack of his pasty lips. "So?"

"I want them to leave me alone!" cries Gloire. "It's only going to get worse, don't you see? I thought it would be over after that guy the other night, but no, there are others and it's all going to start again. I don't want them to start pestering me again. Can't you understand that?"

"Fine," says Béliard, "fine. Calm down."

Then she plunges her face between her hands: "I just want everyone to leave me the fuck alone," she says again, but in a different tone, in a voice like the downward spiraling of a parachute.

She sobs for two or three minutes, while Béliard mechanically pats her on the shoulder, throwing worried glances all around for fear the woman's cries have attracted attention. "Let's think about it," he says. "We'll find a solution."

"I've thought about it," she finally breathes into her hands.

"What have you thought about?" says Béliard, but she shrugs her shoulders without answering. "What have you thought about?" the homunculus insists.

"Nothing," she says after a moment. "And anyway, I can't."

She has blown her nose. She speaks in that voice of desperate, disillusioned anger that certain little girls in tears have, brave but jaded. "Anyway," she repeats, "it's not even possible."

"All right," says Béliard, "what's not possible?"

That she doesn't answer immediately might mean she doesn't dare. In spite of the fact that she treats Béliard rudely, that she often complains of his presence and wishes for his departure, it seems that

Gloire always needs his opinion, his consent, even his encouragement. At first, Gloire is afraid this opinion might be negative; then she finds that dependency humiliating. Finally: "I want to go away," she says softly. "I'd like to go away."

Béliard maintains a clinical silence.

"I'd really like to leave here," Gloire repeats, raising her head. "But no way, huh?"

More silence, then: "Well, why not?" Béliard says calmly. "It should be doable. I don't see any obstacles."

"You think?"

"Of course," Béliard repeats, "of course. Personally, I don't see any reason you couldn't."

Gloire looks skeptically at the homunculus, who continues: "Not only is it possible," he progressively warms up, "it might even be desirable. You've paid your dues, that's enough. You've done enough. It's all right. You can go. Here's what you do: you cash in your holdings and then skip off to the tropics, far away."

"No," says Gloire, incredulous.

"Yes," says Béliard, "yes, since I said so."

"All right," Gloire says cautiously after a brief pause. "All right, I'll do it your way. That's what you said, right? The tropics, far away?"

"That's exactly right," says Béliard. "And I'm coming with you."

"Hold on there," Gloire perks up, "hold on a moment. I can go perfectly well by myself."

"You're out of your mind," says Béliard. "Here's to the good life."

10

"In other words, she's out of her mind," concluded Boccara, cautiously fingering the gauze confetti scattered over his little wounds.

"In any case," said Jouve, "she seems to know how to handle herself."

"That's right, make jokes," Boccara objected. "How long will these things take to heal?"

"No time at all," said Jouve. "Three days, tops. Tell people you cut yourself shaving. What do you make of all this, Personnettaz?"

From his adjacent stool, Boccara cast an apprehensive eye at Personnettaz, who was rigidly seated in the armchair facing Jouve's desk: a thin, reclusive individual, austere though oddly costumed as a whimsical insurance agent, in a sand-colored suit and chocolate-brown shirt with light-green tie. Coppery, almost red hair in a military cut, sunken cheeks, and lined forehead; two long wrinkles parallel to the jawline could have passed for gashes or initiatory scarifications, and his icy stare gave Boccara the creeps. His face reflected a major preoccupation, or perhaps a great moral suffering, or maybe a chronic illness—an ulcer or something of the sort. He was attentive and serious as if at the doctor's. He had said nothing until then.

"It doesn't seem like much at first glance," he finally uttered without moving his lips.

"You're joking," said Boccara. "She's dangerous. She's completely gonzo."

"It didn't seem like much to me, either," said Jouve, "I know. At first I didn't even want to bother you. But now there's that Kastner business that's got me worried. Almost a week without a word; it's aggravating. I want to know what happened. I hope she didn't hurt him—I *am* his employer, after all. Now it's not only for the client's benefit that we need to find her. So how about it, then? Will you do it?"

"You know how I work," said Personnettaz. "I don't do anything without an assistant. And I've lost my assistant. I'm looking for another one."

"Well, take Boccara," suggested Jouve, "there's nothing he'd like better. He's very good."

"Sure!" exclaimed Boccara, "choose Boccara. Top quality, no defects. Don't think twice before saying OK!"

Personnettaz gave him the same grim look that he gave all things, the technical and disaffected gaze of someone judging distance on a rifle range. "Fine," he said, glancing at his iron wristwatch, "we'll try it. We leave in three hours. Before that I have to stop at my place."

Shortly afterward he walked across Boulevard des Batignolles, up the fraction of Rue de Rome that borders and overhangs the train tracks flowing into the Gare Saint-Lazare. Below the street ran some twenty parallel rails that the tall buildings overlooked in a sheer drop and on which trains passed from time to time. Riveted here and there to the protective fence, enameled plaques warned people not to touch the electric wires (mortal danger) or throw garbage onto the tracks.

Leaving the sidewalk of Rue de Rome, Personnettaz turned right onto the Pont Legendre, suspended over the tracks for thirty yards by a structure of cast-iron latticework. As he reached the middle of the bridge, the little convoy of four silvery wagons that linked Rouen with Paris appeared: seemingly made of tin plate, they ran over their rails following a northwest-southeast axis. Since Personnettaz, for his part, was following the bridge on a southwest-northeast axis, the paths of man and train intersected at a right angle, and for the space of one one-hundredth of a second his body was superimposed over that of the woman, inside the train, whom he had just agreed to find.

After her conversation with Béliard, Gloire had quickly organized her departure. She made a list of things to do. Housecleaning and straightening up in the morning, disposal of crab remains and putting to death of the rabbit. In the afternoon, gathering of her clothes and effects, which she had at first tried to sort before shoving them all into a polyeurethane bag that she immediately deposited by the door, in the spot reserved for trash. Drafting of a note for the landlord, which she would mail accompanied by a check and the two sets of keys. Purchase of a bottle of cognac. Preparation of rabbit marengo.

Early the following morning, she had taken the first train for Rouen, then the bus to a rest home located in a former convent on the outskirts of Rouen. After a short wait at the end of a corridor, a well-dressed old man, bright as a button, had shuffled up on the arm of a nurse. Gloire had kissed him. "Miss," the old man had said, "you are absolutely charming, but I don't believe we've been properly introduced." The nurse in the background nodded her head.

"Here, Daddy," Gloire had said, "I've brought you some cognac." The nurse in the background shook her head.

"You are infinitely kind," the old man lit up, "but I fear they might well confiscate it."

Then she had returned to the station and taken the second train toward Paris, Gare Saint-Lazare. She was coming back now. She was going home.

She had kept her miserable appearance and, despite the first-class ticket, retained her fourth-class clothes. Her travel bag was nearly empty, containing only a healthy sum of money in five-hundred-franc bills, which she went to count once in the train lavatory. She studied herself in the mirror, shoulders hunched forward, face stubborn. That was sufficient now; she had seen herself that way long enough—but soon it would be the end of that look. Patience, old girl.

At the Gare Saint-Lazare, as she passed into the field of the surveillance cameras, she noticed once again her poor silhouette, full-length this time, on the monitors mounted above the information boards: it had been a while since she'd seen herself onscreen. Gloire hadn't watched herself often, in any case, in the short time of her instant celebrity, which had set like a sun after having barely risen. On television it had first been three or four variety shows that were never rebroadcast, just enough time to lip-sync "Too Too Too" followed by "We're Not Taking Off," then immediately afterward, during the trial, a few brief appearances at the end of the news, always in the Celebrity or Crime updates. After that she had never again appeared on a TV screen. Had never seen herself on one again except in the household appliance sections of department stores, on the screens of video equipment being demonstrated for private individuals or, just before her departure from Paris, on the monitors that show the platform comings and goings of similar private individuals to the Metro conductors.

But from now on, Gloire would avoid the Metro. A taxi brought her to a small, quiet hotel on a small, quiet street on the fringes of Montparnasse. The hotel didn't look like a hotel but, instead, like something halfway between a family pension and a trysting place. No reception desk to speak of, only a living room in which a discreet and distinguished woman, tailored suit and pearl necklace, handed her a key with no questions asked—no numbers on the room doors, either. Gloire set down her bag and immediately went back out, then headed up Rue de Rennes on foot.

Near Sèvres-Babylone, three or four afternoon hours would suffice for her to reconstitute a wardrobe without worrying about the cost: a raincoat and two skirts, two pairs of trousers, four permanent-press pleated skirts made in Japan, two similar pairs of rope sandals with platform heels. Then, passing by Guerlain, she went in to buy herself a few light products, almost no makeup, tonic and cleansing lotion, a small atomizer of Jardins de Bagatelle. On Rue de Grenelle, finally, Gloire bought two expensive leather handbags in which to stuff her new acquisitions.

After she returned to the hotel to change, barely made up, a second taxi dropped her in the ministerial quarter, in front of a low, elegant building with no sign to indicate its business. Two globes of shrubbery framed a door of translucent glass and wrought iron. Once she had slipped into a white robe on the ground floor and climbed a flight of stairs, the man one floor up made a concerned face when he saw her coming but evinced no surprise; he would ask no questions. “It’s me,” said Gloire.

“Of course,” said the man. “So I see.”

Comb-name: Caesar—a large pensive bird with metal-rimmed glasses and the shaved head of an atomic scientist. He pointed her toward a chair. “Do sit down,” he said. “I’m delighted to see you again. May I offer you some coffee?”

She took her place before a mirror and Caesar, without uttering the slightest commentary, passed three fingers through her hair, lifting a lock, thoughtfully gauging another and reserving his diagnosis. “Dear me,” he finally said in a distressed tone. “It wasn’t you who cut this last time, was it?” Gloire nodded, smiling. “I see,” went Caesar. “So? Do I try to make the best of what’s here, or do I take it all from scratch?”

“All from scratch,” said Gloire, “just the way it was. The same color as before.”

He stood behind her, looked her in the eye in the mirror, having placed his hands delicately on her shoulders. “How long has it been,” he asked gently, “three years?”

“Four,” said Gloire.

Those eyes bathed her in an affectionate gaze that was dismantled, then discreetly rebuilt into a sarcastic one. "You haven't changed a bit," he said. "I don't mean your hair, of course." He reached for his scissors.

An hour and a half later, the sun was about to set when Gloire crossed the Seine via Pont de la Concorde and walked up the Champs-Elysées. The light was silky and blonde, and so was Gloire. She had regained the status of tall blonde; she stood straight; she hardly seemed crazy at all. Once again men turned their heads as she passed by.

On Rue de Tilsitt, between the Belgian embassy and the Zimbabwean embassy, the offices of Bardo, attorneys at law, occupied an entire second floor. Brown carpeting and abstract art in the reception area. Having asked to see Mr. Lagrange, Gloire waited a few minutes, alone in a room huge enough to produce an echo. A very nervous young lawyer appeared, short and austere as a printed form, who soberly requested that Gloire follow him to the padded door of his office, but who, once the latter was shut, began dancing frenetically around the young woman, throwing his head back and beating the air with his arms, all the while exclaiming that it had been so long, that he was so happy, that she hadn't changed a bit. Gloire smiled: people's opinions concurred.

Lagrange calmed down progressively, the way a superball gradually stops bouncing, before sitting back at his desk where, for a few minutes more, he continued to bobble on his chair. Even after he had settled down, Lagrange remained an essentially feverish man, mounted like Donatienne on supercharged batteries and swarming with facial tics; under the effect of this agitation, his small man-tailored suits wore out more quickly on him than they would on others. Four or five times, six years earlier, Gloire recalled having shared his bed: all night long he was everywhere at once. He was basically a lawyer without a cause and was not especially looking for one, having enough money behind him to take on only risky cases and still drive an Opel. But honest. With Gloire, at least. It was to him that had befallen the task of managing the young woman's assets and overseeing her interests, free of charge. "My little Gloire," he said, "I'm here, you know I'm here. I Am Here." He had known her since childhood, or just about; he was more or less the only one aware of the entire situation. Unlike Caesar, he asked a lot of questions. Gloire was free to answer as she wished. But for the moment, what she mostly wished was to go away.

"Where?" asked Lagrange.

"As far away as possible," she said.

"As far away as possible," Lagrange repeated dreamily. "Apart from New Zealand, or Australia, I don't really see . . ."

In Gloire's mind, in fast motion, Alain's Australian adventures suddenly paraded by. Fauna, flora, aborigines, pearl divers; steaks with jelly and primitive minds. "Fine," she said, "let's say Australia."

"You sure you're sure?" worried Lagrange.

"Yes," said Gloire, "and I'd also like some new identity papers. Find me another name."

"Money first," said the lawyer, pulling various bank records from Gloire's file. It emerged from his perusal, first, that spread out over stocks, bonds, and rental units, the fortune at Gloire's disposal was rather sizeable. And second, that this capital had considerably accumulated lately, as the monthly checks Lagrange sent to Brittany were well below the interest earned by these investments. Perfect. To which Gloire responded, first, that she would be needing much larger sums during this trip. And second, that no, there was nothing new in her life, in particular no new man; she simply felt like getting away. She refrained from mentioning Kastner's visit and its sequel. Perfect.

Then they examined the Australian future. Lagrange would take care of everything: airplane tickets, visas, wire transfers, reservations, General Delivery. "And don't forget my name," Gloire reminded him, "and my papers."

"Fine," said Lagrange. "It might be a bit complicated, but I'll manage. What kind of name would you prefer?"

"Whatever you like," said Gloire. "You choose."

"Fine," said Lagrange. "Can I take you to dinner?"

As Béliard had not shown his face that entire day, Gloire felt more inclined after dinner to down a drink and then another drink and then a final drink with Lagrange, and then, one thing leading to another, the sperm of Lagrange, but she returned to her hotel fairly early and went to bed quickly, imagining the other end of the world. Envisioning at the other end of this vile world an undiscoverable, inviolable, unreachable retreat. A marsupial's pouch in which to snuggle, and then hop, hop, ever farther toward a better horizon to forget even her own name, all her names.

11

It would be nothing like that. Gloire would see no kangaroos, koalas, or anything. Just one evening, in a gutter on Exhibition Street, she would notice the remains of an opossum lying between the front fender of a Holden Commodore and the rear fender of a Holden Apollo.

She had taken the Paris-Sydney flight via Singapore and Jakarta, which then continues on to Nouméa. In this airplane, freed from their military duties, twenty New Caledonian conscripts were heading home. *So long*, damp barracks; *so long*, nasty climate: the young men abundantly celebrated their discharge with shouts, libations, speeches, and songs. Once returned to civilian life, they had swapped their military effects for more whimsical uniforms of Rastafarian inspiration: stripes and shoulder braids for pendants and badges depicting Africa, a cannabis leaf, or Peter Tosh; khaki forage caps for ample woolen bonnets shaped like twenty-four-egg omelettes, hand-woven in green-yellow-red tricolor. The joy of seeing their native country again sometimes translated into a few minor exactions. Thus, when the beverage cart paraded by, pushed by a stewardess, it was with one hand that they snatched up a whole raft of burgundy and bordeaux, then, once the cart had passed, with the other that they affectionately smacked the rear end of the stewardess, who stiffened slightly under the impact, then turned around with a constrained smile. "Easy, easy," the two noncommissioned officers charged with bookending them then intervened, debonnaire. "Take it easy, guys."

One of the NCO's happened to be sitting next to Gloire. Native of Wallis and Futuna, he was a massive top sergeant who overflowed his seat when asleep, but who, when awake, made a little conversation with her. Placid smile and bull neck, a drinker of water, the top sergeant had taken part in all the national military expeditions of the last twenty years: from Comoro to Lebanon, from Niger to Gabon, from the Persian Gulf to the Red Sea. From his operations in Chad he kept a mixed impression, each mission having required him to back a different side. The other NCO, whom Gloire liked immediately, was a tall, handsome black with soulful eyes whom the top sergeant introduced as a heavyweight boxer for the French army. A great hope in his category. So Gloire addressed him a look full of hope. The transfer of the dismissed back to hearth and home required such heavy-duty measures, the sergeant explained, without which, left to their own drunken devices, they never failed to cause diplomatic incidents at the stopovers.

Then it was time for the meal trays. Gloire ate what they gave her, drank what she wanted, even after the lights went out and the movie began. The passengers had screwed their headphones into their ears, except for Gloire and a few others who, with no other soundtrack than the engines, distractedly leafed through magazines on their knees. Two hours later, everyone was asleep; even the conscripts had settled down. Discreetly, Gloire stood up to go to the lavatory, casting on the way a sober but precise glance at the handsome heavyweight from the French army, who joined her there twenty seconds later and kept her company for twenty minutes. Later, in Singapore, she visited only the duty-free shops in the airport, while locals dressed in apple green disinfected the Boeing; then, at the stopover in Jakarta, a sleeping Gloire saw nothing at all.

Time is always approximate on long-distance flights; one never knows exactly where one is among the various time zones. On the other hand, near Porte Dorée it was five P.M. sharp when Jouve, returning from the address indicated by his brother-in-law, stopped in to see Salvador. The latter paid scant attention, preoccupied as he was with a central theme (warm tall blondes versus cool tall blondes) of his project.

"A fellow named Lagrange," said Jouve. "He didn't want to tell me anything, claims he doesn't know her; he tried to pull the professional confidence routine, that whole business. But I'm sure he knows something. I think I'll try going about it a different way."

But Salvador, eager to see Jouve out: "Very good," he said, "do as you think best." Jouve gone: "Take this down," he said to Donatienne. "Here we go."

Certain incandescent tall blondes rush forward into the world with open arms. They speak vivaciously, laugh freely, think quickly, and drink heartily. They look proudly at the world, toss it terrible and generous smiles. Sometimes the world becomes flustered at the sight of them, sometimes it is intimidated by that sure, confident, low-necked way they have of rushing toward it, toward you, arms wide open in the direction of your own. The gaiety, the fearsome gaiety of those solar tall blondes.

"You might note Kim Novak in the margin, for example. What photos do we have of Kim Novak?"

They owned several stills of the bell tower scene in *Vertigo*, among them a vertical shot of the staircase (combination of tracking out and forward zoom), but Salvador is himself very prone to vertigo, so prone that even the slightest image of a steep plunge makes him nauseous. "No," he said, "find something else. That's enough for today."

"Right," said Donatienne. "And what about the cool ones?"

"How's that?" said Salvador.

"The cool tall blondes," she specified. "For the moment, you've only talked about the warm ones."

"We'll get to them later," said Salvador. "Can't do everything at once."

A little later, having reached her destination, Gloire settled into a hotel near Darling Harbour where, via a telex from Lagrange, a room had been reserved for her with a balcony overlooking the bay of Port Jackson. To counter the unease of the time change, she had first slept fifteen straight hours, then, on awakening, had made herself comfortable on the balcony, spending the majority of her time there in a deck chair in the company of Béliard.

The latter, who had not been around since Gloire's transformation, had reappeared the moment she found herself alone in her room. Inspecting her from head to toe: "Ah," he'd exclaimed, "I must say I like you better like this." Those first days, in short-sleeved shirt and Bermuda shorts, lying full-length across the footrest of the deck chair, the homunculus seemed to be in tip-top form. Wearing sunglasses made to his size, he trimmed his nails while whistling, gazing at the bay crisscrossed by fat, dark, ramshackle metallic ferries, and sunbathed in maximum-protection sunscreen.

For the Aussie sun is not like other suns: it burns you before you've even gotten warm, a vengeful blowtorch even in cool weather. And its path is not typical, either: jumping up in the morning, carbonizing everything in its rapid wake, it rushes to set at the precise moment in ten minutes flat, without dusk or any sort of protocol, and then night falls like a stone. Refreshing the cool drinks, the bellboys cautioned Gloire against it, advised her to protect herself, adjusted the opening of her parasol. She seldom went out. Everything was just fine.

And yet, less than a week after their arrival, it seemed that Béliard was starting to get restless. His mood seemed to have changed. He scarcely answered when Gloire talked to him, gave his opinion of the weather less frequently. Then one afternoon, when he opened his mouth, it was to posit that he was getting a bit fed up with that goddam sun and to suggest they go out for a walk, that they forget about this goddam balcony for a while. "All right," said Gloire. But outside, the sun was just as much of an issue. As Béliard was still invisible to the eyes of common mortals, he and Gloire had hardly gone a hundred yards toward the harbor when they collapsed into the first deck chair and under the first umbrella they found, annexes to a milkshake parlor. After a moment, Gloire had dozed off. When she opened her eyes again, Béliard was nowhere to be found: it seemed he had taken advantage of the open air and the young woman's nap to slip away. As if he needed that, she puzzled as she returned to the hotel. Thus, it was all alone that she would spend the following days.

12

"Bless you, Gilbert," said Personnettaz.

"I think I'm catching cold," Boccara observed, pinching his sinuses.

"We're wasting a ton of time," noted Personnettaz. "This is annoying."

"Jesus Christ, this thing is tight!" cried Boccara. "It looks like it's totally stuck."

Personnettaz's only response was to grimace one more notch, shrugging a shoulder already practically dislocated by the effort. Boccara pushed down on the crank as hard as he could, but the nuts seemed welded to the threads, riveted to the shanks. The fine, cold rain mixed with his tepid sweat in a warm, salty cocktail that blurred his vision, running over his eyes toward his lips: everything was conspiring against his attempts to change that right rear tire.

Crank in hand, Boccara was kneeling before his flat, whose rim spewed out some flaccid sections of wall. His palms, darkened by engine grease the moment he had grabbed the jack, now sprouted a few blisters as well. With all his weight, the young man bore down on the tool, standing up from time to time to try to unstick the whole mess with huge kicks, in vain: detaching itself from the bolt, the crank then rebounded noisily into the landscape where Boccara went to fetch it while cursing, scattering the accessories lying around him.

He and Personnettaz were on the shoulder of a six-lane highway—two times three separated by a divider sown with comatose plants and bordered by tumescent guardrails—cut off from the rest of the world by a fence between whose links danced scraps of plastic, fabric, and dirty, crumpled papers agglutinated at the feet of the road signs. Beyond this frontier, the world couldn't decide between fallow field and construction site. Not a single walking human to be seen.

Earlier than usual, under an iron sky, drivers in the fast lane had turned on their headlights, whose beams dimmed the daylight still further. Meowings of the vehicles and hissing of their tires on the slippery surface, intermittent gusts of wind and shivers down the spine. It was Tuesday, ten minutes before noon.

Standing behind Boccara, holding a light retractable umbrella, Personnettaz struggled to shelter the young man and himself—a task compromised by the insufficient diameter of the umbrella, which was shaken by the squall and occasionally upturned, and most often protected nothing more than a small uncertain zone between them, while they got soaked.

"You want me to try?" Personnettaz offered now and then.

"Skip it," went Boccara.

Unless a sensitive soul lent them a strong hand, their combined efforts must have succeeded, for two hours later they were back on the road, headlights on bright as they raced down the left-hand lane. Boccara's fingers left blackish traces all over the interior, hardly noticeable on the seats and wheel but very distinct on his shirt collar, his forehead, his eyelids, and the wings of his nose, which were lighter in hue.

Returning from their mission without having found anything but Gloire's deserted house, the two men were silent: Boccara was pouting; Personnettaz was never very talkative. They switched on the radio for the news, which was at the forecast segment. The person responsible for it contented himself with quantifying the lousy weather that was visible through the car windows. Apparently exposed on the front lines to the very storms he was describing, his hoarse, febrile voice guaranteed the soundness of his pronouncements.

Stiff with exhaustion, Boccara also shivered inside his rumpled suit. Bad taste in his mouth, as if he were emerging, sticky and disheveled, from a long, sleepless night in midday. At first demoralized by the narrowness of the world, twenty miles outside Paris he tried to lift his spirits. Even though Personnettaz scared the willies out of him, he lowered the volume on the radio, then—perhaps in an effort to exorcise his discomfort—"So how about girls?" he asked with a joyless smile. "Do you get many opportunities, in your work?"

But he refrained from going further. The other, immobile and mute as usual, stared fixedly in front of him with an air of annoyance, or worry, or suffering. In a very bad mood or simply desperate, hard to say. One could sense his negative thoughts without really being able to divine their content. Not daring to pursue the matter, Boccara thought he might try distracting him with a variation on the same theme. To pick up girls, for example, how did he, Boccara, go about it?

"Simple," he answered himself, "simple. I sit alone at an outdoor cafe, I order a beer, and I pull a long face. And it never fails. Inside of a half hour, there's always one who comes by and sits down. And off you go."

Without emitting the slightest commentary, Personnettaz shot him a rapid glance, a brief composite look in whose heart envy, skepticism, and reprobation glared at each other. Then he turned the radio back up: Shostakovich. Boccara didn't dwell on the subject. They listened to Shostakovich. He's not so bad, Shostakovich; some of his quartets are really very nice. Then once in Paris, near the Opera, Personnettaz had him stop the car in front of a telephone booth. "Wait for me here," he said, opening the door. "I'll report in to the client." At around two-something p.m., the sky had calmed down, the shops reopened. The neighborhood proved to be abundant in salesgirls returning from their low-calorie lunches, their liter-and-a-half of Evian under their arms: Boccara modified the tilt of his seat the more comfortably to watch them heading back to their work stations.

But Salvador, who had just had himself delivered a club sandwich and a beer in his office, was in no mood to answer when the phone rang. Before his eyes, the tall blondes file was open to the delicate point of artificial blondes. "Right," he said quickly, "yes, so it's a bust? How should I know? Ask Jouve." He hung up quickly so as not to lose his train of thought, trying to explore this point, thinking aloud. Taking dictation on the other side of the office, Donatienne simultaneously projected photos of Stéphane Audran, Angie Dickinson, and Monica Vitti on a wall screen to stimulate Salvador's reflections. The latter paused briefly, distracted by the telephone call. Then: "Every blonde, one day or another," he resumed, "faces the suspicion that she's a fake. Every one of them is exposed to this doubt; each one runs the risk they'll be suspected of being artificial. Now, the artificial blonde is sometimes more pertinent, more representative than the true one, what do you think?"

But today, Donatienne didn't feel like thinking, or even like talking at her usual speed.

"Depends," she said. "Can you expand on that?"

"I think so," said Salvador. "We'll come back to it. Let's move on. The artificial blonde is thus a specific category, a style apart. Which the artificial brunette isn't. In any case, the artificial brunette is improbable, we can't see any reason for her to exist. She doesn't create an event the way an artificial blonde can, who has chosen her color with this one objective in mind. So coloring your hair only scandalizes in one direction, you follow me?"

"Whatever you say," yawned Donatienne. "Go on."

"I saw one go by," Boccara announced when Personnettaz got

back in the car. "You should have seen her teeth when she smiled, the way they shined. I've never seen such white teeth, I'm telling you, it was like a whole bathroom."

"Go on, drive," uttered Personnettaz.

"Sorry," said Boccara.

They headed via Saint-Lazare toward the Europe quarter, where the light often reminds one of Eastern Europe; where in streets more open than elsewhere, via more obtuse perspectives, an undercurrent of chilly air persists even in warm weather; where noises sound as if they were coming from a bit farther away. A few of those streets, the most introverted ones, retain a slight air of vacation or penury all year round: for example, in front of Jouve's office, there were loads of places to park.

Symmetrical to this office, another, larger office housed the headquarters of an association of women each more beautiful than the next. When Personnettaz and Boccara entered the foyer, it appeared that a general assembly of this association was being held; Boccara poked his nose through the half-open door.

"Go on, move," said Personnettaz.

"Sorry," said Boccara.

Jouve was awaiting them for the debriefing. They informed him of their failure. "I'm not surprised," he said. "She's obviously cleared out. Anyway, too bad. We'll try something else. You'll need to go someplace, I'll explain where, but you'll have to do it rather discreetly, if you see what I . . ."

"Yes," said Personnettaz, "I see what you . . ."

A little later, furnished with Lagrange's address, they left the office while the general assembly of magnificent women was in full swing; in a riotous climate, they feverishly resolved to put matters to a vote.

"What—now?" asked Boccara. "Are we going right away?"

"Why?" said Personnettaz. "Did you have something better to do?"

The same, a little later still, Rue de Tilsitt: "You want me to try?"

"Skip it," went Boccara.

Standing behind him now for some time, with flashlight in hand, Personnettaz endeavored to illuminate Boccara, who was completely absorbed in his task. He only partially succeeded. Under the effect of the prolonged immobility, his wrist occasionally weakened, causing the beam to veer toward an intermediary space between them, at which point they couldn't make out a thing. Boccara protested. Personnettaz raised the flashlight back up with two hands. It was ten minutes past twelve, already Wednesday.

Still fairly damp outside. On the tall windows of Lagrange's office, the increasingly fine rain, now almost fog, intermittently came to beat softly against the panes, the way gentle waves rumple sand. From Rue de Tilsitt rose a sporadic but sustained sound of traffic. Midnight at Place de l'Etoile: the more muffled halo of the surrounding boulevards farther on, ambulance siren here, car horn there. Nothing to do but listen to all that; nothing to see beyond the beam of the flashlight. Through the door leading to the office, a small glow from the streetlights weakly shone, barely accentuating the contours of the furniture without actually illuminating anything.

They had set up in the little annex to Lagrange's large office, a closed, windowless space of about fifty square feet. Fax machine and metal file cabinets, copy machine and sink, old-model safe: Boccara was kneeling on the carpet before the safe. Files were lying on this safe, from which a few onionskin sheets tried to escape. Sitting next to Boccara was a bag containing small tools, punches and pliers, probes, a larger apparatus shaped like a suction cup, and a stethoscope. Sometimes Boccara donned the stethoscope, listened to the mechanism while counting the clicks, while trembling a bit—trembling sometimes to the point of botching a turn, having to start his calculations from zero, but also sweating at least as much as he was trembling; his moist fingers lost their hold on the slippery knob, and then there was that other guy behind him who lowered the flashlight just at the wrong moment: everything was conspiring against his attempts to open that safe.

The other one behind him, leaning over his shoulder, saw his assistant perspiring.

“You should have remembered to bring some rags,” he said. “Are you sure you don’t have any rags in your bag, there? You didn’t bring any Kleenexes for your cold, did you?”

“No,” Boccara huffed, “no, no, no. Goddammit, this thing is slippery. I can’t believe how hard it is to get a grip—Jesus!”

Interrupting his labors an instant to take a breather, he stifled a sneeze in the palm of his hand.

“Calm down,” said Personnettaz. “You’re wasting time.”

“It feels like it’s going into my chest,” sniffled Boccara. “I can tell already. Then it’ll be months before I can get rid of it. To hell with your blessings, Mr. Personnettaz.”

13

After taking his French leave, Béliard hadn't shown his face again. Gloire wasn't bothered that much by his absence, although sometimes she missed his conversation. Fair weather, in any case, over the entire South Pacific.

That Wednesday, day broke with its usual suddenness. After a rapid shower and a quick breakfast, the young woman quickly left her room. A cover for symphonic, well-trimmed rock orchestra sputtered affectionately in the elevator, and Gloire exited the hotel under the already harsh sun. She took the Pyrmont Bridge, for pedestrians only, up to the large aquarium. Then six hundred yards beyond rose a building in Anglo-antipodal style—luxurious shopping galleries all in lusters and balusters, copper and display windows, rugs, paintings, moldings—and facing it stood a pale marble statue of Queen Victoria. Gloire took the escalator to the top floor and sat at a low table glued to a varnished handrail beside a sheer drop, near a bridal boutique named Seventh Heaven. From there, her eye plummeted down three levels of art galleries, concessions of international couturiers, and dealers in luxury items, recent antiques, and heterogeneous souvenirs.

Once a bartender, sporting a Walkman, had brought her what

she desired—coffee, ashtray—Gloire observed the traffic of fiancées who came and went around Seventh Heaven. Young or already not so young, the fiancées never came alone but always flanked by an attendant: mother, best friend, sister, or sister of the groom-to-be who was out there somewhere, drinking his last few beers with his oldest mates while waiting out the countdown. Installed on white leather loveseats, the attendants proffered or leafed through advice and catalogues. The fiancées seemed rather sure of themselves during the fittings. One could make out some belated hesitations on the faces of some, while the looks of others remained cold or else preoccupied with clandestine thoughts, and a few seemed embarrassed at not being able to hide their contentment; even though for the most part they weren't anything special, at least they'd managed to find someone. Through the shop window, Gloire watched them pose in their getups. Then, in mid-morning, as the boutique had emptied out, she entered.

Pale green or pale pink veils, deep purple and pearl rugs. Cylindrical satin-velvet display racks loaded with hats, necklaces, and shoes multiplied by large full-length mirrors with ornate frames. From among the hangers bearing processions of immaculate, frothy, effervescent gowns, Gloire chose a classic model, high-waisted, long, with lateral pleats, discreet scoop-neck whose obtuse angle would leave little more than her collar bones exposed. She shut herself up in the minuscule dressing room.

By magic she reemerged a quarter of a second later, encased in the gigantic outfit, followed by a squadron of salesgirls carrying far behind her several yards of train—the way a magician pulls out of his opera hat a dove fleeing a cat fleeing dogs followed by horses, camels, and elephants that shuffle placidly toward the wings while bleating, meowing, trumpeting, and defecating along the way; then by cohorts dressed in regional costumes who parade while saluting the public under their applause, waving hats and flags, announced by fanfares and trailed by village bands—and, all things considered, not very well fitted out, spangled with tags, mounted all lopsided on white high heels.

Gloire then let the salesgirls adapt the apparatus to her body, adjust her waist, fix her shoulders, knot a tassel around her groin, make a white lace hortensia blossom between her breasts, dress her hair with a twist of ribbon foliage, spread the veil over her face, adjust the cascades of fabric, smooth out the wrinkles, insert pins in every direction, and sign the whole thing with three rows of pearls. That done, wedged into her gown, she attempted a few careful movements, little precautionary reverences addressed to her image, the single bride in the mirror. "Well," she said, "I'll have to think about it."

Dressed again, Gloire spent the afternoon on one of the ferries that join up with the circular dock in Manly, then returned to her hotel; after dinner, since she didn't feel like going to bed quite yet, the concierge gladly provided her with the address of a club in which she could kill the rest of her night.

She easily found the establishment, frequented particularly by Westerners of the Northern Hemisphere, among them a fair number of Westerners of the Northern Hemisphere who were drunk, including a tall, thin Swiss at the bar with a sad smile beneath his mustache. An organist could be heard in the background. Through the fog of conversations, as if from behind a waterfall, the Hammond organ discreetly inflected sticky sounds, nasal arguments alternating with coughing fits and bellows blasts. The Swiss, who dealt in environmental issues, offered Gloire a glass of local champagne; then they chatted, or more precisely the Swiss painted a somber portrait of Australia: more and more tourists on the ground, less and less ozone in the sky. He seemed to have his work cut out for him here.

Gloire had no sooner emptied her glass than the man immediately, without interrupting his soliloquy, had it refilled, several times. Gloire smiled, a lot of people smiled, the organ continued to talk through its nose, spreading its chords with marmalade or panting like a beast of burden. Just back from Labrador, the Swiss now discoursed on the fate of Labrador seals, mass-exterminated so that their pelts could be made into slippers and key holders, and especially into little jointed toys shaped like Labrador seals. Gloire herself was getting rather drunk and seeing the world through glass, all perceptions anaesthetized, like a blaze cooled by the television screen. When the glass began to cloud over, it was time to go home. The Swiss man was very nice, but no, not tonight; perhaps she'd come back tomorrow to see if he was still there. Gloire stood up carefully, thanked the man, and left the establishment.

The silence in the street, when she came out, was the kind one listens to like a sound. Relieved to see herself walking fairly straight, to clearly read two in the morning on her watch, Gloire preferred to walk home rather than take a taxi. The nightclub was located several blocks from the aquarium, beyond which, via the Pyrmont Bridge, she could get back to her hotel. Not too many people at this hour near the aquarium; not a soul on the Pyrmont Bridge.

But alas, actually there is: shortly after she sets foot on the bridge, a distant soul comes to set foot in the opposite direction. At first indistinct, gradually becoming sharper, this soul is about fifty years old, hefty and dressed in dark blue; male gender. The man advances at a leisurely pace on Gloire's left, while she keeps to her right without raising her eyes. As they are about to cross paths, the man suddenly veers toward her and utters several words that she does not understand. Never was very brilliant in foreign languages, that Gloire. More or less able to manage in a hotel porter's English, but completely unequal to holding a conversation, especially at this hour, and given her present state and the Australian accent. As she shakes her head—*don't speak English*—and quickens her step, the man turns and begins following her, walking alongside while repeating the same formula, this time in a more pressing interrogative tone, and soon gripping her arm just above the elbow. Gloire begins walking more quickly still, shaking her head—*leave me alone*—and trying to free herself with a few icy looks. The man then grabs her by the shoulder, forcing her to stop, and spinning her toward him he grabs her other shoulder.

Gloire tries to struggle, but the other holds her firmly, pulling her toward his large, perspiring body as he edges toward the retaining wall. And then Gloire's strength abandons her; then she is too afraid even to cry out in that place, which in any case is deserted; already nearly asphyxiated by the sweat and breath of this man who is emitting hissed, enraged words. She is incapable of altering the course of events. Everything seems lost when Béliard, out of nowhere, suddenly rises from the young woman's shoulder and begins to yell, face contorted in hate. "Destroy the bastard!" he screams. "Rip his balls off! Tear his motherfucking eyes out!"

Gloire will never know if the man noticed Béliard's warlike presence. Whatever the case, for one instant he seems confused, loses his balance, then more forcefully resumes his grip, spitting at Gloire's face short, new words that she can't understand, but of which she nonetheless gets the gist. But such is Béliard's power that he regenerates cells, multiplies energy: immediately afterward, under the force of a new resistance, an unexpected counterattack, the man finds himself abruptly thrown to the ground and his head thuds dully against the pavement. He cries out, tries to get up. Perhaps he already intends to admit defeat; perhaps he'd let the matter drop with this woman and her tenfold strength if Béliard, stamping his feet on her shoulder, didn't keep exhorting Gloire, who jerks the aggressor upright. Without giving him a chance to run, she shoves him against the retaining wall and slaps him violently, many times over, and the man's look, which swings crazily between pain and astonishment, finally comes to rest on the young woman with an air of exhaustion, as if saying fine, OK, that's enough, you win.

The whole thing might have stopped there. Gloire would have ended up letting the man go if Béliard, up against her ear, weren't screeching at her to annihilate the piece of shit, rip him to shreds. So that in the wake of a final slap, she brusquely hooks the man's shoulder, twists his arm behind his back to the point of fracture, and turns him against the wall; then, grunting briefly like an animal, she knocks him with her shoulder over the guardrail and pushes him into the void. Dumbfounded, eyes open, the man falls without having understood anything about anything, so surprised that he doesn't even think to cry out. The waters of Port Jackson silently engulf him twenty yards below. All things considered, Béliard can certainly come in handy from time to time.

But twenty minutes later, after returning to her hotel still shaking with hatred, excitement, and fear, still pumped up by this energy, downing two whiskies one after the other—twenty minutes later everything turned around: Gloire collapsed in tears, prostrate on the edge of her bed, driven to despair by her irrepressible habit of throwing people from windows, cliffs, or bridges. Béliard, sitting nearby, stared thoughtfully at her. "There now, there now," he said in a consoling voice.

At first, Gloire was unable to utter a single word. Then: "Didn't have to do that," she sobbed, "we didn't have to do that."

"Skip it," said Béliard, "enough with the conscience. Sometimes you have to set an example. They'll never find out, in any case, but still we should probably think about going somewhere else. I'll do some checking into flights tomorrow. And as for you, you're going to get some sleep now, all right?"

"I can't," said the young woman.

"I'm not surprised," said the homunculus. "What have you got left in the way of pills?"

Gloire went to get her pouch of hypnotics, from among which Béliard mixed a potent cocktail, and a little while later everything was calm and the woman was asleep, finally seeming at peace; the little blue veins on her temples throbbed tranquilly. Far from the world she floated: perhaps nothing had happened at all.

But the next morning, when the wake-up call came a bit too early, there was no longer the slightest trace of Béliard in the room. Nobody. Gloire even looked for him under the bed. Still, he couldn't have been very far: when she got out of the shower, the bathroom was nothing more than a block of opaque steam. And Béliard's finger being of small format, it was in fine characters that he had traced on the foggy mirror the words SYDNEY—BOMBAY VIA HONG KONG, CATHAY PACIFIC AIRWAYS FLIGHT 112, 10:30. Then, having copied this information onto the back of an envelope, when she went back to change in the bathroom all the moisture was evaporated: the mirror was newly virgin.

But an hour later, at Kingsford Smith Airport, her seat was indeed reserved in club class, smoking section, window—Béliard really could be handy. At ten o'clock, Gloire walked on to the airplane for Bombay dressed in a beige linen suit of vaguely colonial inspiration and shod in summer sandals with rope wedges. Hardly made up, as had been the case since leaving Brittany, her face was barely visible beneath large black sunglasses and a very concealing bob wig from which, as in the good old days, a few short blonde wisps jutted here and there.

14

And that same day, at the other end of the world: "It appears," Salvador continued, "that tall blondes possess an acute awareness of their singularity. This sense of being special, of constituting the product of a mutation, a genetic phenomenon, even a natural catastrophe, can foster a certain tendency toward self-dramatization. Yeah," he said, "anyway. Maybe. What do you think?"

Yawning again, tugging on her skirt with the other hand, Donatienne suggested putting this point off until later, turning instead to some reliable elements in the population under study. For example a little sidebar on Jean Harlow or, I don't know, Doris Day? "All right," said Salvador, "go find me some photos."

Donatienne crossed the room toward the door, gently swaying her hips before the ringed eye of her employer. All around, a sonorous environment in the acute register—car horns from the street, cheeps from the trees, and in the adjoining studios magnetic tapes fast forwarding: the only low note at that moment was Salvador's mood.

As Donatienne turned the knob and pulled the door open, she nearly ran into Personnettaz who was standing in the hallway behind that same door and who, symmetrically, was pushing it at that very moment. One leaving the room as the other was about to enter, they first took a step back, then, classic misunderstanding, both of them rushed simultaneously into the space freed by the person opposite, jostling each other slightly in the axis of the doorway. Brief, furtive contact, immediately retracted: the man, having inadvertently brushed the young woman's arm, jerked back his own and recoiled. From his desk, Salvador saw the horrified face of Personnettaz, aghast at having touched a high-tension cable, amazed at having survived. Salvador saw Personnettaz's body shaken by strong emotions, as if by one of those twin-release, twin-speed ocean waves that drown you with no questions asked. All this had lasted not three seconds, after which Personnettaz stepped backward, his face suddenly white with fatigue. Donatienne flashed him a candid smile before heading off toward the photo archives.

Personnettaz, looking exhausted, ill at ease, quickly turned away to address Salvador, or rather Salvador's right shoulder, as if he were appraising a stain, three motes of dust, a fallen hair from one of Béliard's cousins.

"Right," he said finally. "We have the information. We know where she is now. We think we know."

"So?" went Salvador. "What are you waiting for?"

"Well, it's far away," said Personnettaz. "It's pretty far away."

"So what?" went Salvador. "What's the problem?"

"Well, it's expensive," said Personnettaz. "The trip, I mean. It's really pretty expensive."

"Of course," sighed Salvador, pulling a checkbook from his drawer. "Business class, I assume?"

"No," said Personnettaz. "Economy will do fine, for two."

While Salvador signs the check and detaches it from its stub, Personnettaz contracts his jaws as Donatienne returns from the archives. She has a sheaf of photographs under her arm as well as a Dunhill, its filter smeared with thick carmine, in the corner of her lips. As she stands leaning next to the open door, waiting for them to finish, Personnettaz pockets the check and rises stiffly. Scrupulously keeping Donatienne just outside his visual field, reaching the exit while describing a discreet arc at a constant distance from her person, he leaves under her still-smiling gaze. But he no longer walks with his natural gait when he knows he is being pursued by a gaze: he stands too awkwardly straight, exaggeratedly contracts his buttocks, his legs parody themselves and his thorax pitches more than necessary; in short, his body follows its own will, and the more he tries to control it the less it obeys. Heading for the elevator, Personnettaz walks like this the entire length of the interminable corridor, sure that Donatienne is still looking at him long after she has shut the door.

As if he were being watched even at a distance, he continued to walk like that on Rue des Martyrs a half hour later, having parked his car on the boulevard. Arriving in front of Boccara's building, he looked up the entrance code in his address book and pressed it in on the keypad next to the street door, several times but in vain: the door remained of stone. Already troubled by Donatienne, Personnettaz felt a nascent exasperation rising in him, made all the sharper by the fact that the nearest phone booth was a good five hundred yards away.

"Personnettaz," he announced. "They gave me a code. What is the code?"

"Er, I don't know, what code have you got?" answered Boccara's intimidated voice.

"Wait a moment," went Personnettaz, leafing one-handedly and with some difficulty through his address book. "They gave me 89-dash-51."

"Ah," went Boccara, "that shows Jouve hasn't been here in a while. Yeah," he recalled, "that 89-dash-51 was a good code, I liked that one. It sounded like a basketball score, and besides it was easy to remember, you know? The French Revolution and Pastis 51, what more could you ask?"

"Fine," said Personnettaz, "so what's the new one?"

"And on top of that, two prime numbers," Boccara continued.

"No," said Personnettaz. "Eighty-nine is, but not 51. Fifty-one is the product of two primes."

"You're right," said Boccara. "Anyhow, they changed it on us."

"Fine," repeated Personnettaz, "so what's the new one, then?"

"Oh, it's completely ridiculous," said Boccara. "8C603, you see how handy *that* is."

And indeed, once 8C603 was punched in, the low click of the electronic doorman sounded without further ado. Elevator. Mirror at the back of the elevator. Avoid looking at it.

"So," went Boccara, "how's it going? Have you recovered from the other night? I really can't go to bed late like that, I'm bushed. I should also warn you I'm a bit depressed today. Anyway, good thing we found the thing. Some coffee? I've made fresh."

"No," said Personnettaz. "Or actually, sure, why not. Show me the thing."

"Here," said Boccara. "One lump or two?"

The thing consisted of life-size photos of the documents that the two men had found, photographed, then put back in their place in Lagrange's safe: names of foreign cities followed by numerals—dates, addresses, telephone numbers, fax numbers. "Good," said Personnettaz. "We leave tomorrow."

And the next day, Boccara was still saying he was depressed when they boarded the same Boeing for Sydney that Gloire had taken. But we know that she has left Sydney, we already know the deal, so let's get this over with quickly and move on. At the hotel in Darling Harbour they found no one, the weather was miserable, they didn't have time to see anything, they turned back immediately.

In the airplane, Boccara dozed off intermittently. With fifteen hours of flight in one direction, then the other, exhaustion and 180-degree double jet lag, sleep and digestion problems, it didn't help being shaken by nausea when the Boeing hit turbulence. At first demoralized, six hundred miles outside Paris he tried to lift his spirits by resuming the conversation begun several days earlier in the car, on the way back from Brittany. He turned toward Personnettaz, who seemed to be absorbed in the worldwide weather report on the closed-circuit TV.

"It wasn't even true, what I said the other day," Boccara confessed. "The truth is, my sex life stinks. If you knew how sick I am of balling widows in high-rises."

"Well," ventured Personnettaz, "at least there's that."

"You can't imagine what it's like," Boccara continued. "Waking up. The mornings. Going home without even a shower in the highway traffic, in shitty weather, to a freezing apartment. Turning up the heat and keeping your coat on while the coffee perks. You can't imagine how little self-regard that takes."

"So stop seeing them," Personnettaz recommended. "Leave them."

"I never leave anybody," said Boccara. "It's too tiring. All things considered, I'd rather they left me. Keeps me from having to decide. In any case," he developed, "it's never as simple as that. You never really know who's leaving who. You think one of the two is taking the initiative. But the one who's really leaving isn't always the one who seems to be."

That said, Boccara stuck the headphones back into his ears, seeking out a little music among the available programs while toying with the knob embedded in his armrest. Coming upon Shostakovich again, he modified the tilt of his seat the more comfortably to watch the stewardesses at their workstations.

At Roissy, Personnettaz headed for the first booth he saw, but Salvador was still in no mood to answer when the phone rang. On his desk, his main project was again open to the chapter concerning artificial blondes—bleached, peroxide, and so on. "Right," he said quickly, "yes, so it's another bust?" Then, without paying much attention to the other's explanations: "Just a moment."

And leaning toward the pages spread before him, he briefly noted in the margin of one of them that nitrogen peroxide is also used in the manufacture of certain explosives, the propulsion of certain rockets: that could prove useful. Good. Be sure to develop this point.

15

That evening at eleven p.m. in Bombay, in the bar of the Taj Intercontinental, you notice that there are, as in the nightclub in Sydney, very few natives. Almost exclusively foreigners, strangers to the city as they are to each other: strangers squared.

You spot two women who have just entered the bar laughing very freely, laughing as no one ever laughs in a public place; two very gay young women holding a bouquet of large white flowers, which they pass back and forth every five minutes. At first glance you find them beautiful as the light of day, then upon reflection as two different days, two holidays in the heart of opposite seasons.

They had met that same morning on the Sydney–Bombay flight. Seated next to each other by chance, they had traded magazines, cigarettes, and beauty tips, drunk a fair amount, and spoken as only two strangers on a long-distance flight can, thirty-five thousand feet above the rising land masses. Rachel, like Gloire, was traveling alone; like Gloire, she said little about the goals and motives of her enterprise. In the days to come, they would not leave each other's side.

They had arrived in Bombay in late morning with no particular destination in mind, immediately crossed the city in a taxi, then got off at random to pace the streets. They walked through a mass of compact, predominantly sweet odors. Dense like a cumulonimbus with variable geometry, these odors emanated from all sorts of spices, incense, essential oils, and fruits, from flowers and fritters, from smoke, burnt horn, mothballs, and tar, from dust and rot, exhaust and excrement. Then, near Marine Drive, when the young women happened upon some crematoria, the smell of bodies in combustion momentarily blotted out all the others—nuanced, depending on the social class of those bodies, by the scent of the logs between which they went up in smoke: sandalwood or banana for the rich, mango for the hoi polloi. And so they had spent the entire day until dusk.

This evening, alone with your glass at the bar of the Taj, you witness how these two very gay women who have just entered immediately meet—surprise—two men similarly disposed. The gayer of the two immediately chooses the more amusing swain, leaving the other pair to make do as best it can. You watch the scene from afar. It seems to you that this newly constituted foursome does not always express its views in the same language, each member speaking his or her own with copious gestures. You wait a while longer, hesitate, then decide against another drink, and you leave at precisely the moment when, in the mind of the foursome, the idea takes hold that linguistic barriers hardly matter since love is universal. Still, if you were to climb the stairs toward room 212 the following morning at around eleven o'clock and crack open the door, you would find not, as expected, one of those couples, nor the second, but Rachel and Gloire sleeping pressed against each other.

After several days, bored with doing the town, they sometimes ended up spending entire days in their room, since they had all the time in the world—always lying close, sleeping (or not) beside the open window on whose ledge perched enormous crows with insolent stares. Rachel had a minuscule tattooed star somewhere, and the crows emitted raucous hawkings of the throat like a man about to expectorate. And from morning until night, through that window, rose the voice of some believer droning a sacred air whose harmonies largely resembled those of "Working Class Hero."

Often they did not go out until day's end, after the worst heat had subsided, to take the air near the Elephanta ferry wharf or to buy liquor in some dark stall with a meshed-in window at the back of an alley on the far side of an abandoned building. But near the wharf they also got to know the young men who hung around all day not far from the hotel, between the Taj and the Yacht Club, among the paid ear cleaners. Small fellows who were polite and properly dressed, shadowed by future mustaches and long-term plans; debutant businessmen who gravely spread the fan of their wares—substances to inhale, substances to inject, boys and girls to fuck, bills to change. Without resorting to their services, Rachel hit it off with a receiver named Biplab, apparently fell in love with him, and disappeared a few days later—exiting Gloire's life as suddenly as she had entered.

After that, alone in Bombay, it was different; the city seemed noisier. Gloire spent two full days without leaving the hotel, wasting her time with the boutique keepers on the ground floor. When she tried going out once on the third day, several beggars pursued her more aggressively than usual, emitting the same throaty calls as the crows; legless cripples launched in her wake cut her off from behind. Gloire returned to her room passably demoralized. She was starting to miss Béliard. He had not shown his face the entire time she was with Rachel—understandably. Still, now that she was alone again, the least he could do was reappear. But no. She began to wonder whether the homunculus, finding a better opportunity, hadn't stayed behind in Sydney.

Whatever the case, the best thing to do was go away again. Rachel had spoken to her of a town in the south where life seemed mellow, and of a quiet, genteel, English-style residence. Gloire had jotted down the address. She had the concierge reserve her a seat, in air-conditioned class, on the next train heading south, and left the following morning.

A quiet little town, in these latitudes, means at least a million feverish inhabitants, but the Cosmopolitan Club was a venerable institution located on the outskirts of the center, in the legations neighborhood. Its main entrance adjoined the Burmese consulate and, in back, a rear gate looking out on the corner of Cenotaph Road and Archbishop Vincent Street led to a residential stretch of great white villas bordered by gardens, enclosed by walls. There Gloire could feel sheltered.

A wide, low building, the Cosmopolitan Club was composed of a huge foyer and several salons, a restaurant, a smoking parlor, bridge-, pool-, and ballrooms, a bar, another bar, a third bar. Its roof terrace was capped by a dodecagonal pinnacle, topped by an infundibuliform urn. Decorated with official photos of the Queen and other, more recent ones of the Prince of Wales, the foyer extended into a porch and then beneath a pale cement canopy, under which heavy Ambassador limousines and big-engined Hindustanis discharged the club's empty-stomached members by the hour, before repocketing them soused to the gills a quart or two later. To the left was a swimming pool filled with fresh water, to the right a library filled with stale volumes. Then an isolated building, with two floors of rooms and suites served by a rosewood elevator: that was where Gloire would stay, not far from the side entrance with its unimpeded view of Cenotaph Road. All of it in a silken silence, even if from the bustling neighborhoods farther on came a monotonous rumble, hardly noticeable but uninterrupted, acrid like a guilty conscience and giving the silence its contour.

The establishment was like a cross between a luxury hotel, a family pension, and a sanatorium. Unchanged since British times, the bars were mahogany, the wall lamps copper, the silverware silver, the tennis courts red clay, and the servants white. Visible from the restaurant dining room, beyond a porch as long and wide as the upper deck of an ocean liner, fifteen gentle stairs led down to a park planted with peepuls and margosas, populated with mongeese and parrots, bordered by a river prone to flooding. The sun was shining. Perfect.

Immediately upon Gloire's arrival, the superintendent showed her to her room. Exaggeratedly large, it was equipped with a black and white Texla television, a sky-blue refrigerator, and a huge air conditioner between the two windows, with three fans on the ceiling. Above each nightstand, four little glass mounts displayed little birds (*Chloropsis cochinchinensis*), while a large glass mount above the bed depicted four large birds (*Porphyrio porphyrio*). Better and better.

The superintendent, a thin young man with a fine, cold mustache and fine, icy smile, disappeared the minute she signed the register. In the following days he would prove to be very discreet, not so much absent as fleeting. On the other hand, the somewhat aged bellboys proved exceedingly attentive. The wife of the nicest bellboy, the one in charge of the morning ministrations, was temporarily in the hospital, so Gloire slipped him two thousand rupees. Then, once she had hung her clothes in closets a hundred times too big, walked around the park, crisscrossed the empty salons, and gotten her bearings, her days began to take shape.

Each one the same. At seven a.m., the heat awoke her. A little before eight, the hospitalized woman's husband set the tray with morning tea on a low table and drew back the curtains. Sliding together along the curtain rods, the metal rings rang *zing zing*, to the left, to the right, like a knife being sharpened. Gloire then ate her breakfast on the balcony, alone, occasionally tossing to the ground fragments of toast that were coveted equally by the numerous giant crows and ground squirrels that charged onto them all in a heap. Nine times out of ten the squirrels beat a retreat before the arrogance of the crows, more powerful and better organized, beneath circles that eagles described in the sky. After that, Gloire rested a moment in her room, seeing nothing before her but two lizards, short, pink, and immobile on the wall. Only once did she try to catch one.

A number of rickshaws were permanently stationed by the gate, ready to transport the club's pensioners. Gloire took the first one she saw—a yellow scooter with hastily suspended roof, three wheels, two seats in back, and a nonworking meter—toward the center of town. She lingered a moment at the fabric merchants', in the temples, or at the massage parlors, daily entrusting her hands to specialists, surface and depth, chiromancer and manicurist by turns.

Not without curiosity, the locals watched her, unaccustomed to tall blondes; few of them grow in those climates. Meanwhile, far away, Salvador jotted down vague ideas on the subject—tall blondes in Austin Minis, tall blondes and scorched-earth policy—while keeping in the corner of his eye, just in case, the reproduction of a work by Jim Dine entitled *The Blonde Girls* (oil, charcoal, rope, 1960). At the same time, Personnettaz labored, in vain for the moment, to pick up the trail of Gloire who was spending her afternoons on a poolside lounge chair, if she wasn't taking a stroll around the park, stopping at times by the generator near the pond, in which a hundred calm toads, at all hours, silently snapped up any insect below a certain caliber.

In the evenings, Gloire dined alone in the restaurant, a book open on her table and eating with one eye. Then she went to bed early in front of the television, following a Tamil film that wasn't too hard to understand or, turning off the sound, picking up one of the books borrowed from the library, most often encyclopedic works, travel narratives, natural history manuals, studies of customs, or more specialized treatises published by Thacker, Spink & Co. (Calcutta), such as *Animals of No Importance* or *Dogs for Warm Climates.* All of this Gloire read methodically, neither skipping nor retaining a single line. Then, in theory, she went to sleep—although it wasn't always easy, and soon less and less easy to get there. As for Béliard, he still hadn't appeared since Sydney. Trouble with his passport, perhaps?

16

The following week her insomnia intensified. It gnawed Gloire's sleep from both ends, morning and evening in equal measure, deducting a few supplementary minutes every night. Every day, Gloire woke up more tired than before.

At the club bar, she ended up meeting a few Europeans, resident or transient, in particular British subjects representing their firms: an insurance underwriter for the crown jewels, a perfume salesman, an engineer specializing in brakes—a largely neglected device, unknown in these latitudes where they prefer the horn, and thus a huge potential market.

But she spent little time in the bar. In the evenings, to stave off the hour when she would attempt sleep, Gloire stayed awhile by the pond near the gate. After having snapped up every possible animalcule during the day, the toads were now digesting, singing placidly in chorus. To execute their little concert, they split up into three sections, some reproducing the squawkings of fowl, others a police siren, still others a Morse transmitter: a frenetic, simultaneous chorus, without a moment's respite, Morse and siren at an octave's remove, the deep breath of the generator serving at once as basso continuo and pitch pipe. Above the batrachian chorales, from the branches of a rain tree, a winged soloist sometimes projected a brief, melodic utterance in counterpoint, a few riffs in third. Gloire listened for a quarter of an hour, then headed inside to go to bed.

Sometimes she was invited, and sometimes she accepted offers to join the British subjects, who organized parties on Tuesday evenings, dancing the cakewalk on the terrace in Adidas and Bermuda shorts, sweating amid the bottle-laden tables. On one such evening, and one evening only, Gloire let herself go so far as to empty five or six glasses at a shot.

After which she returned stone drunk to the club, where she spent a ridiculous amount of time looking for her room key, then for the lock, and then, once inside, for the night-light switch. She emitted a brief cry after thinking she'd made out, in the semidarkness, a small oblong shape across her bed. Then she got a grip, tried to reason with herself: poor old girl, you're still completely sloshed. But no: at the sound of the slammed door the little shape suddenly bolted upright, stiff as a poker and with arms crossed, looking cross.

"Do you see what time it is?" shouted Béliard. "Is this any time to be getting home?"

"Miserable little shit," said Gloire. "You scared me."

"That's only the beginning," Béliard cried still louder. "If you ask me, things have been getting pretty lax around here. I'm going to have to take things back in hand, you bet I am."

"You're such a shit," Gloire repeated, spotting a chair in the shadows and collapsing into it, a hand over her eyes.

"Watch what you say," cautioned Béliard in a sharp though less assured voice.

"Couldn't you let me know you were coming?" she said after a while, standing with difficulty to go pour herself a last drink.

"I'm not kidding," Béliard tried to threaten, pointing a finger at her glass, then wagging that finger. "You'll get what's coming to you if you don't watch it."

"This is insane," said Gloire. "I haven't seen you in ages. Never there when I need you. I could have dropped dead ten times over."

"I come by when I can," claimed the homunculus, letting his defenses down. "Do you think this is all I have to do? Did you see how I look? With the jet lag, the trip, and all? If you think I'm doing it for fun," he said, pulling a small mirror from his pocket. "I mean it—do you see what I look like?"

And in fact, he was pale and disheveled, suit rumpled, tie and laces undone. And he hadn't shaved. "I can't take it anymore," he groaned, falling back onto the bed. Gloire took a sip from her glass and watched him lying there disarticulated, a cheap doll.

"So what were you up to?" she said. "Where were you? Did you stay behind in Sydney?"

"Let me sleep," yawned Béliard. "I think I need to sleep."

"Lucky you," she said. "I can't even close my eyes anymore. You don't want to know the kind of nights I've spent."

"I'll take care of that," muttered Béliard. "We'll see about that tomorrow."

"Yeah, sure," said Gloire.

But the next morning Béliard was still asleep when she went out, as she did every day, to take a spin around town. Among the rickshaws posted at the club entrance, she had finally settled on a vehicle that looked better maintained than the others, the apparent object of its pilot's devotion. Decorated with lit cones of camphor, it sported a little altar of flowers and statuettes hung over the vehicle's handlebars, above which, on the windshield, were several decals of deities. Painted on the rear of the machine near the reflectors, two mascaraed eyes squinted at a government slogan preaching birth control and, under a roof all patched with duct tape, on either side of the rear seat, were two identical portraits depicting an actor, or a politician, or more likely one and the same.

As for the driver of this rickshaw, he was a friendly, rotund young man named Sanjeev, with linen shirt and pants, and a faded pink cotton handkerchief around his neck. After their first trip, he had offered to put himself exclusively at Gloire's service. His hair was cropped close, except for a long lock on the back of his skull, a handle for pulling him from Hell in case he fell in. He was friendly and very even tempered; he drove well, his meter worked, and his incense was of good quality. Gloire had answered why not. The only problem with him: his chronic cold made him sneeze constantly and blow his nose at every red light into his pink handkerchief, which also served as headband, scarf, belt, compress, rag, bath towel, table napkin, and shopping bag.

When she returned to her room after lunch, Gloire was once more extremely pale, and Béliard showed some alarm. "Get a little rest," he suggested before going back to sleep himself, "try to take a nap." She tried, but sleep no longer existed. It was the same once night had fallen, and again all the following nights, until one fine morning found her utterly exhausted, hardly able to move.

Obviously incapable of treating Gloire's insomnia, Béliard mainly took care of catching up on his own delayed slumber. She spent her days next to him as he slept, lying in her room with the curtains drawn. Staring at the ceiling, no longer thinking of anything, counting the fan's revolutions unto infinity.

For those three days she ventured out of her room only at mealtimes, leaving her breakfasts unfinished, hidden behind dark glasses. As soon as she got up, the crows would swoop down onto the leftovers and divvy up toast, sugar, butter, and artificial marmalade before flying off again to savor their delicacies in peace, motionless on the blade of a fan.

And then there was one evening, at the club restaurant, when Gloire jumped on discovering a very agitated spider in a spoon resting on its convex bowl next to her plate. The imprisoned insect turned around and around, struggled in the bottom of the utensil. An instant of revulsion seized her before she saw wriggling in that concavity only the reflection of another fan above her.

Fans, it appeared, were beginning to occupy too much space in her life. But only at the end of a week, worn out by her sleepless nights, when she began seeing fat frozen mosquitoes in the filaments of electric lightbulbs, did she begin to worry. Béliard, declaring himself unequal to the task, threw up his hands. Gloire confided her troubles to the bellboys.

The bellboys, who had a soft spot for her—a friendly, reserved young woman, not too tight with her rupees, rarely stayed out too late at the bar—the bellboys were very sorry to hear it. After they'd consulted with each other, the hospitalized woman's husband took the plunge and slipped a word to the superintendent. A diagonal smile lightly capsized the mustache of the superintendent, who finally jotted on the back of his card the address of a local practitioner who had a clinic at 33 Karaneeswarar Sannadhi Street, at the corner of a particularly commercial artery.

Béliard, meanwhile, who had not left the room, had been sleeping practically nonstop since his return. Gloire shook him before leaving:

"I'm going out," she told him. "I think I might have found someone for my insomnia."

"We'll see about that," grunted the homunculus, turning over.

Then she went out into the heaviest afternoon heat. Near the gate, in the shade, the rickshaw drivers were asleep at their handlebars. "No problem," said Sanjeev after deciphering the address, before turning the ignition.

They arrived. Squeezed one against the other was an abundance of shops: sellers of pumps, springs, hoses, hardware, plaster, and rope; electricians, plumbers, barbers—the same shops, in short, as anywhere else in the world, except that, not being larger than sixty square feet, all these establishments looked alike under their roofs of braided palm leaves, planks, and straw, and on their packed-earth floors.

Once Sanjeev had dropped her off, Gloire had difficulty finding the doctor's address: the neighborhood buildings, first of all, were not particularly well numbered, and then the contents of the shops didn't always match their signs. So that when she finally located the plaque mentioning Dr. Gopal's clinic, it was attached to the front of a music store in which two men with painted foreheads were arguing bitterly without any trace around them of scores, instruments, or recordings.

She hesitated: on the sidewalk to the left, a stall contained two facing machines, one for typing, one for sewing; while to the right, another offered Xerox-telex-fax services. Above, in back, balancing on scaffoldings made of rope and bamboo, two painters were sketching the design of an advertising panel whose object was still not very clear: liquor or cigarettes, a television or perhaps a washing machine. Sanjeev went to ask the manager of the Xerox-telex-fax, who pointed out the clinic's location: at the back of a courtyard past an L-shaped passage, across from a temple devoted to the goddess of smallpox.

The clinic's reception area, though filled with fans and rugs at death's door, nonetheless boasted state-of-the-art communications equipment. A young woman with a pearl embedded in the wing of her nose and a ring on the third toe of each foot was monitoring the clientele on a screen. As soon as he was informed of Gloire's presence, Gopal appeared, wearing a gigantic gem on his right index finger.

Moreover, despite having the manners of an archbishop, the doctor was a bit slovenly-looking: checkered blouse floating over a green-striped loincloth casually knotted in front, People's Republic of China thongs on his feet. Profusely oiled salt-and-pepper hair curling in ringlets over the nape of his neck, large glasses with marbled frames and lenses so strong that one could see no more of his eyes than two pupils and two irises multiplied by ten.

Once Gloire had explained her problem, she and Gopal exchanged routine questions and answers in English—overall health, childhood illnesses, family history, nature of the symptoms. Gopal showed sympathy for this problem, which could, he said, be remedied with the appropriate ayurvedic mixture. Rifling through a drawer in his desk, he pulled out a box of brown pills, counted out a few, and slid them into a brown paper bag, one at bedtime for ten days and that should do it, a thousand rupees.

As soon as Gloire left the clinic, Gopal dialed the superintendent's personal line. Outside, Sanjeev was waiting for the young woman. "Good doctor?" he asked.

"He doesn't seem too bad," said Gloire. "You should see him about that cold."

"Expensive," said Sanjeev. "Much too expensive for me."

"Here," said the young woman, rummaging through her bag.

"Thank you," said Sanjeev. "That's a lot."

"Not for me," said Gloire.

So no sooner had he brought her back to the Cosmopolitan Club than Sanjeev returned to the clinic at top speed. Gloire, meanwhile, entered her room. Still lying in the same place, Béliard was no longer sleeping; he seemed to have rested, shaved, changed, refreshed himself. He asked about Gloire's doings.

"I wouldn't recommend you keep seeing that guy, if you want my opinion," he advised a little later, pouring the brown pills into his diminutive hand. "If I were you, I wouldn't trust that guy."

That guy, meanwhile, was examining Sanjeev lengthly and minutely: apart from his chronic head cold, apparently of allergic origin, the young man seemed to enjoy excellent health.

"I see what the problem is," he said. "I'm going to prescribe a little product that will surely make you happy."

At the back of another drawer in his desk, Gopal went in search of a vial filled with powder that was also brown, of which he poured a few grains into a sheet of paper folded in eight to form a flat envelope. "Here you go," he prescribed. "Two or three times a day by nasal inhalation and that should do it, ten rupees."

Sanjeev returned to the club and settled into the backseat of his vehicle to inhale a little of the powder, per the doctor's orders. In fact, he immediately felt much better, slumping on his seat and letting his gaze float toward the window behind which Gloire and Béliard were discussing the future. And began, when you got down to it, to find that time passed awfully slowly.

17

To Boccara's big blue eyes, as well, time passed slowly. Nothing to do in life these days except walk up and down Rue des Martyrs, awaiting instructions from Personnettaz.

At the moment, he was walking down. Under his soles creaked and cracked fragments of broken, sometimes tinted safety glass, scattered into little beaches on the sidewalks and in the gutters, flanking vehicles freshly relieved of their radios. He stopped in front of a tattoo parlor whose window displayed a whole range of samples. Alongside lesser designs for the timorous—little flowers, small animals—larger subjects reserved for the true aficionado depicted entire scenes, queens of the night, heroes of the jungle, or body-built leopards. Tempted at first, Boccara finally resisted. In any case, his watch informed him that it was time, from the first booth he saw, to place his daily call to Personnettaz.

The latter seemed to have picked up Gloire's traces without the young man's help: they were leaving tomorrow. "It's pretty far again this time," he said. "Not as far as last time, but pretty far all the same."

"Hold on a minute," said Boccara. "Where exactly are we going?"

(His eyes widened.) "What?" (He inhaled sharply.) "Hey, hang on there, nothing doing. The place is crawling with filthy diseases. When will I have time to get my shots?"

"Don't worry," said Personnettaz, "I've looked into that. It's no longer necessary."

"And what about swamp fever?" Boccara pointed out. "That's a whole preventative treatment right there, swamp fever. With all those mosquitoes, and the humidity besides, and the rain. It rains there all the time. I know."

"I've looked into that," repeated the other wearily. "Monsoon season is over. If anything, it should be rather hot."

"Oh, well then," Boccara mused, "so light cotton clothes. Even so, I'm going to try and borrow a mosquito net. And anyway, you never know with the rain, I'll bring my slicker."

"That's right," said Personnettaz, "bring your slicker."

Given the number of airplanes we've already taken, and the others we might still have to take, no sense describing the one they boarded the next day. In any case, it had nothing special about it. Air India, your basic 747, with no distinguishing features other than the mealtime choice of vegetarian or not, the coral-colored saris of the stewardesses, the leaf-patterned carpet with matching elevator music.

No, nothing special, except that when they landed in Delhi, Personnettaz spotted an unusual phenomenon off in the distance. As he was waiting behind Boccara in the customs line, he noticed that a small crowd was amassing immediately past the booth: a group smiling from ear to ear, though official in appearance, comprised of civilian aviation uniforms and administrative suits, surrounded by flowers and crowned by an incomprehensible streamer, with a few words in Hindi yellowing together on a wire. Personnettaz gritted his teeth when the lively stares and wide smiles at first seemed to be aimed his way. Then as they moved closer it became evident that it wasn't *him* they had trained their sights on, but Boccara. Airsick, not feeling very well, one hand on his abdomen and the other over his lips, the aforementioned Boccara shuffled forward without noticing a thing.

As soon as the young man passed through customs, there was a simultaneous explosion of flashbulbs and applause, accompanied by a brief fanfare. A short, enthusiastic individual with a mustache and dark suit rushed up and warmly pumped Boccara's hand, while with his other hand he groped for the glasses in his pocket and with a third hand reached into another pocket for a scrap of paper that he unfolded and began to read. Boccara, whose mastery of English left something to be desired, spun around in wild-eyed panic.

"What's going on?"

Personnettaz nervously rolled his passport like a last, empty pack of cigarettes.

"He says you're the millionth passenger to take this flight," he translated. "He says they've planned a celebration."

"So?"

"So I suspect we won't be seeing each other for a while."

And, in fact, after the congratulations, the short man enumerated all the various advantages, gifts, and cruises of which Boccara had just become the lucky beneficiary. When they slipped the first garland of flowers around his assistant's neck, Personnettaz rolled his eyes heavenward. Alone in his aisle seat in the airplane heading back, he was in no mood to describe this flight either.

Paris. Beastly cold and raining cats and dogs. Everyone bundled up and in a swinish mood. Even Donatienne, unusually covered, looking not very inviting, has kept her coat on in the office.

"I'm drawing a bit of a blank with these tall blondes," Salvador observes.

"We've been drawing a blank with everything," she says, "since the beginning."

"No angle, I've lost my angle," says Salvador. "Do measurements make for an angle? What do you think of Jayne Mansfield? Or how about an extraterrestrial angle? Something like this: You always thought they'd be little green men. Wrong! They're tall blonde girls."

Donatienne prefers to reserve comment, and it is in silence that two knocks sound on the door, which opens immediately afterward to reveal Personnettaz. The man's features are drawn, his eyes too shiny, his mouth bitter. The man seems tired. He has psychologically prepared himself not to cast a single glance at Donatienne, but he can't help sneaking a few sidelong peeks. His peripheral vision registers a coat. The man finds this oddly reassuring. "Well, Personnettaz," says Salvador. "I thought you were far away."

"I've lost Boccara," says Personnettaz.

Salvador stares at him without comprehending, reestablishing the silence that is immediately pierced in a very shrill register by Donatienne's laughter. Personnettaz, while explaining the facts, forces himself not to train on her the eyes of the assassin that he isn't, having failed the test for that profession.

"Can't you keep looking on your own?" Salvador asks.

"It's not the way I operate," says Personnettaz. "I only work with an assistant. I'd be happy to continue, but you'll have to find me another assistant."

"That's not really in my line," says Salvador. "I don't see anyone around here who could . . ." To Donatienne: "*You* don't have any ideas, do you?"

"Sure I do," says Donatienne.

"You see?" says Salvador. "That's what's so great about her, she always comes up with good ideas. Who do you have in mind?"

"Me," says Donatienne.

"My gosh what a great idea," says Salvador.

"Wait a minute," says Personnettaz, "please. I'd rather not."

"I'll see about the schedules," Donatienne is already organizing, "Odile will see about tickets and Gerard about the visa, it's always faster with Gerard."

"Please," repeats Personnettaz. "Listen to me for two seconds."

But no one is listening to him anymore. His life is about to change, he can see it, he can feel it, he is going to regret it. Boccara annoyed him no end, but Boccara will be missed. Boccara for whom it's surely the good life, flying first-class from palace to palace, thick as thieves with the crew, clinking glasses by the dozen with the pilots, the stereo cranked up full, pulling the stewardesses into the lavatory and doing lines with the steward during the night flights, in the galley while everyone is asleep.

Speaking of which, on Karaneeswarar Sannadhi Street, Sanjeev has just returned to Dr. Gopal's office: "So, feeling better?" the latter asks. "Are you happy with your treatment?"

"Much better," answers Sanjeev. "Very happy, doctor."

And indeed, he seems genuinely happy to be feeling better. His eyes are pink with pleasure, his pupils contracted with joy. His stare is fixedly satisfied. "Really much better," he insists. "I'd like to get some more of that medicine."

"That should not be difficult," says the doctor. "I do believe it's the right thing for you. We're moving along nicely toward a cure, so we're going to modify the dosage accordingly. Increase the amount a little bit. This time I'm going to give you ten grams of the medicine."

"Ten grams isn't much," Sanjeev seems to remember.

"See for yourself," the doctor tells him, thrusting the tips of his fingers into his drawer.

He pulls out a paper envelope folded the same as the other day, but five or six times fatter. Ten grams is much more than Sanjeev thought. Sanjeev is delighted.

"And in addition, you're going to discontinue the inhalations," the doctor prescribes. "I'll show you how to inject it, it's very simple."

"If you say so, doctor," says Sanjeev. "How can I ever thank you?"

"It's nothing," says the doctor, "don't thank me. As you see, it's still ten rupees; I ask nothing in return. Well, actually, perhaps just a little of your blood—you see, it isn't much. You don't mind, I trust?"

"As much as you want," Sanjeev hesitates.

"This must remain strictly between us," Gopal specifies. "It's blood, you see. It's a little like a pact."

"Of course," Sanjeev nods gravely.

"So it's nothing at all, I'll take just a little quart. No objections?"

"No problem," says Sanjeev.

"And then you can come back here as often as you like," says Gopal. "Now, roll up your sleeve for me."

18

"That boy's in pitiful shape," Béliard observed a few days later.

Through the open window, with scale-model binoculars, he watched Sanjeev sprawled over the handlebars of his vehicle in full sunlight, among the green plants by the gate of the Cosmopolitan Club. "Don't you think you should go see what's wrong with him?"

Thanks to Gopal's care, Gloire had found sleep again and had stopped being quite so interested in ceiling fans. It was the middle of siesta time: "Don't feel like it," she mumbled without opening an eye. "Fuck off."

"Go on, I'm telling you," Béliard insisted. "I really think there's something wrong with him."

She yawned as she skirted the library toward the parking area reserved for rickshaws. Following the passage of cargo planes, the sky above her head was canceled by jet exhaust, stitched with white gashes that quickly scarred. Boughs of albizzias shuddered gently in their wake and the toads, at peace in the pond, continued to absorb their animalcules. Gloire crossed through the gate, paused for a moment: from that angle, Sanjeev really didn't look too chipper.

It's true that the young man's services had fallen off a bit recently. Things weren't going well. Contained for two or three days, his cold had not only returned full-blown but was worsening exponentially. He now hunched over when he coughed. Even his wonderful composure was visibly sprouting cracks. Less assiduous, less precise, Sanjeev proved to be more irritable, bitter about his earnings, even secretive. Nonetheless, he still placed enough trust in Gloire—when she came up to shake him gently, ask him if everything was all right, and then, while they were at it, question him delicately about his recent changes of habit—to designate Gopal's medicine as the probable cause, together with the sustained rhythm of his blood donations. Having been quickly initiated into the administration of intravenous injections, his life was no more than a to-and-fro of syringes in both directions. Gloire studied him fixedly, without saying anything at first. "Wait for me here," she then said. "I'll be right back."

"I told you not to trust that guy," Béliard reminded her after she recapped the situation. "You see what he's capable of. Although, when you get down to it, he didn't do such a bad job with you. Hey, what are you up to now?"

"I'm changing," said Gloire, haphazardly pulling three pieces of clothing from a closet. "You were right, but we can't just let it go. The doctor has some explaining to do."

Béliard covered his forehead with his hand: is she crazy or what? "I strongly advise you against it," he said as if it were obvious. "Don't get mixed up in that. What's done is done. Let it be. Don't go. Wait. Come back. Hey, come back!" But twenty minutes later, bathed in sweat, eyes bulging, Sanjeev dropped Gloire on Karaneeswarar Sannadhi Street.

Gopal received her immediately, gaze as voluminous as ever behind his glasses, stucco smile. Without a word she sat down opposite him. "I can see right away that you're feeling better," said the practitioner. "You look much better. I believe the treatment is the right thing for you. We will continue the cure, but today I would like for us to begin with a little relaxation. Relaxation is very good for insomnia."

"I'll give you some bloody relaxation," answered Gloire, "you lousy prick."

"I beg your pardon?" said Gopal.

"You're a complete shit," she continued. "I know what you're doing with the kid."

"The kid?" went Gopal.

"The kid with the rickshaw," Gloire specified.

"Which one?" smiled Gopal.

"You're disgusting," Gloire insisted. "I should turn you in and have you locked up. In fact, I *am* going to turn you in and have you locked up."

"I see," said Gopal, calmly noting this new symptom on a pad, "very well." He was silent for a moment. "I see what the problem is," he finally said. "I understand. But I'm afraid that would not be in your best interests. Let me notify my associate."

"I'm warning you," said Gloire, "don't try anything. They know I'm here."

"Naturally," said the practitioner, "have no fear. My associate will explain everything." Stretching a finger toward the fat telephone, he pressed a button: immediately, at the other end of the room, a curtain pulled aside. Electrified line of mustache, gelatinous smile, and sharp eye, the thin silhouette of the superintendent appeared.

Two hours later, Béliard was lounging on the bed in his underwear when Gloire walked in. Her light makeup was undone; her first movement was to rush over to the minibar and pour herself a drink. "What happened to you?" asked the homunculus. "You should see your face."

Trembling, she aimed poorly, letting the liquor spill next to her glass. "You can't imagine," she said, "you'd never guess."

"I think I would," Béliard said calmly. "You ran into the superintendent, am I right?"

Although in principle he has only the information that Gloire gives him on her comings and goings, it indeed seems that Béliard, through other sources or double vision, is aware of all or part of the young woman's life. The young woman is sitting on the bed, no longer paying attention. "Tell me about it anyway," he says. Well, it's like this. They had done their homework, they seemed to know everything. They knew someone was after her. The inquiries seemed to have been led by the superintendent, who had communicated his information on Gloire to Gopal. Suggesting to her that they were hand in glove with the local police, the two men had threatened her with serious troubles if she tried to interfere.

"But," Béliard exclaimed, "you *did* tell them you've paid your debt, didn't you? You have nothing more to blame yourself for, in theory. No one has any reason to be after you."

Of course she had told them. But: "And what would prevent us from, say, becoming interested in your little visit to Australia?" Gopal had pointed out. Gloire did not have full control of her voice when she asked him what he meant. ("Very clever," commented Béliard.) "I don't mean anything in particular," Gopal had smiled. "We're talking, that's all. We're talking about you, and we can make others talk about you, but we won't do that. We might be needing you."

"What?" Gloire had repeated. "What do you mean? For what?" ("Better and better," noted Béliard.)

"We'll see," Gopal had told her. "You'll see—we'll be seeing each other again. There you have it."

Béliard thought for a moment, then shrugged his shoulders. "He's bluffing about Australia," he said. "Nobody could know about that. I know, I was there. Nobody. They can't do anything to you."

He ran the edge of a fingernail between his two yellowest teeth, glanced briefly at his catch.

"Of course, there might still be a way," he continued. "You want to get rid of them? You know we could always do it. The usual method, a little precipice and sayonara."

"No," said Gloire, "we can't. There are too many of them, and I'm afraid they're well organized."

They certainly were. All day long the many servants passed

through their lodging under the slightest pretext, to water the plants and clean the room, to bring tea, the morning papers, the afternoon papers with still more tea, the laundry, mosquito coils in the evening. Every bellboy seemed a likely informant for Gopal via the superintendent.

The following days were not very jolly. Gloire now spoke only to Béliard, put no more trust in anybody; she began to suspect the librarian, even the hospitalized woman's husband. As at the height of her insomnia the week before, she went back to staying in her room, keeping the door closed to the staff, heading down to eat only when everyone was taking his afternoon nap.

But alas, not everyone was napping. One afternoon, as she was leaving the restaurant at around three o'clock, she noticed Gopal and the superintendent leaning against the adjacent bar. The two men seemed engrossed in serious conversation. Gloire made herself as scarce as possible, passing like a shadow a good distance away. But if Gopal was blind as a bat, the superintendent wasn't. After a quick glance, he whispered briefly to the practitioner, who brusquely turned toward the young woman. "What a delightful surprise!" he said. "Will you take a little refreshment with us?"

But there was nothing refreshing about his statements. "You're just the person I wanted to see," he claimed. "You can't refuse. I'd like to entrust you with an object that I wish to have delivered to my cousin in Bombay. You know that the mail here," he chuckled, "is a little like in your Italy. I'd rather have it delivered by hand, by private courier. Does that sound like something you'd care to handle? We'll pay for the trip, of course."

"I see what this is about," said Gloire.

"I'm sure you do," said Gopal, "but I believe you'll do it anyway."

"No chance," said Gloire.

"No reason to be suspicious," Gopal impressed upon her. "It doesn't commit you to anything, there's no risk involved; naturally I'll reimburse you. All the more so in that, from what I understand, it would not be a bad idea for you to go away for a few days."

Gloire stood up. "What does that mean?"

"I'm just telling you what I know," answered Gopal, "just giving my opinion."

"Let me think about it," she said.

"But of course," said Gopal, "think about it. Even if it won't change anything, it's the least I can offer."

Back in her room, she consulted Béliard.

"We could have seen it coming," he said. "All right, so what do we do?"

"You tell me," she went. "You're the one with the bright ideas."

"My idea is that we do it," said Béliard. "It'll be a change of scenery. And besides," he asked, "what do we have to lose, at this point?"

"I don't know," she said. "Whatever you say."

"Yes," said Béliard, "might as well go away for a while. And besides, we'll be better off in Bombay. It's bigger, more anonymous; they'll leave us alone. Anyway, I've never been to Bombay. Is it nice?"

She didn't answer right away. Sitting crosswise on the bed, legs folded, she thumbed through a copy of the *Bhagavad Gita,* left with a Bible as fixtures on the bedside table.

"Where were you?" she said.

"What, where?" Béliard conjuncted. "When?"

"When I was in Bombay, where were you? Did you really stay in Sydney?"

"Don't get on my case about that," said Béliard. "You know damn well we never talk about that. I have a right to my own life. Go tell him we'll do it."

Then, once Gloire was back in the bar: "I never doubted it for a moment," said Gopal. "Well, then, you leave tomorrow morning."

"So soon?"

"Believe me," said Gopal, "it's in your best interests."

19

As tactless, duplicitous, and corrupt as Dr. Gopal surely was, for once at least he hadn't been lying. The following afternoon, a rented purple Ambassador limousine, sans air conditioner, rolled gently down Cenotaph Road in the direction of the Cosmopolitan Club.

Cenotaph Road is a calm little artery, residential albeit dusty, almost an alley bordered by tall acacias that surge from intertwined bushes. Every hundred yards, an enormous white villa succeeds another, its flat roof capped with a parabolic antenna, its gateway topped with a sign warning visitors against dogs (although one never sees any dogs), and flanked by a booth containing a dozing watchman in unbuttoned paramilitary khaki uniform, belt, badge, and tilted beret. Surrounded by gardens and shut in by walls, these villas never exceed two floors, embellished with terraces featuring steps, turrets, verandahs, and canopies protected by blinds, tarpaulins, screens, or modern variations on moucharaby.

One does not meet many inhabitants of these residences. Sometimes, in the distance, silhouettes clad in light-colored pajamas quickly cross the street from one gate to another. The domestics, no doubt. Beneath a balcony, behind fences braided with shrubbery, a solo, bald, myopic old man with a mustache lets himself be carried back and forth on a swing of feeble amplitude. But as you look at him he looks at you, and you lower your eyes. The temperature nears ninety-five degrees. Everything is calm, almost nothing to be heard. A great white light wears down the contours and colors of things, to the point of confiscating one of their three dimensions. In short, it's Sunday.

At the moment, the Ambassador was the only vivid object in this pale world. Driving at low speed, it encountered few people as it passed. A cyclist transported a bin much too large for his conveyance, but five minutes later another cyclist transported two bins that were just as large. Three women from the less plentiful neighborhoods bound dead branches of casuarina into faggots. From level ground to blue heaven, butterflies flitted, parakeets fluttered, and squadrons of crows darted. A couple of homosexual ground squirrels, before getting down to it in the gutter, risked pusillanimous pecks with their snouts, left, right, left, etc.

Two circling eagles were reflected in the Ambassador's roof, beneath which three individuals were thinking, each in his own way, about different subjects such as sex, for instance, or money. The Western man seated in back was thinking vaguely, still dressed in his wrinkled straw-colored suit. The woman seated next to him—light-colored cotton ensemble bought two days earlier at a tropical outfitter's in Paris—was thinking more dreamily. Only the native chauffeur, in linen slacks and shirt with a dirty front, was speculating more forwardly about the measurements of that lady and the revenues of that gentleman. The gentleman uttered two brief words just before Cenotaph Road met a narrow private drive that disappeared, after a bend, beneath a mango tree; they turned onto it. Having good visibility, they saw that in the distance, at the location of a gateway, this drive was closed off by cement speed blocks next to which, parallel to the raised barrier, a bilingual sign informed the public of the interdiction to enter the Cosmopolitan Club, and of the prosecution that would befall all trespassers. Following two more brief words, the car stopped fifty yards before the threshold.

"Right," said Personnettaz, "I think this is it. I'm going in. Wait for me here."

"I beg your pardon," said Donatienne, "but I'm coming with you."

"No no no no," Personnettaz inflected in various tones, "this part of the job has always been my responsibility."

"But I have to be there," Donatienne insisted, "that's what I'm here for. Otherwise, what good am I?"

"Don't insist," Personnettaz settled the matter. "Besides, you don't have the proper training."

"Stupid jerk," Donatienne muttered as soon as he'd slammed the door. "If that's how he's going to be, maybe I'll just get it on with the chauffeur." But in the final account she did nothing of the sort, immersing herself instead in a tourist guide to the region while the chauffeur, blissfully ignorant of what he had just missed, became absorbed in the Arts and Leisure pages of the *Sunday Standard*.

Trusting the map provided by his informants, Personnettaz headed toward the club annex that housed the short-term guests. His equipment weighed a bit too much in his pockets, but still they didn't bulge: miniature flashlight and ring of keys in the left one; in the right (just in case) a small pistol. He met no one on his way to the annex door, crossed the foyer to the waiting elevator, and entered. This time, for the less than a minute the climb lasted, he studied himself in the mirror that filled the back of the car.

It's in elevator mirrors that you can look most exhausted. And it doesn't matter which direction it's going: whether up or down, your self-image always plummets. You worry, you wonder why, what did you do the night before to deserve this? But you needn't be alarmed, it's only an effect of the overhead bulb. It's that dull, vertical glow that makes the face earthen, deepens wrinkles and draws features, swells the bags under your eyes. Under that low-angled light, the mirror multiplies your unhealthy pallor at the speed of the elevator. It is essentially, therefore, an illusion. But Personnettaz is not aware of this. My god, I've gotten old, he thinks. I never thought it could happen. We might wonder if it isn't Donatienne's presence that is pushing this man, normally so careless of his appearance, to question the mirror this way. We might wonder if he is conscious of that possibility. We might just as easily not give a tinker's damn.

He pushed open the elevator grate: still not a living soul up and down the hallway, which he followed on tiptoe to apartment 32.

Gently he knocked on the door several times, getting no answer. After two lateral glances like a ground squirrel, he delicately gripped the knob, turning it silently. Expecting it to resist, he had selected in advance the appropriate passkey from his ring; but after barely a quarter of a turn the door opened as if on its own. Thrusting a hand in his pocket, Personnettaz closed it (just in case) over the small pistol.

Crossing first through an opaque anteroom, with no other furnishings than two disused clothes hooks on the wall, Personnettaz then entered a large, empty living room. Curtains drawn, furniture arranged, not a single trace of occupancy. A door to the right probably led to a bedroom: indeed; also empty. The man spun around pensively: nothing, at least not a personal belonging in sight. He inspected the shelving, the drawers, the wastebaskets, without finding a matchbox or hairpin, nor a single bill or flyer or crumpled ticket such as people always leave behind in hotels. No cigarette butts in the spotless ashtrays. He opened the numerous closets with no greater success—except for the last one in which rested, folded on the bottom shelf, all the fabrics bought in the afternoons by Gloire when she had nothing better to do. Personnettaz opened them one after the other, without discovering the slightest clue between their layers. Absolutely nothing. Under the influence of spite, he suddenly got the urge to rip one of those fabrics to shreds; and then, under a less precise influence, he thought of bringing one to Donatienne. But in the end he rebuffed both these impulses.

Knowing in advance that he would find not even a hair, his examination of the bathroom was purely for form's sake. He returned to the living room. The silence was absolute, although pockmarked by a distant rumble that multiplied it still more. Evidently the apartment had been emptied with care, but very recently, it seemed, for in it still floated a few nearby echoes of perfume, words, sighs, and the clack of high heels.

A cough sounded behind Personnettaz, who turned his head: a bellboy equipped with a swab and pail was studying him with interest, asking a question that Personnettaz had him repeat. The bellboy wanted to know if he could clean. Personnettaz deemed the place to be quite clean enough already. "Of course," he said nonetheless, "go ahead. In any case, I was just leaving."

In the rear of the Ambassador, Donatienne had dozed off, and on his steering wheel the native chauffeur was asleep as well—a fairly intimate twin slumber which lets us imagine that the young woman might have had second thoughts. But this hypothesis did not cross Personnettaz's mind as he lightly touched Donatienne's shoulder. When she opened her eyes: "Well," he said, "I think it's a bust."

20

From another Xerox-telex-fax office near the Cosmopolitan Club, Donatienne called Salvador the following morning at around nine o'clock. The eighty-five degrees already weighing on the city jumped to 120 in the glass cage with its zinc roof. Donatienne immediately became drenched, while somewhere in the distance, Paris floated in icy darkness, at the hour when late night prepares to change into its early morning garb. No doubt Salvador would still be asleep, but the young woman had no qualms about waking him. And anyway, no, he was not asleep. He hadn't even gone to bed.

High as a kite, Salvador was experiencing some difficulty merely in staying seated at his table, holding on with both hands to the edge of that document-littered surface. Before his eyes, on a large blotter stained with the traces of numerous glasses—interlacings of circumferences that sketched out a dead-drunk version of the Olympic emblem—a few words were jotted in an unsteady hand: the adjectives *brunette* and *blonde* one above the other, then the nouns *cigarettes* and *beer* correspondingly superimposed across from them, with a complicated network of arrows and brackets linking the two columns. In the upper-right-hand corner of the blotter was inscribed the single word *redheads*, in parentheses and followed by a question mark. To all appearances, Salvador's research marked an idle pause that was still more idle than usual. A transistor radio set on a corner of the table broadcast, almost imperceptibly, a continuous program of tropical music.

"Ah," stammered Salvador when he answered the phone, "it's you. Great timing, I was getting kind of lonely here. Where are you? You want to come over?"

Donatienne raised her eyes heavenward.

"Listen," she said, "we blew it again. I swear, it's really something that we can't get our hands on that girl."

"Yeah," Salvador said pastily, "who cares? Nobody gives a damn. Come over."

"Don't be an idiot," Donatienne cried. "Stop it. I'm almost four thousand miles away, I'm dying of the heat, and I'm fed up, you hear?"

"Oh, right, right," said Salvador, apparently not hearing, removing the receiver from his ear for an instant to remedy his empty glass. "Me too," he resumed, "I'm fed up too, you know? More than fed up. That's putting it mildly, more than fed up."

"All right," Donatienne calmed down. "But are you getting some work done? Are you making progress?"

"Man, I'm not making anything," went Salvador. "I'm drawing blanks but I don't give a damn. I don't give a damn, you understand?" he repeated with enthusiasm. "You sure you don't want to come over?"

"No," the young woman sighed, "not right now. I'll call you later."

"Wait, wait a minute," Salvador insisted into the night—well after Donatienne had hung up, left the cabin, and rejoined Personnettaz in the Ambassador.

"So," inquired Personnettaz, "what did he say?"

"Nothing," said the young woman. "He doesn't seem to be doing too well. Where the hell could that bitch have gone to now?" she wondered through clenched teeth.

Naively, that bitch thought they would leave her in peace once she had accomplished her mission. She had arrived in Bombay and taken a room at the Supreme Hotel, where her accommodations were elementary: neither air conditioner nor television, a cement bathroom, a hard leatherette sofa, a single chair, a single table, in a drawer of which Gloire stashed the package given her by Gopal—a painstakingly Scotch-taped package, in the shape of a brick but soft in consistency, as if it contained water, pharmaceutical jelly, or air—before dialing the number the doctor had jotted on a scrap of prescription pad (V.R. Moopanar, 2021947). They apparently had not replaced the telephone since the days of the English; its dial turned with the irritating slowness of a gassed roach. But finally it rang at the other end of the line; someone picked up.

It must have been a huge enterprise for, after Gloire had asked to speak to Mr. Moopanar, a high-pitched operator's voice first advised her to hold the wire. Click. Another female voice, more contralto this time, same request and same advice, another click. Then the uneasy tones of a circumspect young man: double click, after which an older, calmer man, no doubt sitting in a more comfortable chair, desired more information: first name, last name, who referred you? He, too, advised her to hold the wire when Gloire mentioned the name Gopal. Triple click followed by a buzz. Another female voice, more commanding this time, clipped, executive secretary–style: double buzz. More comfortable and jovial, the last voice finally seemed to be that of V.R. Moopanar himself.

"Ah, Gopal," Moopanar exclaimed, "I see exactly who you mean. Now let's see, is he the one in Hyderabad or the one on TTK Road?"

"Goodness," said Gloire, "I don't really know. He's got a clinic on Karaneeswarar Sannadhi Street."

"Perfect," the other cut in, "I see exactly. Where are you staying? The Supreme, ah, well, are you sure you're comfortable there? Well, anyway, we'll meet at the bar, all right? I'm on my way. We're on our way."

He appeared thirty minutes later. Talcumed, ringed, mustache waxed, replete in his raspberry double-breasted suit, Moopanar smiled, smiled, smiled. Each time he smiled, a diamond embedded in one of his canines rang like an electric pinball bumper. Flanking him in the background, his inverse, was a dry, clean-shaven young man squeezed into tight-fitting chocolate brown and suffering from a peculiar strabismus: a killer's steady left eye, a bodyguard's very mobile right one. While he showed only minor interest in Gopal's parcel, not even glancing at it as he passed it to his assistant, Moopanar proved very affable with Gloire, hoped she'd had a good trip, wasn't too tired, welcome to Bombay. Did she know anyone in town, wouldn't she be too alone, wasn't she going to get bored. Unthinkable that she should be bored: might he have the honor of inviting her to a party that he happened to be throwing that very evening, at home? A few friends. A chance to meet people and make friends. His diamond rang four times, followed by the sharp explosion of a free game, as he stressed all the advantages of having friends in Bombay. "I'm not sure," said Gloire. "The fact is, I'm pretty worn out."

"That's only natural," said Moopanar, "I'll let you get some rest. I'll call you toward the end of the afternoon. A car can come by to pick you up."

Back in her room, Gloire consulted Béliard: what should I do? "Why not go," suggested the homunculus. "You never know. What's there to lose? After that, we'll see."

Moopanar occupied the penthouse of a deluxe residence in Malabar Hill. Depending on which end of the terrace one stood at, one's gaze plummeted onto the Gulf of Oman, the bay, the launderers' quarter, or hanging gardens. Tables had been set, laden with enough to souse and stuff two hundred people, though there were but a mere sixty: V.R. Moopanar's immediate entourage. First, all his mistresses and all his brothers and all the brothers of his mistresses and all the mistresses of his brothers. Then Moopanar's colleagues, who seemed to be accompanied by their attendants; certain industrialists; a vice minister; a Congress Party deputy; three Hungarian businessmen without their spouses; and five or six prostitutes. Finally, a few racing professionals—owners, trainers, jockeys. Mixed Western and regional outfits, tuxes and shawls, tailored suits, saris, pajamas and miniskirts, turbans, and pantsuits; no pinky without its gem.

Warmly introduced by Moopanar, Gloire mingled with a few groups, smiling and saying little, feigning not to know English, seeming absent from the conversations. Although all around her they were discussing business rather freely, she had some trouble getting a precise idea of these people's occupations. Then she ended up growing bored: drink in hand, she left the terrace to go tour the apartment.

A wide hallway bordered numerous rooms with brightly painted walls. Through their open doorways, Gloire inspected them one after the other, like a catalogue of sherbets. The floor of each was tiled in matching marble tones, waxed like hardwood, so polished it could be mistaken for linoleum. These rooms were for the most part furnished only with a large bed, a large chandelier, and a large Cuddalore or Masulipatam carpet, or sometimes with a tiger skin still bearing its head and all its teeth. The door to one room was partially closed: Gloire pushed it open before immediately shutting it, having had time only to glimpse a couple writhing on a bed. She walked away, disturbed, then doubly disturbed when she realized that one of the faces of that couple, barely seen, might not be unknown to her. She stopped, retraced her steps, gently opened the door again, and didn't recognize Rachel until the latter began crying out *yes do it up the ass, Biplab, please you know you like it.* "Well, I'll be damned," Gloire said to herself. "She's still with Biplab."

It was so unexpected that Gloire, against all her principles, remained frozen at the door without being able to look away—until Rachel, acting on her word and flopping over on the bed, met her stare and cried out once more in a different tone. Gloire, mortified, immediately turned and left. But she had gone no more than a few yards down the hall when, bare feet slapping the marble, Rachel ran up to her, hastily wrapped in a cotton bathrobe. "What are you *doing* here?"

"It's kind of a long story," answered Gloire. "What about you?"

If Rachel hadn't changed much in such a short time, her life on the other hand had been completely transformed. Tired of traveling without goal or method, she had as we know become involved with the young businessman Biplab, whom she'd met near the Elephanta wharf. Now Biplab, newly recruited in the Moopanar company and quickly risen in the ranks, ensured her an easy life in Bombay, one of unadulterated idleness and royal peace. "He's sweet," she said, "and besides, you know, him or someone else."

"I see," said Gloire. "But what is this company, exactly?"

"What," went Rachel, "you haven't figured it out yet?"

At the end of the hall, wearing new clothes and a wide smile, the young businessman appeared and came toward Rachel, obviously head over heels in love. "Go have a drink on the terrace," she told him. "I'll join you in a minute."

From what she had understood of Gopal's activities, Gloire had expected to meet his counterparts in Bombay, involved like him in the traffic of narcotics and blood. But actually, explained Rachel, these two markets conglutinated into a much larger and more developed network, of which the Moopanar company was one of the nerve centers. From this consortium of various businesses, which constituted an alternative global economy (or perhaps the globe's one true economy), Rachel drew up a table with three headings: goods, services, methods.

The goods: classic commodities, first and foremost, including military explosives, heavy weaponry, currency, alcohol, children, cigarettes, pornographic materials, counterfeit, slaves of both sexes, endangered species. On top of which, new sectors had recently begun to expand rapidly. Human organs, for example—kidneys and corneas lifted from Eastern European battlefields, in the quack clinics of Central America or the subcontinent, more or less healthy blood pumped pretty much everywhere—constituted no less active a market than the one for radioactive products left over from the dismantled nuclear plants in the East: uranium, cesium, and strontium by the shovelful, plutonium like rainwater.

Gigantic poppies, moreover, with miraculous yields, were springing up at top speed around those deboned power plants, helping feed the traditional market for narcotics, another speciality of the Moopanar company. Add some twenty thousand brands of bogus pharmaceuticals, and you've got something that produced masses of good narcodollars and excellent narcomarks, all indispensable for maintaining a voluminous staff of chemists, recyclers, and hired killers.

For the services: The hired killers also contributed their share of rackets and kidnappings, including ransom, extortion, protection money, gambling, and prostitution, redirecting of development grants, misappropriation of international aid or community funds, secret accounts or moonlight labor, investment scams, disposal of toxic waste, forced subcontracts, illicit bankruptcies, and agricultural policy fraud—a whole world, in short.

Yes, the world is teeming with things to do, and for anyone who knows how to do them methodically it is teeming with money. This money is gathered by collectors wearing light-colored ties over dark shirts; then laundered by an arborescence of casinos and palaces, pizzerias and hair salons, massage parlors, coin-op laundries, and service stations; then wired into untouchable accounts in Bad Ischl, Székesfehérvár, or the Anglo-Norman islands. But Gloire had pretty much read all this in the newspapers; she began to grow tired of these explanations. For now, she preferred to take Rachel in her arms.

"All right," she whispered softly in her ear, "but tell me, what am *I* doing here?"

"They'll let you know soon enough," Rachel answered through Gloire's hair, "it won't be long. Come."

They went back into the room, Rachel closing the door more carefully this time, and fell onto the bed. And a few hours later, back at the Supreme, Gloire gave Béliard a rundown of her evening, minus a few technical details.

"I see what the deal is," said the homunculus, "and I know you're having fun. Even so, be careful. Maybe we shouldn't hang around here too long."

21

The day after his party, Moopanar phoned the Supreme to inform Gloire that he'd found her another hotel, better suited to her person. A car would be by before noon to fetch her and her belongings. "The plot thickens," Béliard observed.

The glacial darkness of the restaurant, the bouncers dressed as trainers and the elevator boys as ichoglans, gave a fair idea of this new establishment's prestige. Located on the top floor of a white building rising high above Marine Drive, Gloire's new room was six times larger than at the Supreme, decorated in dark colors and endowed with every modern comfort—refrigerator, television, air conditioner, and bathtub for two. A small balcony overhanging the void supported a lounge chair and a bay window that looked out onto the bay.

Gloire quickly resumed her old habits. Rising late, she spent the ends of her mornings on the balcony, eyes half-closed on the vast and sparsely populated beach strewn with decrepit attractions, rusted slides, and turnstiles. The unclean sea was far away, the sand was only dust. Passersby trampled it in isolation, with no intention of bathing, sometimes behind an ox cart. Occasionally one could see a horse in the background, galloping over the fringe of sea foam.

Lying as usual on the lounge's footrest and wearing only his Bermuda shorts, Béliard soaked up the sun next to Gloire. "Be careful even so," he advised. "Don't let yourself become indebted to them. Don't let them get a hold over you. Insist on paying for the hotel yourself."

Moopanar, however, was very discreet. He called briefly from time to time to make sure that Gloire wanted for nothing, without imposing or even proposing anything—except that she grace the parties he continued to throw on his terrace two or three times a week. These parties were always generally the same; Gloire ended up going only every other time. One day she agreed to accompany Moopanar, with Rachel, to the racetrack where one of his horses, named Telepathy, was running at four to one. Two days later, they watched a polo match that pitted other members of his stables against each other.

But for the time being: sun. Then, at around two o'clock, Rachel would rap softly at the door. "Scram," Gloire would tell Béliard, who slunk off with the sullen eye of a dispossessed voyeur. Sometimes he got up of his own accord as soon as he heard the knock, not waiting for Gloire to kick him out but making a sour face all the same. The young women rested a moment in the room before going to have a leisurely lunch at the hotel restaurant—cubes of marinated chicken and fish, yogurt with bhang. Then, once the worst heat had passed, they went back to galavanting about town as in the old days, near the Chor Bazar or the Banganga Tank, loitering around the reservoirs in the shadows of tall buildings. Monkeys, men, and children played on the roof terraces. Men waving handkerchiefs guided the movements of pigeons grouped in clusters in the sky, the children governed those of their kites, and the monkeys chased each other around the sheer drops of the facades; you never saw any women playing.

When night fell, they dined at the Yacht Club, where Biplab sometimes joined them before going off to resume his functions at Moopanar's. Then, almost as gay as that first evening, they went to down a few glasses at the bar of the Taj, which was still full of foreigners, meeting other young women there—one of whom swore, one evening, that she answered to the name of Porsche Duvall—as well as men and boys. The men were moodier and more forward than the boys, with whom it was easier to negotiate, although the women seemed to have an equal number of friends and enemies in both camps. In short, hardly a care, easy life, royal peace. Gloire didn't even have to fear the maneuvers of Personnettaz and company; Gopal had covered her tracks so well that for the moment they'd lost all trace of her.

Still, it would sometimes happen that she could no longer find her equilibrium, no longer hear herself in the incessant concert of car horns and crows in Bombay—as had been the case, albeit in reverse, when her thoughts stood out too violently in the oppressive quiet of the Cosmopolitan Club. It also happened that she began wondering if she was going to stay there indefinitely, if it wasn't time to go home. On that score, Rachel couldn't answer, Béliard had no opinion, and I myself don't really know. Whatever the case, after three weeks of this diet, Moopanar showed up at Gloire's one morning, unexpectedly: Béliard barely had time to jump into a closet.

Moopanar at first claimed that, having been in the neighborhood, he'd suddenly thought of dropping by just to make sure all was well. He crossed the room, contemplated the bay for a moment, then turned toward Gloire: "Could you do me a small favor?"

"Here we go," a breathless Béliard said to himself, ear glued to the closet door in the darkness.

"What sort of favor?"

"It's very simple," said Moopanar. "I have to send some merchandise to your country. You'd merely have to accompany that merchandise. Make sure everything goes smoothly. Be there, in other words."

"The plot thickens," Béliard repeated under his breath.

Gloire didn't answer right away. It might be an opportunity to go home, as she'd been thinking of doing lately—but, knowing

Moopanar's activities, at what cost, with who knew what blocks of plastique, uranium, or opium stuffed into which private place?

"Please don't go imagining things," Moopanar read her thoughts. "There's nothing complicated, nothing risky. All you have to do is take a plane. I'll assume all expenses, there's nothing you have to do. Someone will be waiting for you over there to handle everything."

"Fine," said Gloire, "let's assume that's true. And what exactly is it you're transporting?"

"Horses," said Moopanar.

"Oh, really," said Gloire. "Horses."

"Yes," said Moopanar, "horses."

"Well, in that case," said Gloire, "if it's only horses."

"Horses," repeated Moopanar. "So you see. Only horses."

Cargo planes were what one used to transport horses from one continent to another. Normally a veterinarian would escort them, armed with a giant syringe in case there was a problem, but, Moopanar assured her, there would be no problems so there would be no veterinarian; Gloire could travel alone with the animals. The day after tomorrow. All right? "All right," she said.

So: Bombay-Saha Airport, the day after tomorrow. Bright sunshine, moderate wind from the northeast. Apart from Moopanar's six horses—of an old Central Asian lineage—the cargo plane would carry the turbine shaft for a hydraulic dam, sent back to France for routine replacement. The whole interior of the plane had been gutted, reduced to the state of an immense hold, with only a windowless cabin installed behind the pilot's cockpit for the escorts. It had six seats in front, along with a microwave oven and a freezer compartment. One door permitted access to the cockpit, another led to a steel stairway that descended into the hold. A steward out of uniform provided limited service. Gloire kissed Rachel and they took off.

Three men in civvies were escorting the turbine shaft, young technicians specializing in the maintenance of enormous things. Three young men in fine fettle and very talkative among themselves, but too bashful to dare speak to Gloire, who distractedly heard them launch into a thousand topics. But it seemed that on each of these topics their conversation, at first quite animated, rapidly petered out before frankly spinning in idle: after the first light, lively, dancing exchanges, it soon got stuck in a rut. Then they would clamber off to dig it out, unfold their collapsible shovels, and stuff branches under the wheels—after which, as soon as it was lifting off and airborne once more, soaring toward another topic, they would jump aboard the conversation at the last second, before it could fly away without them.

Gloire followed their exchange for a moment before dozing off. When she opened her eyes, the technicians were asleep. As usual on a plane, Béliard was unavailable, not even visible: no one to talk to, nothing to see out the nonexistent windows, nothing to read; Gloire was starting to get bored. As luck would have it, the copilot soon appeared, en route to the refrigerator to get something to drink. Seeing her with nothing to do, he invited her to come have one with him and the others in the cockpit. He grabbed a bottle and stepped aside to let her pass.

Equally calm ambience in the pilots' cabin. The captain was asleep in his seat and the flight engineer was leafing through specialized magazines. "Good evening, gentlemen," said Gloire. The captain smiled as he opened a blue eye: his jaws were square and his crew cut white. "I've got the corkscrew," the engineer reminded them. Having settled the young woman in a seat behind the staff, the copilot regained his position before the automatic maneuver dials. The captain sat up in his chair—the back of which was lined with a curtain of ergonomic pearls, of the same model used by taxi drivers with delicate lumbars—then turned toward Gloire. They were flying over Saudi Arabia.

Paris—Charles de Gaulle Airport, three hours later. Cool, drizzle. Gloire left the Boeing with the crew, who went to their reserved quarters to shower and change before heading home while she would go through customs alone with the horses' papers. She calmly handled all the formalities. The documents seemed to be in order; they stamped everything they could stamp. She was told where she could claim her cargo. To do that, she had to leave the terminal and go to a freight hangar. Moopanar had indeed mentioned that someone would be waiting for her in Paris to take care of everything, but if this someone didn't show, what would she do all alone in life with six horses? We'd see.

We see. Barely past the opaque door amid travelers arriving on other flights, among the relatives and allies come to meet them, we spot a face whose mobility made it stand out from all the others. Still devoured by facial tics, but in a more minor key than usual: Lagrange.

"Hey!" said Gloire. "What are you doing here?"

"I'll explain," said Lagrange. He seemed to be in a very bad mood.

"You seem to be in a very bad mood," Gloire observed.

"You're right," Lagrange admitted. "I'm in a very bad mood."

An associate was with him, someone Gloire had never met. Jockey's build, dark clothes, a gap between his incisors that could fit a molar and answering to the name Zbigniew, he coordinated the three vans in which the horses would embark. They waited for the latter, which appeared in the distance. The animals shivered, gave indolent kicks, seemed not very lively, whereas Lagrange showed signs of increasing nervousness all during the transfer. And yet nothing particular caught the attention of the customs functionaries. The final papers, in order like the rest, were stamped.

Normally they send dogs, cats, and monkeys through the X-rays; with no special care they toss their carriers onto the luggage belt with the inanimate valises. But they didn't have any machines big enough to scan the horses, which paraded, in step, from the airplane into the vans. Gloire hadn't seen them when she embarked in Bombay, nor had she gone down to visit them in the hold. Fairly dazed, rings under their eyes, bloated, they did everything they were told; only distantly did they evoke steeplechases and polo matches.

Having locked the rear gates, the associate walked back toward Lagrange, wiping his hands: "All set," he said. "Nice animals."

"Right," said Lagrange, "get moving. I'll see you Thursday. You and I" (to Gloire) "are taking a cab."

They watched the vans drive off, then headed for the taxi stand.

"So," intimated Lagrange, "how did it go with Moopanar?"

As Gloire stopped short, Lagrange took two more steps, then turned around.

"What?" he said. "Come on, let's go."

"Wait a minute," she said. "You know that guy? You work with those people?"

"Come on," said Lagrange. "I'll explain."

They joined the taxi line, but these vehicles were scarce for the moment. By the time they had found the only available one and climbed inside, the flight captain had come running up in freshly pressed civilian garb. Knocking on their window, the captain asked if they wouldn't possibly mind taking him along. "Of course," said Gloire, while Lagrange turned away without answering.

The captain sat next to the driver, sighing contentedly. "This is very kind of you," he said. "You can just let me off at Place d'Italie."

At the wheel was a classic French taxi driver in black and white, yellow cigarette stub, wiseguy accent, checkered cap. "Ah," sympathized the captain, "I see you've got one of those beaded seats too."

"Lemme tell you," said the driver, "this thing saved my life."

"It's remarkable," said the captain, "simply remarkable how relaxing it is."

"It's some kinda Chinese thing," said the driver, "right?"

"I'm not entirely sure," said the captain, "maybe Scandinavian. But how good it feels, how good it does feel."

"Me," said the driver, "I used to get a stiff back like you wouldn't believe."

"Why, so did I," the captain hastened to concur. "But I think that's Place d'Italie now."

"So," said Gloire as soon as he had gotten out, "how are you mixed up in all this?"

"I'll explain," said Lagrange, "but first tell me where you want to go."

"Anywhere," answered Gloire, "so long as I'm left in peace."

"What would you say to the country?" Lagrange suggested.

"Fine," said Gloire.

"Perfect," said Lagrange.

22

They went to the country. Lagrange didn't explain squat.

After the taxi dropped them on Rue de Tilsitt, they immediately left for Normandy in Lagrange's Opel; he remained mute on the highway, then on the smaller roads they took after it. They wound through a copse for three quarters of an hour. At a bend in a single-lane filiform drive, a wrought-iron gate opened onto a prospect of lindens at the end of which stood a small manor in pink brick. They weren't very far from the sea, past Honfleur, somewhere around Manneville-la-Raoult.

They arrived just after noon. Built in the late seventeenth century, the manor stood drily against the yellowed prairies: a tall, brittle parallelepiped, thin and almost transparent. Large windows symmetrically cut in its facades let light pass through from one side to the other. Kitchen and living rooms on the ground floor, and two other floors filled with bedrooms.

The room he gave Gloire occupied the entire top floor. The exposed beams made it look like a capsized boat; the windows were of irregular unrefined glass, lightly tinted, containing small bubbles that distorted the landscape. Antique furniture, modern paintings, and figurines—among which, four miles in the distance, was the spanking new Normandy bridge framed by one of the six windows, a perfect little contemporary sculpture impeccably lit in its showcase.

The young woman looked out the other windows. To one side of the narrow road at the end of the park, a low, whitewashed building in traditional style, with iris stalks on a fringe of thatch, must have served as toolshed and lodgings for the staff. On the other side, beyond a garden, a tennis court with a sagging net, and a tarpaulin-covered pool, horses stood planted in a field. Lagrange and Zbigniew were watching them, their elbows resting on the fence. Gloire went down to join the two men.

The animals numbered around ten and moved little. Three of them nodded their heads together in a corner; two colts wandered around their mother; and the others posed for their statues. Gloire did not recognize Moopanar's horses among them, seen that very morning at the airport. No doubt they were recovering from their journey in the complex of stables and individual stalls framing a bridle path at the other end of the field. They already looked fairly languid as they got off the plane to walk into the van, without fuss or hurry, without anyone suspecting that the first three of them were carrying sixty grams of cesium each and the other three had five kilos of heroin, the latter in plastic wrapping and the former in lead containers. Yes, no doubt they were recuperating after they had had the loads extracted from their entrails, before being brought to conclude this piece of business at the knacker's yard.

"Horses are pretty enormous," Zbigniew pointed out. "You can put all kinds of things inside."

"Shut up already," said Lagrange.

He himself would continue to remain silent for the rest of the day, then the next day; he no longer seemed the same person. In the six weeks Gloire had been gone, Lagrange had changed, and so had the days, now getting longer and longer: the sky was wider, the colors more sustained. And the season, growing milder, must have inspired lighter thoughts, since fairly late on the third night, after the last news broadcast, Lagrange, after having drunk a fair amount downstairs by himself, tried to join Gloire in her room. "No," Gloire said through the door. Lagrange took a clumsy stab at forcing the lock but gave up almost immediately; his unsteady footfalls faded down the stairway.

"What, is he kidding?" Béliard muttered, rolling over under the bedspread. "That's all we needed." The next morning, the sky was black as if the sun didn't want to rise, or as if night had rebelled and refused to give way: here I am and here I stay, you won't get rid of me that easily.

The darkness was more accommodating above Paris, yielding to the daylight at around six in the morning over Place de la République, and finally moving off to get on with its life. On the fourth floor of a building on Rue Yves-Toudic, behind République, Personnettaz had stopped sleeping some time ago. He finally got up, went into the kitchen, and poured two tablespoons of instant coffee into a mug. He opened the hot water faucet, let it run until it was good and hot, tested the stream with a rapid finger to make sure, then filled the mug, which he carried back unsweetened to his room. He sat down at his table and drank this bitter potion in little sips, while reading Jack London's adventures in the gold country. Forty minutes later his radio alarm went off in the middle of a sentence about the Dow Jones, and Personnettaz cut off the next one, devoted to the Nikkei average, before closing his book.

The sound of the shut tome echoed briefly in the room and the man headed, alone, to the bathroom. "You shouldn't keep living all alone like that," the concierge of his building had advised him once upon a time. "Someday you'll be old and sick with no one to take care of you."

The bearer of a Yugoslavian passport, the concierge back then was an elderly man, meticulously dressed, who would bring up the mail every day in pearl-colored suit and purple tie. But that was several years ago. Since then, a fair number of things had changed. Tenants had come and gone, Personnettaz had moved one floor down, and the management had repossessed the concierge's lodge to convert it into a studio, so there was no longer a concierge nor, for that matter, a Yugoslavia; but Personnettaz, despite the advice, persisted in living all alone like that. Chances not to live alone had presented themselves, of course, but he hadn't seized them, and now they were presenting themselves less often, less and less often. There would probably be no one to share with Personnettaz the tail end of an inheritance, seasoned with obscure bonds in manganese or zinc or cadmium, very far away, that he owned from he hardly knew where.

Little supplementary revenues sporadically came in from the operations proposed by Jouve, but on that score Personnettaz found himself technically laid off for the moment. All trace of Gloire had been lost since the attempt in India, and Donatienne had returned to Stochastic. While basically relieved to be rid of her, Personnettaz still phoned Donatienne from time to time, to take stock of the situation.

He threw on a few things without noticing whether they matched, vaguely promising himself to buy some new shoes one of these days—this pair easily had forty thousand on the odometer. But apart from that prospect, there was nothing else to do today; no more or less than yesterday. And nothing can wear you down like idleness when you live in an opaque two-room apartment behind République.

He waited until nine o'clock to make two or three phone calls. First to Boccara, but in vain. Daily since his return, Personnettaz had tried without success to reach the young man. On the off chance he had even stopped by his place but, once in front of the building, he hadn't been able to remember the new door code; he had only a mnemonic recall of the old one. Boccara indeed seemed not to have returned from his cruise, and so Personnettaz dialed Jouve's number. But, once more on the verge of tears from reading a sentimental novel, Mrs. Jouve answered that Jouve was out, as he was so often, as he was increasingly often. Perhaps he would be back tomorrow.

Personnettaz announced his visit for the following afternoon. Then he called Salvador.

Nothing new at Stochastic, either, and Salvador's voice was somewhat less than affable. Personnettaz informed him of his plan to visit Jouve, which served no other purpose than to make him appear active. "Fine," Salvador said with scant enthusiasm. "Well, keep me posted. Ah, I think Donatienne wants to talk to you—I'll put her on."

"No," Personnettaz blurted too late, "no."

"What's this I hear?" said Donatienne. "You're seeing Jouve tomorrow? I'm coming with you."

"There's no point," said Personnettaz. "I really think there's no point. I can handle it perfectly well on my own."

"No," Donatienne said gravely, "you need me and you know it. I'll see you tomorrow."

She sits back down in front of her keyboard, laughing to herself, waiting for the other one to start dictating again; but for the moment the other one is silent. He sits quietly. His face is blank. He is reflecting. He's demoralized. He has come to work on foot from Place de la Nation. Walking by the base of one of the columns that embellish that square, the thought of finding himself one hundred feet above ground level, in the place of Philippe Auguste, brutally rekindled his vertigo. Right now he's on the verge of nausea.

Then Salvador stops bothering even to reflect. He ponders a midge, come from who knows where, that circulates around his desk, also on foot, peacefully skirting the computer and the pencil can, slaloming between the floppy disks, the mineral water, and the bottle of aspirin. Coming and going among these accessories, the midge sometimes pauses more lengthily before one of them, seems to look it over, takes a few steps back and then heads off again, a tourist among the monuments. The contemplation of that insect inspires a few consoling thoughts in Salvador's brain: this isn't so bad, I could have ended up in Manila selling loose cigarettes. He goes back to his reflections. "Let's continue," he says. "Take this down. Warm tall blondes and cool tall blondes, part two."

So alongside warm blondes, there also exist cool tall blondes with measured words, radiographic eyes, and strict tailored suits. They are perhaps more distinguished, more civilized than the warm tall blondes, but the world, for opposite reasons, fears them just the same. At best, lunar, they stiffen in its arms; at worst they evaporate out of them. They run the risk of transparency, expose themselves to the danger of chlorosis. They are seldom lighthearted. Eva Marie-Saint is fairly typical of the genre. There is also a bit of this with Ingrid Bergman, for example.

"How about Grace Kelly?" suggests Donatienne.

"Absolutely," says Salvador, "absolutely. You have some of that with Grace Kelly. Now we're getting somewhere."

23

Her sentimental novel resting on her knees, Mrs. Jouve is sitting very stiffly on the edge of the sofa, alone before her television, which at this hour of the afternoon broadcasts only series produced across the Atlantic or beyond the Rhine. Acted by siliconed actresses with hairdos sculpted from a solid block, laquered and thermoset, the series are also sentimental. So that, regardless of whether she's following the plot on the page or on the screen, regardless of whether she takes off or puts on her glasses, behind them or not Mrs. Jouve's tears are still flowing. She is awaiting the return of her husband. She has not cleaned house very thoroughly: the remains of her lunch lie scattered on the table; on the bed in the next room the sheets are still rumpled.

Rattle of keys in the foyer and Jouve appears, his briefcase dangling at the end of his arm. Entering the living room, the reddened eyes of his spouse make him avert his own and roll them upward. "You can't imagine what kind of day I've had," he claims, listing the succession of obstacles and meetings purported to have eaten away his time. "I'm not asking for an account," his wife answers in a tearful voice.

"But I'm just telling you things, Genevieve," Jouve says gently, "that's all. I just want you to know everything."

He opens his briefcase and rummages inside, looking for nothing in particular. He considers himself above suspicion. No perfume emanates from him; his collar isn't stained with red, nor is his hair too freshly combed: Jouve is pretty well organized. Even if it happens that too great an absence of clues only connotes guilt all the more. The proof: "All you ever do is screw other women," Mrs. Jouve observes painfully.

"Hey, there, Genevieve," Jouve objects, "first of all, I don't only screw other women, all right?" Then, turning toward the half-open door to their room: "You could have cleaned up a little, don't you think? Straightened things up a bit, no?"

"I am who I am," Mrs. Jouve concedes. "I'm sure *they're* more fun to be around."

"Now, Genevieve," Jouve protests, "whatever have you cooked up in that head of yours?"

She turns away when he attempts a small gesture of affection. Changing the subject, Genevieve Jouve is about to tell him about Personnettaz's visit when the doorbell rings and there he is, followed by Donatienne, who is more skimpily clad than ever. If that way of dressing puts Personnettaz ill at ease, Jouve's roving eye, on the other hand, is interested.

While Genevieve Jouve talks with Donatienne, Personnettaz takes Jouve aside. It's inconceivable that a simple matter such as Gloire's shouldn't be easily resolved. It's unbelievable that they don't have a single remaining lead. Just find him one tiny clue and Personnettaz guarantees he'll be back on the case, he'll wrap it up in no time. Personnettaz does not like the constant delays in this operation, nor the feeling of incompetence that he gets from them, nor the enforced idleness that derives from them. It seems to have become a personal issue with him.

Jouve listens while appearing to think, but his eyes continue to glide furtively toward Donatienne. Surreptitiously they divest the young woman of her light textile wrapping. "Fine, I'll see," he finally says. "I'll see what I can do."

Meanwhile, Mrs. Jouve and Donatienne exchange female viewpoints on mostly female subjects, but not exclusively, not exclusively. Turning toward them, Personnettaz notes that Donatienne seems to be getting along very well with Genevieve Jouve. Personnettaz has known his employer's wife for a long time; he feels more comfortable with her than with him. That she should enjoy the young woman's company suddenly seems to him to constitute an agreement, a guarantee, a sanction. In emotional matters, Personnettaz has a pathological need for third-party approval. For the first time he looks at Donatienne differently, but just for a moment. Then he glances at his watch and Jouve, by contagion, looks at his own and, following suit, Donatienne and Genevieve similarly consult theirs. Everyone in fact is wearing a watch; each of them, on the occasion of an exam, a birthday, or a federal or religious holiday, has been handcuffed to time; all four observe, with a few seconds' difference, the same phenomenon of nearly four-twenty. Personnettaz says they'll be going. They're going.

"Did you see what she was wearing?" Genevieve asks after they've left.

"Oh, no," murmurs Jouve, "I didn't notice."

"Like hell you didn't notice," says Genevieve. "Anyway, never mind. I know what that means, when they dress like that."

"Oh, really?" Jouve perks up. "So what does it mean?"

"It's one of two things," states Genevieve. "Either there's a man they're out to attract, or they're completely desperate. But what are you doing? Are you going out again?"

"I'm going back to see your brother," says Jouve. "And believe me, it's not with a joyful heart."

This time, Jouve hails a taxi that heads up Boulevard de Sébastopol, veers in front of the Gare de l'Est, and crosses the Canal Saint-Martin before rounding the Buttes-Chaumont toward the Amérique police station. At the reception desk, the only client is an African in a suit who has a document case cut from the same synthetic fibers in the same color. This African, who would like to procure the requisite forms for a family immigration procedure—"That's right," says the functionary on duty, "bring over the whole tribe"—is sent packing in short order. Jouve goes directly up to his brother-in-law's office.

The latter grimaces disgracefully when he sees Jouve. "And what," he asks, "do you want from me now?"

"Nothing," says Jouve. "The same as last time."

"Oh no, I'm not biting anymore," says Clauze. "I have no reason to help you out."

"All right," says Jouve, opening his briefcase, "listen. I'm tired of this squabble. I'm going to make you an offer for the good of the family. Let's make up, what do you say? I've got the receipt. Here it is, you can have it back."

The receipt consists of three typewritten sheets of tea green onionskin paper stapled in one corner. Clauze grabs it and looks it over. "It feels funny to see this again," he says, shaking his head with an evil smile. "It's been a while."

"I can imagine," says Jouve, also smiling. "I understand."

Clauze leafs through the document attentively. "Hey, wait a minute," he says, "isn't there something missing here?"

"No," Jouve exclaims ingenuously. "You think so? And yet that's all I found in my files."

"You're trying to diddle me," Clauze says bitterly. "You think you're going to stick me in the back."

"I'm not!" cries Jouve. "I don't!"

"All the stuff about the meat is missing," Clauze insists, waving the document in his face.

"I don't know what you're talking about," says Jouve. "But fine, if that's how you're going to be, I'm taking it back." And with a quick motion he repossesses it.

"Wait!" says Clauze. "No, let me have it. It's something, at least."

"Uh-uh," says Jouve, "no way. If you don't trust me, then it's got to be even-steven. I'll let you have it back if you get me more information about the girl."

For a few seconds, Clauze fixes Jouve with a somewhat loveless stare. Then: "Wait here a minute," he finally says. While waiting for his brother-in-law to return, through the window Jouve watches the same branch from the other day limply waving. The same and yet different, for now it's sprouting buds. Five o'clock.

Clauze reappears more quickly than the last time, a new document in hand. Three handwritten lines on a page from an address book specify the address of a geriatric institution in the Seine-Maritime. "Here," he says, "I was able to find this. Now give me back those papers."

"Of course," says Jouve. "Here. I should give Genevieve your love, I suppose?"

"That's right," says Clauze, getting up to open the door. "You give her my love. You give her all my love and then you go straight to Hell."

"Robert," Jouve exclaims plaintively, "Robert, why do you always say that to me?"

24

The days passed, meagerly furnished with short walks in the country (hawthorn, sunken paths, hedges, cows) or by the sea (iodine, jetties, wrack, seagulls), with the soon-wearisome observation of the horses, with inattentive readings and distracted spells in front of the television. Gloire might have taken better advantage of the fresh air, the healthy and varied food, the calm sleep with all windows open; she might have gotten some exercise; but the idea never even occurred to her.

She was finding these days very long, checked the time too often. Never had the march of time seemed so slow. A discouraging slowness, multiplied by itself, weighing at the threshold of immobility. The slowness of grass growing; the slowness of an ai, of glue. If there are words whose meaning determines their career, slowness is no doubt in the first rank: so slow that it hasn't yet found the slightest synonym for itself, whereas speed, which doesn't waste a minute, already has a ton of them.

Béliard, too, consulted his watch ceaselessly, winding it every other minute. Buckled to his wrist, that little mechanism from before the age of quartz was one of the few accessories in his size that the homunculus owned, along with a comb, a mirror, a handkerchief, and a pair of dark sunglasses. At first he had tried to continue wearing those sunglasses, as in the good old days of the warm countries; but, unable to see in the Norman light and bumping into everything, he soon had to give them up. Before long, he started showing signs of moodiness; he pouted, made scenes. He missed his beautiful vacation in the tropics, was getting bored silly, threatened to leave. "Fine, that's just fine," an exasperated Gloire said once, "get lost. Get lost already. I'm sick of you."

Béliard immediately jumped onto his soles while wagging his finger: "I forbid you to use that tone with me," he stamped. "Don't go thinking you're the first one I've ever looked after, eh? I've already advised more important people than you. Famous people. In show business and everything."

"So?" asked Gloire. "Are they dead?"

"Why should they be dead?" Béliard exploded. "I'm good at my job."

As she was expressing surprise that these important people, if they were still alive, should no longer require his services, Béliard began to pout while examining his teeth in his pocket mirror. In a muffled voice he alluded to certain past problems. He did not wish to dwell on the circumstances of his dismissals. "Excuse me," said Gloire, "what was that you said? Can you repeat that?" Grudgingly, the homunculus again mumbled the word *dismissal*. "Wait a second," said Gloire. "Do you mean to tell me you can be *fired*?"

"Of course I can," said Béliard. "You just have to want it."

"But that's what I want," said Gloire. "That's exactly what I want."

"No way," snickered Béliard, sticking out his black tongue in the circular mirror. "You don't want it enough."

"Little clown," concluded Gloire. "Pathetic little fucking clown."

In short, minor conflicts, as always happen when things drag on, and when they drag on too long, you get annoyed over nothing and everything. You get annoyed at Béliard, at Lagrange, and even at Zbigniew. At the horses. You get annoyed that a dog, which is itself being annoyed by another dog, should bark at the other end of the lawn all morning. You also get pretty bored. Like Genevieve and Jouve. And for lack of anything better you spend more and more time in front of the television. You watch movies ("You're going to lose her, Alex. She thinks she's in love with you"), you watch game shows ("And now I'm going to ask for your full attention, Roger. Which flowers does one see most often on balconies?" "Water lilies, no I mean petunias, uh no what I meant to say was geraniums." "I'm sorry, Roger, but I'll have to go with your first answer. So, water lilies"), you watch the news. They never talk about Gloire on the news; moreover, there's no reason they should. And yet she still dreads it. "You're not afraid they'll talk about you," Béliard once suggested, perniciously, "but that they won't. Hey, cut it out!" he cried the next second. "You know I can't stand physical violence."

And so, free of danger but also of future prospects, twelve interminable days passed, not at all as Gloire had envisioned them—sheltered, certainly, but cramped. One evening she tried to get to know Zbigniew, except that Zbigniew didn't really have a lot to say for himself. She had quickly run through the few books lining the shelves in the living room. Béliard continued to sulk, and Lagrange was now drinking every day, beginning earlier and earlier. The time had come to find something to do.

Gloire set about it one bright and sunny morning, before Lagrange got started, by asking him to drive her to Rouen. Just a quick little round trip, they'd be back for dinner. "Gee," said Lagrange, "why not? It'll be a change. Let's go." And so they took the road to Rouen. At Pont-Audemer, while Lagrange filled the Opel, Gloire walked away from the gas station toward a nearby branch of the Shopi supermarket chain.

"What are you doing?" Lagrange said. "Where do you think you're going?"

"I'm going to buy some cognac," said Gloire.

"Excellent idea," approved Lagrange.

The best cognac at the Shopi cost 120 francs and 20 centimes in its stiff box; Gloire swung by the stationery aisle to get herself a roll of tape and another of striped, crinkled paper like seersucker. Back in the Opel, they headed off again; as they drove, she wrapped the box in the seersucker as best she could. It took a fair amount of time, but in the end, sure enough, it made a relatively presentable gift package. Lagrange had turned on the radio, which was playing J.J. Cale, of course, but also Boz Scaggs. Lagrange beat time with his index fingers on the wheel. He did not have the poor taste to ask for a sip of the cognac.

Rouen, then the suburbs of Rouen. Clusters of high-rises, a hospital, a cemetery, a retirement home; they parked in front of the retirement home. "Wait for me here," Gloire said, opening the car door. "I won't be long." Lagrange also had the tact not to suggest going in with her.

At the admissions desk, Gloire asked to see Mr. Abgrall. Kinship: only daughter. "Kindly wait a moment," they told her. At the end of that moment appeared a male nurse. A tall, handsome, young, immaculate type, very attentive, who seemed to know her father well, who spoke of him with affection, who brought Gloire to see him in ergotherapy.

In midconversation with a lady his age, Abgrall *père* stood up from his chair as they approached. Not tall, not fat, line of ashen mustache, looking lost but still elegant in his faded suit—an almost perfect double of Personnettaz's Slavic ex-concierge, but only we will ever know that—he kissed Gloire's hand as soon as it was within his reach. "It's your daughter, Mr. Abgrall," the nurse announced cheerfully. "You're glad to see her."

The old man studied Gloire intently, a hair too lengthily. "Very good," he said, "you've come for the distribution, that's good. You've come for the contribution. Please be seated." He turned to his contemporary: "She's come for the retribution," he confided to her in a half whisper.

Notwithstanding the peaceful activities of the old women all around them—crocheting, knitting, confection of artificial flowers and wicker baskets—a fair amount of noise reigned in the ergotherapy room. In their chairs of dirty plastic wire over rust-speckled tubing, toothless extroverts rocked dangerously while others sang in chorus ("Ah, the delight, the heady delight of the first time in his arms"). The smell was peculiar and the TV on full blast.

"Can't we find someplace a little quieter?" asked Gloire.

"Normally speaking, we can't," said the nurse, "but let me try to work something out for you. We'll find you a corner." The corner was a calm little room, dark at first glance, but the decidedly amenable nurse opened the curtains, revealing a clump of flowers on the lawn. The furniture was waxed, the wallpaper flowered, and the armchairs covered. The nurse disappeared, reappeared with tea, disappeared again. They were alone.

"So," said Gloire, "how are you?" "Personally, I'm fine," answered her father, "but it's the jays, you see." "What jays?" asked Gloire. "It's the jays who aren't doing so well," he specified. "One might even say they are not doing well at all. Well, actually," he amended after a moment's reflection, "they're not really doing so badly as all that." "Are you eating well?" his daughter inquired. "I'm eating better than they are," he winked. "Ten times better," he chuckled, "ten times more." "No," said Gloire, "I mean are they feeding you well? Is the food good?" "It's basically hot," answered her father. "Good," said Gloire, "it's better when it's hot." "That is correct," he said. "Did you see how beautiful it is outside?" she ventured, but her father seemed not to have heard this observation. "Here, I brought you this," she said again. "How very kind of you," he exclaimed, "what is it?" "It's some cognac for you," said Gloire, "you know, as usual." "Ah, cognac," he marveled. "I've never tried it." "Yeah, right," said Gloire, but the old man did not appear to register that comment either. "Well," she said, "I'm afraid I'd better be going." "That's true," he said dreamily, "sometimes one had better." "I'll come back and see you soon," she said. "Of course," he said, "you don't want to make yourself late."

After they had brought Abgrall senior back to ergotherapy, the nice male nurse escorted Gloire to the entrance. She rather liked that nurse. Before leaving, she asked him to keep an eye out that they didn't confiscate the cognac, as she was afraid they had done the previous time. "It's just that, normally speaking, alcoholic beverages aren't authorized either," the nurse smiled broadly, "but we always manage. I'll keep an eye out." Still, if there were to be a problem with the old gentleman, he worried, could Gloire leave a number where she could be reached, an address? She hesitated for a second—she really did like him—but no, she finally said; I'll call to check in.

Gloire left the retirement home and headed toward the Opel, parked on the gravel in front of a small administrative wing. A long ambulance with a sharklike white hood stood parked head-to-foot next to it. Gloire got into the Opel, which started up immediately, maneuvered, passed through the gateway, and disappeared. Five seconds later, the ambulance headed out in turn. On the porch of the retirement home, the nurse pondered this traffic. He stood immobile for five more seconds, then walked down the steps and went through the gateway in their wake. Fifty yards to the left, he entered a telephone booth and inserted into the apparatus a card decorated on the front with a snowy landscape, after absently gazing over the advertisement on the back: WITH THE PASSING OF THE SEASONS, OUTLOOKS AND FEELINGS CHANGE. YOU CAN SHARE THAT EMOTION WITH JUST THE TOUCH OF A BUTTON. This sentiment brought back his handsome smile, and then he punched in Jouve's number.

25

"Your young woman's just been here," the nurse announces. "Yes, she's already gone. No, no, she didn't leave an address, but I've got someone tailing her. I should know by tonight. I'll call you tomorrow. Now, about the money, how do we handle that?"

"We'll see tomorrow," answers Jouve before hanging up and turning toward his wife. "He can be pretty straight sometimes, that brother of yours. His tip worked out pretty well. Maybe we could have him over for dinner, what do you think?"

"Not on your life," answers Genevieve.

"Fine," says Jouve, "well, in the meantime I'll notify Personnettaz."

The next day flashed by at top speed. First Personnettaz showed up at around nine o'clock at the Jouves', who had just finished breakfast. Mrs. Jouve seemed less dazed, less nervous, more relaxed than usual. "You didn't bring the young lady from the other day?" she asked while pouring him the last of the coffee. Personnettaz pursed his lips instead of answering. "She's awfully pretty, you know," smiled Genevieve Jouve. "You're very lucky." Personnettaz tried to compose a detached face, managed only to turn purple and spill a quarter of his coffee into the saucer. Mrs. Jouve batted her eyelashes at this spectacle. Luckily for Personnettaz, the nice male nurse phoned back just then. He gave Gloire's address; Jouve noted the address. Then he asked again about the money; Jouve promised the money.

"So what should I do now?" asked Personnettaz.

"First you check with the client," said Jouve. "Don't forget to tell him about the little supplement for the nurse."

"That's not part of my functions," Personnettaz objected. "I'm happy to bring them up to speed, but anything to do with money is your domain."

"Fine," agreed Jouve. "In any case, you should leave as soon as possible. Are you going alone?"

"I don't know yet," said Personnettaz, making sure not to meet the melting gaze of Mrs. Jouve. "I suppose. I don't know."

At ten twenty-five, Personnettaz left the Jouves and went to the head office of Stochastic, where, as of nine thirty, on the question of tall blonde women, Salvador had decided to change methodology. To take it all from scratch. To proceed in order. And first of all, what is it we call blondness? The French encyclopedias, which united in defining it as the median color between light brown and golden, mentioned no more than two or three shades: Venetian, ash, whatever. The Americans established a finer typology, distinguishing sandy blonde from copper blonde and platinum blonde from honey blonde, not to mention dirty blonde. And others besides. Good. Onward.

But at five past eleven, Personnettaz arrived to interrupt Salvador's reflections. Salvador was there alone; Donatienne hadn't shown up yet. "It's done," Personnettaz informed him, "they've found her. This time it's for real."

"Well, go on then," Salvador said distractedly, "go on then."

"I'm afraid it just won't be that easy," Personnettaz objected. "You've seen how difficult she can be."

"This really is too much," remarked Salvador. "Why is she so wild? We don't mean the girl any harm. Why does she act like that?"

"That," said Personnettaz, "I don't know."

But he does know, or at least he has his little theory. Salvador and his assistant seem to be taken aback by Gloire's behavior, find the harshness of her reactions quite out of proportion to the guilelessness of their project. Personnettaz somehow finds it all understandable. He isn't convinced that dragging someone onto a TV screen is such an innocent maneuver. Still, he lets none of this show.

"Well," suggests Salvador, "take Donatienne with you if you're worried, ask her to go along. It's better if there are two of you."

"Yes," says Personnettaz, "perhaps." He hesitates. He does not like hesitating. Not only does he always have trouble with Donatienne, but she also occupies much too much of his mental space.

And here she is, arriving at around eleven thirty; they fill her in on the situation. "So," she says, "are we going?"

"Well, I mean," Personnettaz hears himself answering, "well, yes. Let's go." They converse for a few minutes more, then head off a little before twelve in Donatienne's car.

But between the heavy traffic on the highway and the time to grab a quick bite en route, then to find their way from the nurse's directions, it was easily three o'clock before they located the manor. They parked the vehicle at the junction of two low walls, affording a discreetly impregnable view of the entrance to the property. When Donatienne pulled a pack of cigarettes out of her bag, Personnettaz lowered the window on his side by a third.

Luck was with them: they didn't have to wait long. After no more than an hour, Gloire appeared alone at the wheel of Lagrange's Opel. They recognized her, followed her at a distance as she turned onto the road for Honfleur. Personnettaz drove very delicately, manipulating the gear shift and steering wheel with the tips of his fingers, avoiding the slightest mechanical creaking as if any sudden movement might compromise the situation—in short, rolling on eggshells. "Really," he thought to himself, "we've traveled to the other end of the world to find her, we've missed her every time, and now here she is, a few yards away."

The weather was still beautiful, almost as beautiful as the day before: at five past four, Gloire sat at an outside table of a bar on the port and ordered a beer. It seemed as if she might have been expecting something or someone. Sitting at a contiguous terrace, Donatienne who was drinking an orangeade and Personnettaz a club soda did not let her out of the edge of their sight. They were pretending to have a conversation, like extras in the movies supposedly talking to each other in the background, inaudible: their lips moved in the void and their dialogues were made of mush. In any case, Personnettaz always had trouble talking calmly with Donatienne, and this fact filled him with suffering and resentment.

Not only did he not know how to talk to Donatienne, but he wasn't sure how to proceed with Gloire either. He was still hesitating. Indeed, what to do? Talk to her. Convince her that they meant her no harm. Make off with her by force. Or by gentle persuasion. Experience had pretty much shown that any surveillance, any attempt to approach or contact her would meet with a violent response. They would see; they would try to do their best.

Gloire stood up at twenty-five to five. They had to follow her on foot. She headed toward the modest, chalky lighthouse that stood not far from the port, toward Trouville, on a small overhang bordering a cliff of modest dimensions. It should be mentioned that Gloire—who had already noticed, the evening before, that a wheezy ambulance without revolving lights had been following them since Rouen—had naturally spotted the unidentified convertible that began tailing her anew near Honfleur. She acted as if nothing were the matter.

At five minutes to five, Gloire will push open the small door at the base of the lighthouse—no smaller than any other door, actually, but looking crushed by virtue of an optical illusion—and close it behind her. In the eyes of her persecutors, this lighthouse is the perfect trap in which to catch her at last: with Donatienne behind him, Personnettaz will enter it in turn. He will climb the 120 spiraling stairs. He will step out into the open air, onto the narrow circular platform above the port. He will have time to notice the more or less parallel waves, coming to beat gently on the shore like written lines breaking against a margin. Nervous gusts of wind, passage of seagulls in an atmosphere that is sharper than on ground level, retracted sunlight too cold to be blinding. Donatienne will appear several seconds later. So it is at five o'clock sharp that Gloire, surging from a slight recess, will surprise Personnettaz from behind and, as she knows how to do so well, forcefully knock him over the guard-rail. We've already said that it isn't a large lighthouse, almost a toy, a prop for a low-budget film. Falling from it would not necessarily kill you. But if you were lucky enough to survive, you could still get seriously hurt and would never be the same.

Everything happened exactly as we have just predicted, except that at the very last moment—5:00:03—as Personnettaz was tipping over into the void, Béliard decided to intervene. He who never appeared in the visible social order had just resolved to publicly display his superpowers. Appearing out of nowhere, Béliard hurled himself toward Donatienne, grabbed her by the waist, and sent her flying in turn toward Personnettaz. The young woman didn't have time to be afraid. As parachutists waltz in free fall in midsky, she joined Personnettaz in the air, gripped him solidly by the shoulders, and led him, still remote-controlled by the homunculus, back to the lighthouse platform. All of it very fast, over in just a few seconds; no one understood a thing—just as after an epileptic seizure, when no one really wants to understand what has just happened. Personnettaz, eyes wild, straightened his clothes; then, getting ahold of himself, made his introduction: Jean-Charles Personnettaz, pleased to meet you. "Gloire Abgrall," said Gloire. They stared at each other without affection but without hostility; everyone seemed very tired. No one saw Béliard quietly slip away, brushing his hands against each other and puffing out his chest, smoothing back his hair on both sides, and that takes care of that.

26

"We don't mean you any harm," said Personnettaz. "I don't, in any case. What will you have?"

They had left the lighthouse for the port. Day was waning. Gently it waned in nautilus pink, a pink of gladiolas and strawberries with cream. It had now gotten too chilly to colonize another outdoor table; they had ensconced themselves in the seats of the Hôtel de l'Absinthe bar. At that hour the clientele was sparse. A bartender wiped off the pedestal table, awaited their order, looked like George Sanders.

"Dry martini," said Gloire.

"Good idea," said Donatienne. "Yes, dry martini."

"Right, so three dry martinis," Personnettaz said to George, showing three fingers.

As a rule, Personnettaz avoids alcohol, but after the lighthouse incident everyone needed a pick-me-up. They were slightly dazed, as if after a match or opening night, when one recovers from one's efforts in the locker or dressing room. One has left behind one's role, one's trunks, one's costume. One redons civilian garb, returns to real life. One catches one's breath. One might exchange peaceable, considerate, muffled statements, but for those first few minutes one says absolutely nothing.

As a rule, Personnettaz also avoids tobacco; but feeling a rare urge, he got up for a moment. When he returned, packing ultralights equipped with three-tiered filters, Donatienne had begun explaining their mission. Detailing her job in television production, her work methods, her plans for broadcasts—among which the one that they hoped to do on Gloire, the reason they had been chasing after her for two months. They were still quite set on it, on that broadcast; Donatienne was very set on it, as was her boss, named Salvador. Would Gloire agree, now, to be part of it? Gloire, without answering, opened her eyes wide.

Donatienne assured her that people still remembered her, that they would be very interested to know what had become of her; Gloire was anything but certain she wanted them to know. "I'm not really sure," she said. "I'll have to think about it."

"Anyway, we won't do anything without your OK," said Donatienne, "never fear. All I ask is that you meet Salvador. After that you can do as you like."

Besides, don't forget that the pay wouldn't be so bad either, you see. They were not short on cash. They had already spent a bundle searching for Gloire at the other end of the world—at these words, Personnettaz lit a cigarette. As Donatienne rapidly summarized this search, no mention was made of its violent episodes. No allusion, for example, to Jean-Claude Kastner, nor to the lighthouse episode from an hour before.

That visit to the lighthouse, furthermore, seemed to have been forgotten by Personnettaz and Donatienne. Unless they preferred not to mention it, not being entirely sure of its reality—one does not mention one's hallucinations, which pertain strictly to one's private life. As far as Gloire was concerned, she was not too keen on having strangers become interested in Béliard, in his little excursions into reality. Moreover, she always distrusted reality somewhat when Béliard deigned to get involved in it. Personnettaz lit a second cigarette, of which, as with the first, he inhaled almost nothing, given the density of the filter.

Donatienne did her best to convince Gloire of the soundness of her offer. Money, fame, success regained, why not the beginning of a new career, and even love while we're at it, and shall we order another round? They had another round, then Gloire stood up to take her leave. "If you want to talk it over some more," said Donatienne, "meet me here tomorrow, late morning. Take tonight to decide, think it over."

Violins erupt at Gloire's departure. First an attack in the minor key when she abruptly stands; then a vertiginous bass whirl when she throws a last look at Donatienne and Personnettaz; finally a series of brief staccato attacks as she moves off toward the cylindrical revolving doors of the entrance. Personnettaz finds himself alone with Donatienne.

"I wouldn't mind one for the road," says Donatienne. "I know it's not the sensible thing, but what the hell, now that we've gotten that over with—how about you?"

"No," says Personnettaz, "I'm fine as is."

Nervously he rips the filter off a third cigarette before reducing it to ash with a single draw. Then he hesitates, not very sure of himself.

"Did you notice anything before, on the lighthouse?"

"Uh, no," says Donatienne. "Why?"

"No," says Personnettaz, "nothing."

Personnettaz, even if he's not sure, nonetheless believes he remembers seeing Donatienne, a little while before, flying through the air to save him from probable death. But he prefers not to insist. "So, we're not going back tonight?" he segues.

"It's late," opines Donatienne. "Aren't you tired? And besides, we might have to see the girl again tomorrow. They must have rooms here. It seems nice, this hotel."

They did in fact have rooms available, and they were in fact nice. Deluxe category as in Bombay, but silkier, more intimate, and with a view of the Channel instead of the Gulf of Oman. Their windows overlooked it from two different floors. They would rest in their rooms for an hour, then would meet for dinner. Personnettaz watched Donatienne walk away toward the elevator.

When he took it in turn, the cabin was better lit than at the Cosmopolitan Club but, under the vertical spotlight near the back mirror, Personnettaz saw himself aging just the same. From the bottom of his heart he never would have thought such a thing could happen to him, ever. Hadn't even imagined it. Proceeding as if it were impossible, as if none of this concerned him, as if he weren't even there, he must have vaguely counted on time forgetting all about him. But time caught up with him from behind, growing ever-larger in the rearview mirror and preparing to overtake him. Personnettaz brushed away this idea. It was just that he had to get ready; it was just that, with Donatienne, he would have to keep himself in check all through dinner.

Personnettaz entered his room and lay down while awaiting the dinner hour. He intended to think awhile on his bed, but he fell asleep, briefly dreamed, then awoke with a start just in time. Feeling some apprehension, he inspected his face in the bathroom mirror before going back downstairs. Less offensive than the one in the elevator, this mirror was still not well disposed toward its user, the proof being that Personnettaz spotted a pimple on the left wing of his nose.

In theory, popping a pimple is no big deal, a matter of a little alcohol on cotton. Having no ninety-percent alcohol in his shaving kit, Personnettaz searched feverishly in the minibar for some liquid to take its place. Rather than amber spirits, such as cognac or whiskey, a transparent alcohol approximating the pharmaceutical kind would no doubt do the trick better: gin, aquavit, vodka. Probably vodka, all things considered, with which Personnettaz imbibed a kleenex and dabbed himself—after which, to bolster his courage, he swallowed the remaining contents of the miniature bottle in one gulp. Which wasn't like him. Already the cigarettes, a short while ago, weren't like him. None of this was normal behavior. Personnettaz didn't recognize himself.

Gloire, meanwhile, had gone off in Lagrange's car; on the road she soliloquized. The Opel's headlights conically perforated the fallen night, projecting the film of the day's events on the twin curtain of poplars. Gloire had barely reacted to Donatienne's proposals, neither accepting nor refusing, saying nothing. She found her rather likable, that girl, fairly attractive in a curvy energetic brunette sort of way. She was undecided. Returning to the manor at around nine o'clock, she ran into Lagrange in the foyer. The half-drunk Lagrange claimed to have been worried, complained that he had waited for her for dinner. "Did you see what time it is," he went, poking his index finger at his wrist, before jerking his erect thumb at the kitchen. "It's all cold now."

"Just give me two more minutes," said Gloire. "I'm coming."

Having vanished from the lighthouse immediately after his lightning intervention, Béliard must have returned to her room. Before anything else, she wanted to consult him.

"So," exclaimed the homunculus as soon as Gloire had opened the door, "was I good or what?"

He seemed content with the afternoon's exploit. Had they talked about it, he wanted to know. "No," answered Gloire, "they didn't say a word."

"Typical," Béliard clouded over. "Still, I wouldn't mind somebody noticing once in a while. Sometimes you need a little public support."

"Yeah," she said, "I don't know. Don't you think we would have been better off getting rid of them?"

Resting a finger on his temple, Béliard explained that he'd considered it, but that he didn't believe so. First of all, he wouldn't have saved Personnettaz if he'd thought him dangerous. And more generally, he deemed that it was time for Gloire to go back to legal methods, to return to human society. It was all right for Jean-Claude

Kastner, even for the guy in Sydney, but they couldn't very well keep on giving intruders the shove forever. Despite all his powers, despite his invisibility, one day or another someone would end up noticing. Wouldn't it be better to come to terms now, try to bow to the common order? It might be a little difficult at first, after years spent living on the edge, but he, Béliard, would be there to help her. So what did that girl want, anyway? Grudgingly, Gloire told him of Donatienne's cathodic proposal. "Perfect," said Béliard, "couldn't ask for better timing. It's the chance of a lifetime."

"You really think so?" murmured Gloire.

"Of course," said Béliard. "Let's go for it. You won't get another shot like this. Go eat something, now. You'll need to be in shape for tomorrow."

Gloire went down to join Lagrange, sitting alone in front of the glasses in the dining room. While they ate their cold dinner, his eyelids drooped several times. He didn't seem to register the announcement of Gloire's departure, found in it only a pretext to pour himself another one. Gloire left the table before he did.

Lagrange was still asleep the next morning when Gloire phoned the Hôtel de l'Absinthe; Personnettaz and Donatienne appeared an hour later. Gloire's bags hopped by themselves into the trunk of the convertible that shortly afterward headed down the western highway. Personnettaz and Donatienne sat in front, while Gloire, sitting to the right, behind them, stared at the road framed by their asymmetrical shoulders; the traffic flowed under a milky sky. After agreeing that they would bring her straight to see Salvador the moment they arrived in Paris, they didn't say much more to each other. Personnettaz turned the pages of a magazine and only once did Gloire's eyes meet Donatienne's in the rearview mirror. "We haven't even discussed money," the latter nonetheless said near Mantes-la-Jolie. "Would two hundred thousand do?" (As Gloire takes her time answering, Béliard appears fleetingly on the seat beside her. Quick wink and rapid smile: he stretches out four fingers and waves them.) "Four hundred thousand," said Gloire. "Four hundred thousand it is," said Donatienne. (Béliard nods, smiles more widely, and gives a thumbs up before evaporating.) They were almost there.

Southern beltway: eight or nine exits separated Auteuil from Porte Dorée, where Gloire got out. Donatienne, who would come back to pick her up a little later, mentioned that they'd reserved a room for her in a hotel near the Mosque. They headed off.

"Where to now?" asked Personnettaz.

"We could always go get a drink somewhere," suggested Donatienne, "or else I can give you a lift where you're going."

It seemed to Personnettaz that he reflected for a long time before hearing himself propose to the young woman that that drink, while they were at it, could just as well be had at his place.

"Why not," she said against all hope, "if you'd rather. Which way?"

"Head toward République," said Personnettaz in a blank voice. "I live right next to it."

All along the boulevards his heart was in his shoes, particularly since it was always difficult to park in his neighborhood. By a lucky break, a spot had just come free in his street, just opposite his building. He tried to think of something to say about that lucky break, about the street, about life; one of those elevated, witty, well-observed pronouncements that beautify existence: but no, nothing for the moment. Or yes, actually, perhaps—but as he was about to open his mouth, someone tapped unpleasantly on the window next to him. Personnettaz turned around: Boccara was grinning broadly at him and making signs on the other side of the glass, notably the sign to lower it. Personnettaz lowered the window.

"What are you doing here?" he asked.

"What a stroke of luck!" Boccara enthused. "I wanted to see you and *voilà*, here you are!"

Back from his cruise, he was appreciably tanned, wearing a new suit that was a bit too yellow and light for the season; he had gained a few pounds. Donatienne looked at him. Personnettaz was embarrassed.

"So just like that," he went, "you're back."

"I had a great time," said Boccara, "and man, you won't believe some of the things I've seen. I'm kind of sorry it's over. I met some girls like you wouldn't believe. I came over to tell you all about it."

"Listen—" Personnettaz began.

"Well," Donatienne interrupted him, grasping the gearshift, "I'll leave you with your friend."

"Hang on," said Personnettaz, then, turning toward her: "Wait, that drink," he whispered, "I thought we'd said—"

"Another time," smiled Donatienne. "You can call me if you feel like it."

"But—" repeated Personnettaz.

She continued to smile as she shifted into first, made a sign with her head before moving off, and was gone. The smile lingered, intact, up to the end of Rue Yves-Toudic; then it would play some more about her lips for the entire length of Boulevard Magenta.

"What's the matter?" said Boccara. "You don't look so good."

"Nothing," said Personnettaz, watching the convertible disappear. "Nothing."

If he is naturally a little annoyed at Boccara, a rival sentiment of slight relief keeps him from holding too much of a grudge against the young man—who is also watching Donatienne vanish into the distance. That's how it is: left to themselves, they watch her go.

"Boy," said Boccara, "she's really stacked."

"Oh, really," Personnettaz said noncommittally while searching his pockets. "You think so?"

"How well do you know her?" worried Boccara.

"A little," Personnettaz answered modestly, pulling out his cigarettes. "I know her a little."

"You son of a gun," said Boccara.

27

"The sun," Salvador says to himself.

He has been seeking new ideas for his project since early morning, without coming up with a single one, as usual. The sky is very overcast; sporadically it rains on Porte Dorée. Salvador is not happy. Whether his mood derives from his mental sterility, the rotten weather, or this wasted time is hard to say. But around noon it begins to clear and the clouds break up. Through the windows the sunlight throws out large bright parallelograms onto the floor, casts trapezoids into the corners with ricochets of reflections. If dazzling weather still does not flood his soul, at least Salvador thinks: the sun.

Let us, he proposes to himself, look into the effects of the sun's rays on tall blondes. Let us ponder. No half measures with it: the sun bronzes you or burns you, it colors or kills. If it generously tans the warm, triumphant tall blondes, it pitilessly carbonizes the refrigerated, chlorotic ones. Too porous and translucent, the chlorotic tall blondes immediately redden, heat up, and shrivel away. Only the triumphant ones remain, the ones whose portrait we tried to sketch in Chapter Eleven. Their denser epidermis, their more resistant complexion give the ultraviolets a hero's welcome. Yes,

Salvador says to himself, let us examine, let us turn our attention to the tanned tall blondes. At that moment the door opens, and lo and behold a tanned tall blonde appears.

Feminine, masculine, neuter: if the sun's gender varies from one language to another, its character also changes depending on the skies. And the fact is that, subjected to the abrupt Australian sun, then to the more enveloping rays of the Indian one, Gloire has browned quite a bit since her departure. Salvador hesitates. For a moment he understands nothing—as if his idea has just been made flesh by magic before his eyes—then he identifies the young woman. Such encounters might provoke a short-circuit, an indraft followed by a blaze; they might unleash fireworks in the heart of a rainbow, accompanied by another cascade of the string orchestra. And that's exactly what happens in the resuscitated spirit of Salvador, who suddenly appears extremely self-conscious. Yes, it's his body that doesn't seem to be in synch: "Oh, right," he lurches up crookedly, "right. Come in."

He bangs against his desk as he comes around to meet Gloire, stops too far from, then too close to, her, can't decide whether to put out his hand, which he finally waves vaguely at an armchair. In the time it takes for him to regain his seat and for Gloire to identify the armchair, we hear quite a number of cars pass by on Avenue du Général-Dodds.

"I was expecting you," Salvador claims.

But he talks to her as if reluctantly, and twenty minutes later Gloire still doesn't know much more than she did the day before from Donatienne. Salvador, meanwhile, is no more relaxed than before. He has given Gloire every possible detail: shooting in late May, travel, commentary, archival documents, film clips, four days in the studio, editing, mixing, broadcast in late September; he has attempted parenthetical clauses, ventured generalities, but without even daring to offer her a drink. So. He wanted her consent, she has granted it, so now what? There remain only silences, averted gazes, composure lost without a trace; the whole thing begins to drag on, and Salvador is abominably perturbed. Fortunately, Donatienne shows up right on time to cut this conversation short. Gloire tries not to appear too relieved. "So, well, then, goodbye," Salvador says awkwardly. "So see you soon, I guess."

Afterward, beneath the reemerging sun, Gloire and Donatienne slice the twelfth arrondissement down the middle, cross the Seine via the Pont d'Austerlitz, then skirt the Jardin des Plantes toward the Mosque. If men talk about women, in cars and elsewhere, we now know that the reverse is also true: as they drive through Paris, the two women swap opinions of Personnettaz—whom they both find somewhat peculiar—then of Salvador, who Donatienne confirms is also a bit peculiar.

Peculiar or not, he tries to get back to work after their departure, but it's no good, he's too distracted. Salvador paces around his office, looks out the window, tries to read a few pages of *How to Disappear Completely and Never Be Found* without managing to get absorbed in it. Shuts the book, which he throws into a plastic bag; folds his notes in four and slips them into his pocket; then gets up from his chair. Decides to go home. Leaves. Walks down into the Metro. Absentmindedly waits for the train without really waiting. It comes; he gets on. Standing, back against the doors of the subway car, once he has cast an empty glance at his neighbors—resigned old people, hirsute readers of computer magazines, a Senegalese girl with ice skates—he pulls the book from his bag. But since the bag prevents him from holding his book comfortably, he tries to get rid of it by putting the bag in the bag, but no, since it's the same bag—shit. No two ways about it, he's rather distracted.

Back home, in his half kitchen, after some leftovers and the evening news, Salvador unfolds, rereads, absently develops his notes; forces himself to banish Gloire from his mind. Let's start again. So, the triumphant tall blondes welcome the sun, absorb it, assimilate it, then wear it. In the form of pigments. Thus, on summer evenings, in nightclubs, crossing their endless legs on high stools, they shine like portable suns. The sun, concludes Salvador, is itself one big blonde.

At that same moment, on Rue Yves-Toudic, Personnettaz is also sitting in his small kitchen, but he has come to different conclusions while puffing on cigarettes. It seems that since yesterday Personnettaz has taken up smoking again. Two empty glasses are on the table before him: recounting his adventures made Boccara thirsty, while drinking made him talkative. At that point, it could have gone on forever, and Personnettaz had begun to worry he might never leave. Boccara has said goodbye only a short while ago. In any case, Personnettaz didn't listen to his whole story, preferring to recall the young man's appraisal of Donatienne, pronounced that very afternoon. After the unabridged narrative of his cruise, Personnettaz had to cut in the moment Boccara threatened to segue into his love life. Personnettaz is finally alone.

He is alone but he is agitated. It's just that feelings are not his strong suit. Up until now, for him, love has always appeared without witnesses. Each time it has occurred, Personnettaz, not very secure in his judgments or his emotions, has hastened to bring it to an end. With no outside opinion, he has given up. But let a witness happen to encourage him—the other day Mrs. Jouve, today Boccara—and anything seems possible. Love, as we know, often passes via third parties, whoever they are and whatever they say. Order or advice, permission or prescription, no matter: the main thing is that it pushes you onward. This said, Personnettaz bitterly admits that it's a pretty unlikely match. There's still the fact that Donatienne is much more beautiful (I mean more beautiful that I am handsome), no doubt much better off financially (which isn't hard), and significantly younger (see above).

In short, things have drifted to such a point in our tale that we now have two men who are smitten with two distinctly different women. What will happen? How will this all turn out?

28

Six months later, during the broadcast of the program devoted to Gloire, Personnettaz seduced Donatienne or vice versa. That Thursday evening he wasn't expecting anything in particular when she appeared unannounced at his door, claiming her TV was on the fritz. She made no comments about Personnettaz's apartment: nearly empty, it didn't lend itself to any. With regard to the only decorative object, a green plant on its last legs, Donatienne merely gave some resuscitation advice. Personnettaz had nothing to offer her but some dregs of kirsch that they split but did not touch. When showtime came, Personnettaz turned on his set, offered Donatienne the only chair he owned, and took his place next to her on an old stool. Then, even if we don't know exactly what phrases, what glances were exchanged, which of those two pieces of furniture first moved toward the other before Personnettaz and Donatienne stretched out on a third, one thing at least is certain: they didn't watch the show to the end.

The following Sunday, Personnettaz moved into Donatienne's, renouncing in a single gesture and with no regrets his little home on Rue Yves-Toudic and his intermittent chores for Jouve. His diet immediately improved, his wardrobe was renewed, his face relaxed a bit—in short, his life was transformed. He even began to cultivate the idea of one fine day marrying that beautiful woman, even if Donatienne Personnettaz might be a bit of a mouthful, as names go.

Since one door closes and another one opens, Jouve, faced with this defection, had to resign himself to replacing Personnettaz with Boccara as his primary agent. In keeping with that promotion, the latter deemed it necessary that they immediately recruit an assistant. Three days later, Jouve found him a new operative answering to the name of Patrick Berthomieux. Patrick Berthomieux was a pensive, reserved, frail boy who in all seasons wore a supernumerary sweater. He was always fearful of bothering people, Patrick Berthomieux—a major drawback when one practiced his profession. He was barely younger than Boccara, who, nostalgic for Personnettaz, saw no better means of honoring the latter's memory than to behave with Berthomieux as the other had acted with him.

Nor, the day after his promotion, on the occasion of a visit to Jouve who was, as usual, out, did Boccara find any better project than to seduce Genevieve Jouve. It occurred to him two days later that this prospect was a dead end, not such a good idea after all. As early as the following weekend, staking out with Patrick Berthomieux the home of an engineer suspected by his firm, Boccara confided his recent woes to his assistant. As he had been used to doing with Personnettaz, he ruminated aloud: "You see, Patrick," he explained, "love is a lot like snow in Paris. It's very pretty when it falls on you, but it doesn't stay that way. And afterward it gets all fucked up. It either turns to ice or to slush, but very soon it becomes more trouble than it's worth."

"Really, Gilbert?" answered Berthomieux. "Do you think so?"

"Yes," said Boccara, "I do think so. But I especially think, and please don't forget it, that it's 'Mr. Boccara' to you."

"Oh, right," Berthomieux caught himself. "Sorry, Mr. Boccara."

Broadcast in prime time, with an average of 16.2 points and a 35.6 percent market share, Salvador's series was a huge success. It was watched in many homes. Genevieve Jouve didn't miss a minute of it on her sofa, nor did Lagrange and Zbigniew in their prison cell at Fresnes. In one stroke, Stochastic Films solidified its positions with the hertzian channels and Salvador had his contract renewed. Given those conditions, he had no trouble negotiating a few weeks away in the mountains, in order to put the finishing touches on a few other projects. Then he packed his bags.

As another consequence of that broadcast, Gloire had to bear the burdens of her new popularity. People once again recognized her in the street, sent her sacks of mail, offered her spots in TV commercials or nude poses in certain magazines, and even the chance to remix her old hits. But we know all too well how fragile she is. After having enjoyed the situation for fifteen minutes, she quickly went back to hiding out, stopped eating, stopped opening her door or answering the telephone. Gloire's behavior ended up worrying the staff of the hotel behind the Mosque, which she hadn't left. Immediately notified, and although quite preoccupied by her new life with Personnettaz, Donatienne flew to her side, became alarmed, and did her best to pacify Gloire before letting Salvador know.

Impressing upon him the fact that he was responsible for the young woman's state, Donatienne ended up convincing Salvador to look after her, take care of her, protect her from others and from herself. At first, Salvador couldn't hide his reticence: this wasn't at all what he had in mind. Deeply impressed by Gloire but burned by life, he would much rather practice prevention than risk needing a cure. Lowering an iron curtain over his feelings, he had scrupulously kept his distance from the young woman during the shooting. But enjoined by Donatienne, he finally yielded. He took the situation in hand.

Before buckling his suitcase, then, he made sure that another room was available in the hotel where he had his reservation: a small, comfortable inn run by two sisters in a ski resort in the Pyrenees. Salvador was known there. "No problem," the older sister answered. "Not many people this early in the season." They left in the car.

They arrived at the end of the day. Gloire's room was furnished in white wood. Sun and detergents had bleached the curtains and the quilt; the sheets were just slightly starched. Through the window, in the distance, she saw two sharp, rocky protuberances standing out in the twilight, scanning the horizon like an encephalogram: the base of one was linked by a funicular to the crest of the other. After dinner, worn out from the trip, she went up to bed early, vaguely counting on a visit from Béliard without really wanting it. But not tonight. Tonight, no one.

The fact is, Béliard was seen less and less often. Since the broadcast of *Tall Blondes*, his interventions had become scarce. And, less regular than ever, in those moments when he did appear it was like a whirlwind. Soon Gloire caught only fleeting glimpses of him, looking rushed like a businessman between two trains, wearing a new suit, checking his watch every five minutes, as well as a little appointment book that she'd never seen before. Nonchalantly, Béliard started hinting at some new contacts.

The day after their arrival, Salvador suggested they go for a walk, counting on the mountain air to restore the young woman's equilibrium. At that altitude and in that season, if the air proved to be a bit chilly at night, in the afternoon it nonetheless donned its summer garb again. Gloire and Salvador walked, not speaking much, not always side by side, as if they barely knew each other. Their exchanges were stamped with the distant courtesy systematically adopted by warring shipwreck survivors forced to share the same desert island. Salvador, who knew the area, occasionally specified the name of a flower they came across, the name of a passing bird; they left it at that. Gloire would have plenty of time later on to look up those names in her little English nature guides.

For a first day, they walked pretty far. Their steps brought them to one of the two sharp protuberances that Gloire could see from her window. They reached the base of it, from which one could take the funicular to the crest of the other. They were dressed in light-colored clothes, and the weather was almost hot. Gloire went ahead first; Salvador followed a few yards behind, jacket flung over his shoulder. Under the pylon, near a small wooden hut—a simple kiosk with penthouse roof and a ticket window—the empty cabin of the funicular looked like an old-model tram in the station or a docked ferry boat. The torso of a man with sun-baked face and thick fingers, dressed in an anorak, emerged from the window frame beside a fat roll of tickets. The surroundings were silent; not a living soul as far as the eye could see, except for Salvador, Gloire, and that man, who also sold postcards of the landscape.

After consulting the posted fees, Gloire buys two tickets just as Salvador joins her. The man inside the kiosk gets up to go activate the launch mechanism. "Wait a minute," says Salvador, "hold on there. I can't get in that thing." Gloire gives him a quizzical look. "I'm a bit sensitive about heights," explains Salvador. "I can't stand to have them under me. It makes me feel ill, if you see what I mean. I'm afraid of them. It's absurd, but there's nothing I can do about it."

Gloire stares at him with a funny, slightly frozen smile. Her eyes are almost liquid. "Come on, come with me," she says in a strange voice. And Salvador, as if devoid of will, follows her toward the cabin. The door shuts behind them as soon as the man outside his kiosk has manipulated handles and levers, then pushed a big green button: the funicular gives a silent lurch, and they lift off. It climbs away. Standing near the machines, the man watches the cabin shrink, while above it eagles, or perhaps vultures, describe new circles in the open sky. A very light wind plays a few intermittent harmonics on the cables of the funicular—whose cabin, halfway up, comes to a sudden halt. Still no sign of Béliard.

You're expecting the worst, and that's understandable. Scared to death, unable to risk the slightest downward glance, Salvador clings with all his might to whatever looks like a handle, squeezes it so tightly that his joints turn white, that he can't breathe. But Gloire is there, smiling at him, moving close and placing two fingers on his shoulder while whispering for him not to be afraid. Her hand comes sliding from Salvador's shoulder to his neck, then to the back of his neck; Salvador's hair is divided between her fingers. And then the next moment, letting go of all his handles, it's the young woman that he squeezes in his arms.

While she is against him, his lips on her neck, Salvador opens one eye and, over Gloire's shoulder, distinctly sees the abyss. Now, miracle number one, no vertigo seizes him, no dizziness; all his cardinal points remain in place, in peaceful harmony with the dimensions. And Gloire, miracle number two, does not at all envision letting this man fall into the void, nor even perhaps letting him fall out of her life in the future. Quite possibly she'll never need Béliard again (assuming he wasn't responsible for these developments to begin with), for between heaven and earth Salvador and Gloire are still kissing. And begin over and over. And do not seem to want to stop. To see their faces this way, their bodies, it appears that neither of them is feeling any pain at the moment, any particular worry. He is no longer afraid of the void. She is no longer afraid of anything.

Piano

Jean Echenoz

Translated by Mark Polizzotti

1

Two men appear at the end of Boulevard de Courcelles, coming from the direction of Rue de Rome.

One, slightly taller than average, says nothing. Under a large, light-colored raincoat buttoned to the neck, he is wearing a black suit with a black bow tie. Small cufflinks with onyx-quartz mounts punctuate his immaculate wrists. He is, in short, very well dressed, though his pallid face and gaping eyes suggest a worried frame of mind. His white hair is brushed back. He is afraid. He is going to die a violent death in twenty-two days' time but, as he is yet unaware of this, that is not what he is afraid of.

The man accompanying him is the complete opposite in appearance: younger, considerably less tall, small, garrulous, and smiling too much; wearing a small brown-and-tan plaid hat, a pair of pants faded in patches, and a formless sweater with nothing underneath. His feet are shod in moccasins marbled with damp spots.

"Nice hat," the well-dressed man finally observes as they are about to reach the gates of Parc Monceau. These are the first words he has spoken in an hour.

"Really?" worries the other. "It's useful, in any case, that's a fact, but aesthetically speaking I'm not quite sure what to make of it. It's salvage, you understand. I wouldn't have bought it myself."

"No, no," the elegant one protests. "It's nice."

"My stepson found it on the train," the other replies. "Someone must have forgotten it. But it was too small for him, you see, my stepson has an extremely large skull, not to mention an enormous IQ. But it's just my size, which doesn't mean that I'm not any stupider—I mean, that I'm any stupider—than the next man. How about a walk in the park?"

On either side of the rotunda in which the guardians of the peace were on duty, the monumental gilded cast-iron portals stood open. The two men crossed through them and entered the park and, for a moment, the younger one seemed to hesitate as to which direction to take. He masked his hesitation by talking nonstop, as if his sole reason for being there was to distract his companion, to try to make him forget his fear. And this was indeed his role. But although he performed it conscientiously, he didn't always seem to enjoy complete success. Before arriving at the park, he had explored various topics of a political, cultural, or sexual nature, without his monologue triggering the slightest exchange, without any of it blossoming into conversation. From the park entrance, he cast a distrustful gaze all around, from the Virginia tulips to the Japanese medlars: waterfall, rocks, lawns. The other man seemed to look at nothing but his own internal terror.

The other man, whose name was Max Delmarc, was some fifty years of age. Although his earnings were quite comfortable, and although he was famous in the eyes of a cozy million or so people and had for the past twenty years undergone all sorts of psychological and chemical treatments, he was, as we said, dying of fright. When the feeling enveloped him to this extent, he would normally fall completely silent. But now here he was, opening his mouth.

"I'm thirsty, Bernie," said Max. "I feel a bit thirsty. How about we stop by your place?"

Bernie looked at him gravely. "I think it would be better if we didn't, Mister Max," he said. "Mister Parisy wouldn't be very happy. And you remember what happened last time."

"Come on," Max insisted, "you're two minutes away from here. Just one little drink."

"No," Bernie said, "no, but I can call Mister Parisy if you like. We can ask him."

"Fine," Max surrendered, "forget it."

Then, noticing to the left a kiosk selling waffles, cold drinks, and jump ropes, he walked briskly in its direction. Bernie, having followed, passed, and preceded him toward the menu posted near the register, quickly glanced over the list before Max could catch up—no alcohol, all's well.

"Would you like some coffee, Mister Max?"

"No," answered Max, disappointed by his own perusal of the menu, "that's okay."

They started walking again. They passed in front of the bust of Guy de Maupassant hovering over a girl, then, on the other side of the lawn, a statue of Ambroise Thomas accompanied by another girl and, farther to the east, Edouard Pailleron towering above still another girl in a swoon. In this park, apparently, the statues of great men feared being alone, for each of them had a young woman at his feet. And better yet, just after the waterfall, no fewer than three girlfriends—one of whom had lost both her arms—surrounded Charles Gounod. But Bernie preferred that they avoid passing by the composer's memorial. Worse than that, from farther away he spotted, juxtaposing the children's play area, the monument to Frédéric Chopin: good God almighty, Bernie said to himself, Chopin. Especially not Chopin. He changed course abruptly, forcing Max to make an about-face and diverting his attention by praising the variety, abundance, and polychromy of the flora, pointing out the great age of the sycamore maple and the substantial circumference of the Oriental plane tree.

"Look, just look at them, Mister Max, look how beautiful it is," his voice filled with emotion. "The world is beautiful. The world is beautiful, don't you think so?" Neither slowing his step nor answering the question, Max pretended to grant this world a look and lightly shrugged his shoulders. "All right," Bernie conceded sheepishly, "fine. But at least agree that it's very well lit."

After dragging Max through every corner of the park, other than the area around Chopin; after trying to make him admire the oval basin, the pyramid with its pyramidion; and after secretly glancing at his watch, Bernie inflected their path toward a park exit, taking Allée de la Comtesse de Ségur, along which sat Alfred de Musset. No problem with Musset, except that the right arm was also missing from the young creature who, leaning over him, rested her left hand on Alfred's left shoulder.

It was seven thirty-five p.m., a hesitant late spring, but the sun was still present. Their faces directed toward its imminent setting, heading west on Avenue Van Dyck, the two men left the park. Since his attempt to cadge a drink, Max had not unclenched his teeth, while Bernie, playing his part conscientiously, did not stop talking or watching him. Max had not left his side but for two or three minutes, just long enough to discreetly go and vomit from fear behind a Hungarian oak. As he had already vomited twice that afternoon, all that came up was bile in a series of highly painful heaves. Now, outside the park, they walked up a service road of Avenue Hoche, taking the first turn on the right—at the corner of which stood a bar, where Max tried once more to entice Bernie in and Bernie silently refused—then a few more yards and there it was, number 252. They were here.

They went in. Stairways, hallways, passageways, doorways that they opened and shut until they reached a dark space littered with cables, pulleys, large open cases, and displaced furniture. In the air floated the noise of a swell or a crowd. It was now eight-thirty on the nose. Max had just removed his overcoat and suddenly, just when he least expected it, Bernie shoved him from behind through a curtain, the swell was immediately transformed into a tempest, and there it was—the piano.

There it was, the terrible Steinway with its wide white keyboard ready to devour you, those monstrous teeth that would chew you up with the full width of its ivories and all its enamel, waiting to mash you into a pulp. Nearly stumbling under Bernie's push, Max just managed to keep his balance. Drowning in the torrent of applause from the packed auditorium that had stood to welcome him, he lurched, short of breath, toward the fifty-two teeth. He sat before them, the conductor brandished his baton, silence immediately fell, and they were off. I really can't take this anymore. This is no kind of life. Although, let's face it, I could have been born in Manila and ended up selling loose cigarettes, or a shoeshine boy in Bogotá, a diver in Decazeville. Might as well go to it, then, since we're here. First movement, *maestoso,* of the Second Concerto in F-minor, Op. 21, by Frédéric Chopin.

2

From the audience, even from the front row, no one can imagine how hard it is. It just seems to happen all by itself.

And in fact, for Max, things do begin moving by themselves. Once the orchestra has embarked on the long overture, he starts to calm down. Then, on cue, as soon as he enters into the movement, everything seems better. His fears subside after a few measures, then fade away with the first wrong note—a good wrong note, in a rapid passage. The kind of mistake that passes by overlooked. At this point, Max becomes liberated. Now he has the situation in hand, he can stroll around, he is in his element. Every half-tone speaks to him, every pause is right, the series of chords touch down like dancing birds, he would like it never to stop, but already it's the end of the first movement. Pause. Everyone gets to have his little cough while waiting for the next one to begin, you rake your throat, you expel the mucus from your polluted lungs, everyone clears his windpipe as best he can and then up starts the second movement, *larghetto*: slow, meditative, extremely exposed, no room for mistakes, and Max doesn't make any; it comes off as easy as pie. You cough some more, then it's the third, an elegant *allegro vivace*, just watch me hand you this one on a platter—ouch, a second false note at around measure 200. I always slip at the same place in the finale, but there again it's lost in the rush. They haven't noticed a thing. We're getting there, we're almost through, chromatic descent and rise, then four punctuations by the orchestra, two concluding chords, and there you go, it's in the bag, bravo, goodnight, bravo, curtain, bravo, no encores, end of story.

Tingling with fatigue but having forgotten all about his stage fright, Max went up to his dressing room, which was flooded in bouquets. "What is it with all these flowers?" he groused. "You know damn well I can't deal with them, chuck them out for me."

"Right away," said Bernie, who gathered up the offending bouquets *presto agitato* and slipped out, loaded down like a hearse. Max fell onto a chair in front of a messy console table dominated by a mirror, in the depths of which, in shadow, Parisy was mopping his neck with a balled-up Kleenex.

"Ah," Max said without turning around, preparing to unbutton his shirt, "there you are."

"That was excellent," beamed the impresario.

"I know," said Max, "I thought so too. But I don't really feel like playing that thing again, I know it too well. And besides the orchestra part's pretty weak when you get down to it, you can tell Chopin wasn't too good at that. Anyway, I'm kind of fed up with orchestras in general." As he undid his top button, it jumped off his shirt and took refuge in the mess on the console.

"Anyway," Parisy said, approaching, "you don't have anything but recitals until summer. You know—Berlin."

Still not turning around, searching for the fugitive button, Max watched the mirror amplify Parisy's massive and balding silhouette, the physique of retractive Jell-O with thick glasses, plaid suit, chronic perspiration, and voice of a light tenor. "Remind me what the program is," said Max.

"Okay, so you've got Nantes at the end of the week,"Parisy warbled. "You have the recital at Salle Gaveau on the nineteenth, then nothing until that business on TV. And then Japan called again, they want to know when you can get back to recording the complete Chausson, they need a date so they can reserve Cerumen."

"I need time," said Max. "I'm not ready."

"What I mean is, they need to know very soon," Parisy accentuated, "they have to plan their schedule."

"I need time," Max repeated. "I'm dying of thirst. Where's the kid?"

The kid had returned, minus the flowers. He was standing by the door, waiting for someone to give him something to do.

"I wouldn't mind a drink, Bernie," Max indicated, still without turning around, while finally snaring the errant button between two empty vases. Bernie opened a cabinet and pulled out a glass and a bottle. After clearing off a corner of the console, he set them on a tray in front of Max.

"I'll be back," said Bernie. "I'm going to Janine's to get some ice."

Without waiting for its arrival, Max filled his glass four-fifths full under the reticent eye of his manager, still framed close-up in the mirror. "Don't start with me, Parisy, if you don't mind. We agreed that I'm allowed after a concert. Beforehand, fine, no problem, but afterward I'm allowed."

"That's not really it," Parisy qualified, "it's just that you haven't left much room for the ice."

"Right you are," said Max, emptying half his glass in one gulp. "See? Now there's room."

Parisy shook his head, searching his pocket for a new Kleenex, and grimaced when he noticed it was the last. He crumpled the wrapper and tossed it toward a wastebasket as Bernie reemerged, carrying an insulated yellow-and-white ice bucket. "Thanks, Bernie, no, no, I don't need the tongs. On the contrary." Max plunged two ice cubes into his glass before running a third cube over his forehead, temples, and neck; then, continuing to address Parisy in the mirror: "Where would I be without Bernie?"

"Good, good," the impresario approved vaguely.

"While we're on the subject," Bernie timidly intervened.

"What," said Parisy.

"Well, the thing is," said Bernie. "I'm afraid I'm forced to ask you, if it's possible, of course, for a small raise."

"Absolutely out of the question," Parisy said stiffly.

"It's just that I have expenses," Bernie elaborated. "For instance, I have a stepson who's very intelligent, I have to help finance his studies. He has a very high IQ, you see, I have to send him to the top schools, which means private lessons, which are very expensive."

"Bullshit," judged Parisy.

"Moreover, keep in mind," stressed Bernie, "that my role is very delicate. I have to second Mister Max in all kinds of situations, watch over his diet" (Max smiled at these words), "buck him up when he doesn't feel like playing. That all makes for a heavy responsibility. And besides," he impressed upon them, "pushing him onstage every evening isn't always easy. Sometimes he fights back. Mister Max is an artist," Bernie concluded. "He owes himself to his public, and please understand that in a certain way all of this happens through me."

"You've got to be kidding," said Parisy.

"Pardon me," Max broke in, "but I completely support the kid's request. He's indispensable to me and I won't take responsibility if I don't have him."

A soaked Parisy squeezed out his Kleenex, looked for another one before remembering that there weren't any, then used his sleeve to wipe off his forehead. "I'll have to think about it," he said. "We'll have to talk about it."

"Why don't we talk about it now?" asked Bernie.

"Absolutely," Max instigated, "why put it off?"

"Let's have a seat, then," sighed Parisy, pulling from his pocket a small rectangular object, like a cell phone or electric razor.

"With pleasure," said Bernie as Max emptied his glass and stood up.

"Well," he said, "I'll let the two of you work it out."

When he left the dressing room, Parisy had just pushed a button located at the end of the rectangular object, which turned out to be a small, battery-operated portable fan, whose rattling click Max could hear all the way to the end of the hall.

3

When Max got home from Salle Pleyel, Alice manifested little reaction, which was no surprise given that she was already asleep. She and Max occupied two large floors in the eighteenth arrondissement, near Château-Rouge—large enough so that each of them could live and work there in complete independence, she upstairs and he downstairs, without seeing each other from one day's end to the next if they didn't want to.

Max closed the entrance door softly before heading into his studio: a grand piano; a small desk; a very small fridge, the kind you find in hotel rooms; shelves loaded with sheet music; and a couch. That was where he spent most of his time, linked to the upper floor of the duplex by an intercom, protected from the bustle of the street by two double-glazed windows. As everything was well insulated for sound, Max could make as much noise as he wanted without the danger of waking Alice and, once he had taken something to drink from the refrigerator, he lifted the fall board of the piano. Setting his glass on the instrument, he stared at the keyboard. It wouldn't have been a bad idea to revisit the evening's two blunders, to isolate those passages, study them, take them apart like little watches, two little mechanisms that you could then piece back together after identifying the damage, repairing the defective gear for next time. But then again, I've really had enough of this concerto. And besides, I'm tired.

So he might as well take a shower, then go back into the studio, pick up his glass, and carry it into the bedroom. Once in bed, Max nonetheless thought some more about his two wrong notes, at the beginning of the first movement and in the second third of the third. It wasn't serious; they weren't bad wrong notes. To flub a note, or even a chord, is inconsequential when it's buried in a huge cascade. In those cases it passes effortlessly in the flood, and no one notices. It would have been more troublesome to have erred on a passage in the second movement, which is less dense, more fragile and more naked; everyone might have heard it. But anyway, enough of that. Instead, think about Rose for a moment, as you do every night. And besides, you've had enough to drink as it is; nobody's forcing you to empty that glass. It's late, let's turn off the light. Good. Okay, now go to sleep. What, it's not working? Okay, fine, take the pill. With a glass of water. I said water. There.

The pill took effect after twenty minutes, and twenty more minutes later sleep became paradoxical: for a handful of seconds, an inconsequential dream agitated Max's brain while his eyes also fidgeted rapidly beneath his lids. Then he woke up earlier than he would have liked and tried to fall back asleep, but in vain: keeping his eyelids shut without managing to reach a true state of wakefulness, he was beset by absurd ideas, shaky reasonings, pointless lists, and endless calculations, with brief dips back into sleep, but all too brief.

Right, now get up, it's after ten. Come on now. Fine, all right, not just yet, but certainly no later than ten-thirty. Sure, go ahead, then, think about Rose all you want. Doubt it'll do you any good, but that's your business.

4

The story of Rose goes back to his days at the conservatory in Toulouse, something like thirty years ago. In her final year of cello classes and endowed with supernatural beauty, Rose owned a white Fiat that was a little too large for her. Every day she emerged from it at the same time in front of the same café where, always at the same sidewalk table, she spoke only with the same bearded and rather fierce-looking individual who (to cut to the chase) didn't appear to be her boyfriend. Every day she was more incredibly beautiful, even if one could perhaps object to a single detail, her nose, which was slightly too hooked. On the other hand, that only made her more attractive: it was the nose of an Egyptian empress, a Spanish aristocrat, or a bird of prey—in short, a real nose. For that entire year, Max had contrived to be seated every day at the same time and at the same café as she, but at another table, neither too far nor too near, from which he watched Rose without daring to speak to her—too good for me too good for me, what in God's name can they be talking about?

Only once had Max taken the plunge and sat at a table next to hers. She asked him for a light, which might be considered an advance, perhaps even an encouragement, but that's just it: it was such a predictable advance, so conventional an encouragement that it wasn't worthy of such a supernatural beauty. It was disrespectful even to have entertained such a hypothesis, forget all that forget all that. So Max handed her his lighter with a detached gesture, painstakingly indifferent, without the spark from the lighter igniting the least speck of powder, and that's where they left it. After that he continued to look at her as she looked elsewhere, without letting himself be too noticed by her, not taking his eyes off her but always with the utmost discretion. Or so he thought. Then, when summer came, Rose left town for the holidays and the cello behind for good. A vacant Max in abandoned Toulouse went to have a drink at the same sidewalk café, also empty, where only a few patrons were to be found—mainly tourists, but also, what do you know, the fierce bearded guy, with whom Max struck up a conversation.

It didn't take long for the talk to turn to Rose. Mouth agape, Max soon learned that it was about him that they had talked. It was Max himself they discussed, she going on about him nonstop, to the point where the bearded fellow sometimes had to suggest she sing a different tune for a change. It turned out that Rose hadn't dared approach Max any more than Max Rose, the latter having only once ventured to ask him for a light. And worse still, according to this fellow, the only reason Rose frequented this café every day was that she hoped to see Max, believing that he was a regular there. At this news, Max remained frozen, in arrest, in apnea, remembering only after a minute that man needs to breathe, to inhale some air, especially when he's flooded by an enormous desire to weep. But where is she now, he pleaded, how can I find her, is there an address where she can be reached? Well, no, the other answered, she's gone now, her studies are over and she moved to God knows where.

Since then, Max had spent a good part of his life expecting, hoping, waiting to run into her by chance. Not a day went by without his thinking about it for a few seconds, a few minutes, or more. Now this isn't entirely rational. After thirty years, Rose could have been living on the other side of the world, already having, according to his informant, some predisposition in that direction. Or perhaps she was even dead, having had, on that score, no less predisposition than the rest of us.

5

Up at ten-thirty, Max discovered his half-full glass next to the bed, went to empty it in the sink, and then, standing nude in the kitchen, made some coffee.

He would wash up only at day's end, before going out to perform or see friends. For now he donned soft, practical, fairly ample garments, such as a sweatsuit or an old wrinkled tan linen shirt and canvas pants that were no longer very white. Moreover, it seemed that, these days, all his buttons were dropping off one by one; his shirts had lived full lives and showed it. Two or three times a week lately, at the slightest excuse, whether overly zealous washing or ironing by the cleaning woman or washing machine, muscle stretch, awkward movement, or spontaneous decay, a worn thread would give way, the button would leave its mooring and fall like a dead leaf, ripe fruit, or dry acorn, bouncing and rolling protractedly on the ground.

Then it's the same daily routine: after coffee, piano. The time is long past since Max did exercises before getting down to business, scales and arpeggios serving only to loosen up his fingers before a concert, like limbering-up exercises to gently warm the muscles. He works directly on the pieces that he will soon have to perform, polishing up a few phrases of his own invention, ruses and technical maneuvers adapted to such-and-such an obstacle, for three or four hours at a stretch. He sits at his keyboard in a feverish mix of excitement, discouragement, and anxiety, although after a while anxiety gains the upper hand. At first lodged in the pit of his plexus, it then invades the surrounding areas, mainly Max's stomach in an increasingly oppressive, convulsive, and pitiless way, until, mutating at around one-thirty from the psychic to the somatic, this anxiety metamorphoses into hunger.

In the kitchen, Max now searched through the refrigerator for viable solutions but, as Alice had done no shopping, nothing stood out with sufficient conviction to sate this hunger on its own. Which was so much the better, since eating at home alone isn't exactly a thrilling prospect; anxiety can then overtake hunger to the point of eliminating it, preventing you from eating, while the hunger, for its part, grows larger and larger—it's terrible. As usual, then, Max went out to eat in the neighborhood, where the ethnic brew had fermented into a proliferation of African, Tunisian, Laotian, Lebanese, Indian, Portuguese, Balkan, and Chinese restaurants. There was also a decent Japanese that had just opened two blocks away. Japanese it is; Max slipped on a jacket and went out. He left his building, headed up the street, and there, reaching the corner, he ran into her. No, not Rose. Somebody else.

This somebody else, let's not mince words, was also a supernaturally beautiful woman. Not the same type as Rose, although, yes, perhaps there was something. Max had noticed her some time before, but he didn't know her, had never spoken to her, had never even exchanged a single glance or smile with her—although she apparently lived in Max's neighborhood, maybe even on his street, perhaps only a few yards away. He had seen her off and on for years, who knows how many—maybe eight, ten, twelve years, or even more; he didn't remember when the first time was.

Always alone, she might be spotted twice in the same week, but months might also go by without Max seeing her once. She was a tall woman, touching and dark and gentle and tragic and profound and, once past these adjectives, which mainly applied to her smile and her eyes, Max would have had a devil of a time trying to describe her. But that smile, those eyes—tightly linked to each other, as if interdependent, and, to Max's great regret, never directed at him, being reserved for other privileged and unknown persons—were not the only attributes of hers that he found intriguing. There was also, in the midst of this lower-class, noisy, multicolored, and overall rather bleak and shabby neighborhood, an extreme elegance in this woman's bearing—in her walk, her posture, her choice of clothing—that one could hardly imagine existing outside of the pretty, calm, rich neighborhoods, and maybe not even then. Anachronistic wasn't the word; anatopic would be the word, but it doesn't exist yet, at least not to Max's knowledge. For him, this unattainable creature was a kind of variation on the Rose theme, a repetition of the same motif. Meeting her in person, Max also tried to meet her gaze, managed to do so for only a fraction of a second without glimpsing any particular sign of interest on her part and two hundred yards farther on was the Japanese. Sushi or sashimi?

Sashimi, for a change. Then he returned home and sat back down at the piano, having no further reason to be out. Two or three times he had to answer the phone, which seldom rang to begin with, and which, as Max almost never called anybody, now rang even less. At around six he heard Alice come in, but that was no reason to interrupt his practicing: he would spend the rest of the afternoon refining a few nuances of two movements, "Presentiment" followed by "Death," of *Piano Sonata 1.X. 1905* by Janáček, after which he'd go up to find Alice busy in the kitchen. "Hmm," he'd say, "fish." "Yes," Alice would reply, "why?" "No reason," Max would say, setting the table, "I like fish. Where do you keep the fish forks?" Then they'd eat together, more or less telling each other about their day, and then they'd spend a moment in front of the television which that evening was showing *Artists and Models*—a film already familiar to Max, who interrupted its progress shortly after Dean Martin had lathered sun lotion on Dorothy Malone's shoulders while singing "Innamorata" to her. Then, each in his or her own room, they went to bed.

6

With a week gone by since the concert at Salle Pleyel, Max still had some fifteen days to live, and one early morning he was speeding back to Paris in a TGV from Nantes where, the evening before, he had appeared onstage at the Opéra Graslin with an all-Fauré program. As usual, the terror of this recital had barely had time to fade from Max's body and mind when, at the prospect of performing again tonight at Salle Gaveau, a new panic had already taken hold of him. In an attempt to dilute it, to give himself something to do, Max left his seat and headed for the bar car, unbalanced by the train's motion, grabbing headrests from behind.

He did not have to go very far to reach the bar, which at this hour was nearly empty. From here you could watch the countryside in peace, even though thick horizontal shafts across the middles of the windows, incomprehensibly placed just at eye level, forced you to bend down or crane up on tiptoe to enjoy said countryside, which wasn't very interesting to begin with. Having ordered a beer, Max reached into his pocket and pulled out a phone, on which he dialed a number.

"Hello," Parisy answered almost immediately, "how can I help you? Oh, it's you. So how did it go in Nantes?"

"Oh, not bad," Max replied, "but the hotel was a disgrace."

"Oh, right," said Parisy, his mind elsewhere, "I see."

"Listen, what were you thinking," Max asked, "getting me a room for the handicapped?"

Indeed: special bed and raised toilets, support bars attached to every wall, openwork seat in the bathtub, window with northern exposure overlooking a section of parking lot that (as symbols on the ground indicated) was also reserved for the disabled. The clinical accommodations had nothing about them to brighten the mood of a man alone, especially of an artist alone, and more particularly of a terrified artist alone.

"I know," said Parisy, "I know, but there really wasn't anything else available. There must have been some kind of convention or something going on in Nantes, all the hotels were full."

"I understand," said Max, "but still."

"You know," Parisy went on, "that kind of room isn't all bad. It's much larger than the other kind, for instance. And did you notice, the doors are wider."

"Why wider?" asked Max.

"Because," Parisy explained, "they need to be big enough to fit two wheelchairs."

"Why two?" Max asked, surprised.

"Even the handicapped are entitled to love," pronounced Parisy.

"I understand," Max repeated, "but, well, really, there wasn't even a minibar."

"The handicapped are sober," Parisy remarked coldly.

"All right, fine," said Max, "whatever. Talk to you later."

And then, having downed his beer, he bought three little bottles of alcohol that he stuffed into his right pocket before returning to his seat.

In First Class, Smoking Section, Max had a group of four facing seats all to himself. One good thing about the TGV, at the time, was that in Car 13, First Class Smoking was next to the bar, which tended to make matters simpler. Coming from the Non-Smoking section, a man walked up to ask if one of the seats was free, adding that he wouldn't stay long, just long enough for one or two cigarettes. "Please," said Max with a gesture of hospitality, as if he were at home. While thanking him and producing cigarettes and a lighter, the man gave Max a slightly prolonged glance, making the latter wonder if the former had recognized him. After all, since his face sometimes appeared in newspapers and specialized magazines, on posters and record covers, it happened occasionally that people came up to talk to him—oddly enough, more often in public transportation than anywhere else. It was never unpleasant, of course, even if sometimes embarrassing, but on this particular morning, in this particular train, Max, who was finding the time hanging heavy on his hands, wouldn't have minded a little conversation. But no: having incinerated his Marlboro, the other man suddenly went to sleep right there in front of him, mouth hanging open, and Max could clearly discern a dark filling in the upper right of his jaw. Oh well, so it goes, isn't that always the way. When you know you're a little famous, you're always a little more or a little less famous than you think, depending on the situation. So what shall I do with myself? Shrugging figurative shoulders, Max dug into his pocket for the first of the miniature liquor bottles.

At the train's arrival, well before it had come to a full stop, the passengers stood up from their seats, retrieved their bags, and crowded around the doors. All except Max, who climbed down slowly from the car after everyone else. Bernie, who was waiting for him on Platform 8 at Montparnasse station, could see right away that all was not well. He rushed up and took Max's arm, laboring to stick to the straightest possible course toward the station exit while talking incessantly, informing the pianist that the reviews of the last Pleyel concert had been uniformly laudatory (anyway, that's what I heard, I never read the papers), that Gaveau would surely be packed tonight, that the States had called asking about a month-long tour, that the honorarium offered by the Fougères festival was scandalously unacceptable according to Parisy, and that, the complete

Chausson being very much in demand, Japan was pressing them to know what date they should reserve for Cerumen studios (couldn't they find something more inviting, as names go?), as well as a bunch of other things.

On the escalators, all this only provoked in Max knowing little snickers, which, in conjunction with the smell of his breath, made Bernie supremely nervous.

"By the way," said Max, "how did it go the other night with Parisy? You know, your raise."

"Well, actually, not badly," answered Bernie, "but it'll depend a bit on you."

"Never fear," said Max, tripping over a step, "it'll be fine. And if it's not fine, we'll get rid of him. You can always change managers. We make a good team, you and I, and Parisy is an idiot."

"Now really," Bernie objected.

"Shut up," Max ordered. "He doesn't know the first thing about music. He has the artistic sense of a yogurt. On top of which," he persisted, missing another step, "he's completely tone-deaf."

"Now really," Bernie repeated, gripping Max's elbow more firmly.

"He is, he is," Max developed. "He's so deaf that his ears are only good for holding up his glasses. And besides, he doesn't understand a thing about my project. But then again," he generalized, "no one understands my project. Not even me."

As it was now twelve-something, after dropping Max off in front of his building in a taxi, Bernie walked down Boulevard Barbès in search of a restaurant. He found one, ordered the daily special, and went downstairs where the telephone and bathrooms cooled their heels as usual. He used the latter, then picked up the former and dialed Parisy's number.

"So?" worried Parisy. "How is he?"

"Not too good," said Bernie. "I get the feeling he isn't too good."

"What!" exclaimed Parisy, "is he soused again? This early already?"

"He's tired," Bernie allowed. "He looks really tired to me."

"Listen, Bernard," Parisy said sharply, "that's your problem, understood? It's your responsibility. You remember what we agreed the other day? I don't have to tell you that if the concert suffers for it, the deal's off. Go do your job now."

After Max had lunched at home at Château-Rouge, where Alice had left some cold chicken in the refrigerator, he dozed off a moment on the studio couch, was startled awake by the return of the fear that he tried to exorcise with a drink, managing only to potentiate it. When Bernie reappeared at his door late that afternoon to escort him to the concert as usual, Max looked even less sure of himself than he had at the station; Bernie had to guide him toward his shower before helping him get dressed. Then, at the corner of Rue Custine, he hailed a cab and they dove in.

"Parc Monceau," Bernie announced.

"Again Parc Monceau?" Max complained. "Why do you always take me there?"

"Parc Monceau is good," answered Bernie. "It's handy, it's pretty, it's easy to get to. It's near where I live. And anyway, it's all I could think of."

A dark gray sky hung over the boulevards filing past. The air was heavy with chilly gusts, little intermittent slaps that entered through the lowered windows of the taxi; Max was constantly opening and closing his raincoat. "Say," he observed when the taxi pulled up in front of the gilded fence, "it's raining."

"Wait a minute before getting out," Bernie anticipated. "I'll cover you. And I'll take a receipt with that, please," he said to the driver before rushing around to the other side of the car, producing a telescopic umbrella. This he deployed above Max, who stumbled as he got out of the cab under the fine rain.

They again entered the park. Bernie had to contort himself somewhat to support Max by one arm while continuing to maintain, at the end of his other arm, the umbrella perfectly centered over Max's skull, as the latter protested, "Cover yourself, too, you're going to get soaked!"

"I've got my hat," Bernie reminded him.

"Listen," said Max, "how about we go to your place instead and have a little drink, just one little beer, where it's nice and warm?"

"No, Mister Max," said Bernie in a firm voice.

"Listen," Max insisted, "you know the rain isn't good for my hands. It plays havoc on my fingers. I'm freezing, I feel my arthritis taking hold, I can feel it coming on. At this rate, I won't be able to play at all."

"Mister Max," Bernie moaned desperately.

Sensing his opponent falter, Max thrust a hand into a pocket of his raincoat, pulled out one of the miniature liquor bottles purchased on the TGV, and brandished it threateningly like a grenade. "Look at this," he said. "If this is what you're afraid of, I have some on me in any case. It can only warm me up. So here's the deal, it's very simple: either a beer at your place or I drink this right here. Would you prefer that?"

"This is not good," Bernie capitulated, "this is not good."

"*What's* not good?" Max persisted. "Where's the harm? And anyway, where'd you say your place was, exactly?"

"Rue Murillo," Bernie answered in a doleful voice, "just over that way."

"I know it well," said Max. "So hey," he snickered unpleasantly, "you live in a pretty fancy neighborhood."

"It's tiny," Bernie protested limply. "It's on the top floor, just enough space for my stepson and me. It was in the family."

"Let's go," said Max.

A resigned Bernie followed more than led Max toward the park's south gate, still taking care, out of principle, to avoid the monument dedicated to Chopin—where the composer, sculpted in mid-action at his piano, continues hammering out some mazurka or other while the inevitable young woman seated beneath the instrument, her hair covered with a veil and her feet curiously huge, apparently quite enthralled, covers her eyes with one hand while in the grip of ecstasy—God, that's beautiful!—or exasperation—God, get me away from this dork!

Number 4 Rue Murillo is in fact quite a handsome building, but Bernie's lodgings consisted of three maids' quarters merged into one, overlooking the courtyard. Bernie ushered Max into the main area, which combined the functions of living room, kitchen, and dining room, and which also contained his bed. Through an open door, Max noticed some very state-of-the-art computer equipment in the room of the very intelligent stepson, who seemed to be absent. Bernie, as agreed, served Max a beer, into which, to his great consternation, the other emptied half the liquor exhibited in the park. Then the little man attempted as usual to distract the pianist, to make him forget the approaching moment of the concert, seeking out arguments and ideas with all the more difficulty in that Max's intoxication worsened with each passing minute—although, to look on the bright side, it seemed to have dampened his stage fright.

At around seven-thirty, holding each other up as best they could, they slowly headed down Avenue de Messine toward Salle Gaveau. And at eight o'clock sharp, after a fair number of efforts to keep Max on his feet, Bernie propelled him toward the piano using his habitual technique. What was not predictable was that the other man walked with a firm step toward the instrument, even though, in his vision clouded by imbibition, the keyboard was no longer its usual single maxillary but an authentic pair of jaws that this time was preparing, as sure as anything, to draw him in, chew him up, and spit him out. Now, as the entire room stood up to applaud him the moment he appeared onstage, in an interminable Niagara of acclaim that was even livelier than last week, and as the ovation grew only more enthusiastic with no signs of abating, Max, who was no longer in full possession of his faculties, deduced that the concert was over. He therefore bowed deeply to the public several times and headed with a no less resolute step back toward the wings, under the horrified eyes of Parisy—but, without a second's hesitation, Bernie gripped Max by the shoulders, spun him around, and, with a hearty shove, vigorously sent him back onstage and so off you go: sonata.

"Well done, Bernard," said Parisy. "That was good. That was really good."

"It's not always easy, you know," Bernie pointed out. "It can be quite a physical job, at times."

7

Two hours later, sobered up by the trial of the concert, nerves at rest but mind at zero, Max Delmarc was dozing on the back seat of a taxi. When it then came to a halt, Max, opening his eyes, recognized his building before noticing, in front of the door, a very large and immobile dog staring fixedly in his direction. Once the driver was paid, the dog continued to stare at Max as he got out of the cab: it was a truly voluminous beast, of Newfoundland or mastiff proportions, apparently peaceful and friendly, who then left, pulled by a long leash whose taut line Max's eyes followed in a tracking shot to arrive at a person of the female sex, viewed from behind. Now even from behind, even from afar, even under street lamps 50 percent of which were burnt out, Max had no trouble recognizing the extraordinarily beautiful woman whom he occasionally ran into in the neighborhood. Here she was now, walking away, followed by her animal, toward Square de la Villette, and at this time of night.

Max is really not the sort to accost strange women in the street, especially at this time of night. It's a matter of principle, of course, but not entirely: even if he wanted to, he would be incapable. Still, maybe as a delayed effect of all the alcohol consumed that day—no doubt, but perhaps not only—he was now starting to follow this woman with the firm intention of speaking to her. He had no idea what he would say, didn't really care, and wasn't even surprised that he didn't care—he'd find something at the last minute. Alas, coming up behind her, he was suddenly surprised to hear her talking to herself, until he noticed that she was conversing with a cell phone. No chance of accosting her under these conditions, so he passed her with a quick step as if he had other intentions, without turning around or even knowing where he was heading, forced to look like he was heading somewhere, improvising a target that would in fact be Square de la Villette three blocks away. Not many people at this hour in the small streets of the neighborhood: the noise of his footfalls echoed too loudly, seemed to ricochet against the dark façades and, as it made his gait awkward, Max uneasily imagined himself seen from behind. Then, arriving at the square, he formulated a very simple plan: he would double back to cross paths with the woman and this time he'd speak to her. He still had no idea what he might say but this point, oddly enough, struck him as negligible.

Having reached the square, then, he retraced his steps and spotted her from a distance coming toward him, the dog walking in front of its mistress in hazy silhouette. As this silhouette became more precise, making it clear to Max that she was still talking into her little phone, he could only abstain once more from accosting her. Head lowered, staring at the tips of his shoes, he passed by her as quickly as possible and fled off to take refuge at home—she must have noticed my little act, at worst I must look like a nutcase, at best like an idiot, and in any case it's shot to shit. He pushed open the main door of his building, registering that the lights were still on in Alice's rooms but not slowing his pace. Then, entering his studio, he tossed his raincoat carelessly on the couch, not lingering awhile as he usually did but heading directly into his bedroom, where he threw off his clothes in a rage and went to bed in a rage. But after a moment of immobility, he was hurriedly throwing them back on again, perhaps inside-out, recrossing the studio, and walking precipitously out. She must be home by now, but you never know, still no idea what I might say but basically what do I have to lose? But wait, what do I see: there she is. She's there, the dog is there, they're there.

Max approached, determined. The dog again began staring at Max benignly, without emitting any growls or showing the slightest bit of fang, seeming as gentle as he was huge—can somebody please tell me what dogs like that are good for? She too watched Max approach, showing no surprise at all, and without the slightest knit brow or self-protective spray made from natural pepper extracts.

"Don't be afraid," Max stammered a little too fast, "I'll just take a second. The thing is, I've been seeing you around for a long time."

"That's true," she smiled. That's good, Max said to himself, she's noticed me, that's already something.

"And I," said Max, "the thing is, I just wanted to know who you are." Cheeky fellow.

"Well," she smiled, "I live at number 55, and as you see I'm walking my dog" (I'm at number 59, myself, Max calculated). "Normally it's my children" (ouch! Max said to himself) "who walk him, but tonight they're out." Silence and another smile. It was high time to wrap this up if he didn't want to look like a . . . Max, who emphatically did not want to look like a . . . , bowed slightly, smiling in turn as broadly as he could. "Well, then," he said, "I bid you an excellent night."

Crossing through the courtyard once more, Max again saw the light in Alice's window but he refrained from going in to say good-night. And yet he often went to see her after a concert, to tell her how it went, how was your day, that whole thing, but tonight, no, no can do. He wouldn't have been able to keep from telling her what had just happened. He had already made enough of an ass of himself as it was, and besides he was too agitated. So he paced for a while around his studio, naturally poured himself one last drink, lifted the fall board on his piano only to close it again, leafed through a newspaper without reading it, and ended up putting himself to bed: long thought for the woman with the dog, barely a tiny thought for Rose, my sleeping pill, and good-night.

8

Over the following days, Max met the woman with the dog at an unusual rhythm, much more sustained than over all the past years. After their brief encounter a few nights before, they now had to greet each other, and even smile at each other since their rapid exchange had transpired in perfect civility. These smiles, however, proved to be of variable amplitudes and models. One evening when he saw her looking more elegant than usual (to be that elegant, she must have been going to some social event, and who knows with whom—you might even wonder if Max was starting to get a bit jealous, things can move so fast in this kind of situation), she gave him an amused smile, almost collusive, or merely indulgent, that seemed to prolong itself even after she had turned her back on him—which had the effect of making Max feel ridiculous, then flattered, then ridiculous at feeling flattered.

Another time, at the end of the morning, he observed her coming from the other end of the street, dressed in a jogging suit—a jogging suit from Hermès, of course, but still a jogging suit—and dragging a shopping cart behind her—shopping cart from Conran, granted, but a shopping cart nonetheless. That morning she was less made-up than usual, her hair less done, less victorious and arched; she must simply have been coming back from doing the shopping and not have appreciated overmuch being spotted like this, because her smile, this time minuscule, struck Max as noticeably cooler. Still another day, he saw her in front of number 55 trying to park her car in the rain—a small black Audi, Max noted—in a space that was somewhat tight for the vehicle's dimensions. Twisted all the way around in her seat toward the Audi's rear windshield, apparently absorbed by her task, she flashed Max a smile that this time had a more complicit nuance, given the difficulty of the undertaking—one of those smiles that make you gently raise your eyes heavenward, that take you aside as witness to life's little challenges, especially since on top of it all it's raining and since this movement of the lips is further softened by the mist and mobile reflections of the streaming windows. Max, who didn't own a car, who hadn't known until then that this woman had one, immediately committed her license plate to memory. In each of these instances the dog was nowhere to be seen and, on each of these occasions, Max made a point of showing himself as discreet as possible, responding to those smiles with a courteous reserve, or a half-tone just below, in short behaving like a perfect gentleman. Still not wanting to risk looking like a . . .

The day of that complicit smile, Max was expecting a visit from Parisy. It was the first time the impresario came to his home, anxious to verify the performer's good spirits before the taping of a televised concert. Prestigious orchestra, exceptional soloists, live broadcast conditions in a studio at Radio-France, and audience by invitation only, but the show would be prerecorded, then aired late in the evening on the cultural channel. Although Parisy, dressed that day in a dark suit meant to absorb and conceal sweat, came on the pretext of having a last look at the scores, of fine-tuning a few technical details, he mainly wanted to reassure himself that Max, nervous as always the past few days at the prospect, was not going to misbehave beyond reason while awaiting concert hour. Normally the impresario delegated this surveillance work, but this time the stakes were too high to be supervised by Bernie alone. Max nonetheless seemed rather distracted, mixing up the figures embossed on the Audi's license plate and the measure numbers on his score.

"Aren't you thirsty?" said Max. "Don't you want something to drink?"

"Listen," Parisy began, "let me just say right off the bat that I'd rather you—"

"Never fear," Max interrupted, "no alcohol today, don't worry. I'm not even sure what's the matter with me, to tell you the truth. I don't even feel like any. Coffee?"

"Gladly," said the other.

Via the intercom, Max asked Alice to make some coffee, inviting her to join them. Then, closing the score, he dropped onto the couch with a yawn.

"Everything okay?" worried Parisy. "Not too nervous?"

"Oddly enough, no," said Max. "TV doesn't affect me the way concert halls do."

"And anyway, it's not live," Parisy reminded him. "You have nothing to worry about. If need be, they can always retake a passage if something goes wrong."

"Yeah, yeah," said Max, standing up to go cast a few sullen glances out the studio window. Under the combined effects of the rain and wind, there was nothing and nobody to see in the street, except that they were still offering the usual 25 percent off the linoleum rolls lined up on the sidewalk, the green neon of the pharmacy cross was blinking as always, and at the thrift shop next door everything was still ten francs a pop. Whereupon Alice appeared, carrying a tray.

Nearly as tall, even thinner, and two years younger than Max, hair as white as his, slightly ill-favored, barely made-up, just ornamented with a thin gold chain around her neck, Alice was wearing a very lightweight, light-colored gray ensemble, very loose-fitting and very neutralizing. Having set the tray on a chair near the couch, she walked smiling up to Parisy, who rose sharply from his seat to bow stiffly before straightening up again. Looking at her gravely, he seemed impressed to the point of starting to stutter and sweating outrageously the moment she addressed him. Max looked on in surprise at his manager, not used to seeing Alice produce such an effect on a man, but amused to see this one so off-balance. Parisy, so as to regain his bearings, forced himself to make a little joke, and Alice immediately burst out laughing. As with some not-very-pretty women, it didn't take much to provoke her hilarity, and so she laughed a bit too often even though her laughter sounded raucous, like a cry of rage or suffering, as if laughing were painful, as if she were trying to expectorate something with great difficulty.

Parisy, however, did not seem to be shocked by this laugh as much as was Max, who normally had such a hard time standing it that he carefully refrained from saying anything even remotely funny in her presence—except that something that wasn't funny at all could still make her burst out laughing, provoking a chain effect of further laughter, in ricochet, increasingly inextinguishable and frenetic the more one tried, more and more sternly, to check the process. Max, in any case, decided to clarify the situation.

"Well then," he said, "let me introduce my sister. I don't believe you two know each other."

9

You, on the other hand, I know perfectly well; I know exactly what you're thinking. You were imagining that Max was yet another ladies' man, one of those classic Lotharios, charming and all but basically kind of tiresome. First Alice, then Rose, and now the woman with the dog: these episodes led you to assume the profile of a man drowning in amorous intrigues. You found this profile rather conventional, and you wouldn't be wrong. But that's not it at all. The proof is that, of the three women who up until now have figured in the life of this artist, one is his sister, the other a memory, the third an apparition, and that's it. There aren't any others, you were wrong to worry; so let's get back to it.

They'd had their coffee, during which time Parisy hadn't taken his eyes off Alice until she'd left the room. Then he'd pointed out that it was getting late and it was time to get a move on and that his car was parked on Rue de Clignancourt, so Max went off to don his pianist's uniform. And there again, even though he proceeded without nervousness, and even with unusual calm, two more buttons chose to desert his garment, one rolling off to hide under a chest of drawers, the other going underground in a crack in the floor. It must have been a season in the life cycle of Max's outfits, some autumn of his wardrobe. But for now, they were too rushed to indulge in long searches. Alice, summoned back, indicated she wouldn't have time to intervene, and Max had to swap his tuxedo shirt for a more ordinary model. It was annoying but he'd make do, and they left in haste in Parisy's Volvo toward the sixteenth arrondissement, which if you leave from Château-Rouge is almost at the opposite end of Paris, the intramural equivalent of New Zealand.

"Rotten weather," muttered Parisy. "We'll try to avoid the center of town."

The rain, in fact, having continued to fall, certainly would not fail to produce its usual coagulation of backups. To avoid losing time by crossing through a congested Paris, they agreed to take the outer roads. They first followed rectilinear Rue de Clignancourt, then took a right onto Rue Championnet to get to Rue des Poissonniers, before reaching the outer boulevards named after marshals, whose sidewalks were sporadically populated with very young women of Nigerian, Lithuanian, Ghanaian, Moldavian, Senegalese, Slovakian, Albanian, or Ivorian nationality. Skimpily clad beneath their umbrellas, they were more or less constantly observed by four categories of men: first the Bulgarian or Turkish procurers scattered about the vicinity, snug and warm in their high-octane sedans, having made the standard recommendations (At least thirty tricks a day; less than twenty-five and we break your leg); secondly the customers for whose benefit, day and night, they declaimed in every tone the same perfect alexandrine, classically balanced with caesura at the hemistich (It's fifteen for a blow and thirty for the works); thirdly the forces of law and order that, for their part, emerged especially at night, though not too aggressively (Hello hello, it's the police, do you have ID papers? Nothing? You sure? Not even a photocopy?); not to mention, fourthly, the television crews making sure that, when the nth report on the subject was broadcast after prime time, in accordance with the law on the protection of privacy, the faces of these working girls appeared duly pixelated on the screen.

These young women, these young girls, who often were not even eighteen, began to thin out as of Boulevard Suchet, then were completely gone by Rue de Boulainvilliers, along which Parisy's automobile glided up to the Maison de la Radio.

Recording was supposed to start at six, but they'd need a little time to get used to the studio, negotiate with the lighting technicians and sound engineers, and go over two or three details with the orchestra one last time, even though everything had been settled after several weeks of rehearsals. Then they'd move on to makeup, filing before the mirrors in groups of three, in the hands of specialists who were often quite pretty and who handled matters with attentive indifference. In any case, they were only putting makeup on the soloists and the conductor; the bulk of the troupe would remain in its natural state, with just a little touch of powder for the melancholics and the sanguines. Although only a minimal space was needed to contain the orchestra, the studio was still much more cramped than it would appear onscreen, but it's always the same story with television: space, screen, ideas, projects, everything is smaller there than in the normal world.

After disembodied voices had given the countdown, the concert could begin. The conductor was fairly exasperating, full of mannered grimances, unctuous and enveloping motions, coded little signs addressed to different categories of performers, fingers on his lips and inopportune thrusts of his hips. Following his lead, the instrumentalists themselves began to act like wise guys: taking advantage of a frill in the score that allowed him to shine a little, to stand out from the masses for the space of a few measures, an oboist demonstrated extreme concentration, even overplaying it to win the right to a close-up. Thanks to several highlighted phrases allocated to them, two English horns also did their little number a moment later. And Max, who had very quickly lost the scrap of stage fright that held him that day and was even starting to feel bored, himself began to make pianist faces in turn, looking preoccupied, pulling his head deep into his shoulders or excessively arching his back, depending on the tempo; smiling at the instrument, the work, the very essence of music, himself—you have to keep interested somehow.

Then, once it was all wrapped up, it was time to go home. Taking advantage of the fact that for once he might look good, Max opted not to have his makeup removed. When Parisy apologized for not being able to drive him back, he headed out on foot. The rain had tapered off and he crossed the Seine over the Pont de Grenelle up to the Allée des Cygnes, a fragment of the river's spine lined with benches and trees that he followed up to the Pont de Bir-Hakeim, via which he reached the Passy metro stop. His plan was to take Line 6 of the urban network, change at Place de l'Etoile, and, from there, head back to Barbès. The elevated Passy stop is very pretty, very airy and chic, overhung by tall buildings as distinguished as flagships, so handsome that they look unoccupied and strictly decorative. Max waited calmly for the train to appear.

Once it arrived, as it was emptying and filling itself by several users, another train pulled in from the opposite direction, heading toward Place de la Nation; it stopped, emptied out and filled up like the others. And once Max was aboard, standing against a windowed door, who did he see, or at least think he saw in the facing train at just the same level as his, which was about to leave? Rose, of course.

Rose, dressed in a dark gray suit beneath a pale-beige, much-pleated raincoat, apparently lightweight, cut from what must be called soft poplin and belted at the waist. The garment wasn't familiar to Max, naturally, but that aside, she didn't seem to have changed much in thirty years.

10

Emergency. Although the warning signal had just sounded, Max rushed perilously out of the car: he jumped off in profile, Egyptian-style, to avoid the doors that briefly slammed into his shoulders and had closed before he landed on the platform. From there, he tried again to make out Rose through the superimposed windows of the two trains, one of which, his, was now rolling toward Etoile. It left the other one more visible for an instant, before the latter started off toward Nation two seconds later, and without Max being able to verify that it in fact contained Rose. He wasn't completely certain it was she but, for the space of an instant, the resemblance had struck him as indisputable; a resemblance wearing a raincoat in which Max, while he had never seen it before, recognized what he believed he'd surmised of Rose's sartorial tastes, thirty years earlier.

Nothing is certain, but you never know. Max started to run down the platform toward the long transfer corridors, bounding up the stairways four steps at a time to reach the opposite platform, where he waited for the arrival of the next train. Which took a ridiculous amount of time. The whole enterprise was absurd. You don't follow a subway. But then again, why not? While waiting, to make time go faster, he feverishly reread the metro regulations—making sure that the five categories of passengers who ride for free still included, albeit in last place, unaccompanied persons who have lost both hands. The train arrived, Max got on. Although this train abounded in unoccupied seats, Max remained standing, posting himself next to a door through the window of which he could inspect the platforms of the upcoming stations. Once they had left Passy via the Bir-Hakeim bridge, he had another opportunity to examine the Seine, after which, between the ensuing stations, he could also ponder the city.

It's just that the Etoile-Nation line, which provides the link between the affluent and working-class neighborhoods—although these adjectives, melding together to the point of leapfrogging over each other, of taking themselves for each other, are no longer what they used to be—runs above ground for the most part, enjoying like no other line the light of day, from which nearly one station in two benefits. It constantly emerges from the earth only to plunge back down again in a sinusoid, sea serpent or roller coaster, ghost train or coitus.

But already, the platform of Bir-Hakeim station, first stop after fording the river, bore no trace of the raincoat. Nor was there any glimpse of tan at Dupleix, a clear and well-lit station beneath a sky of double-sloping glass; and as they began to pick up speed beside the buildings, eye-level with kitchens and bathrooms, living rooms and bedrooms and hotel rooms, and as dusk began to fall and electric lights threatened to go on, Max began to see his enterprise as highly dubious. Although the building windows were most often masked by curtains, drapes, or blinds, he caught fugitive glimpses of the scenes in the apartments. Three men sitting around a table. A child under a desk lamp. A woman passing from one room to another. A cat, or maybe a dog, lying on a cushion. After not finding the slightest trace of Rose at La Motte-Picquet-Grenelle, Max's doubts about the viability of his project deepened further. He was almost at the point of giving up, but no, he persevered. Better that than doing nothing.

After a while, he accorded no more than a summary glance to the station platforms parading by. Instead, he inventoried what came between them, the individuals and objects decorating the balconies and terraces that he saw from the rushing train at a downward angle—laundry stretched on a line or a clothes horse, mopeds leaning against a lowered shutter, shopping carts, baby carriages, and washing machines beyond use, soaked cardboard boxes, lawn chairs, rugs, ladders, footstools, plants and flower boxes in which geraniums claimed the lion's share, old broken toys, plastic basins, washbowls, and pails with mop handles thrusting out at an angle. Not to mention, months after New Year's, the old Christmas trees of which only a rusty spine remained, nor the parabolic antennas all facing in the same direction like vertical fields of sunflowers, nor the idle women in various states of dress, leaning on their elbows against railings and watching the elevated metro pass by, full of single men like Max who stared back at them.

After Pasteur station, Max, who had lost all hope of finding Rose and ended up taking a fold-down seat, cast only an absent eye toward the platforms. As long as the metro remained elevated, he observed the landscape and, when it plunged underground, he pondered the two men on the seats opposite his, but in that regard there was nothing very attractive to see: one, with a suitcase at his feet, offered a view of the cut on his scalp; the other, with a dead face, was consulting a brochure entitled *How to Recover Your Alimony Payments.* Max opted to study his subway ticket.

As nothing special is happening in this scene, we might as well take the time to look more closely at this ticket. There's actually a lot that can be said about these tickets, about their secondary uses—toothpick, fingernail scraper, or paper cutter, guitar pick or plectrum, bookmark, crumb sweeper, conduit or straw for controlled substances, awning for a doll's house, micro-notebook, souvenir, or support for a phone number that you scribble for a girl in case of emergency—and their various fates—folded lengthwise in half or quarters and liable to be slid under an engagement ring, signet ring, or wristwatch; folded in six or even eight in accordion fashion, ripped into confetti, peeled in a spiral like an apple, then tossed into the wastepaper baskets of the subway system, on the floor of the system, between the tracks of the system, or even cast out of the system, in the gutter, the street, at home to play heads or tails: heads magnetic stripe, tails printed side—but perhaps this isn't the moment to go into all of that.

When the metro re-emerged from underground, Max might also have absorbed himself in the viaducts they were rumbling over, good old handsome viaducts, good solid iron architecture, intelligent and dignified, but no: as his plan of pursuit came undone before his eyes, soon wilted like a poppy, here he was getting off the train at Nationale station. Then, as he had nothing left to do, he began to walk, without imagination, still following Line 6 but in the open air, crossing the savage, cursory, and poorly laid-out space that runs beneath those viaducts like a path. This space sometimes contains various peddler's carts, flea markets, stalls, or impromptu basketball courts, but it's mainly a place for the relatively anarchic parking of cars: a cold narrow corridor, a no-man's-land beneath the prickly metal noise of the convoys, where no one ever ventures without a vague sense of disquiet. And so Max walked, following this route up to the Seine, which he crossed in the opposite direction from before, then continuing up to Bel-Air where, exhausted, he waited for the next train.

11

Bel-Air is an elevated station isolated between two tunnels, an island that hangs over the depopulated Rue du Sahel like an oasis. Supported by two rows of five columns, awnings of painted wood shelter the platforms, extended by glass canopies. These platforms appear shorter than in other stations, and overall Bel-Air gives off an aura of humility. It calls to mind the train station of a small village, poor cousin or disowned sister of George V.

We would have no reason to linger on this station, except that it was here, against all likelihood, that Max believed he again recognized Rose. This is how it happened: Max arrived on the empty platform, Nation-bound side, when a train pulled in from the opposite direction, heading toward Etoile—this train business never ends. Passengers got off, almost none got on, then the train rolled away. Max distractedly glanced at the travelers as they made their way toward the platform exit before disappearing into the stairway. Now among them, from the rear, in three-quarter view, it indeed appeared to be she again, other than the fact that this time she was wearing navy-blue slacks and an apple-green zipped-up jacket, or something like that, he didn't really have time to look, all of this transpired in a mere couple of seconds. Still, Max did not take the time to reason it out, to deem it odd that Rose should be getting off a train in that direction whereas he, less than an hour earlier, had begun tailing her in the opposite direction—not to mention that she wasn't even dressed the same. Neither space nor time nor clothing matched, but never mind, let's go. Run for it.

He began running under the twenty-four pairs of uncovered neon lights that reached to just above his skull. He ran skirting the classic attributes of a metro platform, monitor screens, fire extinguishers, plastic chairs, mirrors, pictograms warning against the dangers of electrocution, and trash cans—four trash cans on the side going to Etoile while only two on the Nation side, why is that? Does one have less to throw away when coming from the rich neighborhoods? Max did not have time to deal with this question right now, but even so, as he rushed back out of the subway, the idea flashed through his mind that he'd just used up a ticket for nothing.

When he found himself back on Rue du Sahel, once again there was nothing to be seen, to either the left or the right. He decided to take the footbridge at the edge of the station, straddling the tracks and protected by a fence against which rested empty and more or less battered containers (Orangina, Coke, Yoplait), six pebbles, a liter bottle with star-shaped cracks, an unusable pair of Air-Force-blue espadrilles, a little green plastic sand shovel without its pail, all surrounded by a palpable silence, the famous silence of the twelfth arrondissement.

And in the midst of this silence, nothing and no one as far as the eye could see. Right. Let's analyze the situation. It's one of four things. Either it was Rose at Passy in a tan raincoat. Or it was Rose at Bel-Air in a green jacket. Or it was Rose in both instances, having changed clothes in less than an hour to take the subway twice in opposite directions, which wasn't very likely. Or it was she in neither instance, which was all too likely. Go back home. Take the metro again, plunge back underground. That's right, buy another ticket. And stop making that face.

And for the entire duration of this long return, fourteen stops and two transfers, the metro seemed to him dirtier and more depressing than ever, despite the zeal of the cleaning services. We all know that in the beginning (historical factoid) the immaculate tiling of the subway system, modeled on that of clinics, was intended to lessen or even eliminate worrisome ideas injected by the subterranean depths—darkness, dampness, miasmas, humidity, illness, epidemic, collapse, rats—by disguising this burrow as an impeccable bathroom. Except that they ended up with exactly the opposite result. For there exists a malediction of bathrooms. Even a slightly dirty bathroom always looks dirtier than a much dirtier non-bathroom. It's just that on any white expanse, be it ice floe or bed sheet, it takes almost nothing, the tiniest suspect detail, for everything to turn, just as it only takes one fly for the entire sugar bowl to go into mourning. Nothing is sadder than a stain between two white tiles, like dirt under a fingernail or tartar on a tooth. Once back home, Max didn't even feel like taking a shower.

But the next morning, as he emerged from his building, he again ran into the woman with the dog. This time she was displaying her customary elegance—neighborhood elegance, halfway between that of her supposed evenings out and the outfit in which she did her shopping—and no sooner had he spied her than she walked straight up to him.

"Good morning," she immediately said. "I saw you last night on television, by chance, as I was channel-surfing." She paused for a moment to smile, as if in apology for this verb. "Ah," she resumed, "I didn't realize we had a famous musician in the neighborhood. I'm going to tell my husband" (ouch! Max said to himself again) "to buy your CDs." She smiled at him again, differently this time from all the other times, before walking off on her very narrow high heels, and Max, turning back to protractedly watch her move away, thought that you can say what you will, but music has its advantages.

12

Several days later, Max had to attend a benefit for he wasn't sure what, but something that Parisy deemed couldn't hurt in terms of public image. A series of musicians were to succeed each other onstage for brief performances; Max knew most of them, almost all pals, relaxed atmosphere, zero stage fright. The ambiance in the hall was also much more relaxed than usual for a concert: families paying very little attention, huge number of kids, not exactly the typical audience profile for classical music. When it came time for Max, who was in fact scheduled to play Schumann's *Scenes from Childhood*, he sat at the piano in an astounding ruckus: from the seats came a cacophony of calls, chatting, laughter, and crinkled wrappings that he had never experienced while playing—for, despite what they say, the public for classical music is fairly well behaved; even when it disapproves, it generally keeps quiet.

Without letting the noise deter him, Max thus attacked "From Foreign Lands and Peoples" in an environment so festive that he could barely hear the first measures. Still, as he continued to play, he felt the hubbub begin to dissolve like a cloud, open onto a silent blue sky; he noticed that he was circumventing the audience, drawing it to him like a bull, focusing it, holding it, pulling it taut.

Soon the silence in the room was as loud, magnetic, and nervous as the music itself; these two fluxes bounced back and forth and vibrated in harmony—without Max mastering in the slightest what his ten fingers were doing on the keyboard, without him knowing where this was coming from, from his work or his experience or from some other place, like lightning, like a great unexpected ray of light. The phenomenon is rare but it can happen, and twenty minutes later, no sooner had he finished "The Poet Speaks" than, after a pause, an instant of suspended amazement, an ovation burst out that Max wouldn't have traded for a triumph at the Théâtre des Champs-Elysées.

Champagne. It was the least he could do, he had to recover a bit. Champagne, of course, but soon the program organizers came up, asking Max to sign a few disks by popular demand. Of course, said Max, just one more little glass and I'm all yours. He went back into the room where they had set up a small table for him, behind which was a chair, and in front of which a rather considerable waiting line had indeed begun forming. Very quickly, the *Scenes from Childhood* that Max had recorded two years earlier would be out of stock, then almost as quickly Schumann in general, then any other Romantic music they had on hand. These went to a long line of intimidated men with smug smiles, moved women with available smiles, and even very well-groomed children with serious smiles, and Max signed, signed, signed, ah, all the times in one's life that one has to write one's name.

After a while, the turn came for a man of rather handsome appearance, with an open face and tailored suit, who deposited three disks in front of Max while leaning toward him. "You don't know me," he said, without a smile, "but you know my wife and my dog."

Max, immediately understanding what was what, thought his hour had come. We ourselves, knowing that his death is nigh, might have reason to believe that his passing was imminent, but no, nothing of the sort—we could even say things went rather well. The man's spouse must have told him about their rapid nocturnal encounter, apparently without this triggering any reaction of jealousy or homicidal vengeance. The man himself, he explained, practiced a profession that was not unrelated to the artistic sphere.

"What name should I make them out to?" Max asked hopefully.

"They're for me," the man said. "My name is Georges and I came alone, without my wife and children." It would not be that day that Max learned the name of the woman with the dog.

Everything went fairly well, then, but Max was still a little nervous when leaving the site of the benefit concert. While he hadn't, for lack of stage fright, felt the need to drink before playing, he had on the other hand downed a fair amount of champagne afterward with his colleagues, in decreasing numbers until none remained and he had to leave in turn. Then he passed alone through several bars that he also successively closed down, after which, my word, it was indeed time to go home to bed.

It is late, it is cold, it is drizzling or dribbling, it's still with a fairly steady gait that Max advances in his empty street at this hour of the night. Then, as he approaches number 55 en route to his building, he casts a semicircular glance ahead to verify that the husband of the woman with the dog isn't lurking in a recess, having reconsidered and lain in wait for Max's return with evil on his mind. No, no one. But would that Max had cast that glance behind instead, for suddenly he feels himself grabbed by the collar of his coat, thrown down onto the sidewalk, and now he's lying stretched out on his back with two guys mounted on him, masked by scarves—but, scarves or no, Max has thrown his forearm over his face in protection—who undertake a systematic rifling of his person. To do this, they tear open his raincoat violently, with so little care that two or three new buttons jump off and roll together toward the gutter—no doubt about it, it's plain to see, this really is the season of buttons.

The guys methodically extract everything they find in Max's pockets and, after a moment, as the latter deems that this is all beginning to drag on, it occurs to him to cry out, oh, not cry out for real, cry out just a little bit, you know, for form's sake, in case it could summon someone. But first, he manages to emit only a feeble and timid whine, like a slightly peevish whimper, and second, he feels a hand clamp onto his mouth to shut him up. He could, of course, push that hand aside to keep shouting; it's only a small hand of adolescent size. But he's afraid that another hand, not necessarily larger but holding a weapon, might administer a more radical treatment, and more to the point, he notices the briny, grimy taste of that hand on his lips, which he prefers to shut tight out of hygienic reflex.

And besides, truth to tell, he decides it's better just to lie back, to simply let himself go, let things take their course. He is suddenly enveloped by an almost comfortable, almost shamefully voluptuous resignation, in the renunciation of all and the vanity of everything. It works the same as when you decide, screwed if you do and screwed if you don't, to give yourself over to the anesthesiologist, who fixes a mask over your face in the perfect scialytic light and ideal calm of the operating theater, under the eyes of skullcapped surgeons. And correlatively, even though this entire process unfolds at top speed, time seems to Max to distend and multiply, as if all this were happening in slow motion despite the nervous fever of the two fellows installed on top of him.

He knows he shouldn't do it, but sometimes one has troublesome reflexes: Max stops protecting his eyes to see who these guys are—they're obviously very young, but what do they look like?

But their faces are hidden by scarves, and Max, seized by a jolt of exasperation and before he realizes what he's doing, rips one of them off. He uncovers a rather indistinct, and indeed very young, face, on which he barely has time to glimpse an expression that quickly veers from panicked to furious, indignant to vengeful, then the time to notice a foreshortened arm raised above him, prolonged by a stiletto that the unmasked young man, surely no less horrified than Max, drives deep into his throat, just above the Adam's apple. The stiletto first pierces Max's skin, before its momentum carries it through his tracheal artery and esophagus, damaging large vessels of the carotid and jugular type, after which, gliding between two vertebrae—seventh cervical and first dorsal—it severs Max's spinal cord, and there is no one left on the scene.

Everything is dark in the surrounding buildings; all the windows are black; no one is looking at anything except the dog of the woman with the dog, still awake at this hour on the fourth floor of number 55. He's a sweet and meditative dog, as Max had immediately noticed, a good pensive dog who, suffering from bouts of insomnia, sometimes stares out the window at night to pass the time, and who has just witnessed this regrettable incident. If the beast's dreamy nature predisposes him toward visions, perhaps he will now see, as a little encore, Max's soul rising gently into the welcoming ether.

II

13

No.

No, no ascension, no ether, no big to-do. And yet it seemed that even after he was dead, Max continued to experience things. He found himself naked in a single bed that occupied about a quarter of a small, dark room whose walls, painted ochre with patina effects, absorbed the light of a weak bedside lamp standing on a night table, the dimness accentuated by a fringed maroon cloth spread over the beige lampshade. Once he had opened his eyes, and after several minutes spent looking around without seeing much of anything, Max pulled away the cloth without this revealing a great deal more of his new environment. A few more minutes passed, during which he mustered feeble efforts to understand what could possibly have happened, but in vain. Giving up, he finally got out of bed, fighting off a brief dizzy spell before gathering up his pants, which he found carefully folded over the back of a chair. He pulled them on, then headed toward the door that he assumed, for no particular reason, would be locked.

It wasn't. But although this door opened without difficulty, it led only to a long, empty corridor, punctuated by other closed doors between which, at regular intervals, sconces gave off the faint halos of night-lights. The corridor was so long that you couldn't see either end of it; so empty that it was nothing, revealed nothing, provided no more information than if the door had in fact been bolted. Max, bare-chested, was about to close his door again when he noticed, far down the corridor to the left, an indistinct figure wearing a yellow bathrobe who detached himself tentatively from the wall, evidently venturing out like Max. Max was hesitating about which course to take, whether to wave or hide, uncertain as to the nature of this figure, when he saw it jump back at the arrival of another silhouette.

White in color and emerging from who knows where, this second figure seemed gently but firmly to admonish Yellow Bathrobe, who immediately vanished. Apparently White Silhouette then noticed Max, who watched it walk toward him; become transformed in its approach into a young woman who was the spitting image of Peggy Lee—tall, nurse's blouse, very light hair pulled back and held with a hair tie. With the same implacable softness, she enjoined Max to go back into his room.

"You have to stay in here," she said—moreover, in Peggy Lee's voice. "Someone will be by to see you soon."

"But," started Max, getting no further, as the young woman immediately negated this incipient objection with a light rustling of her fingers, deployed like a flight of birds in the air between them. When you got down to it, she did look phenomenally like Peggy Lee, the same kind of big, milk-fed blonde, with a fleshy, dimpled face, full figure and broad forehead, invasive cheeks, wide mouth, and excessive lower lip forming the permanent smile of a zealous camp counselor. More reassuring than arousing, she exuded complete wholesomeness and strict morals.

Back in his room, Max examined things more closely. There wasn't enough space for much furniture other than his bed and the nightstand, both made of mahogany; a minuscule armoire, perhaps made of oak and containing a few spare clothes in Max's size; an elegant little table roughly the size of a sideboard; the chair on which his pants had been folded, and that was it. No decoration on the walls, no knickknacks, no magazines, not a book in sight, no Gideon Bible in the bedside drawer or tourist brochure that might indicate where he was, what he could do there, what there was to see in the area, with all the usual timetables and fee schedules. In sum, a sober, comfortable room, the kind probably found in certain abbeys that have been refitted as spiritual retreats, intended for souls who dispose of equally comfortable incomes. An air-conditioned space, perfectly quiet owing to the fact that, alas, there were no windows, and still more so because it contained neither radio nor television. A door made of some translucent material led to a reasonably designed bathroom, even though there was no mirror above the sink. As Max tried to see his reflection in this translucent material, he vaguely made out a dark patch at the base of his neck. But something made him hesitate before bringing his hand to it, and in any case, at that same moment, the door to his room unexpectedly opened to reveal a visitor.

The visitor was perhaps a bit taller than Max, clearly a bit thinner, nicely built and of elegant bearing—things that Max would ordinarily find rather irksome. The man displayed a casualness bordering on insolence, reminiscent of a fair number of clowns Max had known in his professional life: art directors or publicity heads of record companies, critics or producers of specialized festivals in some narrowly defined subcategory of Baroque. His light, loose-fitting clothes also fit him a bit too well, tan linen suit over an anthracite T-shirt and docksiders. He seemed excessively aware of his appearance; his hair denoted just the right amount of negligence, thick and brushed back with one discreetly rebellious strand falling forward. With his manicured nails, weekly ultraviolet treatments, and exfoliated skin, he radiated gym clubs, hair salons and beauty salons, fitting rooms and tea rooms. "Hello, Max," he uttered without warmth, "pleased to meet you. My name is Christian Béliard, but you may call me Christian. I'll be looking after you."

All of this—and those who know anything about Max can see it coming—does not augur well. Max does not particularly like it when a stranger calls him by his first name right off the bat, like an American; he does not appreciate very much that this stranger is addressing him in a nonchalant tone and hardly looking at him; and he especially does not care for the relaxed, professionally indifferent attitude displayed by this stranger who, while talking to him, is casting distracted glances around the room as if conducting an inspection. On top of which, Max really doesn't see why this chump, for whom he feels an immediate dislike, claims to be looking after him, or who the hell he thinks he is. He would prefer that someone first explain to him, politely, what he's done to deserve all this distant solicitude, and what they, in fact, are actually doing here, and particularly what he, Max, is doing here at all. But, dislike or not, the man must be fairly intuitive, or at least sufficiently trained to understand what is rumbling spontaneously through Max's nervous system. "Not to worry," says the aforementioned Béliard, who breaks into a half-smile while sitting at the foot of the bed, "everything will be just fine. I'll explain briefly."

It turned out from his explanation that Max was, right here and now, in transit. Right here, in other words, in a kind of specialized Orientation Center, or so he gathered. Something like a triage area where his fate was to be decided. The time needed to rule on his case, which would be handled by a duly appointed committee, should not exceed one week, during which Max could rest and enjoy the Center's facilities at his leisure—you'll find, incidentally, that the cuisine is excellent. As for the decisions that this committee would be handing down, their nature couldn't be simpler: there were only two possibilities, following the either/or principle. Depending on the outcome of their deliberations, Max would be sent to either one or the other of two predetermined destinations. "But don't worry," said Béliard, "each one has its good points. In any case, you'll have a better idea of what I'm talking about in five minutes. Kindly get dressed."

They left the room and headed down the corridor, along both sides of which were aligned doors identical to the one to Max's room, separated by those sconces that were like little torcheres of gilded wood. These unnumbered doors were closed, except for a single one, half open, that afforded a glimpse of a cell also identical to his own. It seemed that someone was cleaning it, for from behind, through the opening, Max fleetingly noticed two chambermaids in action, dressed in immaculate bodices and remarkably short black skirts, with a metal cart behind them holding an array of cleaning products and piles of clean sheets, pillowcases, washcloths, and towels, as well as bundles of rumpled sheets, pillowcases, washcloths, and towels, all of it under the muted whine of a vacuum cleaner and in a light perfume of deluxe disinfectant.

Then, to their left, another door opened and out came the nurse whom Max had met half an hour earlier, and who stopped at their passage. Max greeted her with a respectful nod, then turned toward Béliard, whose face tightened.

"Number 26 is a bit agitated," the nurse said in a concerned voice. "I don't know what to do with him."

"Listen," Béliard said coldly, "you know perfectly well that 26 is a bit of a special case. Do you know the treatment or not?"

"Of course I know it," said the nurse, "but I've tried everything. Nothing seems to work with him."

"That's not my department," said Béliard. "That's *your* area of expertise, isn't it? Assuming you have one," he added in a cutting tone. "And besides, can't you see I'm busy? Go see Mr. Lopez if you can't handle it, maybe they'll give you a transfer. I think they might be short-handed in the kitchen. Later."

They parted without warmth. "That girl," Max ventured to remark, "she's really not bad. It's amazing how much she looks like Peggy Lee."

"She *is* Peggy Lee," Béliard said indifferently.

"Come again?" went Max.

"Yes," said Béliard. "I mean, she was Peggy Lee. Why, do you know her?"

"Well, gosh," said Max, no longer astonished by much of

anything, "she was pretty famous, after all. I've seen some of her movies. And I even think I had one or two records."

"Oh, right," Béliard said indifferently, "that's true, you were in music, weren't you?"

"Not exactly the same type of music," said Max, "but even so, I was interested in other things, too. I mean other types."

He fell silent for a moment, looking at his hands, planting a diminished seventh chord in the empty air. "Besides, I have to admit I'm eager to get back to it," he continued. "I start to miss it pretty quickly when I'm away from my instrument."

"Ah, as for that," Béliard interrupted, "I'm afraid that's going to be a bit difficult. You'll have to reconsider the matter."

"I beg your pardon?" went Max again.

"What I mean is," Béliard specified, "you're going to have to change professions. That's how it is when you come here. It's not my decision, you understand, the same rules apply to everyone."

"But what do you expect me to do?" worried Max. "I don't know how to do anything else."

"We'll find you something," said Béliard. "We find solutions for everyone. Take Peggy, for instance. She had to change jobs, too. She needed to find another trade. So fine, she chose health care, and she's not doing too poorly. Besides, she has the right physique—though no matter what we do, she can't quite rid herself of her little movie-star habits. She gets like that now and again, and sometimes we have to take her down a peg."

"I see," said Max. "I thought I noticed some tension between you two."

"It's not just that," said Béliard. "It's also that I don't really like that kind of girl."

"What kind?"

"Oh," Béliard said with a wave of his hand, "big blondes and such. I know them all too well."

At the far end of the corridor they could make out a bend, past which they reached a kind of vast foyer where the light of day finally entered, pouring in through two large picture windows that faced in opposite directions. One of these windows looked out on a city that could have been a sister to Paris, as it displayed the same classic landmarks—various towers bespeaking different periods and uses, from Eiffel to Maine-Montparnasse and Jussieu, basilica, assorted monuments—but seen from very far away and on high. It wasn't possible to determine which angle they were seeing this city from, or precisely where they were, as such a view of Paris was not possible from any standpoint Max could envision. Whatever the case, this Paris, or its twin, seemed to be smothered under a black, synthetic rain expelled by clouds of pollution, brownish and swollen like udders. The light arriving from that side was opaque, depressing, almost extinguished; whereas it flowed in gently, affectionately, and brightly from the other side. This other side overlooked an immense park, a vegetal mass with soft contours forming a vast array in every shade of green, from the darkest to the most tender. Undulating at various points beneath a more clement sky, the expanse seemed to spread into infinity, as far as the eye could see, with no perceptible boundaries.

"Basically, this is what's awaiting you," said Béliard, indicating the two opposing axes. "These are the two possible orientations, you see, the park or the urban zone. You'll be assigned to one or the other. But again, don't worry, there's no bad or good solution. Both sides have their good and bad points. Anyway, as I mentioned, residence at the Center is limited to about a week. Which means that since today's Thursday, you should be all set by next Wednesday."

"Aha," Max said unenthusiastically. "And couldn't I just stay here? It's not so bad here, I think I could get used to it. I could even help out a bit."

"That's completely out of the question," Béliard shot back. "This is just a way station."

"Yes, but what about Peggy, for instance?" Max insisted.

"Peggy is a special case," said Béliard with an evil smile. "She's an exception. She has protection, you understand? She managed to get herself placed. The system has loopholes. Favors are done here just like anywhere else." Max didn't dare ask from whom or thanks to what Peggy Lee could enjoy such preferential treatment.

As Max, thoughtfully rubbing his chin against the grain of an already noticeable beard—which hadn't been shaved in how long, exactly? How much time separated the scene on the sidewalk from his awakening? Could one get information on this point?—was about to run his hand mechanically under the collar of his shirt, Béliard promptly braked his movement.

"Don't touch your wound," he said. "We're going to take care of it. On top of which," he added, knitting his brow, leaning closer to Max and examining him with a professional eye, "we'd better take care of it sooner rather than later. We can't leave you like this. In the meantime, you'd best keep to your room. You know the way."

"Yes," said Max, "but now that I think of it, I'm kind of hungry. Couldn't I have something to eat?"

"With the shape your throat is in," said Béliard, "I wouldn't advise it for the moment."

"What's wrong with my throat?" asked Max. "I don't feel anything. I feel perfectly fine."

"That's normal," said Béliard. "You're being given a special treatment until we perform the operation. You can eat afterward. In the meantime, you're forbidden to swallow anything whatsoever; in any case, it wouldn't go through. But I'll take care of all this; someone will come see you in a little while."

14

Max went back to his room, which they had taken the trouble to clean up a little in his absence, bringing it to a relatively high-starred level of comfort. The little table now held a tray of exotic but forbidden fruit under cellophane—kiwis, mangoes, bananas, with a preponderance of papayas—plus a matching bouquet of flowers. Easy background music also played at low volume, a loop of placid, traditional, non-threatening works, no doubt selected by a middle-brow sensibility, its volume adjustable via a knob integrated into the nightstand.

As a dozen books were also piled up on the nightstand, Max examined them. They were all identically bound in reddish leatherette as if they came from the same book club, and apparently had been chosen following the same principles as the music. It was a selection of classical works: Dante and Dostoevsky, Thomas Mann and Chrétien de Troyes, things like that, despite the jarring presence of a copy of *Materialism and Empirio-Criticism* that had wandered in, and that Max leafed through for a few minutes. After he had again tried in vain to see his wound in the frosted glass of the bathroom cabinet, he decided to lie on the bed, resisting the temptation to peel a banana, abandoning Lenin to open at random *Jerusalem Delivered* in the old Auguste Desplaces translation (1840).

He didn't have time to pursue his reading very far, as someone soon knocked at his door. Béliard again, no doubt, but no, it wasn't he. It was a valet classically dressed in black and white who entered his room smiling, Good day, Sir, except that in place of the habitual meal platter balancing on his open left hand, he carried a metal stem attached to a bag filled with translucent liquid, from which emerged a flexible tube ending in a needle—in other words, what is commonly called a drip.

This valet was another tall young man, with wavy, gelled black hair and a Latin smile, ironic and charming à la Dean Martin. Up close, in fact, he looked exactly like Dean Martin, down to his dancer's bearing and brown eyes sparkling with blue reflections. He bore such a resemblance to Dean Martin that Max, at the point they were at and given the precedent with Peggy Lee, began wondering if he wasn't the genuine article. Knowing that this was delicate territory, he nonetheless decided to broach it.

"I beg your pardon," he said, "but you wouldn't by any chance be Dean Martin, would you?"

"Sorry, Sir, afraid not," the valet answered, his smile more Martinesque than ever. "Sad to say. I wish I were."

"It's amazing how much you look like him," Max remarked in an apologetic tone.

"So I hear," the valet smiled modestly. "People have actually told me that on more than one occasion. Now, if you would kindly roll up your sleeve. No, the right one, if you don't mind."

For the following hour, Max remained lying on his bed while a hydrating solution of glucose, vitamins, and mineral salts spread through his system. Then there was another knock on his door—God in Heaven, don't they ever quit—and this time it was again the smile of Peggy Lee, exuding more than ever an aura of vegetarianism and Christian Science. Still fresh and perky, she was followed by a young man dressed like a stretcher-bearer, who, for his part, didn't look like anyone famous. They asked Max to get undressed and to put on a kind of smock, clap a bonnet on his head, and slip on shoes made of blue synthetic fabric that crumpled like paper, then to lie down on a very tall gurney, upon which he again headed, pushed by the young man, down the long row of corridors. This time they took the opposite direction to a service elevator as huge as in a hospital, as fast as in a skyscraper: they must have been descending at top speed from a very high altitude, since from the heights of his gurney Max had to force himself to swallow several times to open his eardrums, blocked by the race down to Basement Level 3.

Then new corridors flooded with white light and pierced by wide swinging doors, one of which opened onto an operating room that was no different from any other operating room; nor did the surgeon call to mind any celebrity. "Just a little repair job," the doctor explained, planting another needle in Max's forearm—the left one this time. "We're going to fix you up with a small cosmetic procedure, since of course vital functions are no longer an issue." It would just be a matter of cleaning the wound, sewing up the pieces of his lacerated throat, then reconstructing the damaged elements, especially around the spinal cord—a delicate area—before plugging up and masking the hole created by his attacker's weapon. Max plunged into chemical sleep before the other had finished his explanations.

He awoke with a start, took a moment to recognize his room, but immediately identified Peggy Lee at his bedside, sitting on a chair and flipping through the pages of a magazine. As he was opening his mouth to ask a question, she gently placed her right hand on his lips, posing on her own a finger of the left. "Don't try to talk," she said softly, "it's too soon, it could hurt. But don't worry; it will go very quickly from now on. In your condition, it heals pretty fast. You'll see, you'll feel better by tomorrow." Although he didn't understand a word of what she was saying, Max nodded with a knowing air, glanced briefly at the IV that was lodged once more in his right arm, then dropped off to sleep again like a stone.

The next time he opened his eyes, there was no one in his room, which he now recognized instantly. No sound came from anywhere: they must have disconnected the background music to ensure that he get some rest. No way to know what time it was, evening or morning, day or night. For lack of anything else to do, Max reviewed all the information he had gathered since arriving at the Center, making a synthesis, then reflecting on what was now liable to happen to him—what zone they were going to assign him to. By all appearances, aesthetically speaking, the park seemed to be a good solution, even if it would be smart to check it out more closely. Since Béliard had indicated the decision would be made by studying his file, Max envisioned the future with optimism, having a fair amount of confidence in the balance sheet of his life.

For it seemed to him that he had always behaved rather well. Taking a survey of his existence, he came to the conclusion that he hadn't seriously lapsed in any domain whatsoever. Naturally, he had suffered from doubt, alcoholism, and acedia; naturally, he had occasionally succumbed to laziness, allowed himself a few minor tantrums, or indulged in bouts of pride, but what else could he have done? Overall, it all seemed decidedly venial. If one was granted access to the park based on one's merits, Max couldn't really see what might stand in the way of his acceptance, but it was no doubt premature to speculate on his fate before getting more information—and at that moment, the door opened to reveal Béliard.

15

"Well," proffered Béliard in the martial tones of a head resident, "how are we feeling this morning?" So it was morning. The next day, unless it was the day after that. But before Max had a chance to answer, someone knocked at the door: this time it was the valet carrying an actual meal platter.

"You've noticed everything moves very quickly here," noted Béliard, handing Max a pocket mirror. "Don't even need a bandage, the healing is almost done." And in fact, in the mirror, Max saw at the base of his throat only a slight pale line bordered by a barely perceptible row of dots. "You're going to be able to start eating again," Béliard added, pointing to the valet, who promptly cleared the table before setting down the platter, then busied himself with removing the IV. After extracting the needle from Max's forearm, he briefly swabbed the area with alcohol, the swipe of a dust cloth over a varnished canvas, and zip zip zip, a little square of Band-Aid on top, and end of story. "There," said Béliard, "that's taken care of. Now you can get dressed."

"It's just a light meal, Sir," the valet apologized under his breath as Max slipped on his shirt. "Because of your operation. A little convalescent diet, not very exciting, I grant, and I sincerely hope you won't hold it against us. You'll soon be able to enjoy more varied menus." In fact, this one consisted of white rice and steamed vegetables, a slice of boiled ham, yogurt, and fruit compote, washed down with mineral water. "Will this be to your liking?" worried the valet, while meticulously arranging the silverware in parentheses around the dish.

"Cut it short, Dino, cut it short," exclaimed Béliard, who seemed to derive great pleasure from bossing the junior staff around. He tried to dismiss the domestic abruptly, the moment the latter had finished his task, but Dino, since Dino he was, took his sweet time with a distant, smiling, indifferent, calm indolence.

"Now that you're recovered," said Béliard, "I'll show you around the place a bit." They took the same elevator that had carried Max to the operating room and, as they headed down, Max tried to worm some information out of Béliard about Dino.

"Why?" the other asked coldly.

"I don't know," said Max, "I like that young man. I find him very pleasant, even rather special."

"I can't answer that," said Béliard. "He doesn't like people talking about him. He prefers not to have anything known about him personally, which I respect. People have this right in our institution. But I won't hide the fact that he annoys me sometimes. Truth be told, I find him a bit too casual."

This time, the elevator stopped three floors above the surgical level, at the ground floor of the Center. They followed a new network of corridors, wider, better decorated—fresh bouquets of flowers on console tables, neoclassical statuettes on pedestals, fantastical landscapes—and more populated—chambermaids and factotums, secretaries wearing glasses and buns who, hugging their folders under their arms, gave Béliard timid and respectful greetings when crossing his path, which he vaguely answered with a brief movement of his chin. Corridors and more corridors that finally ended at a gigantic foyer lit *a giorno* by gleaming crystal-and-bronze chandeliers framed by oblong pastel windows, and from which rose a monumental staircase with two revolutions. "Here we are," said Béliard. "This is the entrance of the Center." Past a revolving door, one could in fact make out, punctuated by water fountains and clumps of vegetation, the kind of vast stretch of gravel that one often sees in front of grand mansions—usually strewn with long automobiles, stained by oil from their crankcases, and furrowed with traces of their tires—but here, as far as Max could tell from where he stood, there was no stain, no trace of any tire, no car beneath the clear sky.

Nor did there appear to be a security guard on duty inside the foyer or in the surrounding area. No sentinel, no watchman, not a single video camera, ah, wait, there's something: hidden behind the architecture of the staircase, Max spotted a small, discreet booth, in frosted glass to waist level and containing a desk, behind which a sexagenarian dressed in traditional grand hotel concierge garb—black frock coat over white vest, his lapel sporting two crossed keys—seemed to be in a dream, oblivious to the world.

"It doesn't look like you have a very large staff," Max observed. "People can come and go as they please, can they?"

"It's not quite that simple," Béliard moderated, "but it's a little like that. We work on the honor system, if you like. Surveillance is very low-level, everyone is responsible for himself. I'll show you around the park tomorrow, if that sounds all right. In the meantime, let me introduce you to the director. Would you like to meet him?"

"Oh, yes," said Max, "good idea. I'd like to meet the director."

"Let me go make sure he's in," said Béliard, heading toward the concierge's booth. "Good morning, Joseph, is Mr. Lopez in his office at the moment?"

At Joseph's affirmative reply, they took the staircase, on the landings of which several grooms stood or circulated—very young subjects, barely pubescent, dressed in woolen dolman jackets and striped trousers, white collars, gloves, and caps, and engaged in apparently farcical activities that Max and Béliard's passage momentarily disrupted. On the second floor was a large double door guarded by an usher who, with a grave salute to Béliard, let them pass. They crossed through a string of vast rooms that were sometimes empty, sometimes sectioned off into cubicles separated by glass partitions behind which, here and there, one could make out a silhouette bent over its job. After they had crossed another antechamber, Béliard knocked on the next door, which immediately opened onto a huge directorial office. We'll choose not to describe this office in much detail; let us simply note that its furnishings and decorations matched—perhaps in a slightly duller and sadder way, and a little less well maintained—the style of the rooms Max had thus far walked through.

Directorial or not, the office was occupied only by one thin, stooped, standing man, bent over thick bundles of yellowish documents spread out over a desk. This person was of average height, tightly dressed in inexpensive gray. His long, waxy face denoted a poorly balanced diet; his gummy eyes were teary. He sported the anxious air of an underpaid clerk, depressive, apologetic more than displeased about being so anxious, but resigned to it. He must have been a secretary or accountant, or one of the undersecretaries or under-accountants working for the director, whom he was, no doubt, going out to notify.

Or maybe not. "Mr. Lopez," Béliard uttered gently and with deference, "this is Mr. Delmarc, who has recently joined us. He was admitted this week and he wanted to meet you."

"Ah," the other said confusedly, raising an intimidated eye toward Max, "well, welcome." He did not even ask Max a few questions for form's sake. At first glance, he seemed a bit frightened; his questioning look made him appear overwhelmed by events—although one might wonder if this wasn't some kind of ruse, a trick he used so as to be left in peace; if in fact he knew, better than anyone, all about Max. "What did you say his name was?" he asked Béliard, who repeated Max's last name for him, spelling it out. "Yes," said Lopez, "I see. Just a moment." Bending once more over the desk and rifling through the scattered documents, he eventually pulled one out and handed it to Béliard. The latter first skimmed it rapidly, then, in the general silence, began rereading it more closely.

Standing at a cautious distance, Max nonetheless glanced over at the object. It was a rectangular, lined index card, 5 × 8 format, its edges yellowed and slightly frayed, almost entirely covered in a fine, close handwriting traced in brown ink: apparently it was not of recent vintage, like most of the documents piled up on Lopez's desk. It was reminiscent of those other index cards that people used to consult in public libraries, back before their catalogues went digital.

"Say," Max allowed himself to observe, "you aren't computerized here?"

"Did I ask you anything?" Béliard answered without raising his eyes.

Meanwhile, Lopez had sat down, brushing imaginary dust with the back of his hand from the surface of his desk, which he stared at vacantly. Then Béliard, having finished reading, glanced quickly at Max before handing the card back to Lopez. "Right," he said, "I think I basically get the picture."

"What's with them?" Max asked himself. "What's there to see, in particular?"

Two fried eggs were waiting for him in his room, accompanied by a beer and a slice of melon, the first discreet sign of an improvement. As of the next day, in fact, his lunch would offer more depth, then dinner would be frankly worthy of a five-star restaurant. Max had to spend that entire second postoperative day in his room, leafing through the books he had, but without enthusiasm and not really able to read, at first distracted by anxiety over the index card he'd seen in Lopez's office, then, as of early afternoon, more profoundly distracted by boredom. Dino still handled the service with his smiling and detached discretion, although it was still impossible to make him be anything but even-spoken; then Béliard came by for coffee. When evening fell, Max fretted to him about his schedule in the days to come.

"It's just that I'm starting to go kind of stir-crazy here," he had to admit. "Couldn't I just go out for a little walk now and then?"

"But you're absolutely free," Béliard assured him. "Your door is open. At this point, nothing is stopping you from coming and going as you please in the establishment. As for distractions per se, we'll see about that later. Cigar?"

16

The start of the next day would prove to be pretty depressing. It's just that it was Sunday and, even in a place as cut off from the world as the Center, Sunday produced, as always and everywhere, its effect of indolence and emptiness, of pale expanse and hollow, sorrowful resonance. First there would be an interminable morning, during which Max would keep to his room, pondering the matter of Lopez's index card, until somebody served him one of those cold meals that you get when there's no one in the kitchen. Besides, it wasn't even properly served to him: when he started feeling hungry and opened his door to watch for Dino's arrival, he found the platter set down in the corridor at his feet like a doormat. And Béliard, like Dino, was no doubt taking advantage of his weekly day off, unless he already had lunch plans, since he didn't show up for his daily coffee with Max. Max now felt fully recovered from his operation and, once fed, he decided to go take a spin around the Center. With a little idea in the back of his mind.

It wouldn't exactly be easy. He had to reconstruct, by himself, the path he and Béliard had taken the day before. Emptier even than usual, the corridor on his floor gave off the glacial echo of a deserted boarding school during holidays, when all the others have gone to be with their families and you remain behind, alone with the staff, whether out of punishment or orphanhood. Except that Max didn't come across any staff. He could have sworn he made out the rumbling of a vacuum cleaner in the distance, the dim clanks of a mop in an empty pail but, as there was no one to be seen, these could just as easily have been slight auditory hallucinations produced by the silence itself. He had no trouble finding the elevator and, once its doors had closed behind him, as the mechanism made no sound, Max was shut into a higher silence, a silence within the silence, a cubed silence that didn't bespeak anything good. It was with a troubled index finger that he zeroed in on and pressed the button for the ground floor; then the descent was long enough for his entire life to pass before him, until the concluding *dring* of the elevator brought him back with a slight start.

As on the day before, the elevator doors opened onto the same network of hallways that were better decorated than upstairs. The rooms from yesterday were now deserted, and Max could linger at the thresholds, looking at what must have been offices, exhibit halls, and conference rooms furnished with coffee machines. He ventured into what looked like a reception hall, a huge space whose decoration suggested a vaguely Soviet aesthetic: stucco and moldings, thick damask drapes, carpets with indistinct designs, and large ungainly furniture, heavy with good will and coiffed with table mats. At the far end of the room, there was even a piano. A concert grand. Well, well.

Seeing it, Max realized that for the past several days he had almost forgotten about music. And yet music was his life, or at least it had been. But he had hardly even mentioned it to Béliard, just long enough for the latter to intimate that he would now have to give it up. Max remembered, moreover, that he hadn't been particularly devastated by this news at the time, but the piano, well after all. A piano. Max approached it very slowly, as one might draw near a wild animal, as if the instrument were threatening to fly off with a squawk at the slightest sudden movement. Taking advantage of

Béliard's dominical absence, he felt the desire to see what this model had under its hood, the urge to make it talk. But first, prudently halting a few feet away, he tried to make out its label. Neither Gaveau nor Steinway nor Bechstein nor Bösendorfer nor anything: no signature on the gold plate under the music desk. A big, anonymous machine, black, sleek, shining, solitary, and closed. Inching closer on tiptoe, Max silently turned his hands supine but, when he gently risked the tips of his fingers toward the instrument to open the fall board, he noticed that it was locked, making the keys inaccessible. Max insisted, trying to force the cover, but no, nothing doing, it was bolted. Bernie, among his many talents, would have been perfectly capable of prying open the lock in two beats of three movements, but there was no more Bernie. Bernie, too, had been his life.

Max had to be content with circling for a moment, not more than two or three times, around the closed piano. Without much conviction, he also tried to lift the instrument's lid, if only to examine its sounding board and wrest plank, caress the strings and run his fingernails over them like a harp, but in vain: locked shut like the rest. During these two or three turns around the piano, the little idea grew in the back of Max's mind.

This idea led him to retrace fairly quickly and easily the path toward the main entrance. He moved forward in the same thick silence that, not merely amplifying the sound of his steps, also brought forth other various and indistinct sounds, distant moans and grunts, whines, creaks, and buzzings that stopped dead the moment Max became aware of their untraceable origin, their possible genesis inside him, his skull acting as their echo chamber. When he found himself back in the foyer, the latter was equally devoid of any guard: even the concierge was absent from his glass booth. Max nonetheless made a show of examining the place as nonchalantly as you please, distracted but exhibiting a complete curiosity, like a tourist set loose in a chateau without his guide, coming and going with no discernible method on open-house day. Nevertheless, a goal directed his wanderings: to amble closer, by concentric circles and oh so casually, to the foyer's revolving door; and then, having reached it, to give it a slight prod to make sure it wasn't blocked; then, this being verified, to push it more firmly, slip into its space, and stroll out as naturally as could be. He experienced a brief sensation of claustrophobia when he found himself, for the space of three seconds, enclosed in the door's rotating airlock, while the once little idea now left the back of his mind to swell and invade this mind completely—I'm getting out of here, God help me, I'm getting the hell out of here.

To go where? No clue. Once outside, the main thing was to get as far away as possible; after that, we'd see. The exterior consisted in a minimal landscape: past the graveled esplanade that stretched before the Center, a summarily blacktopped pathway opened up, its pavement gradually splitting into plates of asphalt that were increasingly unconnected, among which grew tufts of weeds. This pathway soon became a stony dirt road, barely suitable for traffic and lined by dry shrubs with outlines like stick insects, with nothing in sight but sterile undulations on either side, stretching to infinity.

Nothing in this landscape suggested either of the ones Max had seen from the windows: it was an intermediate stage, gray, neutral, and chilly in nature. Max decided to follow this dirt road, shivering a little, and in any case having no choice, nor the slightest idea of where he was going. After roughly five hundred yards, he thought to turn around and get a look at the Center. It was, as the elevator had defined it from within, a very tall building, almost a skyscraper, about forty stories high, gray in color and flanked with long, low wings and annexes. The whole thing must have been able to house a huge number of people.

He walked another mile or two along this deserted road in the middle of the countryside before he made out the faint whine of a rather shrill engine, no doubt a two-stroke, slowly growing louder behind him. Max took pains to act as if there were nothing untoward until he heard the engine slow down right near him, behind his back, humming gently in idle. At that point he had to turn around and look: it was a service vehicle of a model unfamiliar to Max—moreover, as with the piano, no manufacturer's mark was visible. Halfway between a Mini Moke and a golf cart, it was a small, topless, all-purpose conveyance, rather stylish in its very simplicity. Max had no trouble recognizing Dino sitting behind the wheel, even though he'd swapped his valet's livery for an electric-blue business suit of good cut. He was also wearing a hat that he pushed back slightly while opening the passenger door with the other hand, not saying a word but grinning irresistibly with the full width of his enamel.

It was clear that there was no discussion to be had; Max could only get in quietly and sit down. Dino maneuvered the vehicle and they headed back with no comment toward the Center, at first in silence. Then, as if sensing that this silence might begin to weigh on them, Dino began delicately humming a melody that Max immediately identified: "The Night Is Young and You're So Beautiful"; then he started to sing it for real, with lyrics, at halfvolume, while improvising a rhythm section by tapping his fingers on the steering wheel. Not only did Max recognize the song, but he recognized more and more precisely the timbre of Dino's voice—that crooner's voice, a bit ironic, nonchalant, and gifted, but aware and making fun of its own nonchalance: obviously Dean Martin, of course Dean Martin. It was no less indisputable than it was intimidating—because, after all, Dean Martin.

But it was also a chance to know the artist a little better, even while not letting on that he'd been recognized, the other having made it very clear that he wished to remain incognito. If Dino didn't want to be identified, that was his business, and Max wasn't going to pester him about it. Still, they could talk a bit, broach a host of other subjects, like, jeez, I don't know.

"Dino," he said once the other had finished singing, "would you like to have a drink one of these days? I'd enjoy getting to know you better."

The other, who up until then had been nothing but relaxed and friendly, suspended his smile for an instant, albeit without hostility, and, turning politely toward Max, he answered calmly, "No one can know me, Sir," before redeploying his dazzling whites. Max took care not to insist: Dino was a tranquil and secretive man, and as Béliard had said, one had to respect that.

As they drove toward the Center beneath a sky that was almost as white as that smile, Max began to ponder the awful trouble that was surely awaiting him on his return. He could hardly imagine the disciplinary measures that might follow his attempt to run away or escape—the very nature of his crime was still to be defined—but there must be a punishment for such conduct. What? Penitence, imprisonment, reprimands, forced labor, appearance before a disciplinary committee followed by expulsion pure and simple—although where could they expel him to? And yet, for the moment, none of this seemed worth worrying about if you judged by Dino, who continued to tap his fingers casually on the steering wheel—although it wasn't really sympathy that emanated from his behavior, more like he didn't seem to give a shit, and more generally didn't seem to give a shit about anything, and not only seemed, at that.

Still, arriving back at the Center, Max was not greeted by a row of impassive armed guards or nurses brandishing syringes, nor dragged to a jail cell or before an assembly of men in black. Dino merely accompanied him back to his room, where Béliard, sitting on the single bed, was waiting calmly while looking at his watch. Max feared remonstrations or even threats, for on top of everything else, he had probably ruined Béliard's Sunday, his one day off all week—but no, the other proved to be as benevolent and detached as Dino. And even fairly thoughtful. As Max was about to launch into jumbled explanations, Béliard preempted him with a wave of his hand.

"Don't worry about it," he said. "Everyone has tried at some point. Well, not really everybody," he qualified. "But you know, we don't really have anything against this kind of initiative. On the contrary, it's very healthy, it's a good reaction. It's especially a sign that you're completely healed. And now, if you'd be good enough to get your belongings ready," he added with a circular gesture.

"I don't have any belongings," Max reminded him, worried.

"Forgive me," said Béliard, "it was just an expression. It's only that you're going to change lodgings."

Max was still expecting the worst—dark dungeon, padded cell, cooler—but instead, no, not at all, it seemed that they had even decided to upgrade him. Located on the same floor, larger and especially better lit than the first, his new room included double French doors leading to a balcony, from which one could enjoy an unimpeded view of the park. That evening, Max would again have dinner in his room, and Béliard, having invited him to lunch at the restaurant the next day, lent him a pair of binoculars thanks to which Max, while the daylight lasted, could get an overall idea of how the park was laid out.

Bringing Max's platter, Dino, who had redonned his livery, marveled at the new room, sparing no praise for the furnishings, the functional arrangement, and the color of the walls. "It's much better than my place," he observed. "And just look at that view. *Wow!*"

Uttering this interjection, he looked so much like what he obviously was that Max, no longer able to stand it, cried out, "Come on, Dino, please, I'm begging you, just admit who you are."

"Who I am?" The valet darkened.

"You know perfectly well what I mean," Max said, exasperated. "I'm sure it's you. I know you, I saw you a bunch of times in the movies, I even saw you in a Tashlin film on TV not more than a month ago. I owned some of your records. Come on, admit it, it'll be our secret."

"Sir," Dino declared firmly, "I like you, but I would appreciate it if you did not bring this subject up again. *Okay?*"

17

The next day at around half past noon, Béliard came to find Max, saying it was time to socialize him a bit. "It's not good for you to stay all alone in your little corner; you can't keep yourself cut off from the world. A little conversation never hurts." This would therefore be Max's first meal outside his room, at the door of which they met Peggy in the corridor. There she was, apparently just hanging around with nothing special to do, as if she were just waiting to run into Max. And although the latter, as we have said before, had never exactly been what you'd call a seducer, never been sensitive to the more or less subliminal signals that might have been addressed to him, since he was never sure enough of himself to consider them such, it seemed to him that Peggy looked at him more closely, smiled at him more acutely. Even her makeup and her gait, suppler and more light-footed than usual, weren't the same as the other times, as if something—well, who knows. Anyway, what are you rambling about? Who do you think you're fooling?

"It's not the only restaurant in the Center, of course, but this one isn't bad," Béliard stated, leading Max through yet another network of corridors that this time did not pass by the elevator doors. "Otherwise we could never manage," he continued. "In fact, there's one on every floor. We're divided into sectors, you see, with people grouped by geographical area. The ones you're about to see didn't live very far from your neighborhood. You might even run across some fellows you knew. In any case, they're only here for a week, like you."

"Fine," said Max, "but why only fellows?"

"Ah," went Béliard, "I neglected to mention that the Center isn't coed. The women's section is somewhere else. I know that sounds a bit old-fashioned. The point has been hotly debated with the management team, but for the moment that's how things stand. We'll see. We have time. We have all the time in the world. Besides, here we are. After you; I insist."

They entered a space able to contain some two or three hundred persons, sitting around about forty tables that were each set for six. There were especially elderly men, of course, who ate slowly and little without looking around, but there were also some younger ones, sometimes of Max's age, who gaily asked for more wine. Among the latter, one could count a higher proportion of accident victims, murder victims, and suicides who for the most part exhibited souvenirs of serious injuries—puncture wounds, impacts from projectiles, traces of strangulation, and skull fractures. Of course, the surgeons must have treated these lesions as they had operated on Max's, making their scars barely visible, but nonetheless some of these stigmata remained distinguishable and, depending on how each man looked, one could have made a game of guessing what had happened. Whatever the case, past events did not seem to ruin the appetite of any of them. "Well," said Béliard, "I'll leave you now. You'll be taken care of, and I'll see you later."

A maitre d' in fact came up to them, leading Max to a table where a free seat was available. As Max didn't recognize any of his tablemates at first glance, and as none of them took the initiative to speak to him, he used the opportunity to study the place, and after it the staff. It was, then, a room of huge proportions, monumental angles, and vast perspectives, but in no way reminiscent of a refectory, mess hall, or company cafeteria. On the contrary, everything suggested the decor of a very expensive restaurant: pleated drapes, loaded chandeliers, cataracts of hanging green plants, immaculate embroidered napkins and tablecloths, heavy engraved silverware, prismatic knife-rests, fine porcelain monogrammed with indecipherable interlacing, gleaming crystal, and guilloched carafes, with small copper lamps and assorted bouquets on each table.

The service was supervised by a headwaiter wearing a black tuxedo, starched shirt with wing collar, black bow tie and white waistcoat, black socks, and matte black shoes with rubber heels. He was assisted by front waiters in black evening coats, waistcoats, and trousers, starched shirts with wing collars, black bow ties, black socks, and matte black shoes with rubber heels. These latter oversaw a brigade of second waiters in white checkered spencer jackets, buttoned-up black vests, black trousers, starched white shirts with wing collars, white bow ties, black socks, and matte black shoes with rubber heels. As for the sommeliers who constantly verified the levels in each glass, they wore black tailcoats, vests, and trousers, starched white shirts with wing collars, black bow ties, and aprons of heavy black cloth with patch pockets and leather strings; an insignia depicting a gilded bunch of grapes was pinned to the left lapel of the tailcoat.

Lower down in the hierarchy, servers assisted by busboys provided the link between the tables in the service of their second waiter and the kitchens, unseen areas in which, under the authority of a head chef, as in any worthy establishment, there must have been an army of sauciers, pastry chefs, coffee makers, silver polishers, dishwashers, glass washers, cellarmen, wine stewards, and fruit arrangers—and at the top of the pyramid, gliding along the margins of the tables and keeping a discreet eye out for trouble, the restaurant manager was wearing a jacket and vest of gray fabric with black flecks, a starched white shirt and collar, a gray tie, striped trousers, black socks, black shoes, and impeccably silver hair.

No doubt having arrived at the Center before Max, thus necessarily better informed, the fellows around the tables seemed much more knowledgeable than he about their two possible destinations, park or urban zone, each one wondering about his own fate without neglecting to comment, sometimes rather cattily, on that of the others. They were speculating big time, bets were placed under the table, and Max listened. Before learning of the gender segregation, he had briefly nurtured the ever-possible idea of finding Rose at that restaurant, but let's not go into that. Drop it.

Since the stays lasted a week, some, already there for the past five or six days, had had time to start conversations and had gotten to know the others. Max felt like the new kid who needed to be broken in. They passed him the salt without a glance and barely said a word to him. It seemed that the only glimmer of sympathy he received was from the meat slicer in immaculate kitchen togs who, circulating among the tables with his little chrome cart, sliced the roasts to each diner's specifications after having presented to each the various cuts: it seemed that the choices that day were spring chicken à la Polonaise or saddle of venison with Cumberland sauce. Once he had opted for the spring chicken, Max consumed what was on his menu, through coffee, simply waiting for Béliard to come fetch him.

Later, in the elevator: "So," asked Béliard, "did you run into anyone you know?"

"No," answered Max, who, having spotted no familiar faces in the restaurant, but whom the presence of Peggy and Dino at the Center—even if the latter clung to his anonymity—had impressed, hinted at his disappointment in not meeting other celebrities.

"On that score, you needn't waste your time," said Béliard, who explained that, while one of the Center's principles was to recycle old personalities as part of the staff, there were nonetheless quotas to be respected. The whole thing was carefully regulated: no more than two per floor. "For instance, on the next level down," he specified, "they've got Renato Salvatori and Soraya." Some of these past luminaries found themselves exempted from the choice between urban zone and park and were appointed in residence. Their status was without risk, of course, but also without much of a future.

Max was about to have him develop this point about the future when the elevator's discreet bell notified them that they had arrived. We won't elaborate on the new corridors that led, this time, to an entrance vastly different from the one through which Max had tried to escape. Here, there was no revolving door reminiscent of an old colonial hotel, no booth, no vista onto a graveled courtyard: here, two high, wide glassed doors led straight out to nature.

"Come on," said Béliard. "Follow me. A little after-dinner stroll, what do you say?"

"With pleasure," said Max.

To start, they climbed up a hill from which Max could view the overall structure of the park. It was a huge verdant expanse, roughly circular in shape, but of such vastness that a tour of its horizon seemed to exceed the usual three hundred sixty degrees. It was composed of remarkably varied landscapes, felicitously combined, a montage of every imaginable geomorphological entity—valleys, hills, steep slopes, canyons, plateaus, peaks, and so on—among which snaked a very complex hydrographic network: here and there, transient or fixed, areas of brilliance revealed or suggested rivers, streams, lakes, ponds, basins, spouts, waterfalls, and reflecting pools, at the horizon of which one could make out a seashore.

Once they had arrived back at the foot of the hill, Max saw a green profusion begin to stretch toward that horizon, a concert of trees and plants in which cohabited every species growing in the most varied climates—pine juxtaposing elm and yew rubbing against terebinth—as one sees in certain Portuguese gardens, but much more exhaustive, to the point where not one of the thirty thousand varieties of trees inventoried in the world seemed to be missing.

"Let's keep going," said Béliard. "We'll take a closer look."

They embarked on a path of a style quite different from the one Max had taken the day before, abundantly floral, bordered by fruit, ornamental and forest trees, and prickly, intertwined vines. In the heart of this vast flora, of course, the fauna was not to be outdone. Rabbits bolted in the bushes like furtive little machines; flights of iridescent hummingbirds striated the sky between the branches; and at mid-level buzzed deluxe insects, hand-picked—varnished dragonflies, lacquered ladybugs, metallic beetles. Further on, certain ill-mannered monkeys hung from the vines screeching like morons while other monkeys, calmer and better disciplined, gathered fruit in the pear trees, the handles of lovely wicker baskets nestled in the crooks of their elbows.

After a while, and seemingly at a great distance, small houses set far apart could be distinguished among the trees, as varied in appearance as the latter. These constructions bespoke various cultural origins, from traditional hut to yurt and from isba to tea pavilion, but one could also make out more modernist edifices, gas-inflatable structures, concrete dwellings with glass appendages, one-piece abodes of diverse materials, monoshell capsules made of plastic, and even a prefab bungalow. Every one of them had two peculiarities. First, each one was of reduced size, designed to house one or two people at most; and second, each one seemed like it could be quickly dismantled and rebuilt on short notice, when they weren't simply mounted on wheels. Seeing Max's surprise, Béliard explained that geographical mobility was a way of life among park occupants, a nomadism encouraged by its ample dimensions. Scattered throughout the landscape, these mobile structures generally stood at a decent remove from one another, although certain more sedentary residences, installed in the tree branches, might form a network linked by suspended catwalks, running from plane tree to sequoia. But Max could only see these houses, in which one occasionally glimpsed an occupant or two, from too far away to really make them out in any detail.

"Couldn't we get a little closer?" he asked.

"No," answered Béliard, "we can't. We mustn't disturb them, they don't like that. They value their privacy. And besides, you have visitor status, you see. I can't let you mix with the residents. I can tell you in any case that they're comfortable, all of them at home in their own little spaces, which they designed themselves. It's a very popular solution. Since the park is so vast, they can live here in peace, without being on top of each other. But sometimes they get together. They have the use of sporting equipment. There are golf courses, tennis courts, yacht clubs, the works. I have to say, the amenities aren't bad. They also organize small concerts from time to time, little shows, though of course no one is required to attend. Everyone does as they please. Actually, I *can* take you to visit one of the units closer up. We can go have a look; it's unoccupied at the moment."

He guided Max toward a minuscule English-style cottage flanked by a modest garden teeming with roses and anemones, phlox and devil-in-the-bush, cleomes and poppies, under fleeting rainbows unfurled by the automatic sprinkler system, in the shadow of mastic and sweet gum trees. "Just look how lovely that is," marveled Béliard, "they can even tend their gardens. And besides, there are as many fruit trees as you could want in the park, you see, you can eat anything you like. Well, when I say 'anything,' in reality it's mainly papaya. There are practically no seasons here, the climate is ideal. So it grows constantly, papaya, it never stops. Just between you and me, it helps if you like papayas—personally, I have trouble digesting them. But here, let's have a look at some more exotic houses. We'll take advantage of the fact that no one's in them right now. No surprise, really, since they aren't nearly as comfortable. They mainly serve as stopovers."

And so Max was able to admire, by turns: a lodge built on oak pilings, with chestnut beams and willow poles, the whole thing thatched with layers of pine needles arranged on a wicker trellis; a circular shack whose frame, walls, and roof were formed of interlaced reeds, bamboo, and rushes; a low-lying shed covered with palm fronds woven together with goat's wool, and in which the heavy canvas of the walls and roof were stretched and held in place by thick, braided cords; a conical hut with A-shaped rafters built on layers of brick that were slathered with a mortar composed of mud, mashed grass, and horse manure, and bonded together with a cement made of peat and cow droppings.

"I grant it all smacks a bit of a natural-history museum," admitted Béliard. "It's fairly ethnographic. That's enough of these. But you also have less exotic things, look over there." Max in fact noticed, as they walked, miniature Mediterranean villas, fisherman's cottages, worker's units, and even, still more roughly assembled, refurbished caravans, station wagons, or minivans, customized bunkers and blockhouses, and inverted boat hulls. "You see," said Béliard, "there's a little of everything. Whatever the client wants."

"Yes," said Max. "And how are they heated?"

"The climate is carefully regulated," Béliard smiled. "You don't need heating here, ever, any more than you need fans. Anyway, there it is," he concluded. "This was just to give you some idea of the park; in any case you'll be assigned tomorrow. But you can see how comfortable you'd be, no?"

"Oh yes," recognized Max. "The only thing is, I'd be a little afraid of boredom."

"Ah," said Béliard, "there's the rub, of course. Right. Well, it's getting late, time to be heading back."

As he was returning to his new room, Max again ran into Peggy in the corridor. She stopped alongside him, all smiles, will you be needing anything? "Everything's fine," Max assured her, "everything's just fine."

"So, you were able to visit the park, you saw how pretty it is?"

"Magnificent," certified Max, "truly gorgeous."

"Well, I'll let you go, I've finished my shift," Peggy indicated, "so I'll say goodnight."

"Goodnight," said Max, "goodnight."

They parted company with prolonged smiles, intent looks. Max hadn't been in his room three minutes when there was a knock at his door. It was Peggy again, who entered on a flimsy pretext, claiming that the chambermaids had left something behind, looking for that something in vain, then turning impetuously toward Max and, against all odds, rushing into his arms. And that was how Max Delmarc, one fine evening, possessed Peggy Lee.

18

Night of love with Peggy Lee

19

The next morning, Max woke up very late and alone in his bed. As he turned over, eyes still shut, the first spontaneous movement of his brain was to recall the previous night. At first, the episode with Peggy seemed so highly improbable that he suspected it was just a dream. But once he opened his eyes, then sat up with a start and gave his sheets a quick once-over, the state they were in confirmed the reality of the facts. He fell back again, pulling the covers over himself and letting out a contented sigh. Then, after revisiting the high points of the evening, came the second movement of his brain: it was today, he remembered. It was today, according to Béliard, that he would be informed of his fate.

In anticipation of the verdict, Max attempted once again to take stock of his life, as he had done after his operation but in a more strictly canonical fashion: exhaustive examination of conscience following the accepted protocol. Let us recapitulate, then: I've never killed anyone, practically never stolen anything, no memory of bearing false witness, and I rarely swore. I always made sure to rest on the Sabbath, and as for my parents, I think I did the best I could. While I never had a chance to explore the question of adultery very fully, there was certainly the more general matter of coveting my neighbor's goods, wives included, on which I perhaps haven't always been entirely above-board. But fine, nothing excessive. Then, of course, there's the problem of divinity, which I believe I handled reasonably well. Skeptical but honest. Hesitant but respectful. Apart from that, I really can't think of anything. I admit I sometimes had occasion to drink excessively, but first of all, given my profession, I think there were extenuating circumstances, and besides, it seems to me that nothing in the Ten Commandments directly addresses the question of alcohol. What else? Overall I believe I can say that I behaved, yes, rather well. It should be fine. It should go smoothly. Although the park, well, I don't know that it appeals all that much, but we'll see.

Basically satisfied with this panorama, Max then reprojected the film of his night with Peggy. She really was pretty amazing sexually, very imaginative as far as he could judge—he who, for lack of experience, since he had never known much in his life other than two or three unhappy love affairs and a few call girls, could only suppose that she had in fact been full of ideas. Even though in this domain one can rarely surpass the ten or twelve possible deployments with their many variations; after that, it's always pretty much the same thing. For example, during a good part of the night, she had performed long and remarkably sophisticated blow jobs that Max, back when he would listen to her singing, would never have imagined she could conceive of, despite her artistic talent. He would never have thought of her that way.

It was a little before noon and he, still in bed, was at this point in his reflections when Béliard entered his room with an unaccustomed albeit very discreet look on his face, halfway between reprobation and amusement. "Is everything okay?" asked Béliard. "Did you sleep well?"

"Not bad," answered Max, wondering if by some chance the other could know about the details of his night.

"Good," Béliard said abruptly. "I have your results. I've come to give you the report; they ruled this morning."

"Go ahead," said Max.

"I'm terribly sorry," said Béliard, "but you're being sent to the urban zone."

"Well, all right," said Max, wondering again if by chance his night with Peggy might have weighted in the verdict, constituting an infraction of the non-coed principle that might, just as easily, extend to a more generalized intolerance of sexuality. Just as easily. Still, despite the slight reticence he had exhibited about the park—which was in fact only a bit of coyness, based on his certainty that he'd been assigned there from the get-go—anxiety seized him. When you got down to it, they hadn't really told him anything about the urban zone, and besides, what was up with that idiotic name that they'd taken from an old subway map? "To be honest, I don't really understand," he said. "It seems unfair. With the life I lived, my devotion to art, I thought I could expect a little more indulgence."

"You know," Béliard softened, "I won't deny that there's always some measure of subjectivity in these deliberations. It's not automatic. It often happens like this, it's almost standard practice. And besides, we have to maintain the quotas," he added without further details.

"And there isn't any way," Max coughed, "there isn't any way to appeal?"

"No," said Béliard. "That, on the other hand, is not at all standard practice. But don't worry about it, don't take it badly. And besides, frankly, just between you and me, the park isn't always a cakewalk. You can definitely get bored at times. Sure, you've got the sun all the time, but I'm sure you'll agree that the best part of sunlight is the shade. There are even some who have a very hard time dealing with it at first, and then eventually they get used to it. Fact is, they don't really have a choice."

"Fine," said Max, "I'm willing to go along with the program, but what exactly is this urban zone about?"

"Very simple," said Béliard. "People form all sorts of ideas about it, but you'll see it isn't so bad, either. In a nutshell, we're sending you back home, there you have it. Well, actually, when I say back home, I mean to Paris, you understand."

"Until when?" worried Max. "When does that part end?"

"That's all there is," said Béliard. "It will never end. It's kind of how the system works, if you like. But if it makes you feel any better, remember that it never ends for those in the park, either." And as Max was about to console himself that returning home would at least allow him to find his loved ones again, see people again, resume normal activities, Béliard immediately intercepted his thought.

"There are only three basic rules in the urban zone," he specified. "First, it's forbidden to contact people you knew in life, forbidden to make yourself recognized, forbidden to renew contacts. But that," said Béliard with a knowing air, "shouldn't be a problem."

"And why is that?" Max wanted to know.

"We're going to modify some small aspects of your appearance," Béliard announced, "just some little things. But don't get upset, it's very subtle."

"But I don't want that!" Max protested vehemently. "I refuse."

"I said not to get upset," said Béliard. "When we put you back together the other day, we already took care of a few details."

"What details?" panicked Max, running his hands over his face.

"You see?" said Béliard. "You didn't even notice. You're going to have a little more plastic surgery, nothing very complicated, just a few finishing touches, some minor touch-ups here and there, and after that no one will be able to recognize you. As far as your appearance is concerned, we'll handle the entire thing. As I said, nothing too drastic. And let me reassure you right off the bat, it won't change much of anything for you. People can't imagine how peaceful it is to be incognito.

"The second point is that you also have to change identity, naturally. *That* will be your responsibility to take care of. You'll have to see about obtaining identity papers and such."

"Hold on a minute," Max objected plaintively, "give me a break. I don't know anything about that stuff. I wouldn't have a clue how to go about it."

"That's not my problem," Béliard said harshly, with his former abruptness. But, seeing how lost Max looked, he ended up digging into his pocket and pulling out an address book, which he leafed through. "I could give you an address," he said, "but it's in South America, and I'm not even sure it's still good. Still, I'll try to arrange a little side-trip for you."

"But I don't know that part of the world," Max repeated. "I don't even know how to get there."

"We'll give you a hand at first," said Béliard, "but after that it'll be up to you to find your way. Right. The third rule, as I've already mentioned, is that it's forbidden to resume your old activity. In the broad sense, I mean. That includes any professional practice related to the one you used to have. You won't be able to play artist like before, you understand, you'll have to hold down a real job like everyone else. You'll need to find something. But there again, you'll have a little help at first."

"And what about money?" asked Max.

"We've thought of that," answered Béliard. "We'll also give you a little something to start off with. Well, I think I've covered everything. Your operation is scheduled in twenty minutes, and you'll be leaving immediately afterward. I'll come back to fetch you in a bit."

No sooner had he shut the door behind him than it opened again on Dino, whose smile was a notch below its habitual register. "So you'll be leaving us, Sir," Dino said gravely.

"Yes," Max said in an anxious tone. "They're sending me back home. I don't really know what's going to happen."

"So I heard, Sir. I'm sorry."

"Dino," Max suddenly thought, "could I get a little something to drink? I think I could use one right about now."

"I'm afraid that would be difficult, Sir," said the valet. "Your stay here is over. To tell the truth, I just came to prepare the room for the next occupant, you understand, they never stay empty for long. That's the problem with this job, the turnover is very fast and you never have much time to get to know people."

"I understand," said Max. "I understand."

Béliard reappeared just then, accompanied by the stretcher-bearer, and Max said a quick farewell to the valet. "Right, well, so long, Dino, thanks for everything and sorry to have bothered you."

"Bothered me, Sir?" said Dino. "Come now, not in the slightest, never."

"Yes, I did," said Max. "You know, that question I asked you."

"Really, Sir," went Dino, again displaying his classic smile, this time seasoned with an unaccustomed wink—a direct quote from a scene with Raquel Welch in the film *Bandolero!*, which explicitly answered the question.

"Come on, come on, let's go," said Béliard impatiently.

Back in the operating room, Max was offered no commentary by the surgeon, who in any case wasn't the one from the other day. Nor, to put him under, did they use an injection, as he expected: this time it was an anaesthetizing mask, promptly clamped over his face, that once more plunged him into artificial slumber, without leaving him time to wonder where, when, how, or even if he would someday wake up again.

the next occupant, you understand. They never stay empty for long. That's the problem with this job, the turnover is very fast, and you never have much time to get to know people."

"I understand," said Mrs. [illegible]. "I understand."

Richard reappeared just then, accompanied by two stretcher-bearers, and Max said a quick farewell to the [illegible]. "Goodbye, [illegible]. Doing the best [illegible] everything, and sorry to have bothered you."

"Interesting, Sir?" said [illegible]. "Come now, not in the slightest [illegible]."

"Yes, I did," said [illegible]. "You know, that question I asked you."

[illegible] again [illegible] playing the classic smile, this time [illegible] with an [illegible] — a direct move from a [illegible] Welch in the film [illegible], which [illegible] answered this question.

[illegible] question, is it?" said [illegible] impatiently.

[illegible] the [illegible] Max [illegible] no [illegible] by the surgeon [illegible] the [illegible] the other day. Not [illegible] under [illegible] the [illegible] of this [illegible] was [illegible] the [illegible], [illegible] fact, that [illegible] into [illegible], [illegible] leaving [illegible] wonder [illegible] when [illegible] or even [illegible] would [illegible] up again.

III

20

He was awakened by the chaotic bucking of a hydrofoil, a small yellow craft in the white of dawn slapping over a wide river the color of glue. Opening his eyes, Max noticed, in the distance to his right, a city of respectable proportions and shabby appearance built near the water. "Iquitos," the pilot soberly announced—a young fellow with a pencil mustache, a face of ochre marble, and dark fake Ray-Bans treated with iridium.

Now immobile, the hydrofoil rocked gently on the surface of the waves, in the extreme heat already rising at that hour of the day. After a few minutes, the young fellow clicked a latch on the door, pointing with his chin to a motorized canoe that approached at top speed and then came to a halt next to the vehicle's floats. Max thanked the pilot with a wave of his hand before jumping onto the canoe, which immediately started up again toward the port terminal located upstream from the city. The canoe driver was as uncommunicative as the hydrofoil pilot, and Max was carrying only a small bag of unknown origin, containing a few basic toiletries that he didn't recall having purchased. Nothing else, no change of clothes, just an envelope holding a small bundle in a local currency unfamiliar to him, along with a slip of paper bearing the address of a hotel and a telephone number preceded by the name "Jaime." This bundle might be enough to live on for a short while in a country with a weak exchange rate, which at first glance, from afar, the rather miserable aspect of the place suggested that it might be. Max didn't dare ask the canoe driver where exactly in South America they were; it might have sounded strange, and in any case Max spoke neither Spanish nor Portuguese. Whatever the case, he'd have to figure out how to buy something to wear, for at the moment he had on only a shirt, a pair of canvas pants without a belt, and yellow shoes that pinched his feet.

Located to the northwest of the South American continent, at equal distance from three borders, squeezed between the tropical forest and the Amazon River, Iquitos is a city of three hundred thousand inhabitants built on the right bank of this considerable estuary. It was officially designated an Amazonian port by the sole clause of Law no. 14702 on January 5, 1964. Its average temperature is 96° Fahrenheit. Surrounded by the river and several of its branches, Iquitos might also appear to be a kind of island, since no road leads there; the only way to reach it is by air or water. Along the bank is a series of small docks like the one they were approaching, at the far end of which sat a Ford occupied by two men named Oscar and Esau, who eventually extricated themselves from this vehicle to come greet Max.

Much younger than Esau, more talkative and round, short-sleeved shirt and a gold chain around his neck, Oscar spoke excellent French. Without explicitly naming Béliard, he intimated that he was aware of his influence and the formalities Max needed to handle, before inviting him to get in the car. They turned onto the dilapidated road that must have led to the center of town. Dark suit, tie, slicked-back hair, thick glasses with large frames, Esau contented himself with driving, silently and slowly, the dented old Air-Force-blue Ford. The seats and steering wheel of the car were covered in a yellowish plush, and a horizontal band along the bottom of the windshield was covered by a protective runner of quilted red velour with gold fringes. As this unstable runner constantly slid from its support, falling at the slightest pothole, Esau spent most of his time patiently setting it back in place with one hand, his primary concern apparently being the maintenance of this object that Oscar sometimes helped readjust. Constantly distracted by his task, Esau drove at an average speed of twenty miles an hour, with a fair number of dips to about twelve. When for no apparent reason one of the two windshield wipers spontaneously began working, scraping the heavily pocked windshield with a raucous screech, Esau vainly tried every knob on the dash to shut it off before letting the matter drop. It was getting hotter and hotter in this car with no air conditioning, and as for the protective runner that continued to slip off, Esau let that drop, too.

In Iquitos, at the corner of Fitzcarrald and Putumayo, the room that they had reserved for Max on the second floor of the Hotel Copoazú was as elementary as could be, its window looking directly out onto a solid wall. Iron single bed; little hospital-style TV attached to the flimsy wall; plastic chair; a nightstand holding a lamp, a telephone, and the television remote: nothing more. The bathroom was meager, and Max put off as long as he could checking in the mirror to see what he looked like now. Lying on the bed, the back of his neck twisted by the skinny pillow propped against the metal head rail, he skipped through some forty public and private channels of local, neighboring, and North American origin. The three national stations broadcast election results, which Max, although he grasped very little of the language, seemed to understand were being contested. Still, he couldn't stop thinking about his face, with a mixture of fear and impatience, dreading what he desperately wanted to see.

He finally decided to have a shave, comb his hair, and brush his teeth as an excuse to get himself into the windowless bathroom. As the neon light above the mirror naturally didn't work, he could only view himself in silhouette, but from that perspective, at least, nothing appeared significantly different. He waited another long while in front of the television before calling the front desk to ask in his rudimentary English if someone could come replace the bulb—*Please could you change the light in the bathroom, it doesn't work—Sí, señor*—which also took a fair amount of time. Then, once the repair was made and Max was alone again, he took a deep breath before daring to go look at himself.

Nice work. They hadn't messed up. While Max was patently unrecognizable, you couldn't attribute his transformation to anything in particular. Not his nose, forehead, eyes, cheeks, mouth, or chin—nothing had changed. Everything was there. Rather, it was the arrangement of these features, the relations between them, that had been imperceptibly altered, although Max himself couldn't have said exactly how, in what order or which direction. But the fact was, he wasn't the same anymore—or rather, he was the same but incontestably someone else: his face might appear vaguely familiar to someone who had known him, but it would surely go no further than that. He tried opening his mouth wide to make sure they had left him his teeth: they had. He recognized his old fillings and his little crown, but there again an indefinable new maxillary order seemed to reign.

Perplexed, at once relieved and horrified, Max opened the faucet to pour himself a glass of water. But on the one hand, he was trembling so hard that it took several attempts to fill the vile cup, and on the other the water from the tap, which under European climes has to pass sixty-two quality parameters to be deemed potable, must in Iquitos have had only a tiny little dozen, tops. So Max called down to the front desk again to have them bring up an *agua mineral.* And while they were at it, considering that this kind of thing doesn't happen to you every day, judging moreover that after his week of relative abstinence at the Center he certainly deserved one, why didn't they also bring him a bottle of pisco, with ice and some lemon. Sí, señor. While waiting, he went back to look at himself some more in the mirror. He'd get used to it. He didn't have any choice, of course, but fine, he'd get used to it, maybe even faster than he thought. He switched off the neon, left the bathroom, and, just as he was turning up the sound on the television, someone knocked at his door.

It was the manager with his tray, holding everything Max had asked for. Once the manager had left, Max uncapped the bottle of pisco and eagerly poured himself a drink, but the taste of the alcohol was repulsive, vile, unbearably emetic, and Max had to run to spit it out in the sink. What's going on here. Very strange. And yet pisco is actually quite good. Whatever the case, after having washed and carefully wiped off his glass, Max rinsed out his mouth with agua mineral, opened his bag, removed the envelope, opened the envelope, took out the piece of paper with the telephone number jotted on it, sat down on the bed, pulled the telephone toward him, and dialed.

21

After hanging up the phone, Max left the hotel with his empty little bag, which he spent the afternoon filling by doing some shopping in the streets of Iquitos: clothing suited to the climate—light jacket and shirts, cotton trousers, batch of underwear; basic necessities, such as a belt, razor blades, soap, and shampoo; as well as a larger bag to hold it all plus the folded smaller bag. Back at the hotel, he ate alone, the clink of his silverware producing sinister echoes in the empty restaurant dining room. Then he went upstairs and soon got into bed. He slept fitfully and, having risen early, decided to leave this establishment without further ado.

That morning, Max quickly found two rooms to let in the dilapidated mansion of a former rubber tycoon. The façade of this residence was covered with glazed ceramic tiles, beautifully decorated though now mostly cracked; *azulejos* that, in the days of his splendor and Iquitos's prosperity, the tycoon had had shipped from Portugal via fluvial and maritime routes, on the same ship that carried his dirty laundry each week to the Lisboan cleaners'. The barred windows looked directly out on the Amazon past Avenida Coronel Portillo and, from his room, Max could thus enjoy a view of the wooden houses built on the river itself, some floating, others on stilts. Large seagoing vessels passed by in the distance, motorbikes spluttered on the avenue blacktop, birds circled above the canoe traffic, and small children played in the rubbish. Max absently surveyed this spectacle, daydreaming, developing his thoughts in two directions. First, he would have to get used to living with his new appearance, while waiting for the documents bearing his new identity that they would deliver in a few days at the airport cafeteria, as agreed the day before on the phone. Second, while his rent for the two rooms wasn't exorbitant, Max had nonetheless felt a twinge of worry when calculating the fraction it deducted from his little bundle. The identity forgers surely weren't in it for the good of the cause, and what he had left wouldn't take him very far. We'd see.

Resigned to spending his money, he soon came across a place where he could take his meals: the Regal restaurant, located in an iron building on Plaza de Armas, above the British consulate. The iron had the drawback of amplifying the heat like a cymbal, but you could eat fish from the river while watching the girls who strolled across the square in tight, inaccessible groups and the men who gathered around the sewer drains, amusing themselves by fishing for rats with some line and a bit of omelet tied to the end. And here, as in every tropical restaurant in the world, you could see huge fans reflected in the concavity of the saucers, spoons, and ladles like gigantic insects or tiny helicopters. Max stared at all of this with an interested but detached eye, the eye of a man resuscitated, restored to the world and looking at this world as if through a pane of glass.

As he didn't speak to anyone and no one spoke to him, his main activity consisted in systematically and thoroughly perusing the local and national press, which soon gave him an elementary grasp of Spanish. On the heels of an obviously fixed recount, the controversy over the electoral results still occupied the front pages in bold headlines, but Max was more interested in the back sections. Entirely photographic, these related in detail the social lives of the local and neighboring ruling classes. Thus one could see, in the context of various inaugurations, receptions, premiers, marriages, and cocktail parties, groups of personalities flashing wide smiles at the paparazzi with glasses in hand. Evening gowns, tuxedos, champagne, and pisco sours, general gaiety, dizzying multiplicity of faces, none of which, of course, was familiar to Max. The latter, whose stay at the Center had neither made him forget his cares nor lose his habits, continued to verify automatically if Rose might perchance figure in one of these photos. Naturally, such a hypothesis was highly improbable, but when you got down to it, having disappeared so completely, she could just as easily turn up married to an Argentine banker or a Guatemalan industrialist, or maybe a Paraguayan senator.

One can get used to Iquitos fairly quickly—more so than to those yellow shoes that Max still hadn't managed to replace. It's fairly easy to get around, and one finds oneself not too badly off. Apart from his money worries, which he kept putting off thinking about seriously, Max felt like he was on vacation by the end of his third day. But that was the day of his meeting with the identity broker, at Francisco Secada Vigneta Airport, located two and a half miles from the center of town. To get there, Max had to take one of those motocars whose drivers offered him their services pretty much nonstop. The motocar, a covered scooter with a seat in back, is the Amazonian equivalent of the rickshaw, though lacking the side panels and with a slightly different body from its Indian counterpart. Unlike the latter, it is not spangled with political or pious decals—just a tiger or two, at times, painted on the seat—and isn't equipped with a meter. But as we all know, a rickshaw meter isn't worth much. We all know just how unreliable it can be, and so the fare for a ride is debated from the start no less bitterly with a *motocarista* than with a Tabul rickshaw-wallah, a Beninese *zemidjian,* or a Laotian *túk-túk* driver. As for the comfort provided by each of these vehicles, it is more or less comparable in every case.

Arriving at the airport, Max had no difficulty finding the cafeteria nor, virtually alone in the middle of it, the aforementioned Jaime to whom he'd spoken three days earlier on the telephone, sitting before a steaming double espresso. Jaime must have been about Max's age; the small, ironic spectacles of a presbyopic filtered his knowing gaze. Left arm in a cast buried under a sweater buried under a jacket buried under a coat buried under a scarf buried under a hat—but, despite the steamroom atmosphere, these superimpositions did not seem to bother him overmuch. No sooner had they started talking than an old shoeshine boy, haggard and dressed in rags, came to squat at Max's feet and, without asking his permission, immediately began to furbish his shoes, which Max let him do without overseeing the operation.

"Right," said Jaime, "everything is almost ready. All we need now is an ID photo. If we could have it by the day after tomorrow, the papers could be ready at the end of the week."

"Fine. And tell me," worried Max, "do you know exactly how much this is going to cost?"

"Hard to say just yet," Jaime eluded. "We haven't drawn up the final invoice."

Then, concerning the shoeshine boy who had finished his task and was now standing, trembling lightly in silence and staring fixedly at Max, the latter asked the same question.

"And what about him? How much should I give him?"

"A one-sol coin will do," decreed Jaime.

Max paid the shoeshine boy without looking at him and arranged a second rendezvous with the forger, who then walked away. Left alone, Max cast a glance at his shoes. For lack of yellow shoe polish, no doubt, Max's footwear had been made violet, a beautiful and spectacular violet. Maybe they really weren't any worse like that, but still. Max stood up and left the airport, staring at the new color of his feet. Well, if one was going to change identity, might as well start from the ground up.

22

The days that followed didn't go nearly so well. Time passed ever more slowly and Max grew ever more concerned about money. For whatever one might think, despite his stay at the Center and the tragic event that had preceded it, his personal situation did not prevent him from experiencing the classic feelings and needs of the organism. Hunger, heat, thirst (even without pisco), the desire for elementary creature comforts—all this raises problems that only money can solve. The humblest lifestyle is still subject to a budget. But Max could see his resources dwindling visibly, inexorably.

Added to this was an increasing sense of isolation. While discovering Iquitos had initially been enough to occupy him without his needing to speak to anyone, by now Max had had tourism up to here; by now he couldn't stand the solitude of this godforsaken hole anymore. No way to share a few words with anyone on Plaza de Armas, neither the pretty girls nor the rat fishermen. And if he sometimes managed, in his budding little Spanish, to chat a bit with natives, mainly the aging waiters of the Regal, it was only to hear pessimistic and resigned news of the city: exploding suicide rate, omnipresence of religious cults, massive drug traffic, practice of black magic, and then some. All this was pretty discouraging and didn't exactly inspire Max to try to settle here. He had bouts of depression, days of boredom, the kind of listless boredom engendered by the union of solitude and modest means. He sometimes lost all desire to walk around Iquitos, what's the point, and once he even spent the entire day shut up in his two rooms, pacing restlessly between them, a caged beast who only stopped now and then to contemplate, through the bars of his window, the river with its unchanging colors.

That day, to take his mind off things, Max decided to write to his sister, thereby breaking the strict regulations that Béliard had recited to him. He spent a good hour composing his letter, in which he explained everything, recounted everything, complained about everything, and even had the nerve in conclusion to ask Alice for money. But once he had signed, read, and folded his letter, slipped it into an envelope and licked the adhesive strip, the annoyances began. First, Max cut his upper lip on the flap of the envelope—a wound that, although very fine and benign, proved to be disproportionately painful; second, the rancid fish taste of the glue spreading through his mouth was abominable; third, Max stopped to think about the trouble he was courting if Béliard were to press an investigation, now that he'd left behind some compromising saliva—the Center's doctors surely hadn't gone so far as to alter his DNA. And finally, reflecting on, fourth, the extreme distress Alice might feel on receiving it, Max opened the envelope, read his letter over one last time, then ripped it up and burned the pieces.

At the Tropical Paradise Lodge on Putumayo Boulevard, where he had gone to swipe a few leaflets for reading matter, he was offered the opportunity to take his mind off things by enjoying a canoe ride down the river. It would be another expense, of course, but what the hell, the half-day was still within his means. From several angles, the dark blocks of the Amazonian forest sometimes called to mind certain areas of the park he'd visited with Béliard. Infested with mosquitoes, the waterways were lined with trees that grew following a bizarre logic, as if prey to a hereditary insanity, which went no small way toward fostering a sense of unease. They came across other canoes, rowed by silent locals transporting crates, bags, trash bins, or chickens in cages. They saw dogs, and once a fat iguana on a protruding branch, or more precisely a fat, female, pregnant, flabby iguana, which the canoe driver tried to capture to steal her egg—nothing tastier, the man assured him, than soft-boiled iguana egg.

On the appointed day, Max took another motocar back to the airport. Jaime was there, again swaddled in the convection-oven temperature, this time sitting before a hot chocolate. He handed Max a small pouch made of embroidered cotton—local craftsmanship, handmade, he pointed out, a gift—containing the perfect copy of a French passport in the name of Salvador, Paul André Marie, French nationality, born on the same day as Max with Max's photo beneath, accompanied by zero children on page four and authentic French fiscal stamps on page five. On page seven, in the first empty space reserved for visas, there was even a stamp attesting to his arrival in the country's capital, several weeks earlier, at Jorge Chávez International airport. It all looked impeccable.

While Max leafed through this object, Jaime withdrew from his pocket and handed him a folded sheet of paper on which a long number was inscribed. This number, the amount of the invoice for the passport, corresponded precisely, down to the last centavo, to what Max was carrying that very moment in the pockets of his new pants: apparently they had kept close tabs on him, watched over his slightest expenditures, meticulously calculated what he had left, and now Max was utterly broke. As this must have shown on his face: "What's the matter?" said Jaime. "Is something wrong?" Max didn't have time to answer before the other, smiling as if he had been waiting only for this, was already making him a proposition so classic and devoid of imagination that it's embarrassing to report it. It would involve, as is only too common in this sort of caper, transporting a certain something abroad—to France, as it happened—for a certain remuneration. The situation is so clichéd that there isn't even any need to specify the nature of this something, enclosed in a lizard-skin valise with locked, gilded-metal clasps, that Jaime, bending down, pulled from under the table and set on top.

"Here, this is all you'll have to carry," he explained. "It's nothing. Discreet, easy work, and paid. Not in local currency, trust me on that. You'll get dollars, the freshest bills around."

"Sure," said Max, "I don't mind, but when would I be going?"

"Right away," answered Jaime. "Your plane leaves in forty-five minutes."

"And what about my things?" worried Max.

"No problem," said Jaime, bending down once more, "I've got them right here. They stopped by your place to pick them up after you left." He handed over the belongings, carefully folded in their bag, and here are your tickets and here's your money. Max took a moment to count this money: dollars indeed, but very few of them, barely enough to last two or three days in Iquitos, in other words two or three hours in France. But for now, what else could he do?

"Right," said Max. "Sure."

23

Max, his valise, and his bag did not have long to wait: immediate boarding. In the lounge at Iquitos airport, locals departing for Lima crossed paths with clusters of vacationers come to tread the limbo of the Amazonian forest, study the natives, consult their shamans, and have their minds exploded by the ingestion of *ayahuasca*. The luggage of both groups was carefully and suspiciously sniffed by two dogs kept on a leash and muzzled, whose absence of reaction at the passage of the lizard-skin valise at least allowed for the hope that it didn't contain any narcotics. Then, as soon as Max was seated in the small plane, the latter began moving at top speed, attaining its altitude and cruising velocity in the blink of an eye, attesting to the professionalism of the pilots. This country, in fact, maintains a long tradition of virtuoso aviators, taking off at the appointed time and landing at the exact moment without getting bogged down in considerations or niceties—never hesitating to dive toward their goal, for instance, almost on a vertical trajectory and ignoring the stages of decompression entirely, heedless of the passengers who clap their hands in unison over their eardrums and yowl in pain.

On the other hand, Max had a longer wait in Lima, where he passed the time by reading through the newspapers, pleased to note his dazzling progress in Spanish but anxious about what awaited him in Paris. Then, once on board, he dispensed with the mimodrama of safety precautions performed by the stewardesses, who then distributed among the passengers orange juice and candies, blankets, and headphones featuring various musical programs. A knob embedded in the armrests allowed one to choose among these programs: selections of easy listening, jazz, ethnic, and classical music. As the airplane began to taxi, Max put on his headphones to have something to do, automatically stopping at the classical selection where he immediately identified an *Impromptu* by Schubert in midstream, the Allegro in E-flat from Op. 90. But no sooner had he recognized the work than he also recognized his own performance, recorded five years earlier at Cerumen. He pretended not to notice, the way one feigns not to see a bothersome acquaintance in the street, except that this time the acquaintance was himself. He immediately changed programs, then finally gave up; in any case the headphones were hurting his ears like an ill-fitted prosthesis. Max preferred listening to the sound of the Boeing engines, which was deep and penetrating, fundamental like an endless breath, not like those little Airbus motors that give off the sound of an old rototiller. Then he eventually fell asleep.

It was raining hard in Paris when the airplane touched down at Roissy-Charles-de-Gaulle, the kind of heavy rain that seems to fall from very high up and that Max had noticed, several days earlier, from the windows of the Center. After customs, where, nothing to declare, no one bothered to inspect the contents of his bag and valise, he passed through the doorway to the main hall unimpeded. There, facing the flow of arrivals, several individuals seemed to be waiting: two wives equipped with children ready to throw their arms around the first available neck, three unknown persons holding cardboard signs with names on them. Max did not immediately react when he spotted, on one of them, his new identity written in capitals; then, remembering, he walked straight up to it.

The unknown holding it was absurdly wearing a beard, hat, dark glasses, and a raincoat buttoned to his Adam's apple. Still brandishing Max's name card even as he watched the latter approach, he dangled at the end of his other arm a suitcase of moderate size that he immediately held out to Max, without, for lack of available prehensile organ, shaking his hand.

"I'm Schmidt," he said, "and here are your belongings. I trust you have the valise."

"Here," said Max, handing it over.

"Good," said Schmidt, taking it. "Let's go get a cab."

A fairly short waiting line at the taxi stand, after which the so-called Schmidt gave the driver an address, an odd number on Boulevard Magenta. Max discreetly studied this improbable Schmidt, with his exaggerated surplus of anonymity attributes—although in truth, he wasn't certain they were really artifices; all of it could have been entirely normal for him. Then, deciding to cut short his contemplation—Schmidt probably didn't much appreciate people looking at him—Max turned in the other direction to ponder the landscape. It felt like he was coming home after a very long absence, even though his combined stays at the Center and in Iquitos had probably lasted no more than two weeks, but under the circumstances it was understandable to think that way. Through the taxi window, he saw the flat low-rises and tall towers of the eastern suburbs that are visible around Bagnolet, when you return from the airport on Highway A3. Max had always found it hard to believe that these buildings contained real apartments housing real people, with real kitchens and real bathrooms, real bedrooms where they authentically coupled, actually reproduced—it was scarcely imaginable.

But as it happened, the lodgings picked out for him by the services of the Center would be hardly more desirable. Schmidt, after remaining mute on the highway, specified the route to follow once they hit the peripheral boulevard and, on Boulevard Magenta, halfway between Place de la République and Gare de l'Est, the taxi pulled up at a hotel. While not exactly luxurious, this establishment, named the Montmorency, wasn't quite a fleabag, either. It possessed a lobby, two conference rooms, and a bar. They didn't take the elevator: without stopping at the front desk, where a shapeless receptionist was marking time, Schmidt immediately signaled Max to follow him up a steep staircase that did not appear to have been built for the use of the clientele. On the uppermost floor, two rows of brown doors, opposite each other and very closely spaced, filed down a dark yellow hallway. Schmidt pulled a key from his pocket and the fourth door on the right opened onto a narrow room, wallpapered with faded flowers and garnished with skinny furniture plus an overly large bed, with a sink as its sole sanitary facility.

"Here you are," said Schmidt, "this is your home. There's a shower down the hall and toilet on the landing."

Max walked up to the French window, pulled back the curtains, whose metal rings squeaked on the metal rod, and opened it onto the tumult of the boulevard that immediately began roaring and bounding into the cramped space.

"One problem," Max reminded him, immediately pulling the window shut. "I have practically no money."

"The first month's rent is taken care of," Schmidt indicated. "After that, it'll be up to you to pay out of your salary."

"Salary," Max repeated uncomprehendingly.

"Of course salary," the other confirmed. "You've been assigned to the bar. I'll show you."

They therefore went down to the cellar of the establishment. As the bar was empty at that hour of the morning, Schmidt introduced him to his future work area, the multicolored collection of bottles, the glasses of all sizes, the utensils, saucers, shakers, strainers, citrus presses, and spice racks. On a hanger in the closet hung a worn red jacket; a gilded metal rectangle was already pinned to its lapel with the name Paul S. engraved on it.

"Here you are," said Schmidt, "your work uniform. You have two days to get over jet lag, and on Monday you start. The management knows the story, if there are any problems you take it up with them. We will surely not have occasion to meet again, good luck."

Back up in his room, Max pulled from his bag the items he had bought in Iquitos: garments that were too exotic and lightweight for the climate here, still impregnated with tropical aromas that he breathed in nostalgically before putting them away in the narrow white melamine armoire. Then he opened the valise that Schmidt had given him. It contained a dark gray suit, a pair of black pants, two white shirts, a black tie, and three pouch briefs, as well as a pair of black shoes wrapped in a newspaper from the day before. All these clothes, of synthetic fabric, approximate size, and mediocre quality, seemed to have been worn by countless others before being put through numerous industrial washes. Welcome to the urban zone.

24

Max spent his two days off walking around Paris. First he tried a few experiments in his old neighborhood of Château-Rouge, as a way of verifying the effect produced by the plastic surgeons' work. He went incognito to see the shopkeepers he had habitually frequented, whom he used to call by name, and who for their part had ended up, despite his not exactly sociable nature, considering him a nominal regular. He observed their reactions when he entered their shops, making a few small purchases—a pack of Kleenex here, the evening paper there—looking them in the eye more and more intently, but without the others ever showing the slightest sign of recognition.

It even happened on the first day that, as he was leaving his ex-pharmacy, he ran smack into the woman with the dog, flanked by the latter to her left and her husband to her right. It was the first time Max had seen the three of them together; they looked rather content to be that way but showed no reaction when they crossed his path: they even met his gaze for a few seconds, then walked off as if he didn't exist. Only the dog, after a brief latency period, turned back toward Max with a perplexed face, braking for an instant and knitting his brow—that odor reminds me of something, confound it, I've already sniffed that somewhere, but where? To give himself time to study the question in depth, the animal even stopped to piss lengthily against the right rear tire of a Fiat Panda while examining Max, who for his part, wanting to verify once more the transformation of his appearance, leaned discreetly and symmetrically toward the vehicle's left rearview mirror. Then, yanked by his leash, the dog seemed to drop the matter, letting his attention drift toward a band of soaked, hirsute, rumpled pigeons who—the proof that they're aware of their filth—had come to take a lustral bath in a gutter of flowing water before flying heavily off again.

Since he was in the neighborhood, Max decided to brave it still further by going to see his sister. He would just try to get a look at her, without making contact, merely to reassure himself that she was all right. He would proceed carefully, without exposing himself to Alice's view, for, despite the know-how of the Center specialists and given what had just happened with the dog, it wasn't far-fetched to think that his own sister—blood thicker than water, etc.—would recognize him for real. Accordingly, he took up a position not far from the entrance to his building, inanely hidden behind a newspaper; and in fact, after an hour or two of waiting, he saw Alice come out, stop in front of the doorway, and look at her watch. And then, surprise surprise, here was Parisy emerging from the building in turn to come join her and take her arm. Parisy's bearing, a slight nonchalance in his suit along with something lighter, more familiar, in his behavior, suggested that the impresario had finally made it with Max's sister, perhaps had moved in with her, and perhaps had, troubling perspective, even taken over Max's studio. It nonetheless seemed to Max, from a distance, that Alice was speaking a bit harshly to Parisy, who answered while waving his other arm in agitation—in short, it seemed like they were already fighting. Max watched them walk away, not following them, then set off again. He continued to look at all the people he came across in the street, wondering about each one's status: maybe there were others like him, who had passed through the Center before coming back here;

maybe there were many of them; maybe, when you got down to it, they were even in the majority.

Once his two days of recuperation were over, Max, as scheduled, began his new vesperal service as a bartender. It turned out that the bar was not only empty in the morning; it was that way almost all the time. Not empty enough, however, for Max to take it entirely easy: there was always, at some advanced hour of the evening, one customer or other, sometimes alone but much more often accompanied by a woman. And Max, noticing that it was usually the same woman but not the same customer, and that their brief stays at the bar (whispered confabulations in which numbers played a part) most often concluded with the ordering of two drinks or a bottle to be brought to a room, soon understood what was what. So there weren't a lot of people there to pass the time with, which didn't keep him from being asked now and again for atypical cocktails that were a real pain to make. Alcohol itself was no longer something to pass the time with: it seemed that, since his attempted pisco in Iquitos, Max's appetite for it had curiously evaporated.

And every night at around one-thirty, he returned to his room after having counted the till and wiped down the bar. He took off his red jacket and the rest and immediately went to bed, reviewing his cocktail recipes in a specialized book and taking pains to memorize them. Then he had trouble falling asleep in his large bed, for large beds, let's not forget, are made for two people to find each other in beneath the sheets, and these sheets themselves are designed to be folded as a couple. Just see how a man trying to fold his large sheet alone soon ends up in an awkward position, entangled in himself as much as in the sheet; see how his short arms struggle to attain the required breadth. Whereas a couple, folding the sheet together while talking about other things, have it much easier—not to mention the additional interest, the intimate strategy, of anticipating, on either side of the dividing sheet, which direction the other will turn it in so as to harmonize with his or her movement.

But then see, too, how things work out. After several painful weeks of solitude in the depths of his red jacket, Max ended up meeting someone. As often happens in life, this would occur at his place of work, at the hotel itself. The receptionist. Not at all as shapeless as he had originally thought. She was, on the contrary, a tall reddish-blonde, not super great-looking but not too bad, always dressed fairly sexy, with high heels up to there. He might have noticed her earlier, but the truth is, during his first days at the Hotel Montmorency, Max hadn't noticed anything at all, not even that it was raining all the time.

Now one day, when the sky was good enough to clear up, Max ran into the receptionist not far from the hotel, right in the street, lit by a shaft of gentle sunlight. She was with a small boy in the four-five range who was complaining in an anxious voice that something black kept following him, that something was there and it didn't want to go away. "It's just your shadow, sweetie," the young woman explained. "It's nothing. Well, it's not nothing, but it's just your shadow." That sentence convinced Max, who felt pretty shadowy himself, to take an interest in this young lady. He would proceed gradually. He had time.

He had time but things nonetheless went faster than expected. One Wednesday Max suggested they go for coffee—okay. Bought her some flowers—very okay. Then invited her to dinner, next Sunday when he wasn't on duty at the bar—all the more okay in that the receptionist's son would be spending the night at his grandma's. Risked complimenting her overtly—absolutely okay, and Max, as it happened, neither restrained nor recognized himself: you're so feminine, he told her, tracing rounded figures in the air, you're the very definition of feminine. To which she responded with a very pretty laugh. She was a single mother named Félicienne. What a beautiful name, Max enthused. And how well it suits you. So well, in fact, that their evening ended in a hotel, neither very far nor very different from the Montmorency.

25

Then, after his shift the next evening, Max went to see Félicienne at her place, and on the nights that followed he would no longer sleep much in his room at the hotel. The receptionist lived in a three-room apartment, hardly bigger than Bernie's on Rue Murillo: a living room and two bedrooms, the larger one being occupied by the kid, whose IQ they hadn't gauged yet and who answered, or didn't, depending on his mood, to the name of William—though in general, they just called him "the kid."

At first, Max spent only his nights at Félicienne's, joining her after having closed his register and changed jackets, but always escaping from her place the moment he woke up. After breakfast in a nearby café, he would go back to the hotel to take a shower, then head off again to walk around Paris, sometimes stopping in a movie theater—better to see a film than to watch the time pass on the ceiling of his inhospitable room, stretched out on his bed as if dead. But little by little Félicienne persuaded him to have breakfast with her, use the bathroom after her, accompany her to the babysitter's to drop off the kid, then escort her to the Montmorency. Not quite to the entrance: no sense in the whole staff knowing about them. They usually separated one block beforehand.

That was in the first stage, for it happened that things moved quickly—very, then too quickly. Max soon found himself being given a copy of the door key, along with a shelf in the closet for his change of clothes, which would rapidly land in the laundry hamper next to the washing machine, after which, since according to Félicienne Max had nothing to do all day long, he saw himself being handed the clothes iron. Responsibility for this iron was soon followed by the bestowing of shopping lists, on which figured a fleet of cleaning products whose directions Félicienne taught him to read and then apply, having already introduced him to the mop and broom closet, which would keep him busy until it was time to go pick up the kid at the babysitter's. From that point on, Max went to the movies less often, now spending the free time he had left after shopping and cleaning in front of Félicienne's VCR, taking advantage of her subscription to a video club.

This evolution is hardly enviable, but then again, since things were going okay with Félicienne sexually, this shared life was basically as good as any other. For lack of other alternatives, at least there was this. And so the time passed. Getting off his shift, Max joined Félicienne who was asleep, who on awakening gave him a little love before heading off to the hotel to receive the customers and answer the phone, leaving Max, sorry, leaving Paul to take care of the housework, and returning home just as he was heading off in turn to don his red jacket and concoct spritzes, bronxes, manhattans, and flips for a clientele that, truth be told, was rapidly deteriorating. Plainly put, the vague provincial businessmen who took advantage of their brief stay in Paris to buy themselves a girl for the night were being replaced by a growing population of locals who fancied that kind of girl, and who often weren't even guests of the hotel; in short, there were more and more hookers, often the same ones and often quite nice. Max wasn't offended—on the contrary—by this shift in population, which paid less attention to the dosage and quality of the cocktails that he still had some trouble mixing by the book.

Given their work conditions, Félicienne and Max hardly saw each other anymore, except on Sundays when they took the kid out for some air—which kid, initially standoffish with Max, ended up letting himself be won over to the point of becoming very familiar, then more and more familiar, and soon much too familiar for Max's taste. They went to the Champ-de-Mars on Sundays, they went to Les Halles, to the park, they went for a walk down the Champs-Elysées. It always gave Max a funny feeling when Félicienne suggested Parc Monceau. He no longer dreaded the statue of Gounod next to the drinking fountain, nor even the one of Chopin not far from the children's playground, where the kid constantly stamped his feet to have yet another turn on the whatever.

Nonetheless, Max began to feel bored. While he'd grown accustomed fairly quickly to his new physical appearance, strangely enough he had much more trouble with being called Paul, but perhaps someday he'd get used to that as well. And so time passed as if in a waiting room, with a sense of leafing through magazines as worn-out, faded, and mind-numbing as Félicienne herself. On top of which, what did he really know about Félicienne, other than that she dwelled on insane claims about the past, bitterly insisting that in her youth she'd had measurements to kill for, a gift for languages, and perfect pitch? But, raised in modest surroundings, she'd had to enter working life early, thereby sacrificing a triple career as a world-famous top model, international interpreter, and renowned concert performer, having been forced to abandon the piano. Max, slicing the Sunday roast, masked with his indifference the intense relief produced by this third bit of information.

Indifference, yes, they would reach that point. Soon the arrangement with Félicienne would no longer be working so well. It's just that love—well, when I say love, I'm not sure it's the right word—is not only evanescent, but soluble. Soluble in time, money, alcohol, daily life, and a host of other things besides. Sexually, for example, it was not at all going well, Félicienne refusing his advances more and more often. In fact it was going so badly that Max, often, dreamily played a record he'd found one day at a discounter's near the Porte Saint-Denis, *The Best of Peggy Lee*, about which Félicienne, demonstrating a real hostility as if she suspected something, would sourly ask him how he could waste his time listening to that shit.

"No, no," said Max, "no reason. I just like it."

Nor did it help matters that he found it harder and harder to stand the kid, who, technologically very precocious, demanded the VCR for his own exclusive use, depriving Max of being able to watch one of the two videos with Dean Martin—his all-time greatest roles, in *Some Came Running* and *Rio Bravo*—purchased that same day at the same discounter's.

Several increasingly lackluster weeks flowed by like this until one night when, in the bar, while turning over and over the different ways of putting an end to this business with Félicienne, Max was artlessly preparing an alexandra—the composition of which is not all that complicated: three equal parts cognac, whipped cream, and crème de cacao. As he was struggling with the whipped cream, which was too firm after a prolonged stay in the cooler, he saw a man come in at the far end of the room, fairly short in stature and flanked by an immense redhead dressed in almost nothing.

Max knew the redhead a little, one of the new regulars he liked well enough, a sweet girl who ran on whisky-fizz, which is a refreshing drink served directly in a tumbler, very simple to prepare. Too absorbed in his task, he paid no attention to her new admirer, who sat down with her at a little table in the back, then who, standing up again after a few seconds, started walking toward Max, no doubt to impart what he wanted to drink. Now, Max had better things to do at that moment than to take an order, having just spilled all the whipped cream into the shaker, and, head down, he was just about to rebuff the outsider, when: "Mister Max?" went the outsider.

26

Max jumped, sending the whipped cream spewing even farther and raising his eyes to the outsider. Bernie.

"Mister Max," Bernie repeated with delight. "What are you doing here?"

"It's a long story," said Max, wiping a spurt of cream from his sleeve. "But how did you recognize me?"

Bernie didn't seem to understand the question. "Well, it's you," he said. "Why?" (One's true friends, Max melted inside.) "I'm really happy to see you," declared Bernie. "I've often wondered what became of you."

As he didn't seem to know about any of it, Max avoided going into the matter. "And how about you?" he asked. "What have you been up to?"

"I had some problems with Parisy," answered Bernie, "didn't he tell you? I got fed up, you see, he wasn't true to his word, and I left right after your concert at Gaveau, do you remember? I haven't seen him since."

"Of course," eluded Max, understanding that Bernie, who still maintained he never read the papers, must not have heard about what had happened to him, neither his disappearance nor, of course, the rest.

"But I immediately found something much better," Bernie continued. "I'm in show business now. I've completely broken with the classical crowd. I organize shows. Well, not exactly—I'm a concert promoter, if you like, and it's going pretty well. Ah, I never would have expected to find you here."

"Yes," said Max, "I needed to get away from what I was doing before, you understand, the milieu and all that. I needed a break myself."

"Right, right," Bernie said dubiously. "So you're happy here?"

"Not really," said Max, "but it's just for now. It's temporary."

"Even so, a man of your stature," lamented Bernie, "ending up here. I've never been to this place, but it doesn't strike me as all that great. I was just coming in for a drink with my friend."

"Of course," said Max, with a wide smile for the friend, which caused Bernie to glance down at his shoes.

"Listen," he said timidly, "if you ever wanted to make a change, I might be able to help."

"You think?" Max pretended to wonder with a detached air.

"Oh, definitely," said Bernie. "I'm sure I could find you something. Are you still playing the piano?"

"Well, actually, that's a bit complicated," said Max. "But anyway, what can I get you in the meantime?"

"It's mostly cocktails here, right?" went Bernie.

"Alas," admitted Max.

"Well, in that case, I'll have a rainbow," Bernie stated. "Hold on a minute, I'll ask my friend what she's drinking."

"Skip it," said Max. "I think I know."

When Bernie returned the next day, alone, Max was wiping his tumblers while casting distracted glances at the two or three girls settled in that evening with their clients. While he was relieved that someone had finally recognized him, he was also a bit concerned over flouting Béliard's instructions. But after all, he himself hadn't done anything; it was Bernie who had recognized him, Bernie who had acted on his own, Bernie who was coming back to see him. It was also Bernie who had looked into things: an acquaintance of his named Gilbert had just opened an establishment off Rue d'Alésia.

"Very up-and-up," stressed Bernie, with a gesture toward the girls. "Not at all like here. Kind of a nightclub, very distinguished, very quiet, and they're looking for a pianist. What do you say?"

"In principle, I really shouldn't," said Max, "but what the hell." Yes, what the hell, what would the staff of the Center know? Of course, it would again mean working in a bar—which, given Max's past, bordered on just retribution, or repetition compulsion—but it was perhaps, and particularly, a welcome chance to rid himself of Félicienne. Although he didn't quite know how to go about it, as he explained in detail to his former bodyguard. "I tell you, Bernie, I can't take any more of that woman. And I don't have the first clue how to get away from her."

"Nothing could be simpler, Mister Max. Here's what we'll do."

27

And the following Sunday, after they had walked the kid, Max announced to Félicienne that he was taking her out to dinner that very evening, which would give him an opportunity to introduce her to an old friend of his.

They met in front of a large seafood restaurant on Place de l'Odéon. Bernie was already waiting, very elegant, standing very straight in a chic black unstructured suit, nothing like the outfits Max was used to seeing him in. The latter only had the sordid gray combo left by Schmidt to put on; a striped tie bought by Félicienne failed to raise its sartorial level. From the moment they went in, the staff treated them with an attentiveness that rivaled the restaurant in the Center. Félicienne, impressed by the setting and Bernie's elegance, tried not to show it. As she went to powder her nose before they were shown to their table, Max briefly took Bernie aside.

"There's just one thing I forgot to mention," he said.

"Yes, Mister Max?" said Bernie.

"Listen carefully, tonight you don't call me that, okay? Just call me Paul. I'll explain later."

"That's fine with me," said Bernie. "It's my stepson's name. It'll be easy to remember."

It must be obvious by now that Max is not exactly the world's jolliest fellow, the most relaxed or talkative person around, but as soon as they sat down at their table, he became someone else. Maintaining a smile that was by turns affectionate, complicit, seductive, kind, relaxed, and generous, he took the floor from the start and did not let it go, segueing gracefully between myriad anecdotes and light pleasantries, attentions and compliments, bon mots and witticisms, subtle observations and rare quotations, imaginary memories and historical comparisons, without ever getting bogged down or seeming like he was hogging the spotlight. Bernie writhed in laughter at the slightest word out of Max's mouth, while Félicienne, dazzled, looked at him with new tenderness and wide, emotion-filled eyes.

From aperitif to dessert, Max thus staged a spectacular performance. Hanging on his every syllable, Félicienne and Bernie smiled and laughed nonstop, she turning several times to Bernie to take this charming friend of Paul's as witness to her happiness, Paul's charming friend sometimes laying a discreet hand on Félicienne's shoulder to punctuate his hilarity. At times both of them looked at each other, delighted like enthusiastic spectators sitting in contiguous seats by the luck of the ticket sales, who spontaneously, without knowing each other, connect in their enchantment. Charming ambiance, delectable evening. From the diners sitting around them to the waiters themselves, the whole room threw seduced, almost envious glances at this trio led by a Max in excellent form.

When suddenly, at the turn of a phrase, he immobilized both the fork above his plate and his smile, freeze-frame on the image, his gaze fixed on Félicienne and Bernie in a glacial stare. Disconcerted silence around the table.

"No, really, both of you," he said in a changed voice, "you think I haven't noticed your little game? You seriously believe I don't see what you're up to? You somehow imagine I'm going to put up with this right under my nose?"

And, standing up, Max pulled from his inside pocket a wad of bills that he dropped on the table before taking his leave forever, without another word, wearing a bitter expression of wounded pride.

And the next morning, he met Bernie in a café near Châtelet.

"So," said Max, "how was I?"

"Excellent, Mister Max," said Bernie. "You were perfect."

"I owe it all to you, you know," said Max. "It was your idea. How did she take it?"

"The poor woman," said Bernie. "She didn't know what hit her. She needed consoling, so I took it upon myself. I saw her home and then, you know how it is."

"Very good," said Max, "you did well."

"So there you have it," said Bernie. "I'm seeing her again on Thursday."

"Just be careful," Max warned. "She's not exactly an easy customer."

"Oh," said Bernie, "I'm used to that. But now where are you going to live?"

"I don't want to go back to the hotel," Max indicated.

"No problem," said Bernie, "you can just come stay at my place."

"I've been to your place," Max recalled. "It's kind of small."

"I've moved since," said Bernie. "Now I live on Boulevard du Temple. It's not as fashionable as Monceau, but I have a lot more room. I have the income for it now—you saw my suit last night, didn't you?"

"Speaking of which," said Max, "I owe you for dinner."

"Oh, don't worry about it, Mister Max," said Bernie. "We'll deal with that later. In the meantime, let's go see Gilbert."

The establishment that Gilbert had recently opened was large, dark, and silent at this hour, as was Gilbert himself at all hours. The decor was elegant, sober, and distinguished, as Gilbert turned out to be as well.

"So you're a pianist," he said.

"Gosh," Max qualified, "let's say I used to be."

"Mister Max is a great artist," Bernie testified, his eyes bulging.

"You see," said Gilbert, "the fact is, I need someone reliable. I know all about the problems you can have with musicians. Would you mind submitting to a small audition?"

"Really, Gilbert," Bernie said indignantly, "you can't just insult him like that. You forget you're dealing with an artist of international stature."

"No problem," said Max, "as you wish. What would you like to hear? Classical or piano bar—whatever you prefer."

As Gilbert left the choice up to him, he performed the chain "Laura," "Liza," "Celia," followed by one or two polonaises.

"That should do perfectly," judged Gilbert, but just at that moment the door to the establishment banged open and, visibly furious, Béliard made his appearance.

28

Without a word of greeting, without a glance at Gilbert or Bernie, Béliard walked straight up to Max with a determined step.

"What did I tell you?" he started screaming. "If you think we're not watching, you've got another think coming. What you're doing here is a double violation, it's not right, it's a double infraction of the rules. Not only did you let yourself be recognized—"

"You can't blame me for that," Max interrupted him, pointing to Bernie. "*He* recognized *me.* It's your doctors' fault for not doing their job properly."

"Maybe so," shouted Béliard, "but then on top of it you're practicing your former profession."

"Not in the slightest," pled Max, pointing to the piano. "I was just showing these gentlemen what I can do."

"Fine," said Béliard, calming down a bit too quickly, "I'll let you off this time."

He had changed since the Center. He no longer displayed the haughty, distant, and condescending composure that had antagonized Max as of their first meeting. He now seemed hypertense, on an emotional hair-trigger, flying off the handle just as quickly as he'd then let the matter drop. Gilbert and Bernie chose to move away from the piano, sidling over toward a back room.

"Let's get out of here," Béliard decided, jerking his head in their direction. "We'll be able to talk more freely outside."

They went out. The street. The cars passing by. The various kinds of music escaping through the lowered windows of the cars. Sometimes it was just rhythmic blips, sometimes heavy bass lines that sent a shiver up the spine. At first they walked without saying anything; then Béliard resumed speaking.

"I've come to set things back in order," he stated calmly. "So now you're going to do me the favor of going back to your job at the bar, all right? At the hotel where you've been assigned."

"Absolutely not," Max declared in a firm voice. "I don't ever want to go back to that bar. I don't think I've done anything to deserve that."

"You're starting to piss me off, Delmarc," Béliard started shouting again. "You're making my life very difficult. You're not a very easy fellow to deal with, do you know that?"

"First of all, what are you doing here?" asked Max. "I thought you always stayed at the Center."

"They reassigned me," said Béliard. "I've been rather tired lately. And anyway, as I said, I needed to deal with you. I'm going to stay here a few days, just long enough to put you back on the straight and narrow. And besides, I have another, more important problem to take care of. I've got someone who escaped from the park—you remember the park?—who I have to bring back. It's work, it's really a lot of work."

"First you should get some rest," Max pointed out. "What hotel are you at?"

"I don't know," said Béliard, ready to collapse, "I just got here, I haven't had time to deal with it. Do you know of one?"

Advising him against the Montmorency, Max recommended the Holiday Inn on Place de la République. "It's not bad," he emphasized, "it's comfortable and centrally located. And on top of which, I've got a friend who's offered to put me up on Boulevard du Temple, which is just a stone's throw from République. We'll be right near each other, we can get together whenever you like."

"Maybe," said Béliard, letting his shoulders sag, "I don't know. I'm exhausted. Yeah, maybe that's what I'll do. Is République far from here?"

"A bit," said Max. "You'll be better off taking a cab."

"Fine," said Béliard, "all right." Then, pulling himself together and wagging his finger: "But don't go getting ideas about being a jerk behind my back, all right?"

"No being a jerk," said Max. "Go get yourself settled. You get settled in, get some rest, and I'll call you in the morning, all right?"

"All right," said Béliard. "That's what we'll do."

Max hailed a taxi that the other man entered without another word and that Max watched drive away. The fact is, Béliard seemed utterly depressed.

"It was nothing," said Max once back at Gilbert's, "just a friend who's going through a bad patch. Anyway, where were we? Shall I play you something else?"

"That won't be necessary," said Gilbert. "I thought you were very good."

"Right," said Max, "so when do I start?"

"How about Monday?" suggested Gilbert.

"Ah, I'm so happy," Bernie exclaimed ten minutes later, in another taxi that was carrying them toward Boulevard du Temple. "Mister Max, I'm proud of you."

"I should be thanking *you*," said Max. "Furthermore, you can call me just plain Max from now on. Or Paul. Whichever you like."

Bernie's new apartment, at number 42, was indeed roomier than the one on Rue Murillo but also much noisier, as it looked directly out on the boulevard. Since the stepson's room was still unoccupied—"He's in Switzerland now," explained Bernie. "A big private school in Switzerland. He just keeps getting smarter and smarter"—Max moved into it without bothering to fetch his things from the hotel. An advance from Gilbert would allow him to buy all new clothes as of tomorrow, after he had met Béliard as arranged.

The latter was decidedly less agitated than the day before. "I slept well," he informed Max. "I got some rest. I needed it." Without Max having to plead his case, he made no more fuss about the new employment at Gilbert's. "I admit that business with the Montmorency was a bit harsh," he judged. "Basically, you can do as you wish, I'll smooth things over with Schmidt. I'm going to take advantage of being here to do a little sightseeing. Do you have plans for this afternoon?"

"Just some shopping," said Max, "for some new clothes. But we can have dinner tonight if you like. Why don't you drop by Bernie's, he'd be happy to meet you."

So Béliard dropped by Bernie's, got along with Bernie, came back the next evening then the evening after that, to the point of dropping by for dinner almost every evening until they eventually got used to his being around.

While Max persisted in his newfound sobriety, it seemed that Béliard, on occasion, gladly yielded to the call of the spirits. One excessive evening, he opened up a little, evoking in a jumble his daily life at the Center—"It doesn't seem like much, but it's hard working there. You might not think so to look at him, but Lopez can be a holy terror"—and a few episodes of his professional career. As he emptied glass after glass under the worried eyes of Max and Bernie, he pastily alluded to a so-called mission during which he'd had to look after a young woman in dire straits. He was just starting out at the Center back then, he labored to explain, he was in training and it was especially horrible to be a trainee, he assured them, pouring himself another one, they force you to be small, ugly, and mean, I who love only what is beautiful and good, but anyway, he'd had to go through that stage. He was clearly delirious.

As the days went by, Béliard, who had started drinking a lot, at times from early morning, dropped by Boulevard du Temple on a daily basis, to the point where they soon had to take care of him full-time. Bernie freed him up another room and they took him for walks, brought him to the Louvre or the Musée d'Orsay, dragged him out to the Mer de Sable amusement park and the Palace of Versailles, made him breathe the clean air of Buttes-Chaumont park. Having no further objection to Max's job at Gilbert's, Béliard accompanied him there every other evening, sitting at a table right near the piano with an infinitely refillable glass and insisting on loudly giving his opinion of the music afterward.

But this saturation soon twisted him up, as is sometimes the case, in knots of depression. When Béliard started complaining nonstop about his loneliness, despite the fact that he was constantly on their backs, they scrambled to find new solutions. Bernie even offered to introduce him to girls. Not difficult girls, he hastened to add, but nice, simple girls, the kind you might for example find in abundance at the bar of the Montmorency; but Béliard flatly refused. "My condition," he slurred with a drunkard's gravity, "forbids me."Without making any comment, Max deemed his refusal to associate with mortals rather snobbish.

They went through a difficult period, then, in which Béliard started moaning so much, and so constantly, that they ran themselves ragged trying to help him. They recommended he see someone—but in spiritual medicine he had no confidence. Max, who remembered going through similarly difficult periods, offered to obtain antidepressants of all kinds, things with lithium that back then had brought him a little relief, but Béliard refused these as well. He refused everything they suggested. They didn't know what do to with him.

29

And then, who knows how or why, the situation gradually improved. After several weeks, Béliard started feeling better. Without going so far as to swing into a manic state, the classic alternative to depression, Béliard's mood took a more serene turn: they saw him begin to smile again, start conversations, even take some initiative. Soon Max and Bernie no longer needed to wrack their brains finding distractions for him: he went out all by himself in the afternoons, the entertainment listings in his pocket, and they didn't see hide nor hair of him until it was time for the aperitif—toward which, moreover, he seemed to be practicing a certain moderation.

He who, since his arrival at Bernie's, had never lifted a finger to help out with day-to-day life, might now come home carrying—self-inspired—some shopping for dinner. Truly Béliard was making progress, tucking in his bed as soon as he got up, helping with the dishes and the housework, rinsing out the tub before leaving the bathroom. Willingly he accompanied Max to the supermarket, nor did he hesitate to change a light bulb or cart the empty bottles to the green receptacle on the corner of Rue Amelot, even without anyone having dared to ask him. The ideal guest: pleasant, cooperative, and so discreet that sometimes Max, coming home late from his job at

Gilbert's and consequently rising late as well, didn't see him for the entire day.

On one of those days when Béliard had disappeared—to the Sainte-Chapelle, the Grand Rex, or the Drouot auction house—Max took advantage of his free afternoon to go to the Printemps department store, with the prosaic goal of undergarment renewal. Having quickly dispensed with this, he wandered around the store's different floors, with no desire to buy or any aim other than to pause here and there in front of things for which he had no need whatsoever, a multifunctional shower head, a wide-screen plasma TV, or a panoply of knives—for vegetables, tomatoes, bread, ham, and salmon; for deboning, slicing, or hacking. All the while, he listened vaguely to the various loudspeaker announcements, which might encourage shoppers to check out this week's special on curtains, discounts on household appliances, 20-percent-off awnings, or Madam Rose Mercoeur to please report to the customer service desk on the ground floor.

Of course, it wasn't that rare a first name, but then again, why not? Nor had it been, at the time, Rose's family name, but anyone can get married. In short, it was even more improbable than at Passy or Bel-Air, but he had plenty of time to kill, so why not go have a little look? Still, the situation was clearly making him nervous, and he advanced discreetly toward the escalator without seeming to be in a hurry, with the same detached air over pounding heart as if, having just committed a robbery, he was afraid of being watched—careful not to give himself away by suspicious behavior under the eye of the surveillance cameras. On the escalator, Max continued to display this nonchalant slowness; then, having reached the ground floor, he searched a bit more feverishly for the customer-service desk and, once he had found it, go figure that this time it was she, it was absolutely she.

It was immediately apparent that Rose, who hadn't changed much in thirty years, in other words, no more than would be expected, had had her nose remodeled, about which Max experienced a wisp of annoyance. We recall that this nose, back then, might not have been her loveliest feature, but even so, even so. Slightly too hooked, it was so well framed by a perfect face that it ended up being, at the time, all the more endearing. Fine, well, now it had become as pretty as the rest; it was kind of a shame but why quibble. It was, in any case, a handsome job of plastic surgery, wholly worthy of the surgeons at the Center. As for Rose's outfit, she was wearing at the customer service desk none of the clothes he had spotted the day of his pursuit in the metro. It was fairly classic, a camel-colored cashmere twin set and speckled tweed skirt—Max noted with a pang of emotion that the label of the twin set, having escaped the cardigan, was flipped up on the nape of her neck.

She was alone. She appeared to be waiting. Max wanted to go up to her, but she surely wouldn't recognize him—understandable, given the time gone by, not to mention the treatments he'd undergone at the Center. So she obviously wouldn't identify him, but then again, trying to seduce her with his new name and appearance might even be rather exciting after all these years. Max was dying to approach her, but something held him back; he was embarrassed by his pathetic clutch of shrink-wrapped underpants no less than by the risk, as always, of looking like a . . . —although that risk, this time, seemed less likely than it had with the woman with the dog. He nonetheless waited awhile, giving his heart time to stop pounding so hard and himself a moment to imagine how he might dare go up and speak to her.

It was then that, from across the store, Max saw Béliard cross the entire length of the perfume department and walk up to Rose, accosting her frontally and without preamble, as if he'd known her forever. Between Chanel and Shiseido, they immediately launched into an animated discussion, easy and smiling, at the start of which Max, horrified, witnessed Béliard fold the label of Rose's sweater back inside with a familiar movement. After which he seemed to be stressing a point, making his case with eloquence and with the use of gestures, always the same gestures and therefore, no doubt, always the same point. As the conversation went on, Rose for her part showed more and more signs of acquiescence, provoking in return wider and wider smiles from Béliard.

Max could not help starting to walk toward them, like a ghost, but let's not forget that he is only a ghost, then stopped several yards away. As Béliard noticed him at that moment, he signaled him to come closer, maintaining his wide smile, come over here so I can introduce you. "This is Paul," he uttered, "a friend of mine. And this is Rose, an old friend I hadn't seen for quite some time," Béliard smiled more and more broadly. "I had almost given up ever finding her again." Max bowed clumsily to Rose, who, as anticipated, gave him merely a slight nod without showing the least sign of recognition. "Well, we'll be leaving now," Béliard announced. "We have a small errand to run."

"Wait just a minute," said Max. "Excuse me, but this person—I think *I'm* the one who was supposed to find her."

"Yes," Béliard said with a cold smile, "I know. I'm perfectly aware of all that, but I'm still the one leaving with her. You see, this is what it's like in the urban zone. This is what it consists of. In a sense, it's what most of you call Hell. So, are we agreed?" he segued, turning back to Rose. "I'm bringing you back to the park? My dear Paul, I bid you so long for now."

Standing frozen by the customer-service desk, a crushed Max watches as Rose and Béliard head toward the glass doors, push them open, and leave his field of vision; then, as if in a trance, he sets into motion as well. Once outside the store, he again spots them walking up Boulevard Haussmann in a westerly direction, but he stops there, follows them only with his eyes, without trying to catch up. At the corner of Rue du Havre, Béliard looks back to give him a little wave, and Max, deader than ever, sees them resume their walk, growing smaller on the receding boulevard before turning right and disappearing into Rue de Rome.

Running

Jean Echenoz

Translated by Linda Coverdale

1

The Germans have entered Moravia. They have arrived on horseback, on motorcycles, in automobiles, in trucks, but also in light horse-drawn carriages, followed by infantry units and supply columns as well as a few small half-tracks, and not much more. It's too early to see any big Panther and Tiger panzers driven by tank men in black uniforms, which will prove quite practical for hiding oil stains. Overhead fly a few reconnaissance aircraft, single-engine Messerschmitts called Taifuns, but since their orders are merely to confirm that things are going smoothly, they're not even armed. It's only a quiet little lightning invasion, a minor annexation, no muss, no fuss, not yet what you'd call a real war. It's simply that the Germans are arriving and settling in, that's all.

Those in charge of the operation move around in Horch 901s or Mercedes 170s, the rear windows screened off by tightly pleated gray curtains that obscure the generals' faces. Officers of lower rank ride in the more open carriages, wearing long overcoats, peaked caps, and Iron Crosses tucked under their chins. Horses carry other officers or haul field kitchens. The trucks carrying troops are Opel Blitzes, and policemen in helmets with metal throat guards are piloting the heavy sidecar Zündapp motorcycles. All these conveyances sport decorative red flags with white circles displaying the rather distinctive black cross that no longer needs any explanation, and which the officers also wear on their armbands.

When this whole crew showed up in the Sudeten Mountains six months ago, the German-speaking population of the area welcomed them more or less warmly.[1] Now, however, having advanced through Bohemia into Moravia, the invaders are meeting with a noticeably chillier reception under a leaden and overcast sky. They enter Prague to stony silence, and no one crowds the Moravian roads to salute their passage, either. The few venturesome onlookers observe this parade with less curiosity than wariness, if not outright antipathy, but something tells them it isn't a good time to show this, that it's no joking matter.

Emil is not among these spectators because he has plenty of other things to do. In the first place, having left school three years earlier when his family couldn't pay the tuition anymore, he works as an apprentice in a factory, no joking matter either. Then, after work, he takes courses in chemistry, with an eye to improving his job prospects. And lastly, whenever he has time to go home, he helps his father out in a garden that is not simply for show, where they must grow what they eat, and that's no joking matter at all. Emil is seventeen, rather handsome, rather placid, a tall blond boy with a triangular face who smiles all the time, and then you see his big teeth. He has limpid eyes and a high voice; his pale skin is the kind that dreads the sun. Today, though, zero sunshine.

2

So, in Moravia now, the Germans settle in and occupy Ostrava, a city of coal and steel near the town where Emil was born and where Tatra and Bata, two leading companies in that heavily industrialized area, each offer a way of getting ahead: cars or shoes. Tatra designs very beautiful, very expensive cars; Bata manufactures not too pricey, not too bad shoes. Anybody looking for work goes to one or the other. Emil wound up in the Bata factory in Zlín, a hundred kilometers south of Ostrava.

He's a boarder at the technical school and a factory hand in the rubber department, which stinks so much everyone tries to avoid it. The workshop where he started out produces 2,200 pairs of crepe-soled tennis shoes every day, and Emil's first job was to trim those soles to one size with a toothed wheel. But the movements were tiring, the air unbreathable, the pace too swift, the slightest imperfection punished by a fine, the least little delay taken out of his already meager salary, and he was rapidly overwhelmed. So he's assigned to the preparation of shoe lasts, which is no less arduous but smells less awful, and he can handle it.

All that goes on for some time and then things look up a bit. Emil's endless studying pays off with a job at the Institute of

Chemistry, something of an improvement. Even though he's only brewing cellulose in a freezing shed packed with carboys of acid, Emil likes that much better. Of course he would prefer laboratory work, improving viscose or developing artificial silk, but he makes it clear in the meantime that he's happy where he is. So happy that the chief engineer, pleased with Emil, encourages him to take courses at the graduate school in the evening. A nice little career as a Czech chemist is slowly taking shape.

Only one problem at the factory: always eager, understandably, to sell still more of the shoes they export throughout the world, and not content with having pushed the rationalization of their industry as far as possible, the bosses at Bata also wish to publicize the company name by every possible means and through every imaginable medium. Among other initiatives, they've organized their own factory soccer team, which will carry the Bata colors from stadium to stadium. Emil doesn't pay much attention to all that but unfortunately, every year Bata also organizes a footrace called the Zlín Run, in which all the technical school students must participate, rigged out in jerseys bearing the firm's name. And that Emil just hates.

He loathes sports in general, anyway. You could almost say he looks down on his brothers and pals who spend their spare time kicking a ball around like idiots. When they force him to play the occasional game, he does so grudgingly, clumsily, hasn't a clue what the rules are. Even while feigning interest, he looks off into the distance, trying discreetly to avoid the ball, the trajectory of which he can never figure out. And if the thing unfortunately lands at his feet, Emil gets rid of it with a huge kick in any direction at all, and all too often toward his own team's goal.

So, the Zlín Run, Emil couldn't care less about it, participates only under duress, tries hard to get out of it—but in vain. Even though he limps around every year for an hour before starting time, claiming an exemption because of some grievous injury to his ankle or knee, no matter how enthusiastically he winces and moans, the doctors never fall for it. He's got to run. Fine, he does. Emil is all the less inclined toward sports in that he has inherited his firm antipathy for physical exercise from his father, who considers it a sheer waste of time and—above all—money. A footrace, for example, now that's really the cream of that crop: not only is it perfectly useless, Emil's father points out, but it also requires the repeated resoling of shoes beyond what is strictly necessary, thus straining the family budget.

This budget (carpenter father, housewife mother, seven children, no money), Emil knows it well. On the subject of sports, Emil agrees with his father who, by the way, would rather have seen him be a schoolteacher than a factory hand. Emil was ready to take the examination, but ever since the eighteenth century, schoolteachers in Czechoslovakia have traditionally been cantors whose chief task is to make children sing, to have them listen to and learn about music. Emil, alas, sings like a bleating trombone: a non-starter. Which left Bata.

Bata where, aside from that unpleasant business with the Zlín Run, Emil's future would be shaping up nicely, but the thing is, the Germans have turned up. Nazi flags have taken over the city: standard-bearers are parading around its squares, along its streets, even into the offices of the shoe factory, where they seize control as they do everywhere. They cut off funding for laboratory research, suspend any trials in progress, forbid all experiments. For Emil it's back to studying for his exams and, in the meantime, back to the factory.

3

National Socialist propaganda has taken hold in its various forms. Censorship of the press, films, books, songs. Edicts against listening to foreign radio broadcasts. More or less compulsory attendance at meetings and conferences; distribution of leaflets; bill-posting on a massive scale. The streets are plastered with newspaper murals, photo-reportages proving that the army of occupation could not possibly be better behaved. Moreover, there is no occupation. The German army respects all persons and property. The German soldier is a friend to children.

At the movies, when Emil has the time and money to go, he can watch, along with the usual short documentaries (and presented as such, in the guise of sober evidence based on serious information), the latest newsreels: seductive images of harmony, accompanied by a friendly voiceover affectionately addressing Emil to proclaim the return to normalcy, peace, fraternity, and cooperation.

Thanks to freshly created youth organizations, propaganda is also going full steam ahead in schools and universities. One of the occupiers' first initiatives is to provide young people with sports events, athletics, and competitive games, and there again, attendance is essentially obligatory.

The first race in which Emil takes part is therefore a nine-kilometer cross country run held by the Wehrmacht in Brno, pitting impeccably equipped German contestants—tall, lean, arrogant athletes all in the same *Übermensch* mold—against a starveling bunch of raggedy Czechs, haggard young peasants in long undershirts or weekend soccer players in need of a good shave. Emil's heart isn't really in this endeavor, but he's a conscientious young man, he buckles down, does what he can. Since he finishes second without really noticing it and to the keen displeasure of the Aryans, a trainer from the local club takes an interest in him. You run funny but you don't run so badly, he tells him. Actually you definitely run funny, says the trainer, shaking his head in disbelief, but hey, not badly. Of these two pronouncements, Emil hears and half listens only to the second.

Since his pals figure that even running funny, Emil's not bad, they invite him to start running with them, but he refuses. He likes running now and then—who doesn't?—but that's about it. In spite of this fluke success in Brno, Emil doesn't think much of his abilities, in fact he doesn't think about them at all; it's not his thing and anyway he can clearly see that most of the other guys run faster than he does. In the mornings, when they're coming back from gymnastics, he'll do a few sprints with them but it's just to be nice and he always ends up way back in the pack. So he says no, he'd rather not, it doesn't interest him, besides he really—truly—won't have anything to do with competitions.

Well, everyone knows how he is, Emil: when he says no he's smiling. He smiles all the time anyhow, so everyone likes him and they insist. He resists but he's not that hard to convince, a weakness that bothers him a bit. No matter how often he explains that he's not that eager to join in, he can never hold out for long. Oh all right, fine, he caves in at last. And he goes along.

Against all odds, he soon starts enjoying himself. He doesn't say anything but seems to be getting into it; after a few weeks he even begins running on his own, just for the pleasure of it, which astonishes him, and he prefers not to mention this to anyone. After nightfall, when no one can see him, he does the round trip between the factory and the forest as fast as he can. Although he doesn't breathe a word about this, the others catch on in the end, pressure him again, and, too nice a guy to resist for long, he gives in since it means so much to them.

Well, nice as he is, he begins to realize that he likes a good fight: the first few times they let him loose on a track, he goes for all he's worth and easily wins two races, of 1,500 and 3,000 meters. People congratulate him, encourage him, reward him with an apple and a slice of bread and butter, tell him to come back again and he goes back again and starts training in the stadium, at first for a laugh but not for long. Wedged into the industrial area of Zlín and plug ugly, the stadium sits across from the power station, downwind of all the dust, soot, and smokestack fumes that blow into the athletes' eyes. Despite those drawbacks, Emil finds himself growing fond of the stadium as well, where the polluted atmosphere is still far cleaner than the air in the factory.

In the factory, moreover, there's been a turn for the worse. After some sort of unpleasant situation, Emil has been assigned as punishment to the crushing of silicates. This job is even more dreadful than the others: breathing the white powder that covers him, he looks like a ghost in a permanent state of apnea. When he complains and applies for a transfer, the head of personnel obligingly offers, if he's not satisfied, to pack him off to a work camp. Emil lets the matter drop.

4

Ruling by terror now throughout the protectorate, the Germans endlessly slaughter, deport, burn, and destroy, so perhaps continuing to run is a way to think about something else. Given that Emil has just been honorably beaten—by two seconds—over a distance of 3,000 meters, finishing second, an editor puts his name in print for the first time in a local newspaper that isn't allowed, in any case, to print much else. Emil rereads the article ten times the way one does in such cases, but it's that name he looks at most intently, that strange name he hasn't encountered in print before, has never seen like that; it's a peculiar feeling, finding himself with this new public identity. Although public identity, at twenty, in Zlín—he doesn't particularly see what that could mean.

Another thing he doesn't understand, it's how the other guys, at the stadium, talk solemnly about each race, as seriously as if they saw the whole thing that way, whereas running has more or less become a pleasure for Emil, even though he also realizes that this pleasure is an acquired taste. Result: he's the one who starts overdoing it. During the winter off-season, he trains recklessly while the others are resting up at home. Every day he barrels down the road to the neighboring village, a nonstop round trip of eight kilometers, and he's constantly going back to the stadium even though it's tiring and he's hurting. He goes at it so hard that the others begin to worry about him. You're completely sick, Emil, they protest, you're wearing yourself out. Work on your form instead. No, no, he says, form is all nonsense. And besides, my problem is that I'm too slow. If you're going to run, might as well run fast, right?

He therefore refuses to work exclusively on his endurance, the goal of runners who've chosen to concentrate on long-distance or middle-distance races. Reversing the system, Emil focuses more and more on his speed, over short distances repeated indefinitely, which starts to work pretty well.

Well enough to consider going up against other runners besides his old pals from Zlín. At the Prague Championships, a competition between Bohemia and Moravia, Emil enters his first official 1,500 meter race, taking on the three best Czech middle-distance runners. That trio has carefully worked out a joint strategy against the record holder, one Salé. This plan is simple. They will run as fast as possible from the very start so that the aforementioned Salé—known to be a "kicker," who counts on catching up at the end of a race—will eventually slow down and give up the chase when he finds himself lagging too far behind the front runners. Simple it may be, but the three Czechs' plan seems ready to pay off: Salé is growing discouraged, the three Czechs are pleased. But they've forgotten about Emil, who has his own ideas about a proper strategy. First he settles for running respectfully behind Salé; then, seeing him begin to falter, he allows himself to pass Salé and come up behind the three leaders, whom he leaves one by one in his wake. Two hundred meters before the finish, he puts on a burst of speed, knowing he can do this because he trained for it: he wins.

In those days, individual runners always tried to pace their efforts evenly throughout the race. Anxious to conserve their strength, they didn't believe they could—and above all didn't dare—save their full speed for the last straightaway to unleash their greatest power at the very end. Well, that's the whole point of training over short distances as well as long ones: Emil has just "invented" the final sprint.

Having become quite attentive to his pulse rate and degree of fatigue, Emil would like to understand the limits of his endurance. He keeps training all fall, all winter, and not only at the stadium. In the street, along roads, in forests, fields, everywhere, to the point of injury and in all sorts of weather, he runs less like a man than like one of those animals more gifted at it than we are. Emil walks along a lane lined with poplars on his way to the factory and back every day, which gives him a new idea. The first day, he holds his breath until the fourth poplar; the next two days, until the fifth; then the sixth, and so on every two days until he can finally get to the end of the lane without breathing. But once he gets there, he passes out. He passes out another time while taking a cold shower after twelve straightaways taken at top speed. He gives up such eccentricities but finds it all very interesting. He always wants to know *how far*. . . .

That's how he winds up setting a new record, in Zlín, where he becomes the first in his country to run 5,000 meters in under fifteen minutes. Excitement, exaltation, notification of the national press, but the guys over in Prague don't believe it. First they think it must be a Teletype error, then that the stopwatches at Zlín have been tampered with. And Zlín, after all, what kind of backwater is that. What kind of jerk is this guy. What kind of swindle is this. Nevertheless, after beating his own new record locally, Emil goes off to Prague itself some time later to run the 2000 meters and breaks another record, his third for the year. The guys in Prague, well, they're forced to admit they were wrong.

5

Hard times have come to Zlín. It's been a tough winter. The November bombardments caused heavy damage in the city. There's no heat anywhere, and everyone's freezing while waiting for the war to end, which people say shouldn't be too long now, perhaps. Ever since the beginning of spring, in fact, the chimneys of the occupied city hall have constantly belched greasy brown smoke, spreading its stench everywhere, which hasn't helped the air quality in the stadium. The Germans, it seems, have set to burning their archives. This destruction of secret documents gives some idea of their uneasiness, and it's not a bad sign. People feel vaguely hopeful. There is no other hearth, no other source of heat in Zlín—icy white and sooty black—except the room in the technical school where Emil and his pals have patched together an old stove found amid the rubble. Despite the threat of death by hanging for such offenses, they've scrounged pieces of wood from the ruins and that's how they spend the winter.

This spring, since the front is drawing ever closer, no one is allowed to train or indeed do anything else. But now that the sun is back, and with it that longing for fresh air, Emil can't resist going to take a few turns around the track. Finding the stadium shut tight, he scales the wall, nips through an unlocked window into the changing rooms, and gets out onto the cinders. The track is in wretched shape, what with weeds springing up everywhere and the clinker surface crumbling, but it's still there.

Emil has begun trotting back and forth, monitoring his breathing, when the sirens go off. Over the course of the war, he has learned to decipher their code with precision: this time, he knows that their prolonged notes are warning that tanks have been spotted. Perhaps this signals the long-awaited arrival of the liberating forces. Indeed, a series of explosions begins jolting the air all around: positioned on the slope above the stadium, the German anti-aircraft battery has just opened fire. Emil prudently leaves the track but before going home, as long as he's there, he returns to the locker rooms to pick up his friends' tracksuits. Hugging the walls of streets emptied by the alert, he must stop at one point to huddle in the doorway of a building near the church on the main square when a column of vehicles races past, heading west. The occupiers haven't wasted any time in trying to escape, haven't lost all hope of somehow pulling through, but one can see the fear in their faces. Somewhere between the city and the forest, bursts of machine-gun fire start up, indicating that serious fighting is going on and that the Soviet army might really not be far away.

Still intent on delivering the tracksuits to their owners in spite of everything, Emil runs to the technical school as soon as the coast is clear but finds the doors locked, since everyone fled into the cellars at the alert. On the opposite side of a street he is about to cross, two houses collapse, hit by a bomb. Hastily retreating, Emil finds a cross street to return to the school and hears someone somewhere shout that yes, the Russians have arrived, they've begun shelling from the forest.

Right in the middle of the boarding school garden, in fact, there they are: soldiers in unfamiliar uniforms looking nervously all around as they advance. Now Emil begins shouting and runs to meet them; he's the first to talk to them, to tell them everyone's been waiting for them, that he's glad to see them, he's welcoming them, he's saying whatever comes into his head. Their eyes darting elsewhere, the soldiers reply briefly, but they do reply. The two sides don't have many words available to make themselves understood but there are quick handshakes, they clap one another on the shoulder, communicate through gestures and expressions, they get on well enough like that.

Soon, emerging from their holes one after the other, the inhabitants of Zlín draw near. The Soviet soldiers with the frank, tired smiles are anxious to know where the Germans are. Already gone, mostly, people tell them, pointing to where the last vehicles have sped away. But the score hasn't been completely settled yet: some of them must still be hiding in the area. They'll have to be rooted out. Arriving that evening, a few Soviet units halt at Zlín. Decisions are quickly made regarding command posts and the emplacement of batteries to begin the mopping-up; a few minutes later, howitzers begin addressing the problem.

With nightfall, things calm down; at home in bed, Emil can't manage to sleep. Just when he has finally dozed off around midnight, a first shot startles him awake to hear a chorus of machine guns return to the fray. *Soli*, *tutti*, *en contrepoint*, a solid barrage of artillery has just engaged an enemy doggedly determined to extricate its last surrounded troops.

So nothing has really been gained yet and the population remains gripped by fear, desperately worried about its fate should the German rescue attempt succeed, because they know what comes next: hostages, reprisals, and so on. They stream back down into the basements and shelters while the defenders stand their ground, strike back, then regain the upper hand and, after a while, it seems the forces of the German occupation have been repelled. Emil, who hasn't taken refuge like the others, watches what's going on. Arming himself with a field shovel to help the soldiers out as best he can, he joins them in digging trenches; he's not particularly useful, but it's something, anyway. Moreover, things seem to be going well when the Germans suddenly begin shooting furiously once more, seeking their victims on the expanse of open slopes behind the city and there's just no end to it all.

The fighting goes on throughout the night. Entrenched in the woods, what's left of the German infantry struggles to hold on, to inflict the maximum of casualties before trying to find a way to fall back, but while their positions are being precisely located, contained, then bypassed, the auxiliary forces specifically summoned as reinforcements rapidly arrive. It takes only a few hours: by the time the sun rises, Soviet mortar fire has wiped out the last pockets of resistance. Silence falls once again over Zlín. The war is over.

6

Since the war is over, everyone rearms. Restored to its former borders, Czechoslovakia rebuilds its army, and when Emil is called up, he leaves the Bata works without regret. Right away, he prefers garrison life to the factory. In tiptop shape, he finds the daily drill a breeze, likes going on maneuvers out in the Moravian countryside, climbs hills with his regiment, enjoys marching in step through nature and breathing the fresh air unsullied by silicate dust.

And his running doesn't suffer, either: since the liberated republic organizes military championships, staff officers with a keen eye for athletic ability allow Emil to go participate in those events, where he calmly sets two new records. Upon his return he is "mentioned in dispatches" for having brought distinction to his unit. Life in uniform isn't going badly at all, in fact Emil considers entering the Military Academy to become a career officer. Officer, not so bad, why not. Besides, anything rather than returning to Bata. He pretends to hesitate for five minutes but when encouraged, he applies and is immediately accepted. Anyway, given its appetite for athletes, the army has had its eye on him for some time and welcomes him with open arms.

Glancing out a window the day he arrives at the barracks, he sees a courtyard encircled by a running track that also seems to be smiling up at him. Things are off to a rather good start, even if life at the academy is no bed of roses but, well, Emil does what he's told, studies what he's told to study, never misses a day of training. When the other cadets are resting, though, Emil suits up and goes out running, which pays off yet again: a few weeks later, in Prague, he breaks his own records for 3,000 and 5,000 meters, leaving the rest of the field far behind.

At this point in his life, Emil naturally has no experience with international meets. The occasion now presents itself to go up against the world's elite runners in the 2000 meters, especially Sundin, a Swede who seems to run effortlessly, tirelessly, his trim, light step adjusting his speed up or down at will. Emil's style, it has to be said, isn't one bit like that. For half the distance, Emil keeps up with Sundin, watching him closely to keep from being left behind, but when the Swede makes his move, Emil can't manage to step up the pace and he hits the tape just behind him. So he hasn't won, although he does break the Czech record.

Some time later, in Brno, he runs a 3,000 meter race with the Dutchman Slijkhuis, Europe's swiftest and most elegant runner, whose smooth stride delights the public. Again, not really Emil's style, yet the Czech battles anyway for every centimeter until the finish, but in vain. Prolonged applause rings from the stands: once more, Emil hasn't won, but he has broken the Czech record.

He isn't too pleased with himself, feeling he still has much to learn. When he's invited to Oslo, for the first postwar European Championships, he doesn't feel up to the job and so would rather not accept. Since Czechoslovakia is determined to participate, however, Emil reluctantly takes a plane to Sweden with four comrades. It's the first time he has ever been out of his country.

Emil, and this hasn't been noted enough, is a young man with an inquiring mind, quite curious about the new things to be seen abroad. But in Oslo, billeted in the little neighborhood where the athletes stay, he hasn't time to see much of the city. In this bivouac of champions, meeting rivals he's known only as names shining with glory, Emil finds a bunch of ordinary guys: Wooderson looks like a law clerk, Slijkhuis is a complete innocent, Nyberg's rather funny, Reiff, a little too standoffish, and Pujazon is quite pleased with himself. But above all, Heino is there, the fabulous Viljo Heino, the one they call the wonderful runner of the deep forests, champion of Finland and world record holder, the relaxed man of few words who has revolutionized the art of running by rejecting all stylistic flourishes in the systematic search for an efficiency of minimum effort. Emil approaches him as if he were a god, timidly touching his legs as though they were holy relics; the other man, silent as usual, never looks at him once.

All those ordinary fellows, seeing as they're from Western Europe, are quite well dressed—their tracksuits look wonderful—and the five Czechs feel slightly uncomfortable among them. The war hasn't been over long, there are still shortages, a lack of funds, and their country either can't or won't equip them adequately. Without the proper warm-up suits de rigueur during the parade of international champions, the Czechs must appear in their skimpy running togs and they feel somewhat naked, it's rather humiliating.

For the first time in his life, Emil thus finds himself at the starting line with the best athletes in the world, before a tense crowd of spectators from many nations eager to see new records set. The great champions, all well known, are greeted with cheers, Wooderson by some fans, Heino by others, Emil by no one and he feels weak in the knees.

The public falls silent, a calm shattered by the starter's gun—and the fight for the 5,000 is on. Certain competitors establish an extraordinary pace right from the start, a speed Emil finds hellish as he looks around for Wooderson, the heavy favorite in the event. The Englishman is staying far back in the pack, however, and no one knows why. Not too sure of himself or anything else, Emil wonders what tactic to follow. If he stays close to Wooderson, any faltering in the Englishman's pace could prove fatal to his own, so without thinking too much about it, Emil joins the runners who've taken the lead.

They're constantly changing places, now surging ahead, now hanging back, making it impossible to predict a winner. Sometimes Emil finds himself in sixth place, sometimes in fourth, it depends—and has nothing to do with him, really. At the third kilometer, Slijkhuis is out in front, followed by Wooderson who's gaining ground with every stride. During the next-to-last lap, Slijkhuis tries to settle matters by improvising a sprint that puts him well ahead of his adversaries. Wooderson hasn't let down his guard, though, or let his rival open up too much of a lead. Relying on his usual strong finish, the Britisher pours on the speed two hundred meters from the tape. His judgment is sound: he passes Slijkhuis and beats him to the finish by five seconds.

Throughout his first important race, Emil has kept himself among the front runners, an honorable performance. Although he's had no illusions about winning, he would still have liked to come in third. But the more seasoned Scandinavians Nyberg and Heino, who have more wisely husbanded their strength, move ahead of him by a few tenths of a second at the end. Emil comes in fifth; once more he has not won, while beating the Czech record.

This fifth place is still a success, Emil could be proud of himself, but as usual he isn't. It all reminds him that he must go even faster, marshal his efforts better, save some energy for the finish and, above all, carefully study his adversaries' tactics to improve his own. And then there's his form, which everyone is always criticizing; maybe it's his running style that makes him lose, he'll have to think about all that. He'll see.

He arrives back at the Military Academy the next day at noon. One hour later, the candidates must report for inspection; the program includes gymnastics. Emil could really use some rest but he never even thinks about it, quickly changes his clothes, and joins the ranks to take part in the review.

7

Never mind that he doesn't win all his races: by piling up records, unassuming Emil has still become the idol of his countrymen. In the eyes of the Czech public, what he now represents is quite simple: all it takes is a brief notice in the morning papers that his starting time on the track will be six o'clock—and that evening twenty thousand fans will fight to get into Masaryk Stadium.

He is asked if he will represent the Czech army at the Allied Forces Championships to be held in Berlin. Strongly supported by his superiors, his request to participate is granted. Fine, says Emil, great, I'm going, and one Friday, in his army uniform, he leaves alone by train for Berlin, with a change of trains in Dresden. The championships are to begin on Saturday, and at midnight, he's only just arriving in Dresden. Practically destroyed by the bombardments, the city is nothing but collapsed buildings, precarious ruins, cratered pavements. Almost the only thing left is the station, and Emil sets out through the unlighted, devastated streets, trying to find his way through the rubble with no one to give him directions. He's hungry, worn out, tired, and apart from that, it's raining buckets.

Finally he runs into an American lieutenant who takes forever to recognize his uniform and figure out what he's saying, but then agrees to guide him. Emil follows him to a kind of waiting room, a former air-raid shelter where a few sentries are hanging out. At loose ends, the soldiers are glad to relieve their boredom by welcoming a new arrival, especially one rigged out so weirdly. They're curious, but given the state he's in, Emil doesn't much feel like talking about himself. He's got to run the next day, as he understands it; the train for Berlin leaves at five in the morning and it would be nice to rest a little if he doesn't want to arrive at the stadium exhausted. The sentries couldn't care less, and keep asking questions Emil doesn't understand but tries to answer with gestures that become ever more dilatory and evasive. Discouraged, the soldiers leave him alone at last, pointing to a bench; Emil lies down on it and sleeps for an hour or two.

He doesn't reach Berlin until the following afternoon, more tired than ever, still completely on his own and dying of hunger. Managing to learn where the stadium is, he hurries there so as not to miss the start of his race. He's all in. Then he has to go through a whole song and dance to be allowed into the stadium, a huge building where he can't seem to get his bearings. Now it's his turn to ask questions no one understands, and without understanding anyone's attempts to answer him. Emil finally manages to find one of the organizers of the events and is relieved to hear that his race won't be run until the following day.

That's not all, though: he must still sign in, which means finding the organizer in charge of this formality. Someone eventually points out the man in charge of the list, and this time it's an English captain. What country? asks the captain. Czechoslovakia, replies Emil. Right, says the captain: How many competitors? Well, says Emil, me. Yes, got that, says the captain, but besides you? Well, me, repeats Emil, just me. Oh really, marvels the captain, nodding his head, just one. Yes, confirms Emil, just one. Me. Fine, says the captain patiently, and for which race? The 5,000 meters, says Emil. So, the 5,000 meters, says the captain, who's about to write his name on the appropriate list. Then he hesitates, pencil poised, and studies Emil, whom he doubtless finds a touch untidy, all rumpled, unshaven, his hair tousled—in short, not too prepossessing. And you've already run 5,000 meters, he says with gentle insinuation. That, yes, says Emil, adding, several times. Very good, says the captain, with increasing unction, and what was your time over that distance? Let's see, replies Emil simply, I ran it in 14:25.8. Excuse me? exclaims the captain: Is that even possible? You can check for yourself, says Emil, it's easy: Oslo, the European Championships. Naturally, of course, says the captain, hurriedly scribbling down Emil's name.

Leaving the stadium, Emil can't find any cars, but gets a ride in the back of a truck that takes him over to the military camp of huts assigned to the contestants. It's a crummy, muddy camp where Emil wanders around lost again until he gets himself assigned to some wretched garret where a drunken and unkempt soldier eventually brings him a few lukewarm dregs of tea, which he drinks. Then he sleeps like a log and the next day returns to the stadium.

It's the one built before the war for the Olympic Games, where the Führer refused to shake the hand of Jesse Owens because he was black. Jesse Owens has since retired from competition but Larry Snyder, his trainer at the time, is among the honored guests for the present events. The Americans have decorated the stadium just as it was for the prewar games, and there isn't a single empty seat in the stands, which are filled mostly with soldiers. It's starting: a parade of athletes from all the nations taking part in the championships will open the competition. Each country's name is written on a sign carried by a soldier walking ahead of that country's team of contestants. They're about to begin.

Emil looks everywhere for the man carrying the sign for Czechoslovakia and when he spots him, he goes up to him and holds out his hand, smiling as always. It's another American soldier, who stares at Emil the way the captain did the day before, then looks behind Emil, sees no one else, and asks, What, just one? You'd think Emil would be getting used to this but no, he's embarrassed, he nods. Yes, he replies finally, just one. The soldier's name is Joe and he can't hide the contempt he feels for this pathetic jerk. At first he'd thought it was sort of sharp to parade around in front of a band of athletes; now he feels foolish, having to march in front of only one. Joe's enthusiasm has suddenly hit rock bottom. He's almost ashamed. He'd rather drop the whole thing, now, but it's a little late.

Too late: a fanfare tackles the first notes of an opening march. Joe manages a twisted grin. Okay, come on, he says bitterly, as if deeply insulted. Let's do it. Hustle up. The athletes enter the stadium through the main gate, begin to parade past the stands amid the shouting, all loudly applauded in their handsome warm-up suits. But when a single individual appears behind the sign for Czechoslovakia, alone and dressed only in running shorts and a faded tracksuit top, the entire audience bursts out laughing. Everyone stands up to get a better look. Special correspondents pull out their notebooks and lick their lips, deploying flurries of adjectives to really capture the scene, while cameramen and reporters gleefully film and photograph it from every angle.

Although Emil is by nature a cheerful man, he has still been rather hurt by the enormous hilarity he has just provoked. So there he is all on his own, feeling quite alone and pretty unhappy since Joe dropped him cold right after the end of the parade, swearing and throwing his sign away over his shoulder. Emil listens to the opening speeches without getting a word, while he stares idly at all the national flags waving or else hanging limply. (I don't know if there's any wind that day or not.) Emil is sitting in the shade in the corner of one of the stands; he's a trifle hunched over, contemplating his feet, then the track, his feet, the track, waiting for something to happen.

As it happens, a Czech émigré who'd joined the American army has spotted him and figures it's a good chance to limber up his native tongue. He comes over to sit next to Emil and chats with him a moment. So, he finally says, what distance do you run? Five kilometers, replies Emil in a tired voice. What? shouts the other guy, appalled. Don't you know they already called the runners for the 5,000 a while ago? They've even called them three times: look, in that far corner, everyone's there already.

Emil gasps, jumps up, leaps out of the stands and streaks diagonally across the stadium like a demented sprinter. As he runs he tugs off his jacket, blinding himself for an instant and almost falling flat on his face; shouting and waving his arms, he tries to attract the attention of the men gathered at the starting line, where, luckily, he arrives in time.

Who the hell's this guy? Hardly a warm welcome. You, you want to run too? And where've you been? They look for his name on the list; they don't find it. When he wrote it down the day before, the captain—perhaps rattled by the 14:25.8—forgot to add the change to the starter's list. A few foreign competitors who are there have already seen Emil in action; they recognize him, vouch for him, and he's finally allowed to run.

All right, fine, grumbles the starter, fine, but in that case go over there, behind, in the second row, in that lane. Emil, this time, has had just about enough, and takes the liberty of protesting. As he's trying to prove he has a right to an inside position, the other runners, as one, back him up. They're familiar with Emil's record, know he's quite good and deserves a position on the inside. Okay, groans the starter before he raises his pistol. So, here we go.

Since Emil, annoyed by such treatment, decides to start right out at a punishing pace, it doesn't take him long to get rid of his most powerful adversaries. His speed is even such that he has soon lapped the slowest runners. Eighty thousand spectators then rise shouting to their feet, in one movement, because Emil is showing them something they've never seen: having already lapped all his adversaries, he now sets out to pass them again, one after the other, and as they realize what's going on and slow down, Emil just keeps going faster. Open-mouthed or screaming, driven out of their minds as much by his performance as by his impossible running form, the fans in the stadium are beside themselves. On his feet like everyone else, Larry Snyder himself is bewildered by Emil's unconventional style.

It's unnatural, he thinks, it's completely unnatural. This guy does everything you're not supposed to do and he's winning.

More than two laps ahead, yells the astonished announcer as Emil hurtles past, and to make this quite clear, he thrusts two fingers toward him at the risk of poking out his eyes. The stands are jumping with jubilation: people stamp their feet, shiver, howl, and all the soldiers chant Emil's name in chorus. The last lap, crows the delirious announcer, clearly more out of breath than Emil himself, and the starter, wild with joy, fires his pistol in the air as Emil keeps on accelerating, picking up his pace even though all his competitors are now impossibly far behind.

When he heads at last into the final stretch, the public is on the verge of fainting, and as he breaks the tape the stands begin to roar with applause that seems as if it could simply go on forever. No one, because who gives a damn, thinks to note that Emil has incidentally just smashed the Czech record.

And he, Emil, not in the least tired, grinning ear to ear, continues trotting nicely on after his finish, as if to cool down after that little jaunt. But he doesn't get away with that for long—people are now all over him, peppering him with questions, putting clothes on him to keep him warm, removing them again to get a better look at him, everyone taking pictures from every side, everyone all trying at the same time to tell him he just did something unbelievable. His name isn't well known yet outside of his own country, and the crowd seems to think he doesn't even know it himself because people keep calling his name in every possible way, as if to enlighten him on that point. Emil—it's clear by now how simple and modest he is—is baffled by all this admiration coming at him from every direction. He keeps assuring everybody that no, it's very nice of you but really, no, there's nothing miraculous about his running, he came in only fifth in the European Championships.

But the happiest guy of all, the one bursting with the greatest joy, is the humiliated soldier with the sign. Joe's heart, at that moment, swells with pride. In a short time, Emil will march in the final parade, his medal pinned to his tracksuit jacket. Before he lines up with the other athletes, Emil spots his American soldier waiting for him impatiently, sign in hand; as soon as he can, proud as punch, Joe rushes over and hugs Emil. Just one, he shouts, laughing till he cries, just one, just one. He pats him, embraces him, pokes him, kneads him, he's so happy he could hit him. When he sets out shortly in the parade, walking in front of Emil, Joe will glow with triumph and delight, knowing that he is now envied, that all the other sign carriers in the world envy him no end. Dear God, just one.

8

His form, in fact . . . impossible. Larry Snyder isn't the first one to have noticed. To have wondered how Emil does it.

There are runners who seem to fly, others who seem to dance, still others who look as if they were parading, and some appear to be advancing as though they were sitting on top of their legs. There are those who simply look as if they've been summoned and are hurrying as fast as possible. Emil, nothing like all that.

Emil, you'd think he was excavating, like a ditch digger, or digging deep into himself, as if he were in a trance. Ignoring every time-honored rule and any thought of elegance, Emil advances laboriously, in a jerky, tortured manner, all in fits and starts. He doesn't hide the violence of his efforts, which shows in his wincing, grimacing, tetanized face, constantly contorted by a rictus quite painful to see. His features are twisted, as if torn by appalling suffering; sometimes his tongue sticks out. It's as if he had a scorpion in each shoe, catapulting him on. He seems far away when he runs, terribly far away, concentrating so hard he's not even there—except that he's more there than anyone else; and hunkered down between his shoulders, on that neck always leaning in the same direction, his head bobs along endlessly, lolling and wobbling from side to side.

Fists clenched, torso writhing chaotically, Emil just lets his arms do as they please. Now, everyone will tell you that you run with your arms. To best propel your body along, you must use your upper limbs to take your own weight off your legs: in long-distance races, minimum movement of the head and arms produces the best results. Yet Emil does exactly the opposite, seems to run without paying any attention to his arms, whose convulsive momentum begins too high and plays out in strange movements, the arms sometimes raised or thrown backward, dangling or left to flop in ridiculous gestures, while his shoulders twitch around as well, and his elbows, too, are held exaggeratedly high as if he were carrying too heavy a load. Running, he looks like a fighter busy shadowboxing, so that his entire body resembles some kind of machine breaking down, going painfully to pieces, except for the harmonious churning of his legs as they voraciously bite off and chew up the track. In short, he doesn't do anything like other runners, who sometimes think he does simply anything at all.

But it's not enough to run any way you like, because you have to train, too. Well, he trains that way as well.

On the question of training, theories flourish throughout the world. The early Finnish system, called terrace training, divided workouts into alternating periods of exercise and rest, with each spell of effort building on the previous one, like the steps of a terrace. Swedish fartlek—"speed play"—advocates jogging on a soft surface in a natural environment, interrupted by bursts of running at various speeds for different lengths of time, with varying recovery periods. The Gerschler system recommends time trials, gym exercise, and training in intervals that emphasize speed work and efficient recovery. Emil has carefully studied each of those methods and made them all his own, incorporating them one by one into a single system, Emil's do-it-yourself method, which gives only a slight nod to pure physical culture.

All those other techniques recommend pauses between sprints, for example, relaxed periods that most runners spend walking.

Emil, no: he opts to jog between strenuous efforts, convinced that the body thus learns to rest while still racing and to maintain the necessary pace even during a state of great fatigue.

The standard training methods are also, without exception, based on the principle that the greatest expenditure of energy should be reserved for the challenges of competition: one should safeguard, during less rigorous workouts, the strength one will need during a race. Emil thinks that, on the contrary, one should train as vigorously as possible, tackling ever more demanding spells of effort so that the competition itself will later seem easier.

Emil feels that all these systems, in the end, fail to instill adequate willpower because they allow the runner to ease up when he finds himself faltering. Emil does not agree at all. On the contrary: if he feels tired, if he detects the slightest indication of a drop in speed, he immediately pushes himself to go faster. Luckily for him, he enjoys physical discomfort: he knows he can rely on himself and on his love of pain. He never permits anyone to give him a massage.

This training method allows him to exhaust his adversaries through a great number of interpolated sprints, while conserving energy for the end of the race, which is always extremely violent. He constantly varies his pace, running in raggedy tempos with subtle changes in speed that draw bitter complaints from those who run in his wake. For not only is it almost impossible for them to follow that short little bumpy, uneven, wildly fluctuating stride Emil whips up, not only do those constant variations of rhythm complicate their lives no end, and not only does his strange, exhausted style, driven by the rigid gestures of an automaton, hoodwink and thus discourage them, but to top it all off, the perpetual head-bobbing and those constantly windmilling arms make them dizzy to boot.

Never, ever, anything like the others, even though he's just a guy like everyone else. Of course people insist that he has an enlarged heart of above-average diameter that beats at an abnormally low rate. Of course they claim that his lungs absorb an unusually rich supply of oxygen. But meeting in Prague specifically to address such questions, a committee of medical experts discounts all those rumors, affirming that, not at all, Emil is an ordinary man, he's simply a good Communist and that's what makes all the difference.

In short, nothing is certain except that he has doubtless learned how to discipline that heart and those lungs, increasing their capacity for great bursts of speed at very short intervals along with equally speedy recovery. That's how he can wind up a long race with an all-out sprint only to dash off a few seconds later, barely winded, to fetch his tracksuit at the other end of the stadium—and the next day, if need be, do it again.

At some point someone will figure out that simply while training, Emil has run three times around the world. Making the machine run, constantly tinkering with it to tease out better and better results, is all that counts and that's why, frankly, he's not a pretty sight. It's because he doesn't give a damn about anything else. That machine is an extraordinary motor around which no one ever thought to mount any coachwork. His style has not achieved perfection and perhaps never will, but Emil knows he hasn't time to bother with that: it would waste too many hours better spent on increasing his strength and endurance. So even though he's not easy on the eyes, he's content to run the way that suits him best and tires him the least, that's all.

9

Style or no, doesn't matter, Emil is world famous. On the whole, it hasn't taken much: Oslo, Berlin, an Allied Forces cross country race at Hanover, and the records he has piled up at home. In one year, he has gone from a name in small type near the end of a column of athletics highlights in local papers to front-page photos in the international sports press, and soon the international press, period.

He has become what is called a great champion. He is inescapable. His participation in an event is no longer announced; his future triumph, long before the meet takes place, is simply proclaimed. His chances of victory are so absolute at this point that his participation in an event is discouraging, so discouraging that it's sometimes considered undesirable by sports federations. His appearance at this or that meet abroad may wind up cancelled because of his presumed superiority, and the federations are frank about this. We'd prefer that he not attend, some of them humbly admit, just to avoid demoralizing our runners. Or others announce, more hypocritically, He would bring nothing to our cross country runners from the standpoint of technique.

Even the doctors get involved, having long criticized him on the pretext that he runs completely counter to all common sense.

Shaking their heads, they opine that for two years now, they've been waiting for him to expire at any moment. According to them such a phenomenon, who is essentially committing suicide, cannot last long. The doctors can say what they want, remarks Emil calmly, but personally I'm not fond of them. They're supposed to take care of sick people, not guys like myself. The only doctor I listen to is me.

The newspapers gleefully take up this debate, which proves a gold mine for them. Is Emil defying the medical establishment? Will Emil keep going? Isn't Emil running too much? He is becoming the center of fanatical interest and receives whole post-office sacks of hundreds of letters, requests for autographs or advice, with photos for dedications and proposals of marriage. He has earned a nickname: the Locomotive. Things are going just fine.

Result: things aren't going too badly for the Czech regime, which after the war has moved into the Socialist Bloc via the Prague Coup and now begins to see Emil as a splendid propaganda tool. Of that ilk he is the best diplomat, the most effective ambassador; he has become an Athlete of the State, one of those who, like elite workers, are awarded special status, honors, and advantages. In civilian life, such celebrities may receive villas, medals, an honorary position in metallurgy or the textile industry, for example. Emil, who is in the military, will be promoted to ever-higher rank, while his activities will remain centered on sports. So he'll be well taken care of. They're keeping him in the army, obviously, which he likes anyway, while offering him ideal training opportunities, and so, taking advancement too in stride, this simple sergeant rapidly becomes a lieutenant in the tank corps.

In his garrison at Milovice, the new lieutenant is in charge of training the recruits, a duty the press insists is not a sinecure, burnishing Emil's legend with the news that every evening, the military mail is delivered on foot by the greatest runner in the world. Which naturally does not interfere with his regular exercise runs over varied terrain, sometimes in field dress because he likes that, galloping through the snow still wearing his big heavy army boots.

Try running twenty kilometers in those things, he likes to suggest, and later, on the track, when you slip into light shoes, you can't imagine how that changes everything. For the same reason, when he trains indoors, he's careful to use ankle weights to work the muscles harder.

This continues: Emil is everywhere, from international meets—The Hague, Algiers, Stockholm, Paris, Helsinki (where he finally beats the runner of the deep forests)—to simple provincial athletic events like the one in Zlín, one June day, where he notices a girl he likes.

I must say that she's perfectly nice, very pretty, tall and slender, with short chestnut-brown hair, light gray eyes, a quick, sweet smile, and she throws the javelin, besides. Emil asks around a little and learns two things: first that her name is Dana, and second that she's the daughter of his commanding officer. Since this colonel's daughter and her javelin have just improved their personal record on the track at Zlín, Emil shrewdly spots this as the ideal occasion, dashing off to buy a bouquet of flowers with which to tender his congratulations. They chat and, a few days later, when he has a go at yet another of his own records, it's Dana's turn to come compliment him.

They chat some more and, chatting, notice that they have the same birthday, September 19, and are exactly the same age, although she had a six-hour head start on him. Since they're amazed at this coincidence, and since Emil doesn't feel like leaving it at that, Listen, he says after a moment: we'll never see the end of it if we have to go congratulate each other every time we break a record. It'll drag on forever. Because records, you know, I've got the feeling we'll be setting plenty of them. The best way to congratulate each other without having to trot around each time, perhaps, would be to live together, no? What do you think?

While waiting to hear what she thinks, Emil flies off a month later to the Olympics, held in London that year. The city is suffering through a heat wave and on the day Emil must run the 10,000 meters, the atmosphere is sweltering, oppressive, stormy weather that can't quite make up its mind. A thick fog swells the sky to form a giant magnifying glass between the sun and the earth, where it's 104 degrees in the shade.

Emil is the favorite, of course, but there's still Heino, who is there saying nothing yet thinking nonetheless. The man of the deep forests has a thirst for vengeance and no desire to let Emil have the last word. So Emil and Dr. Knienicky, whom he has for once allowed to advise him, come up with a race strategy. It's really rather simple. When the doctor, sitting in the stands, feels it's time for Emil to accelerate, he will just wave a red jersey, Emil's spare: he runs only in red, representing his country at athletic meets exclusively in the color of the proletarian revolution, although whether by choice or by fiat is anyone's guess.

Emil takes off as always with his machine-like strength, his robotic reliability, but this time without the frenzy of Berlin, whereas Heino has started out savagely, quickly surging eighty meters ahead. Emil seems unconcerned, knowing perfectly well what he intends to do and waiting for the signal. He remains in twelfth or fifteenth place during the entire time he allots himself for observing the action, calmly pacing his efforts. It isn't until the halfway point, when he spies the red jersey discreetly waved by the doctor, who has just stood up in the stands, that Emil joins the chase and begins implacably to speed up.

Then he devours the track, brutally pounding along in striking contrast to the smooth stride of his rival Heino. Just when the spectators might have thought he'd exhausted some of his strength, they see a brand-new Emil reborn in mid-race, a fellow bursting with fresh energy, ferocious, astoundingly determined. Panic in the deep forests: dreading his approaching peril, Heino tries to derail the locomotive by arrogantly taking back command of the action. But Emil can't bear staring at the backs of his adversaries and won't tolerate the situation for more than five hundred meters. To avenge this indignity, wipe out the affront, grimacing until his face becomes a fright mask, he sets furiously to work while a madly perspiring

Dr. Knienicky, now standing on his seat, frantically—albeit uselessly—brandishes the red jersey with which he occasionally and distractedly mops his brow or neck. The final sprint . . . and in a few dozen meters Emil has crushed everything, blown everything away: it's the first gold medal in track and field for Czechoslovakia.

At the finish line, everyone thinks that after so great an effort, having displayed such superhuman energy, the diabolical Emil must surely collapse. Well, not at all. On the contrary, he begins frisking about the stadium, takes off—almost skipping—to get a little glass of water, trots back to the victors' podium, thumps the stricken Heino cordially—and respectfully—on the back, then, pirouetting, performs an impeccable handstand, even running a few meters that way just for a change.

The shouting audience surges out of the stands and past barricades to engulf Emil in an ecstatic crowd, in the midst of which, among the joyous faces, he glimpses Dr. Knienicky, the most jubilant of them all, weeping with happiness. After things have calmed down a bit, the two of them wind up in a pub facing two pints of beer at which Emil wouldn't turn up his nose, ditto for the doctor.

Well I must say, the doctor tells him, you seemed to have quite a crick in your neck: you made even worse faces today than in Berlin. Yes, I know, admits Emil, people are always complaining to me about it. Whether I'm training, competing, they all say that. But I can't change, it's not something I'm doing on purpose. I swear it really does hurt, what I do—don't you think I'd rather smile? Still, you could try, suggests the doctor vaguely, raising his hand to get another pint. I'm not talented enough to run and smile at the same time, sighs Emil, raising his hand as well. I'll run with perfect form when they start judging the beauty of a race with a calculator, the way they do with figure skating. But me, for the moment, I just have to go as fast as I can.

10

So: back from London with the gold for the 10,000 meters, which Emil sweetens with a little silver medal for the 5,000, and that's it for this time. There's more to life than the Olympics, however, and not every day is that much fun. A year later he must run in his native region, in the stadium at Ostrava, against sixteen other military competitors.

He'd been in Gottwaldov[2] the day before, as it happens, returning only on the eleven p.m. express. The train was packed for a five-hour trip during which Emil had to stand in the aisle without any refreshment except some cookies and a little beer offered him by a soldier on leave. He's still dead tired and falls asleep on the tram on the way to Ostrava; fortunately, another soldier recognizes him and wakes him up at the stop for the stadium.

When the starter's pistol goes off for this latest 10,000 meter race, Emil doesn't feel like putting on a show; it's not that the stands are rather empty that day, it's just that he's not in the mood. He didn't really train the day before, he's truly exhausted, let's just get it over with. The track's in excellent shape, though, having recently been upgraded, and has those wide turns that always improve performance. But Emil's only going through the motions when he almost immediately gets out in front and rather quickly pulls away from his rivals, steadily increasing his lead.

He runs, he runs without wondering about anything, then the loudspeaker announces that after the initial laps, his intermediate times are better than Heino's. Now, Heino, although beaten in London, still holds his world record. Pleased by this evocation of the deep forests, Emil is nevertheless still fatigued by his train trip and doesn't think he can manage to keep up his pace. After the seventh kilometer, however, he changes his mind and, sensing that he still has some strength in reserve, he decides to try his luck. He goes for it and what do you know, he gets it, he breaks the world record.

World champion: the reaction is immediate and he's promoted to captain and then his troubles begin. Those in high places put their heads together: they definitely consider Emil living proof of the wonders of Socialism. In which case, they should keep him close to home, not waste him, not send him abroad too much. The rarer he is, the better. Plus, it would really be too bad if while on one of those trips he were—on a sudden impulse—to cross over to the other side, the unspeakable side of capitalism and imperialism. So when Emil is invited to run the 5,000 meters at an international meet in Los Angeles, the powers that be have a word with him.

Comrade, they tell him, the military committee has decided that in the future, you will not participate in any sports event without official permission. Fine, says, Emil, but that doesn't change much. Up to now I've always had it, permission. Well that's just it, comrade, they reply: permission, that's now a thing of the past. Dismissed, comrade.

And the committee coughs up a communiqué announcing the news, claiming that too many invitations to competitions of too little importance are distracting Emil from his military duties and preventing him from pursuing his athletic goals.

Emil takes the hit, but he's none too pleased. He says nothing and yet the fact is that, from then on, he begins to lose fairly regularly, finishing third or fourth in races he should easily have won.

Not in the best of shape, it would seem; sometimes he doesn't even show up. At first the foreign press pretends not to understand. They say Emil is unwell. There's talk of a foot wound, tetanus, blood poisoning, speculation that the doctors who criticized him may have been right. Or else people think they understand but couch their thoughts diplomatically: We do not wish to accredit the rumors that Emil fell suddenly ill upon learning that his government had withdrawn its authorization for his projected trip to California.

Still, matters aren't doing too badly, all things considered. One Saturday the sporting press has happier news of him to announce: Tomorrow, Emil faces a new challenge. But it's only his marriage to Dana, taking place the following day. And on a lovely fall Sunday, in his handsome new captain's uniform, he does indeed wed the colonel's daughter, a future Olympic javelin champion. So it is beneath a long arch of those crossed weapons that the wedding procession, drawing huge crowds, brings traffic to a standstill for some time in the streets of Prague. Prague where, apart from that, everyone is scared to death.

11

Prague where, in those years, everyone is afraid, every second, of everything and everybody, everywhere. For the greater good of the Party, the overriding concern is to purge, demolish, crush, liquidate all hostile elements. The newspapers and radio speak of nothing else; the police and State Security Service take on the job. Anyone may at any moment be charged with treason as a spy, conspirator, saboteur, agent provocateur, or terrorist of the—pick one—Trotskyist, Titoist, Zionist, or Social-Democratic persuasion, reviled as a kulak or a bourgeois nationalist.

At any time, anybody can wind up in prison or a camp, usually without any idea why. People generally end up there not because of what they think but because they are in the way of someone powerful enough to send them there. Each day, from the four corners of the country, hundreds of letters arrive at the State Security Service Headquarters to obligingly and imaginatively draw official attention to this or that comrade, colleague, neighbor, relative, all denounced for plotting against the regime.

Here, then, we have reached that same point we'd already found ourselves in, with slight variations, not even ten years earlier. Fearful of speaking or listening to anybody, people systematically shun one another, even within the bosom of their families. The press is gagged as never before, and as before, listening to foreign radio broadcasts can lead to fearsome reprisals. Now that terror has settled comfortably into everyone's consciousness, the choice is simple: silence and resignation, or participation in the personality cult of President Gottwald and in the fanatical demonstrations supporting the regime. Another mainstay—or last hope—is to join the Party, which has grown in a few months by over a million new members, among whom, it must be said, is Emil.

One shouldn't dismiss Emil as an opportunist. Two things are absolutely indisputable: that he sincerely believes in the virtues of Socialism, and that in his position he could hardly do otherwise. He knows that certain intellectuals roaming the corridors of power have him in their sights as they eagerly consider whether his status as a great sports hero might—perhaps inevitably—be tainted by bourgeois individualism, since the unhealthy adoration of any athlete seriously betrays the Stakhanovite ideal.

Although his superiors always cautiously prefer to keep him under wraps, claiming that he's in poor form, tired, or even ill, Emil still doesn't give an inch. When Heino emerges growling from his deep forests and retakes the world record for 10,000 meters, Emil takes it back from him fifty-two days later, leaving his competitors so deep in his dust that the second finisher comes in four laps behind. In the 5,000 and 10,000 meters, Emil definitely remains the fastest man in the world.

A few months later, in Finland, he breaks his own record so thoroughly that the audience, refusing to believe the first announcement of his time, remains silent. When this winning time is confirmed, a storm of enthusiasm rages unabated for twenty-five minutes. When calm has been restored, Emil takes his little victory lap at the clip of a good 400 meter race, as if nothing has happened. And as always when people congratulate him, he insists that he really didn't do much, that he won thanks to the excellence of the track and the ideal temperatures of Scandinavia. And in any case, he claims, individual exploits are not important. What counts is drawing the working masses to the stands. That's what matters. Of course, Emil, of course. That bracing philosophy does you honor.

In other words he keeps on winning almost every time: in rain, snow, icy winds, he leaves everyone in his wake, everywhere. Almost everywhere. Because for the Eastern European meets featuring the USSR and its satellite countries, for the huge Communist rallies in East Berlin, Budapest, Bucharest, Warsaw, or when he goes off to train in the Crimea, there, obviously, there's no problem in letting him leave Prague. When he's invited elsewhere, on the other hand, somewhere in the so-called Free World (enslaved by capitalism, naturally), where he is often invited since he's in demand everywhere, forget it. And what's more, it isn't even Emil who replies, No thank you, it's his federation. Which, what's even more, given the Cold War, doesn't deign to reply all that often.

Even the cross country run sponsored in Paris by the Communist paper *L'Humanité*, an event with solid ideological underpinnings that attracts the best athletes of the Socialist Bloc—even that is off limits for Emil. The thing is, the higher-ups are wary, and for good reason. Let's take for example one Bacigál, a young Czech student, an excellent middle-distance runner they'd allowed to go run that *L'Huma* race. Imagine, he up and decided to skip returning to Prague by staying in Paris and asking for some kind of political asylum. Most unfortunate precedent. Lively irritation in the federation as well as in the corridors of power. Well, fine, they must have decided to keep their response low-key, to take measures and hire specialists, because that young Bacigál obtained a residence permit, joined the Racing Club de France, and that was the last anyone ever heard of him.

No such unpleasantness must ever occur with Emil, so he is closely attended, occasionally extracted from his lair to go on exhibit, even solo, in staged personal performances. On Czech Army

Day, before an audience of fifty thousand watching a soccer tournament final in the Strahov stadium in Prague, he has to run all by himself during half-time. Immediately afterward, he disappears.

So they're hiding him, he's silent, then no one hears a thing about him anymore. He's keeping quiet, keeping his head down these days, doesn't seem to be running. People abroad are lost in conjecture: What could he be up to, what's he doing; will he ever be allowed one day to finally go abroad outside of official competitions; is he secretly working on new records; is he lying low for reasons we don't know; is he ill again; is he finished. . . . Mystery. Always an excellent thing, mystery.

All that lasts for a while until out of nowhere, with both barrels, Emil breaks two new world records, for the 20,000 meters and the hour. He becomes the first man in all of history to run more than twenty kilometers in one hour. And in the course of that exploit immediately hailed as legendary, his fastest kilometer proves to be the final one, a largesse attesting to his ample reserves and suggesting that he could yet do even better. This prodigious performance will not soon be eclipsed, warbles the press. In thus expanding the norms of physical possibility, Emil becomes superhuman, inaccessible to us all, for no one has gone that far. Since those two records had previously been held by the eternal Heino, just imagine the ambience in the deep forests. There had already been talk of a decline, but now the light has dawned: Emil was preparing himself for distances he had never tackled before.

Meanwhile, no one has ever gone so far in the political theater of show trials, either. A massive spectacle, produced by the State Security Service, with the artistic collaboration of Soviet advisors on dramatic presentation, one-hundred-percent attendance by the accused, impeccable sets and costumes, a top-notch audience, lines flawlessly memorized by the entire cast—judges, prosecutors, lawyers, defendants—and the staging of each production worked out to the last detail: a perfect dramatic arc all the way to the show-stopping verdict, hangings galore, sustained applause, numerous curtain calls, long live President Gottwald.

It's against that backdrop that a foreign journalist, a special correspondent from a sports daily, takes it into his head to come interview Emil. Why not, no problem. But before meeting him, one must obtain permission first from his commanding officer and then from the newspaper union and then from the ministry of information. Which represents quite a lot of preliminary interviews, questionnaires, forms to fill out in quadruplicate, with signatures and stamps. Breathless, the special correspondent finally arrives at Emil's home, Number 8 Půjčovny Street, in a recently constructed building next to the main post office. The journalist rings, and it's Dana who opens the door, smiling and simply dressed in a brown sweater and blue skirt.

Unfortunately Emil is not here, she explains most apologetically; he would have been so pleased to see you. The problem is that he must train hard every afternoon, and at the moment he's very busy getting ready to go to Kiev, where he'll be facing a new Soviet hope named Nicéphore Popov. But no matter, come back this evening and you'll see him. In the meantime, she says, do come in, I'll show you around our home and then we'll have tea. I'd love that, says the delighted special correspondent.

The two spacious rooms are prettily decorated: Dana's guitar hangs on the wall among pictures and banners; books and knickknacks crowd the shelves; there are rugs, a framed portrait photo of Joseph Stalin, another of Klement Gottwald, a lamp shaped like a globe, and a large radio. Opening onto a handsome kitchen, these two rooms flank a wide vestibule where one may admire the equipment Emil uses daily for his limbering-up exercises, including a Swedish rib stall clamped to the wall amid countless trophies and medals. And the javelins, Dana points out. My javelins.

The house isn't bad, but Dana is not alone. One of her good friends, actually, is staying there as well, a jovial home economics teacher, a woman who is extremely attentive, helpful, considerate, and who never leaves her side, even when the tea is made. So they busy themselves with the tea while Dana talks about her day-to-day life. Goodness, it's nothing, really, they have a very simple life. She works as a filing clerk for the sports magazine *Ruch*, which occupies her days while Emil carries out his duties as an officer over at the ministry. Then, in their spare time, she works with her javelin while he runs his daily quota of kilometers. Wonderful, says the captivated special correspondent, but you must have a few moments for leisure activities, I suppose.

Naturally, replies Dana. I must tell you first off that Emil insists on answering his mail himself: he receives lots of letters, it takes him quite a bit of time. Then, well, there's reading, she says, gesturing toward the bookshelves. Yes, Emil is a great reader. Plus they do go out sometimes in the evening, plays and all that. And when they stay home, they listen to music or play it themselves: Emil has a very pleasant baritone and enjoys singing old national folksongs late of an afternoon, while Dana accompanies him on the guitar, she says, waving toward her instrument. Charming, says the enthusiastic special correspondent, forgetting what he'd thought he'd read one day regarding Emil's vocal talents. Then, each evening, while he has a little glass of Moravian wine, Emil likes to do the cooking himself, what can you do, he loves that. Of course, who wouldn't, gushes the special correspondent, doing his best not to recall the recent adoption of rationing coupons for bread, flour, and potatoes. And tell me, is he feeling fit these days?

Ah, says Dana, he'll tell you more about that this evening but the fact is that for the moment he's not in top condition. He's been ill, you know, a nasty bout of tonsillitis, after which he had to stop training completely. But, well, he's getting back to it little by little, he's the one in charge, he's his own coach, you know. Naturally—the special correspondent jumps right in—and what does he have in mind for the next Olympic Games? Oh, well, as for Helsinki, replies Dana, he hasn't decided yet. Either he'll run the 5,000 and the

10,000 meters, or the 10,000 and the marathon. But strictly between ourselves, Emil is truly beginning to tire of his fame, you see; he's thinking about his legacy more than anything else. You must have heard talk about Ivan Ullsperger, and Stanislas Jungwirth. I know their names, nods the special correspondent.

Anyway, we'll see, announces Dana briskly. One thing is certain: after the Olympics, we're going to spruce up our home a little. It certainly needs it, and Emil just happens to be extremely handy around the house. That's another thing he simply loves. He's planning to repaint everything, hang some wallpaper, fix the shower, and reupholster the armchairs. The only trouble is, he's so fond of working around the house that he tends to make a mess everywhere, says Dana, smiling in mock complaint, and he's tracked up a few of our carpets, but there you are. He loves puttering about. Ah, sighs the special correspondent sympathetically. But do drop in again a little later, concludes Dana, getting to her feet, and he'll tell you more himself.

When the journalist returns that evening, it's the jovial teacher who opens the door while Dana hovers behind her in the shadows to tell him that they're so very sorry but, well, Emil is already asleep. I told you, he's so worn out. I understand perfectly, says the special correspondent, much moved, and please give him my respects. Then, after he leaves, there's a pause; Dana turns to the other woman. Well, she says, it went all right? Did I say what I was supposed to? The other woman drops all pretense of being a teacher and housemate, shedding her mask of joviality as she goes to open a cupboard, where she presses the stop button on a tape recorder, removes the tape, slips it first into an envelope and then into the pocket of her coat, which she brusquely puts on without a word. I will write my report, comrade, she says. If necessary, you will be informed. She leaves. A midnight-blue Tatraplan T600 four-door sedan pulls up in front of the house. She gets in, and the car drives off toward the headquarters of the State Security Service.

12

The Helsinki Games begin on Tuesday but Emil is not in great shape. At thirty, he is tired, perhaps worn out by having to keep leaving the scene only to storm back in full force. His chest is sunken, his cheeks gaunt, his eyes deep-set in their orbits; his wife has never seen him so thin. It's Sunday and things aren't looking good; streaming sweat but never winded, he returns from his daily twenty kilometers interspersed with long sprints, then packs his bags. And the next day he flies off to Finland with Dana (who accompanies him both as an athlete and an athlete's wife), surrounded by a handful of burly officials, mute giants in red jackets and glowering looks who never leave him, especially abroad.

Helsinki: crisp weather, evenly overcast sky, zigzags of wind, scattered showers. The humidity comes from all around, from the sky but also from the rivers and countless lakes, from the sea that insinuates itself through a thousand meandering ways into the capital. But the air is invigorating and, at this latitude, the short nights coincide with the time spent sleeping: perfect repose. Instead of limiting himself to two long-distance events, Emil surprises everyone by deciding in the end to enter three: 5,000 meters, 10,000 meters, marathon.

This decision does not please everyone and especially not the professionals, even those from fraternal countries. The Soviet Olympic Committee expresses its skepticism, which amounts to a criticism and therefore a disapproval, through the voice of its secretary general. No one, he announces, can deliver good performances in three such difficult races at such close intervals, not even the peerless Paavo Nurmi. An announcement that leaves Emil indifferent but gives him an idea: always eager to see the local sights, he'll go visit Paavo Nurmi.

Before Emil, a quarter of a century earlier, Paavo Nurmi was the greatest runner of all time. Nicknamed the Flying Finn, he's the one who invented training by stopwatch, a stopwatch he kept by him constantly—even running, eating, and sleeping. He became a rich man, having opened a haberdashery in Helsinki considered a place of pilgrimage by athletes from all over the world, who hasten there to enjoy the honor of shaking his hand. He, without a word, merely looks them straight in the eye while selling them exorbitantly priced Finnish shirts or extravagantly expensive silk ties they don't need at all. Having bought his shirt like everybody else, Emil, cleaned out, wears it for a few hours—it's nice-looking but it's a bit too small, it's a little bit rough to the touch, it's just a bit itchy—then changes into his red jersey, number 903 for the 10,000 meters, and they're off.

A quarter of the way through, he takes charge of the race and stays there. Halfway through he accelerates sharply before beginning to break up his pace with his usual sudden variations: abrupt takeoff in the far turn and straightaway, slowdown in front of the stands as if to allow the audience time to admire him, renewed takeoff at top speed. His rivals might still almost manage to follow him if his pace were regular but these repeated moves, these incessant sharp changes in rhythm dismay, exhaust, and demoralize them: their hearts and legs go on violent alert each time, their temples throb and it's really hard for them but he could care less and he wins. Gold medal.

Three days later, he dons his jersey again for the 5,000 meters and they're off again. But as he'd warned Dana and contrary to what people think, Emil really doesn't feel in good shape. He has no hope of victory in this race, which isn't his preferred distance; he would simply like not to come in fourth, he's not asking for more. Fourth, that would be pathetic. No, a tiny third place would suit him fine. But it's stronger than he is: brutally yet methodically, grimacing and gesticulating more fiendishly than ever, he still finds a way to shatter his adversaries' rhythm, to confuse, rattle, disconcert them. One after the other he disorients them to make them lose even their own sense of the race and their abilities. Then while he's at it, when he winds up third in the home stretch the way he wanted, so that he's looking at the backs of just two men in front of him (which always aggravates him a little), he taps into a modest surge of energy he'd set aside, he passes them and he wins.[3] Gold medal.

And four days later, Emil dons his red jersey once more to go run the marathon. His official coaches are against this but he gives as much of a damn about coaches as he does about doctors, masseurs, agents, dieticians, or trainers, that whole bunch he doesn't need. He goes.

The marathon, as everyone knows, began when General Miltiades, pleased at having beaten the enemy on a field of fennel and wishing to let Athens know as quickly as possible, sent his messenger Pheidippides, who ran forty kilometers beneath a leaden sky to die of exhaustion when he arrived. We also know that two thousand years later that distance was officially extended to 42.195 kilometers, namely the stretch between the Great Park of Windsor to the White City Stadium of London. We know—at least we can imagine—that it's a cruelly demanding event. We know that up until now Emil has never run it.

So off he goes. And the spectators get ready to naughtily enjoy the spectacle he usually puts on with his facial contortions, writhing torso, and apparently discombobulated stride. Well guess what. The man whose features convulse with appalling pain, that's the Emil of the running track. The Emil of the marathon runs in complete serenity, without the slightest apparent suffering. At the halfway point, where disheartened runners often give up, seeing as a Swede and an Englishman have escorted him that far with their tongues hanging out, Emil turns to them with a smile. So, he says, it was nice of you to keep me company but here, I take my leave. Got to get going.

He abandons them and goes on alone, enjoying his sense of relaxation. Even stride, peaceful expression. Emil answers the shouts of the public massed along his route with discreet waves, trades a few jokes with the occupants of the support vehicles following him, winks at onlookers still stunned by his overwhelming superiority. It's the first time he has ever smiled while running, showing all his big teeth, as he admires the landscape. He seems almost ready to sign autographs along the way and share his impressions of the pleasant Finnish countryside, a cheerful decor of fir plantations and barley fields, of birches and tumbled brown rocks, and ponds gleaming in the sun.

Seven kilometers before the finish, though, a slight hitch: his jersey is sticking too much to his sweaty chest, so he rolls it up and keeps plugging, torso half naked, radiant. Then, knowing he's approaching the Olympic Stadium, he makes sure his expressive system is in prime working order: to ensure instant recognition, he begins grimacing, but only a little, not the full-blown classic number, nothing on the order of his track performance. Just a tiny twitch of a rictus he sets off only outside the stadium, where it serves him as a passport, allowing him to be identified from the moment he enters by a public glad to welcome his familiar face. Heralded by a trumpet fanfare, he arrives fresh as a daisy, treats himself—amid general satisfaction—to a bit of a final sprint that isn't strictly necessary and that's it, he's won the lot. Gold medal.

Emil, his denigrators will say, didn't even win the marathon: he just went off on one of his good old training runs. That contortionist with his mask of pain turned the dramatic ordeal of supreme suffering into an afternoon stroll. He made sport of it: the exhaustion of the soldier collapsing on the finish line of a duty fulfilled, the sweat and tears, the medical attendants and their stretcher, all that, for him—horseshit. The denigrators are wrong. Emil has just experienced the same martyrdom as the others but he lets none of it show, he is discreet even if his smile, as he crosses the finish line, is that of a man brought back to life. Once he has crossed that line, just breathless enough, without a glance at the stretcher-bearers, he says no, not too tired, just a minor headache but it won't last long.

For fear of repeating ourselves, to avoid growing tedious, we have opted not to describe the reception of Emil's earlier victories in Helsinki: various ovations and hurrahs, eruptions of enthusiasm, the explosion of the applause meter. But now, three gold medals snatched up in ten days by the same guy, that's just unheard-of: a hundred thousand spectators brought to their feet are dumbfounded not only by what's right in front of their eyes, but also by the noise they can make while they're watching it.

13

Back in Prague, Emil is received in triumph, a national hero. Official congratulations in the Strahov Stadium, motorcade before immense throngs jamming the avenues, promotion from captain to major, government flea in President Gottwald's ear proposing Emil for the Order of the Republic. And in the months that follow, Emil is trotted out in factory after factory all across the country to show that he's real, he does exist, no one invented him, or rather, yes: he was invented by Communism on the march.

And that's not all it invented: in Prague, meanwhile, more spectacular than ever, new show trials are beginning against fourteen leaders who six months earlier were conscientious and respected secretaries-general of the Party, ministers, vice-ministers, or section chiefs in the highest circles of the state. Soviet advisors have decided that these fourteen, among whom—it is pointedly noted—figure eleven Jews, should be finally and suddenly unmasked as conspirators, traitors, Trotskyist-Titoist-Zionist spies, bourgeois nationalists, imperialist lackeys: enemies of the Czech people, the popular-democratic regime, and Socialism. The fourteen are worked over ruthlessly until they agree to admit, describe, and assume responsibility for their crimes, and then even beg for punishment to make the torture stop, at which point most of them are hanged; those few remaining go to prison for life, while one or two privileged souls wind up in the uranium mines. Which just goes to show, comes the eager explanation, that Communism on the march proves its matchless superiority: it not only produces the greatest champions, but also flushes out the greatest traitors. And it's in this cozy atmosphere that Emil is summoned to deal with a pressing request from the American government inviting him and Dana to the stadiums of the United States.

Comrade, you will of course refuse this invitation, announce the authorities, handing him a paper, but we'd also welcome a few words from you on the subject. Words, for example, like these. Fine, says Emil, if you want. And on the state radio station, there he is making fun of the American offer, claiming that the poor quality of tracks over there makes athletic meets a circus, adding that he simply laughs at those grotesque and—let's be blunt—anti-sports events. Cold War, Iron Curtain, Emil is obviously not going for a little stroll abroad. The official confirmation comes a month later: he will no longer participate in any competition outside of Eastern Europe.

Already, in Helsinki, people had wondered if Emil was completely free in his movements, if he himself made the decisions regarding his competitions. Right after the marathon, in front of the press gallery, an Italian reporter had asked him if he would be coming to run that autumn in Milan. Emil had looked up and, without a word, jerked his thumb back over his shoulder at one of the red-jacketed officials. Who had merely shaken his big head from side to side, that's all. Got it.

Which leaves what he can accomplish in his homeland; one has to keep busy, after all. During a meeting of the Army's Physical Education Instructors Club, for example, Emil announces that he'd like to break two new world records: those for twenty-five and thirty kilometers, distances rarely contested by professionals, but an important element of which are the intermediate times, the individual running times for shorter distances that allow a runner to bring off several separate performances during a single event. Emil will make the attempt in his favorite stadium, in Stara Boleslav, in the urban center of Hutska, up in northern Bohemia: humid, zero wind, 52 degrees Fahrenheit. And the next day, those world records, well of course he breaks them. And the splits for the shorter distances, well of course they're a cinch. The whole business might almost start to get a wee bit tiresome.

The sports press, moreover, does seem somewhat tired of it. Emil is overdoing things. Winning too much. The public will soon cease to marvel at his victories—or worse, will marvel only if he loses. It even appears that in this regard, the sports papers are busily laying the groundwork. In a few years, they predict, Emil will be only a memory. Such is the law of sports, sigh the papers. You'd think they were already eager to get rid of him.

Besides, ever since his first great success at the London Games, at twenty-six, there has been no one to compare with Emil: he is incomparable. For six years, the next two thousand days, he will be the fastest man on earth over long distances. To the point that his last name becomes for everyone the incarnation of power and velocity, joining that small army of synonyms for speed. This name of Zátopek that was nothing, that was nothing but a funny name, begins to clatter around the world in three mobile and mechanical syllables, an inexorable waltz in three beats, galloping hooves, the throbbing of a turbine, the clacking of valves or connecting rods punctuated by the final *k*, sparked by the initial *z* that darts off already quite fast: say *zzz* and it's speeding right away, as if that consonant were a starter. Plus the fact that a fluid first name lubricates this machine: a can of Emil oil comes with the Zátopek engine.

It might almost be unfair: there have been other great artists in the history of running. If they haven't had such lasting renown, mightn't it be because their names never sounded as good, weren't made for that, didn't cling as closely and tenaciously as Emil's to that discipline—except for Mimoun, perhaps, whose surname sounds like a whispering name for the wind. Result: they've been forgotten, it's that simple, too bad for them.

So in the end, it has perhaps been this name that has brought him glory, or at least contributed powerfully to his fame. . . . We may well wonder. Wonder if it isn't the rhythm of his name, its beat that makes it speak even now to everyone and will make sure that people will speak of it a long time hence; wonder if it isn't this name that created the myth, wrote the legend, for names can also, by themselves, perform great deeds. But let's not get carried away, here. This is all fine and dandy, except that a last name—you can make it say or evoke whatever you please. Had Emil been a grain broker, a nonfigurative painter, or a political commissar, his name would doubtless have proved completely suitable for each profession, equally well denoting rational management, lyrical abstraction, or a chill up the spine. It would have worked just fine every time.

On another note, at the end of the year, a classified ad in the papers offers to sell the scoreboard from the Helsinki Games, an apparatus comprising seven thousand light bulbs in two hundred groups of thirty-five. Another leading light, Joseph Stalin, goes out at the start of the New Year and President Gottwald, beloved guide of the nation, catching a chill at the funeral, dies in Prague right after returning from Moscow.

14

Emil is a little tired. It's understandable; a lesser man would have faltered before now. In addition to the gold amassed in Finland, he has become the man with eight world records over distances longer than 5,000 meters: six, ten, and fifteen miles; ten, twenty, twenty-five, and thirty kilometers; not to mention the hour record. Back in Prague, in top form, he is no longer very active during the months that follow, as if he were resting after his exploits. There are celebrations for him wherever he goes, a museum honoring him has just opened in his native village of Koprivnice, there's a film in the works about his life story, and he's certainly earned the right to catch his breath.

Stalin, then Gottwald, dead; perhaps we'll all get a chance to breathe a tad easier. In fact, there are slight signs that something must be going on in the corridors of Czech power, even if only temporarily. Minor events, no big deal, set the tone. Overnight, for example, here's *Prace*—the union newspaper no one reads anyway except for its sports page—daring to criticize the Office of Physical Culture for its deplorable practice of forbidding Czech athletes to compete abroad. That's news indeed.

As if to prove the union paper correct (unless it was told to pave the way), the authorities announce that Emil will be going to Brazil, to São Paulo, where he will run in the great Saint Sylvester race taking place on the last day of the year. After he has obtained his visa and expressed his pleasure, Emil mysteriously shuts himself up in the bathroom for hours, his only company a packet of Riz Lacroix cigarette papers. The same fragile little Riz Lacroix papers on which, meanwhile, in his cell deep in Ruzyne Prison, one of the men who received a life sentence at the show trials in Prague is secretly writing an account of what really happened there, hoping to slip it to his wife.

From Prague to São Paulo, Emil will touch down once, in Paris, where he gives a press conference in the aerodrome hall at Le Bourget before flying off aboard a Super Constellation. And how does he think the race in São Paulo will go. Well, he says ingenuously, I'm going to win. They haven't told me the names of my adversaries but it doesn't matter because I will win. Whoever they are, I will beat them all and I'm pleased about that. I'll enjoy beating them very much, he says again, showing even more teeth than ever. And that's it. He's annoying, sometimes.

São Paulo: at the hotel where the foreign athletes stay, his usual curiosity sends him hurrying immediately into the bathroom of his assigned room. He turns on a faucet, gets out his packet of Riz Lacroix papers, rolls a few of them into tiny balls that he tosses into the sink. Thing is, he's heard about the Coriolis force and he wants to find out if it's true that in the southern hemisphere, water swirls in the opposite direction than in the North before running down the drain. What do you know, it is true, good Lord. Emil can't get over it. Going back down to the lobby, where a crowd is waiting and jostling to see him, he smilingly grants interviews, gives autographs, fraternizes with his fellow runners.

Nobody else seems to doubt that he'll win either, although there is one small technical question: this event, held on the night that separates one year from the next, is seven very rugged kilometers long, but—more importantly—run by over two thousand starters.

That's the whole problem: breaking free of the mob. Extricating oneself soon enough to avoid being overwhelmed. Starting out quickly only to tire too early risks compromising the end of the race, and a cautious start might leave one drowning in the pack. Well, says Emil, we'll see. Meanwhile, he consults the offices of the *Gazeta Esportiva*, the newspaper organizing the event, for information. And the starter fires a pistol, as usual, I suppose, he inquires. No, they tell him, you begin at the last notes of the Brazilian national anthem. Fine, but tell me, asks Emil: I assume one can find that anthem in a store somewhere. . . . And he buys the record, learns it by heart. You can never be too sure.

To avoid false starts and premature sallies, it has been decided to play the national anthem before the pistol shot intended to punctuate the last note of the music. Some joker tosses an inconsiderate firecracker, however, which inspires ravages of confusion: taken for the expected signal, it jump starts the immense cohort right in the middle of the anthem and that's it, everyone gets going. Emil chooses to take the lead immediately before a million frantic people beneath a giant fireworks display and in a deafening din of shouts, horns, sirens and trumpets, rockets, cherry bombs exploding everywhere, open-air orchestras saluting the athletes as they pass by, with the runners forced to make their way through the narrow passage left open by spectators among the garlands, Chinese lanterns, and popping flashbulbs.

But all this takes place without too much trouble, up to the final and extremely steep hill, where the Czech Locomotive takes off, turns himself into a mountain railroad train, and naturally wins, far ahead of the others, pulverizing the course record by a full minute. The delirium surrounding his person is still at its height, and that evening, at the reception hosted at the headquarters of the *Gazeta Esportiva*, the crush is so monstrous that Emil, threatened with asphyxiation, must slip out of the building by a side door.

The following day, it rains; catching a cold that turns to flu, Emil must stay in his hotel to rest. He turns down ten invitations a day, while four hundred pounds of medals, trophy cups, and statuettes are delivered to his room. But enchanted by Brazilian enthusiasm, and thinking he can count on the cooperation of the sporting authorities, he promises to return the following year. Thanks to the authorization to travel, his victory in São Paulo has brought Czechoslovakia some welcome popularity and seems to have changed the political climate on that score. Then, back in Europe, Emil spends a night in a hotel on the banks of the Seine in Paris, where he also promises to return in six months.

In the meantime, he has become the man to beat, the benchmark, the gold standard of long-distance running. We might even ask ourselves, opine the columnists solemnly, if he is not committing a major psychological error in breaking the world's records at such a relentless pace. Because after all, grumble the pundits, there will come a day when astonishment will give way to polite curiosity, then curiosity to indifference, and when one day the extraordinary becomes an everyday affair, he will no longer be extraordinary at all. Emil will not astonish anyone anymore until he loses. Until that day comes, even despite avid speculation about the runners who might soon manage to dethrone him, every news item about Emil still makes the front page everywhere.

So, six months later, back to Paris for the cross country event sponsored by *L'Humanité*. A royal reception awaits Emil at Le Bourget. Emerging from the huge DC-6 that has just landed on the concrete runway of Le Bourget, he is snugly buttoned up in a large gray gabardine raincoat and sports a rainbow-colored woolen bonnet with a pompom that will be his constant companion from now on. When he removes it in greeting, everyone notices that he has shaved his head, because there's no denying this, Emil is beginning to lose his hair. As photographers and reporters rush up to him, he answers them in good French but in a less triumphant tone than six months ago: in his opinion, he says, it's Kuts who should beat him the next day at the Vincennes Racecourse. This Kuts is quite a good-looking boy, a sailor in the Russian navy, better prepared than Emil (who claims he isn't in good shape), plus above all (there's no denying this either), younger.

The following day, however, Kuts isn't even a threat to Emil. Before a crowd of twenty thousand, taking his time at first to get into action, Emil then covers the distance at top speed, galloping once again far ahead of the others between a double row of spectators. Security guards overwhelmed, track invaded, ovation as usual. Changing their minds again, the columnists wonder if the years can ever slow him down, and Kuts himself remarks that he has never run as well. As for Emil, he says he's ready to come back in two months to Paris, where his curiosity on this trip has led him only to take a stroll around Pigalle.

With this return (and the prospect of the Bern Games) in mind, he begins several weeks' intensive training at Stara Boleslav, where he always feels at home. Training over, press conference at the Palace Hotel where the reporters stay. Questioned about his unusually consistent form, gentle Emil, as he is often called, admits that he, too, is amazed. But I'm not fooling myself, he says for the first time; I know that I'm going into a slow decline. In any case, I'm aiming only at the record for 10,000 meters. For the 5,000 meters, I'm not fast enough anymore. And as for the marathon, it's an event I don't much care for: frankly, it's too boring. In the meantime, I'm going back to Paris. And indeed, in Prague, the Minister of Sports and Culture has approved his appearance at the Jean-Bouin de Colombes Stadium, after a favorable response from the army top brass.

During his last visit to France, however, Emil gave an interview to a Czech daily called *Svobodne Slovo*, the official newspaper of a small Party satellite, created to foster the impression that pluralism exists—and edited by a collaborator with the political police. Comrade, the reporter had asked him, could you tell us first of all how you feel? Fine, replied Emil, just fine, but I believe I've reached a point where it's very hard for me to make any progress. Got that, said the reporter, and now could you share with our readers your impressions of Paris? Of course, said Emil, with his mind on other things, not paying much attention to the matter at hand. Well, let's hear them, said the reporter. So, Paris, what did you think of it?

Right, Paris, replied Emil casually; you know, there's not really much to see. Pigalle, of course, not bad. And then the girls, obviously, damned beautiful, the girls. You see their pictures all over the papers, those splendid girls. And then there's the wine, naturally. But the shops, too, I mean the shops they've got in that country, I'm telling you, I'd never seen that before, there are stores everywhere.

Very good, comrade, thank you, said the journalist, closing his notebook. I'll be happy to write up your interesting remarks in a suitable fashion.

Remarks that, written up indeed in his paper, turned out as follows: I was disappointed in Paris, Zátopek informs us. The Paris of trashy fiction. The Paris of prostitution, of pornographic magazines and photos. The Paris infected to the very heart by an obsession with business and the money-making mentality.

Result: a few days later, the French Ministry of Foreign Affairs issues a communiqué. After his latest visit to France this spring, announces this communiqué indignantly, the runner Zátopek felt obliged to make various uncalled-for observations to the Czech newspaper *Svobodne Slovo* regarding his trip. Considering the injurious nature of these remarks regarding the people of Paris, the Ministry of Foreign Affairs has decided to refuse to allow M. Zátopek into the country.

15

This refusal stirs up a huge controversy but, since everyone weighs in on it, Emil winds up with his visa after all. This incident ought to teach him to keep quiet but it isn't his fault that he has a gift for languages, that he speaks Russian and German well; gets along decently in English, French, Hungarian; and doesn't do too badly in most of the Eastern European and Scandinavian languages. Sometimes I regret my fluency in foreign languages, he laments sheepishly after that visa episode. It's not good to know too many of them. You must always talk, always answer. Yes indeed, Emil.

After that business, he arrives in France rather ticked off, the way he was in Berlin the day the whole stadium laughed at him. And it's perhaps to take revenge that he breaks the world record for the 5,000 meters in the stadium at Colombes. He only breaks it by a second, but it's the last long distance he was missing—which plumps his total up from eight records to nine. Then, when the public clamors for a victory lap, Emil gallops 400 meters more to please them, flat out, as if he'd just run only a relaxed race. Next, despite his baldness, he purchases a nylon hairbrush, a thing unheard-of back home in Czechoslovakia. But it must be for Dana because he also buys a cake of almond-scented soap and a tube of Kiss Red lipstick.

Then, while he's at it, he improves his own world record for the 10,000 in Brussels. Which at this point might seem rather routine, but the Czech authorities are quite appreciative of that particular routine, and in their singular arithmetic they calculate: Colombes + Brussels = Emil's promotion to the rank of lieutenant-colonel.

I don't know about you, but me—with all these exploits, these records, these victories, these trophies—a person might start to think that enough is enough. And just in the nick of time because lo and behold, Emil starts losing.

16

It begins in Budapest, with those 10,000 meters that are his distance, that belong only to him, but where he's beaten by a certain Kovacs. It's almost unfair: Emil so handsome despite his sloppy style and Kovacs so ugly, short legs and torso topped by a bulging head, but who makes up for looking like a stubborn gnome with a tenacity that just won't quit. Anyway, it's a tough break for Emil, especially since he loses a series of other races now that he's on a roll.

He loses a little, he wins, he loses again, he wins back a bit, and people begin thinking that maybe Emil doesn't have what it takes anymore. He's thinking the same thing, moreover, but from now on all those other runners he wiped off the track, they begin cherishing a hope of one day taking revenge. Not a vengeance as spectacular as Emil's exploits, of course, but one sufficient to gently refurbish their self-respect. And so there is speculation, anticipation, prognostication. Emil appears, people say, to be facing the prospect of irreversible decline, of farewell to his supremacy, and the end of his honors. The man believed to be impervious to weakness is betrayed by a body that no longer wants to work, in spite of his powerful will and pride. It's only normal, after all: there are no miracles in that department. He will have to admit that the simple effect of his presence in a stadium is a spent force, that his turn has come to feel the dismay through which, even involuntarily, he held adversaries in his grip.

Which becomes apparent when he goes to run in Switzerland. He has pinned great hopes on the meet in Bern, he has prepared for it as never before. Even though in this case, considering the competition, he's practically a shoo-in to win, he seems uneasy while he waits to do battle, nervous, almost stricken. He walks rather bent over, shoulders hunched, his cap pulled down over his ears without a thought for how he looks. When the Czech team is ritually invited to tour a chocolate factory in Bern, Emil accompanies them politely and from curiosity, as usual, but without appearing to pay much attention. In the drizzle, wearing his raincoat, he seems like a lowly clerk heading off to work. And after the visit, sitting next to Dana during a film the factory shows them exalting Switzerland in general and chocolate in particular, he, the titan of the track, is just an anonymous spectator, humble and obedient, who sits there watching nicely the way he'd watch no matter what. Among his giant teammates, so hirsute and athletic, Emil suddenly looks like a good little boy or a heartbroken old man who couldn't care less about all that.

Still, his curiosity takes him to the zoo in Bern, where Emil is glad to finally see some monkeys, a species that does not yet enjoy the right of residence in Czechoslovakia. But the monkeys look mean, embittered, perpetually vexed at having missed out on humanity by a split hair. Obviously obsessed, they think about nothing else. They'd be quite prepared to take it out on Emil. Who isn't exactly disappointed by this spectacle, but it doesn't cheer him up any.

Even though he continues to surprise his public, they've already begun to talk about him almost in the past tense. Abruptly, practically overnight. Even though in Bern—gleaming track, forest of umbrellas—they find him astounding: a sparkling race, fantastic run, the red jersey setting the pace of the struggle against supposedly formidable adversaries who never even come close. Even though once again in Prague— strong wind, freezing weather—the demonic Emil performs a new number from a repertoire everyone had thought exhausted. But though he still wins now and then, he loses more and more. He can see what's happening to him; he comes to terms with it. He admits it. Right, he says, I'm obsolete but so what. And even, after all, so much the better. I love to run, I still want to run, to run a lot, but it's not bad either to go back to being a normal runner who can lose.

He can't see himself running the 5,000 meters anymore, and decides to give it up. That challenge has become too fast, the exclusive domain of milers, where endurance specialists like himself have nothing left to win. From now on he'll concentrate on the 10,000 and the longest distances. He'd really like, for example, to work on the marathon—in spite of how boring he finds it—with an eye to the next Olympics, in Melbourne.

While waiting for Melbourne, Emil feels like returning to Brazil, as promised, but right after his trip last year, another reporter from the *Svobodne Slovo* had asked him for a little interview. Remembering the one in Paris, Emil had glared at him suspiciously. Comrade, the journalist had said, our readers would be quite interested in your impressions of Brazil.

Listen, Emil had insisted, I would like to be perfectly clear. It's absolutely wonderful, Brazil. I mean it, now: it's really fantastic. In every way. I'm going to enjoy going back there. Have I made myself clearly understood?

Result: a communiqué from the Brazilian Ministry of Foreign Affairs. Emil's visa for Brazil has been denied. There is nothing political, explains the spokesman, about this decision, which applies only to this particular case. The fact is that M. Zátopek, upon his return to Czechoslovakia, made some highly offensive statements about Brazil.

17

Time goes by, the waters of the Vltava flow beneath the bridges of Prague, and rumors ramble on about Emil's fate. Without announcing the end of his road, his repeated losses seem to signal at least the end of his omnipotence. For the Eighteenth *L'Humanité* Cross Country Race, the Czechs and Soviets arrive in Paris on the same Air France DC-4, but this time Emil is no longer the only star athlete awaited at Le Bourget. Also on the plane is the handsome Kuts, who—each of them repeatedly stealing the best time away from the other—had helped Emil break the record for the 5,000 meters before the Czech retired from that event.

Emil is dressed as usual: old gabardine raincoat (green this time), eternal woolen hat with pompom, still relaxed away from the track, but could be he's put on a bit of weight. Yes, he smiles (in every language, as he always does), I've put on four little pounds. You know I've had lots of work this year, so, well, not quite as many opportunities to keep in shape.

Opportunities or not, Emil wins the run traditionally organized by the Party's official newspaper. This internationalist athletic event is attended by the ambassadors of the USSR, Czechoslovakia, Hungary, Poland, and other brother countries, while the French apparatchiks include Jacques Duclos, Marcel Cahin, Étienne Fajon, and André Stil, who face polar blasts and an orgy of long-winded speeches, military marches, and national anthems. To the cheers of the comrades, Emil agrees to say a few words at the podium. I'm happy, he announces, but a little sorry that a young man didn't beat me. Myself, I'm thirty-three now, I don't have the same will to win anymore, I only run these days for the pleasure of running. I thank you. He receives an ovation. What a great guy, people think, *mon dieu*, what a great guy.

Meanwhile, the world of track is proving Emil right. Back in Czechoslovakia, in the town of Budajovice, where he participates in the Army Cross Country Championship, Emil loses to Ullsberger, who happens to be his favorite disciple. Over heavy ground, in cold, dry air, Ullsberger amazes everyone by coming in fifty meters ahead of Emil. It's the first time in ten years that the Locomotive has lost in his own country.

A few days later, in Zlín, even though Emil takes his revenge on Ullsberger, the damage has been done. He tries to get on top of things by announcing that he will challenge his own world record for the 10,000 meters, set in Brussels, and he wants to do it in Hutska, in his favorite stadium, Stara Boleslav. The track there is a small one, 363.76 meters, but it's excellent, well protected from the wind by the neighboring forest, and has been resurfaced by the best local technicians in preparation for the event.

It's been a busy week, however. As an officer, Emil had to take part three days earlier, on the tenth anniversary of the liberation, in the great commemorative parade of the Czech army; it doesn't seem like much, but those things are tiring. And besides, the temperature is sweltering that day at Stara Boleslav, where the nearby trees prove an ineffective shield against violent wind gusts that raise oppressive dust clouds in the stadium. Failure. Emil is betrayed by the wind, the heat, the dust, and by Ullsberger, who was supposed to be his pace setter but takes advantage of that to leave him behind. Panting, red-faced, exhausted by the stifling, stormy atmosphere, Emil gives up at the eighth kilometer and misses his record, even though he's been well within his intermediate times from the Brussels run. Moved, the crowd almost forgets to chant their encouragement.

Too bad. Now what can he do. Well, start getting ready for the marathon at Melbourne. In the meantime, at the antipodes, Australians are already hurrying by the millions to buy their tickets for the Olympics the following year. Also in the meantime, the Czech press announces the creation of a miracle tonic, conceived in the laboratory by a team of researchers and based on Emil's training diet. Immediately dubbed the Zátopek Cocktail, this product leaves one a touch unsatisfied, however, on closer examination: composed of yeast and fruit extract glucose, it resembles nothing so much as the mixture touted at the time by Gaylord Hauser, author of the best-selling *Live Young, Live Longer.*

In spite of yeast and glucose aplenty, things still aren't going well. In Prague, Emil sits out the Army Championships, then loses at the Rosicky Memorial Race. In Belgrade he is clearly beaten because of an intestinal upset, due—as it happens—to eating too much fruit. In Warsaw, a disappointment, Emil drags himself without distinction through the 10,000 meters to get trounced the following day in the 5,000.

No fool, he sees it will soon be time for him to retire. But he doesn't take this badly, mentions it with amusement. He continues to say he's glad that youngsters are outrunning him and getting ready to break all his records. Emil simply hopes to last long enough to get to Melbourne, where he stubbornly wants to put up a good show. Then, he says, his travels will be over. I'll run around my house, I'll keep busy coaching all these kids who love long-distance running, and that's it. He even starts getting around on a moped, a little NSU Quickly given to him in Karlsruhe. Well, it's mostly Dana who rides it, while he just trots along behind it for a laugh when he has to pose for press photographs.

Still, the old Emil sometimes shows up, but that's also because anyone looking for trouble with him will find it. In Brno, for example, he runs a 5,000 meters against a Pole, one Krzyszkowiak, who has just beaten him in Warsaw and already sees himself romping home again. So, getting out in front, the last thing this Krzyszkowiak wants is for Emil to pass him and he even tries to get rid of him, jostling him halfway through to bump him off the track. This infuriates gentle Emil, who dodges the low blow and takes the lead after the turn. But Krzyszkowiak surges back, passes him, pulls ahead, and seems destined to win when Emil, still enraged, grits his teeth and blows past the Pole at top speed just before the finish to wind up with his best time of the year. He wins amid the usual storm of applause, has become once more the hero of the race, the king of the track. No, you see—everything is not completely shot for Emil. But you also see that when he wins, it's by settling for accelerating gradually, as much as he can, during the last kilometers. He never used to do that before.

Winning less often isn't serious for anybody else going through ups and downs. It's just that Emil, always a winner before, has never really experienced inexorable decline. Well, it's perfectly normal that as he grows older he tires faster, takes longer to recuperate, doesn't recover his former strength. He knows this but sometimes still gets his back up, as if he didn't want to hear anything about it. Obstinately, he keeps rolling the dice. As affable as ever and showing no anxiety, he announces his intention to go after his Brussels record yet again.

It still doesn't work. It works so poorly that after a London-Prague meet, Emil, coming in third, seems to draw the obvious conclusions. He announces that without definitively abandoning athletics, he will no longer participate in international meets after the Melbourne Games. It's better to retire when you're still in shape, he observes, stating that he had reached that decision some time before. And then enough's enough, he adds; I've had a good run.

But he's incorrigible, really. In spite of everything, now he gets it into his head to beat another of his world records, the hour, and to do it he goes to Celakovice, a little town near Prague. That's how it is. On a whim, just like that. Emil drops the idea at the last minute because the track isn't ready but, instead, he decides to run twenty-five kilometers to try recapturing the record for that distance, which the Russian Ivanov had snatched away from him a month earlier. And voilà, he runs and recaptures it. This fellow people have been starting to call washed up owns all the world's long-distance records once again, from six miles to thirty kilometers. No one knows what's going on.

No one knows what to think. Some suspect this was his strategy all along, his secret plan for that season: to show signs of weakness, even waning ability, in order to pull off this stunning achievement in Celakovice. Some feel he has chosen to focus less on his chances in the 5,000 and 10,000 meters and to prepare for longer distances, doubtless with an eye to the Melbourne marathon. Because he'd already made that splash four years ago, at another Olympics—coming in with a low profile to run away with all the gold in the world. With him, you never know. You know even less because, like a wave goodbye, Emil publishes his memoirs, *My Training Experiences*, in which the last chapter, "Emil at Home," has been written by Dana.

Dana with whom Emil goes to live for two months in India, where they will give a few lectures and supervise the coaching of local athletes. (Things definitely seem to have changed in Prague; it's getting easier and easier to leave the country.) From Bombay they proceed to Delhi where Emil does seventy kilometers every day, because running a marathon means getting ready. That's how he gets ready, anyway. On his return, moreover, he announces in the *Svobodne Slovo* that in Melbourne, he will line up only for that event. He has finished with the Olympic 10,000 meters, in which he feels he no longer has any chance of performing effectively.

But go figure, he could still change his mind. Following a ritual not unlike that of a music-hall farewell tour, running stars have a knack for alternating between emotional declarations of retirement and impromptu returns to training or even the setting of new records. Emil, in any case, continues his forest runs despite the harsh cold that has enveloped Czechoslovakia.

Then the season returns with a first cross country run in Prague to choose eight runners for an event in Paris. The challenge is forbidding: a little over eight kilometers in seven degrees Fahrenheit. There Emil starts out simply following the pack, led by one Kodak, and pulls away toward the end to win by sixteen meters. That's good, all is not lost. He makes the cut, of course. He calmly awaits the Twenty-Ninth *L'Humanité* Cross Country Race.

18

So he arrives there with his pleasant smile, his knitted hat with pompom on his now completely bald head, and that gaze of astonished delight he always turns on people and things and will abandon only when the starter's gun goes off. But Kuts has arrived there too, awaiting Emil the way one awaits the man to beat, because in spite of Emil's age and even the fact that everybody keeps writing him off too soon, he's still everyone's biggest bogeyman. And Kuts with his blond, unruly hair, prominent cheekbones, powerful shoulders, and that air of having just debarked from the battleship Potemkin—he simply takes off like a shot without letting anyone get close all the way to the finish line that Emil, overwhelmed, crosses only in third place. Fine, says gentle Emil without making a fuss, I have to face facts, I've grown old while these kids were coming along, okay. My time has passed, it's my last season. I still have to train some more to wind it up honorably. Well, an honorable finish has only one name: in eight months, the Melbourne Games.

And he gets back to his training. First in Hungary, at the Tata Camp, then at Stara Boleslav, a track watched over by lofty trees a hundred years old, majestic beeches and tall birches in whose shade

Emil has broken most of his records. He trains there so hard that he winds up neglecting his appearance, wearing a threadbare old tracksuit of indeterminate color, a four-day stubble, and his cap pulled down to his eyes as if he were a tramp. So hard that he also winds up injuring himself, developing a hernia in the right groin that requires surgery.

Hospital, silence. A long silence during which, as always, proliferate all sorts of rumors immediately denied, followed by denials of those denials: Emil is retiring except no, not at all, since he'll be running in the Army Day celebration but again no, he has backed out of Army Day, Emil is very ill and then feels in the pink, he's been banned from the Games for seditious remarks but absolutely not, he'll be going to the Games, then he'll be attending the Games merely as a spectator, then he's not going anymore because he's giving up. Emil's hanging on. He has to have a new operation. He's back training again, he's training as never before. He can't recover his old form, he's not getting anywhere, he's dropping the whole thing, he's finished, he's going to come back, he'll come back. In the past tense, the future, the present but especially the past, rarely has Emil been so talked about ever since people began saying, along with Emil himself, that he was on the way out.

He comes back. In a cutting cold spell, out in stinging hail, he comes back to run 10,000 more than honorable meters in Bratislava followed by twenty-five perfectly sparkling kilometers in Thorgau and the prognosis immediately flipflops again: Well of course he'll be going to Melbourne since he's completely back in form, the official word is he'll be running the marathon, the 10,000 meters, and walk away with a fifth gold medal.

Fine, Melbourne is on, but Emil isn't feeling too optimistic, he doesn't much believe all that talk. As he often does before a big meet, he says he feels tired. Plus he doesn't really connect with the Australian public. He's afraid the Aussies aren't used to athletic events, don't understand their elegant simplicity, favoring instead less abstract sports like motorcycle or horse racing. Besides, deaf to his arguments, his selectors have refused to enter him in the 10,000 meters, letting him run only the marathon.

In short, his mood as he arrives for the second time in the southern hemisphere is not too good. Entering his quarters in the Olympic Village, he does not dash into the bathroom right away to double-check on the Coriolis force. He'll get around to it, sort of, in the next few days, but rather sullenly and without putting too much stock in it anymore. The only thing that tickles his curiosity a little is his brand new camera.

And yet, those first few October days in the antipodes aren't bad, because it's springtime: parks in flower, placid ocean, clear skies, mild nights. But the weather soon changes with rainy days, icy gusts, everyone shivering including the black swans in Port Philip Bay, which take refuge along the shore. Spirits are low, especially since everybody agrees that these games are pathetic compared to the ones in Helsinki: lousy organization, mediocre food, inadequate equipment, uneven track surface. The faucets sputter, the heating is temperamental, while the squeaking beds turn out to be too short, just like the pool, which is eight millimeters shy of the precise Olympic length. And when the wind isn't sultry air from the desert, a real ordeal for long-distance runners, it's a freezing southern blast coming at present from the nearby Antarctic, not so great for them either.

On the day of the marathon, however, to say the sun is out doesn't even come close: it produces an overheated hell, an oven of debilitating violence that weighs massively on the runners' shoulders. For protection, Emil exchanges his woolen cap for a lighter but inadequate cloth one. The course runs along a dry and dusty suburban road without a scrap of shade and where the asphalt, crumbling in places, boils beneath the runners' feet. Small houses with Venetian blinds line this route, called the Dandenong Road, and along it waits an enormous rowdy throng of men red-faced with beer, young women in sun dresses, horsewomen in cowboy pants. Rackets under their arms or wooden bats on their shoulders, women have deserted their tennis courts and men their cricket lawns.

Off goes the starter's pistol (all things considered, it's lucky no stray bullet causes an accident), and off go the runners. They all set to it and during the first twenty kilometers, Emil remains prudently a good ten places back. Not such a bad getaway for him: he's being a smart aleck, tipping his hat to the crowd with a great flourish, even taking time to pose for amateur photographers. It's when the road turns steep that things go wrong, the long climb before the red flag marking the intersection where the route turns back toward Melbourne. But since things go wrong in particular for most of his rivals, who begin to stagger, merely zigzagging along, exhausting themselves and dropping out one after another, Emil manages to move up to fifth place during the next ten kilometers, at which point he's the one who breaks down.

The mechanism gives way at first in little details: a knee that wobbles a tad to the left, a throbbing ache in one shoulder, the beginnings of a cramp behind the right knee; then the pains and problems swiftly intersect, enmeshing him until it's his whole body going out of kilter. Although he keeps trying to run steadily, Emil constantly loses ground, his performance reduced to the incoherent spectacle of an erratic, uneven stride, and soon he is nothing but a livid and flailing automaton with hollow eyes that sink deeper and deeper into his skull. He has tossed away his cap, which had begun weighing on him like a helmet in the brutal sun.

At the thirtieth kilometer, broken and out of breath, he stops at one of the tables set up along the route with buckets of water, sponges, and drinking water. Emil splashes himself liberally, drinks half a glass of water, stares at the route with apparent hesitation, restrains what's left of an initial impulse to get going again, drains his glass, and then sets out. He does so worn down to a bewildered and disjointed puppet, his stride shattered, his body out of order, as if abandoned by his own nervous system. He'll hang on until the stadium but, beaten, the sixth to make it down the final stretch, Emil falls to his knees, drops his head to the yellow grass, and stays like that for long minutes weeping and vomiting and it's over, everything is over.

19

Not everything.

Not everything because, in the ten years following that moment when Emil gazes in extreme close-up at the close-cropped yellow grass on which he is vomiting, quite a number of things will still happen.

First, after his return from Australia, he'll be promoted to colonel. Until now he has moved up the ranks after a victory, but in this case it seems to be for services rendered, to crown the end of his career. Not only has he essentially announced that he is giving up competition, it's also the first time in many years that he no longer tops the list of Czech champions: he's now number five, behind a discus thrower and a shot putter. So he's promoted, then recycled: assigned to educational duties, he is named Director of Sports at the Ministry of Defense.

It would also appear, however, that he hasn't lost his desire simply to keep on running. Six months after Melbourne some of his old pals, who just happen to be the national stars of the 5,000 meters, approach him to ask for a favor. I'd be delighted, Emil tells them, so, what can I do for you. Well, here it is, say his pals: Come running with us, why don't you, just like in the good old days. But

I've dropped all that, Emil tells them, as you know. Oh no, his pals patiently explain, that's not it at all. There's no question of competition, naturally. Naturally they know that Emil has definitely declared himself *hors de concours*. No, they're simply asking him to lead the running, to set an appropriate pace to help them make better progress. Fine, says Emil, who is only too pleased to give them a hand. Fine, if that's what they want. And on the appointed day, in gusts of rain, he sets out nicely with them. But when he looks back five laps before the finish, he sees no one behind him except some blurry, winded silhouettes grumbling down at the other end of the track. It wasn't on purpose, he just can't help himself.

Given that fact, and since others encourage him, Emil will do the rounds a little while longer, with varying results. Running a 10,000 meters at the Third Moscow Athletic Games, on the crushed brick track of the Lenin Stadium, he sprints desperately with a complete unknown to finish in sixth place behind him. It's moving, it's ridiculous, but three months later in Odessa, he triumphs over that same distance as in his glory days. It's moving, it's complicated.

Too complicated: when he's invited to Spain for the Saint Sebastian Cross Country Race, Emil is willing but this time it's for the last time. He flies there, with a stopover at Orly. Deplaning from the Tupolev, he sees a mob of reporters and photographers at the airport exit, behind the customs area. Emil is used to that, he's touched, how kind of them to show up, it's always nice to see you haven't been forgotten. But when he gets through customs there's no one left, only a press intern who's running late, still rewinding his film without a glance at Emil, the rest of the mob having left after taking pictures from every angle of every one of Elizabeth Taylor's curves as she arrived from London only a short while ago.

So it's with mixed feelings that Emil tackles the Saint Sebastian run, an obstacle course over varied terrain. And once again they're off: the wind at their backs, the athletes have made a quick start at the gun. Those who venture to take the lead rapidly lose ground in the recently plowed fields and on the hill right before the racetrack.

That's where Emil decides to make his move, accelerating, while only six runners manage to follow him to the hairpin turn. Now heading into the wind, Emil shortens his stride to battle the gusts and then, grimacing more than usual, transfigured by effort as in the good old days, he runs through the undergrowth and enters the hippodrome to win by twenty meters, saluted by thousands of waving handkerchiefs. They applaud the veteran, they honor him, they respect him, they present him with a sombrero and a Basque fox terrier Dana will name Pedro. Pedro will be with them for a long time.

It's his last victory; best leave it at that. Might as well hang up the cleats for good, now, as planned. Besides, his status has changed: for the last two years, Emil has attended *L'Humanité*'s cross country race only as a coach. Although he still runs every day, it's simply for himself, to keep in shape, in other words, less. And since he trains less, he has more time to take an interest in what's happening in his country.

Which is not without interest. During those ten years after Melbourne, presidents of the republic and first secretaries of the Party have continued to come and go after the death of Gottwald without improving much of anything, even though the name tag has changed: Czechoslovakia has gone from a popular democracy to a Socialist republic, a nuance that's hard to grasp, but never mind. Nothing's really new, still as much fear, still as cold, life still drags on in gray despair, with long lines and anonymous letters.

Well, here comes a new first secretary named Alexander Dubček[4] who seems eager to do some housecleaning. Essentially, Dubček would like a fresher name tag, "Socialist democracy" this time, which barely causes a ripple at first, but he also declares that the country must open the door to Europe. Which, two thousand kilometers to the north-east of Prague, causes the big brother of Socialism to cock an eyebrow.

But Dubček doesn't stop there. He ups and starts doing things no one would have dared imagine. Lifting censorship. Religious tolerance. Rehabilitation of the old leaders condemned during the show trials of Prague. Release of authors imprisoned for thinking out of line. Freedom for everyone to travel abroad. In short, what appears to be a general thawing out. There are unbelievable sights. People watch, on television, as ordinary citizens speak up to question ministers and Party bigwigs, while in Moscow, big brother is now frowning fit to kill.

From then on everything starts shaking seriously loose. As fear drains away, daily life takes on a new look. Folks immediately begin talking to one another, talking spontaneously in the street, at home, at work, where they have always kept quiet and never listened to a soul. People get together, discuss things, argue, comment, feel a whole lot better, you'd even think the weather had warmed up. People will be breathing freely, without that constant, dogged, ancient fear; they'll be able to envisage a new Czechoslovakia, liberal and Socialist at the same time. Communist, okay, fine, since they can't do otherwise, but they'll try to find a new way to live as Communists and—above all—to live better.

Aside from a few nostalgic Stalinists, everyone's pleased by all this. Emil as well thinks it's just fine. He, who was lucky enough to travel, to glimpse abroad a freedom of speech and movement unknown at home, can only closely follow and support the progress of this liberalization. When he compares what Dubček proposes with what Novotný and the others have done, what can he do but back Dubček. When his support becomes public, the effect is all the more spectacular in that Emil remains, even in retirement from the track, the most popular man in his nation. Everyone is feeling more and more pleased.

It lasts a little less than a year, while in the meantime, for his part, big brother is growing more and more impatient. Until impatience becomes anger, and anger exasperation. Until, ten years after Melbourne, one August night in Prague.

20

The Soviets have entered Czechoslovakia. They have arrived by plane and in tanks. First via Aeroflot, a flight that discreetly drops some paratroops in civvies, elite Spetsnaz forces, to take control of the Prague airport. Then via other planes bearing the red star, MiG fighters and huge Antonov An-12s transporting heavy equipment as well as the 103rd Guards airborne division. Those soldiers move toward the center of Prague, taking possession of the presidential palace along the way. Then seven thousand armored and mechanized units of Warsaw Pact troops, massed along the nation's borders, converge on its capital to besiege it with half a million soldiers.

The tanks are T-54s, T-55s, and T-62s; the Spetsnaz soldiers are equipped with Makarov pistols, AK-47s (including some with folding rifle butts), plus RPK-74 light machine guns, SVD Dragunov sniper rifles, and AGS-17 automatic grenade launchers. You might consider such an arsenal appropriate for a war or an invasion, but not at all. Neither are we talking about a quiet little annexation like the one thirty years ago, no. It's simply that the Soviets have come to tidy up a regime in which they feel they have a proprietary interest, the current evolution of which they consider an unfortunate error—and one that should be rapidly corrected. So they arrive with the armies of five of the Warsaw Pact nations and they settle in, that's all.

It takes only about ten hours for the city to fall to the paratroops, after which, when the link with the ground forces has been established, Soviet tanks pile into Prague. And within twenty-four hours the physical occupation of the country is complete.

When this crew enters Prague, they encounter not cold disapproval, but immediate hostility and resistance. Citizens gather in the middle of the night on Wenceslas Square to confront the T-55s parked here and there, motors rumbling. When the drivers try to climb out of their tanks, they're greeted with deafening shouts and jeers. Fired from the roof of the National Museum, a few bullets soon slam into the tanks, whose drivers hastily drop back into their vehicles. The hatch covers slam shut, the turrets swivel, the guns fire in unison. The plate-glass windows of the museum explode as fragments of the facade collapse.

While fire from machine guns and automatic pistols begins to clatter in scattered bursts throughout the city, the demonstrators now rush to the building housing the radio station—still on the air—toward which the tanks are also heading. Firing high at first, then progressively lower, the tanks bump, bash, crush cars parked in their way, clearing a path for foot-soldiers to occupy the building. At eight in the morning, the radio studios are overrun, all normal broadcasting is cut off. It's over.

In the days that follow, the citizens of Prague mount a passive resistance. They do try at first to talk to the soldiers but since that doesn't get them very far, they quickly pick up certain habits. If Soviet soldiers lost in the capital ask for directions, it becomes only natural to point them in the opposite direction. In the same way, people are careful to systematically rearrange street signs to confuse the intruders. And during these first nights of the occupation, the population keeps gathering on Wenceslas Square.

Emil has joined the demonstrators. He will be forty-six next month. Despite his baldness he's still a good-looking man, still amiable, still quite steady of nerve even though this evening, unusually for him, he is not smiling. This evening his big teeth are not on display.

He is recognized almost immediately when he arrives at the demonstration. Say something, Emil, come on, they urge him, you can't keep quiet about this. At first Emil feels a little awkward. It's not that he has nothing to say, of course, but although he has learned how to talk to journalists, he has no real experience addressing crowds. Never mind, he steps up: straining his thin voice, the national hero speaks out, denouncing, condemning the invasion by the Warsaw Pact forces. Speaking as an athlete, and since the next Olympic Games will take place in a few weeks in Mexico, he improvises a short speech in which he invites the army to observe an Olympic truce. Since that seems a bit vague, to really make his point, he even calls for a boycott of the USSR at these Games.

The consequences of such statements are not long in coming. The very next day, Emil is fired from his post at the ministry. And in quick succession he is expelled from the Party, cashiered from the army, denied the right to live in Prague. He isn't the only one: 300,000 Party members are expelled along with him, 300,000 other non-Communists are excluded from state employment, another 300,000 are laid off or demoted.

So Emil is now unemployed. Even though he is obviously no longer permitted to travel, he could certainly try to leave the country, which others are managing to do, but he won't even think about going into exile. Besides, he wouldn't have time to think it over because a few days later, he's assigned to work in a warehouse in the uranium mines of Jáchymov, in the northwest of the country, near the German border.[5]

Jáchymov is an open-pit mine where uranium ore is crushed without any ventilation or sprinkler systems to reduce the radiation, heavy dust, or radon, a highly toxic gas given off by the processing and containment equipment, waste-water tanks, and mountains of debris. The wind blows radioactive particles more or less everywhere, while the sludge seeps into the streams and ground water, contaminating the flora, fauna, and people.

That's where Emil will work at various jobs, which might remind him of his assignments at the Bata factory except that in comparison, this is even less jolly. After the ore is crushed, it's concentrated through oxidation, extraction, precipitation, operations to which Emil is introduced, moving as needed among the washing, drying, and packing workrooms. When required, he also pushes and pulls the tip carts of ore. All this for six years, during which—through I don't know what subterfuge—Emil finds a way three times, in disguise, to go see Dana, who has remained assigned to live in Prague.

At the end of those six years, the big brother of Socialism and his flunkies in Prague, who have turned Alexander Dubček into a gardener, decide to recall Emil to the capital with the intention of making him a garbage collector. That seems like a really good idea, from the humiliation point of view, but it quickly becomes clear that it's not such a good idea after all. First off, when he walks around the streets of the city behind the garbage truck with his broom, the population recognizes Emil immediately: everyone leans out the window to hail and applaud him. Then, when his comrades at work refuse to let him sweep up any refuse, he simply jogs in short strides behind the truck, cheered on as in the old days. Every morning as he goes by, the people of the neighborhood where his team is working come out onto the sidewalk to give him an ovation, emptying their trash cans into the truck themselves. Never has any garbage man in the world ever met with such acclaim. From the flunkies' point of view, this bright idea is a complete debacle.

So, swiftly removed from this job, Emil is tried out in two or three others where his popularity still proves troublesome. At their wits' end, the flunkies finally send him off to the countryside, which has fewer people than the city, where the hope is that he'll be less noticeable, and there he works with a shovel. With the official title of geologist, Emil will now dig holes for telegraph poles. Two more years go by like this. Then Emil is summoned before a committee that no longer calls him comrade. They hand him a piece of paper with the firm suggestion that he sign it.

In this document, he dutifully admits all his past mistakes. That he was wrong to back the bourgeois revisionists and the counterrevolutionary forces. That he should not have supported the reactionary filth of that two-thousand-word charter.[6] He declares himself quite happy with the current situation in general, very happy with his personal life in particular. He affirms that, despite the rumors, he has never been a garbage man or a post-hole digger. That he has never been persecuted, or even dismissed from the army, and that he doesn't need to collect his pension as a colonel in the reserves. That he in fact draws a salary more than adequate for his work in geological exploration, in which capacity he is discovering a new and fascinating world. He signs. He signs his self-criticism, what else can he do to have some peace. He signs and, shortly afterward, he is pardoned. His purgatory is over. He is entrusted with a position in Prague, a job in the basement of the Sports Information Center.

Well, says gentle Emil. Filing clerk: I probably didn't deserve any better.

NOTES FROM THE TRANSLATOR

1. Czech units fought on the Allied side during World War I, and in 1918 Czechoslovakia emerged as an independent republic from the ruins of the Austro-Hungarian monarchy. After Hitler exploited the disaffection of the German-speaking people of the Czech Sudetenland during his rise to power, Western appeasement brought him the Munich Pact of 1938, through which Germany obtained those Bohemian borderlands. The resultant truncated state of Czecho-Slovakia was dissolved in March 1939, when Germany created and occupied the Protectorate of Bohemia and Moravia. After liberation by American and Russian forces in 1945, pre-Munich Czechoslovakia was restored, and the German population was expelled.

2. Zlín is the center of the Czech shoe industry, founded in 1913 by Thomas Bata. Under the Bata family, the city grew into an almost self-sufficient factory community. After World War II the Bata industries were nationalized, and in 1949 Zlín was renamed Gottwaldov in honor of Klement Gottwald, Czechoslovakia's first Communist President (1948–1953). Gottwald came to power in February 1948 through the Prague Coup, and when certain government officials resisted Russia's new influence on Czech politics, Gottwald—a devoted Stalinist—instigated a series of purges (the Prague Trials), which sent many victims to prison and execution. Although in ill health, Gottwald insisted on attending the funeral in Moscow of his idol Stalin on March 9, 1953; he died five days later.

3. Click on the "Archive Video of 5 km Olympic run" link in the Wikipedia entry for Emil Zátopek to see the final moments of this race, with exuberant Finnish commentary.

4. Under Communism, the Czechoslovak economy in the 1960s was in serious trouble. In October 1967, a group of reformers challenged First Secretary Antonín Novotný; one of the leaders of this movement, Alexander Dubček, became the new first secretary of the Communist Party on January 5, 1968, and ushered in the period known as the Prague Spring. Dubček and his fellow reformers sought to create "socialism with a human face" by liberalizing the Communist regime, and Dubček believed that as long as Czechoslovakia remained a loyal ally of the Soviet Union, under Communist rule, the country would be free to pursue domestic reform without suffering the fate of the failed Hungarian Revolution of 1956. On August 20, 1968, however, history repeated itself when Warsaw Pact forces invaded Czechoslovakia. Over a period of several months, the achievements of the Prague Spring were reversed; Dubček was forced to resign as first secretary in April 1969. After his expulsion from the Communist Party in 1970, Dubček worked in the Forestry Service in Slovakia. During the Velvet Revolution of 1989, he supported Václav Havel and was hailed by the Czech people as a national icon of democratic freedom. He returned to politics and in 1992, when he died in what many people consider a suspicious automobile accident, he was the leader of the Social Democratic Party of Slovakia and a member of the Federal Assembly.

5. Jáchymov (Joachimsthal in the original German) is a town in Bohemia in the Czech Republic. The silver coins minted there in the sixteenth century from the local silver mines were called Joachimsthalers, or "thalers" for short, which word later became the word "dollar."Until World War I, Jáchymov was the only known source of uranium, and it was Marie Curie's discovery of the highly radioactive element radium in pitchblende ore mined in Jáchymov that brought her the Nobel Prize in Chemistry in 1911. When radium disintegrates, it produces a toxic radioactive gaseous element called radon. In 1906, the first radon spa in the world was opened in Jáchymov, which thus became a famous spa town like Karlsbad and Marienbad. In 1929, it was established that working in the uranium mines caused cancer. After the Communist Party took control of Czechoslovakia in 1948, a prison camp was constructed in Jáchymov, where opponents of the new regime were forced to mine uranium ore under conditions so harsh that life expectancy in Jáchymov at that time was forty-two years.

6. Charter 77 (1977–1992) was an "informal and open association of people" committed to promoting human rights in Czechoslovakia. The movement took its name from the group's political manifesto, signed by 230 prominent Czech intellectuals (including playwrights Václav Havel and Pavel Kohout) and published in various Western newspapers on January 6, 1977. The next day, Czech authorities arrested some of the signatories and began cracking down on dissident activities. After the 1989 Velvet Revolution—and the peaceful division of Czechoslovakia into the Czech Republic and Slovakia in 1993—many of the members of Charter 77 played important roles in both Czech and Slovak politics.

PUBLISHING IN THE PUBLIC INTEREST

Thank you for reading this book published by The New Press. The New Press is a nonprofit, public interest publisher. New Press books and authors play a crucial role in sparking conversations about the key political and social issues of our day.

We hope you enjoyed this book and that you will stay in touch with The New Press. Here are a few ways to stay up to date with our books, events, and the issues we cover:

- Sign up at www.thenewpress.com/subscribe to receive updates on New Press authors and issues and to be notified about local events
- Like us on Facebook: www.facebook.com/newpressbooks
- Follow us on Twitter: www.twitter.com/thenewpress

Please consider buying New Press books for yourself; for friends and family; or to donate to schools, libraries, community centers, prison libraries, and other organizations involved with the issues our authors write about.

The New Press is a 501(c)(3) nonprofit organization. You can also support our work with a tax-deductible gift by visiting www.thenewpress.com/donate.

www.ingramcontent.com/pod-product-compliance
Lightning Source LLC
LaVergne TN
LVHW030907080826
845145LV00010B/2799

* 9 7 8 1 5 9 5 5 8 9 8 3 5 *